THE LAST SIP OF WINE

A Novel of Tuscany

STACEY REYNOLDS

D1518133

Stacey Reynolds

AUTHOR WORKS

The O'Brien Tales and Novellas (in reading order)
Raven of the Sea: An O'Brien Tale
A Lantern in the Dark: An O'Brien Tale
Shadow Guardian: An O'Brien Tale
Fio: An O'Brien Novella
River Angels: An O'Brien Tale
The Wishing Bridge: An O'Brien Tale
The Irish Midwife: An O'Brien Tale
Dark Irish: An O'Brien Novella
Burning Embers: An O'Brien Tale

De Clare Legacy
His Wild Irish Rose: De Clare Legacy

Spin-off Stand-alone Novels
The Last Sip of Wine: A Novel of Tuscany

This book is dedicated to my husband, Bob. You've made me laugh during the best of it. You've kept me afloat during the worst of it. My rock and my best friend.

Note to the Reader

This is a spin-off story from the O'Brien Tales, but it is also a stand-alone novel in its own right. We first met Dr. Antonio Rinalto in the book *River Angels: An O'Brien Tale*, and it has always been my intent to see Antonio happy. It is my immense pleasure to tell you his story.

"In vino veritas—In wine there is truth." — *Pliny the Elder*

PROLOGUE
GREVE IN CHIANTI, TUSCANY, ITALY—TEN YEARS EARLIER

Marcello Rinalto followed his son down the hallway of their home, arguing as he went. He stopped in the doorway of his son's old room. "Antonio, just stop and listen to me. You act in haste."

"No, Papa. I have thought about this a great deal. It's happening. I just need my football shoes. I won't be back here before I leave. I'll be studying Portuguese intensely with a tutor. I need to find those shoes." The abbess at the local charity hospital had mentioned how much the children at the orphanage love to play football in the garden.

Calcio, his father thought, was the only thing his son loved as much as medicine. "You are worried about your football shoes?

That is the major concern at this point? Antonio, *mio figlio*. You are acting out of grief. Think for once in your life! You don't even speak Portuguese! You can surely stay in Italy. What happened to the job in Milan? You would be only a train ride from home."

Antonio pierced him with hard eyes and said, "I made a commitment, Papa. I will see this through. It's only two years, and I need to get away. I can't be here. I won't be here!"

The look of resentment and anger on his son's face stole his breath. His voice was hoarse. "We should stay together, Antonio. Your mother would have wanted ..."

Antonio cut him off, pointing straight at him. "Do not bring my mother into this conversation. If you had acknowledged what my mother wanted, she would still be here. She'd be alive!" His father flinched, and Antonio wished he could find a way to take the words back, but he couldn't. He was too hurt. Too angry. His father had always held on to his family too tightly, not with loving arms, but with shackles. It had killed his mother, and Antonio wouldn't forgive him.

He packed a small bag, having moved most of his things into the city three years ago. He made his way to his Fiat 500, which was parked in the drive instead of the garage. Their garage held nicer *macchine*. His brother had an old Land Rover, good for driving the property, along with the other maintenance vehicles their small staff used. His father had his baby parked in the garage as well. The car he'd shared with Antonio's mother. A 1960 Alpha Romeo convertible. It was custom painted to the color of their best wine. His grandfather had an old truck parked down by the winery, but he walked everywhere if he could. If town had been closer, he'd have walked there. Right now, Antonio heard him approach, his once-even gait shuffling a little more in his advancing years.

"Were you going to say goodbye, *mi coniglio*?" Antonio smiled and couldn't remember the last time his grandfather had used his childhood nickname. He'd never liked it, a fact that had never dissuaded his family's use of it.

"I was going to come find you after I packed the car." Antonio hugged and kissed his grandfather, who was one of the only stable adults in his life. The others were his nonninas. He hardly ever saw his grandmother Martha. She moved back to England when his other grandfather died. But Giuseppe and Magdalena had been married since they were sixteen and seventeen. They'd inherited this vineyard, like the several generations before them. And they loved each other. They loved their children and grandchildren, but they loved one another more. A pang of affection hit him in the chest. "I said goodbye to Nonna." Antonio smiled. "She told me not to get married. That she'd find me a woman when I returned."

His grandfather laughed. "Don't doubt it, my boy. Now, are you sure about this?"

"I am. I need to do this. Marcello doesn't understand." It was disrespectful to call his father by his first name, but he wasn't feeling particularly giving right now.

"You shouldn't part when you are angry. You think you know everything, but you don't, Antonio. You blame him. He blames himself. But you don't know everything."

"I know enough," Antonio said roughly. It had been several months, and he still had trouble even thinking of his mother. "I have class in three hours. I must go, Nonno. Take care of the grapes while I'm gone. Marco will make a mess of it."

Giuseppe gave his grandson a chiding look. "He's still learning. He wants to please, but he doesn't love it the way your sister does." As if summoned from the depths of the cellars, Catarina ran toward him. Like a little deer, she was all thin legs and speed. Lithe like their mother.

"Antonio!" She flew into his arms. "I almost missed you. One of the nanny goats gave birth. You should see it! It's a girl. She's so cute!"

His sister loved everything about their home and all who dwelled there. She was the heart of this place. He would miss her exuberance. "Goodbye, *little duck*."

"I wish I could go. I wish you'd stay ..." She paused. "I don't know what I wish."

"I wish to find you running this place by the time I return. You are destined for great things, *papera*. I love you," he said. Antonio looked back at his family seat. Viti del Fiume, a successful vineyard and his boyhood home. Or at least it had been for most of his life. He'd miss the gentle slopes and twisting vines. But he had another destiny, and he just couldn't be here anymore.

Università degli Studi di Milano

Antonio looked at his faculty advisor, Dr. Maria Russo, and felt about twelve years old. "Dr. Rinalto, you know that I encourage going abroad to round out your education. I wholeheartedly support it. However, according to your file, you know three languages. Our native Italian, Latin, for educational purposes, and English. And you received mediocre marks in English five years ago." She began, then, speaking to him in fluent Portuguese said, "As far as I know, Brazil is still a Portuguese-speaking country. Why Brazil?"

He shook himself. He'd caught some of it. He said in English, just to salvage his pride, "I can get by in Spanish and French. My roommate is from Barcelona." Portuguese wasn't that different. He was a quick study, despite that mediocre mark in English. There had been a beautiful girl from Abruzzo in his class, and he'd done more flirting than studying. He'd been just out of secondary school. "I've been studying on my own. You said ... something about Brazil being full of Portuguese, by the way. I did understand a lot of it. I hired a tutor as well."

She threw her hands up, an unladylike curse coming out of her. "Why Brazil? Why not America or England?"

"Because I'm needed there." He wasn't needed here. Marco would take over the family vineyard when his father and grandfather retired. Catarina would be the brains, even though no one gave her credit. At sixteen, she already showed signs of a good business head and an unmatched palate within the family. Even better than his. It infuriated Marco that his two younger siblings could pick out those subtle notes so easily. Make a sip of wine a study in layers and flavors. It was genetic, of course. His father groomed Marco, ignoring the gem that lay in his coffers. Catarina could run the vineyard someday, if his father would just listen to reason. And if his brother's pride and need for approval wouldn't get in the way of progress. Antonio was suddenly grateful for his second-son status. Middle children often flew under the radar. He had different dreams.

"You could work in Florence with little effort. Stay near your family. I could make this happen for you. With what has happened this year, I'd thin—"

"I want Brazil," Antonio said, cutting her off. For so many reasons, he couldn't count. "Is there any reason I can't? Because the job is good. I'd leave in two weeks, and it would give me a chance to take the intense language class." Not to mention finishing up about five million vaccines. He would do this. "The private hospital agreed to honor my arrangement with the charity mission. They have a good relationship with the Reverend Mother in charge of the hospital. I'd go there twice a month as the general surgeon resident. It would be minor surgeries. Ones that would otherwise add the poor people and orphans to wait lists. And anything too serious would be farmed out to the closest public hospital. If you check your email, I have the head physician's information. He's willing to work with us."

"It's very adventurous and noble. I suppose I can't say no. It might be good publicity for the program. Buy a good camera. Our webpage administrator will want to give updates on the university blog."

MANAUS, BRAZIL
Two Weeks Later

Antonio stepped into the baggage area, his camera bag and laptop case strapped to his chest and shoulders. He looked around and saw a man holding a sign—*Dr. Antonio Rinalto, Hospital Rio Amazonas.* His stomach jumped with excitement. This was the beginning of something good. He knew it. The person meeting him was a guide of sorts. Someone who would show him some rental properties, assist him with buying a car, and other things that would help him get settled. For now, he'd take him to his hotel. Then he'd pick him up bright and early to go to his new workplace.

The hospital had a good reputation, but his real passion was helping the people who could not afford the private hospitals. And if he had to hobnob in Brazilian society, pay his dues at the surgical unit, he would. His specialty had been as a trauma surgeon, but his duties would be split with general surgery, as they had a need. Residents didn't get to call the shots. Not yet. As he walked out of the airport into the balmy air and buzzing insects flying overhead, the troubles of Italy receded to a corner of his heart that would be locked and forgotten. At least for the next two years.

LONDON, ENGLAND

Sophie Bellamy climbed the steps to the headquarters at New Scotland Yard, willing her body to stop shaking. Her parents bracketed her, a shield of protection and love. "Such strength, my sweet Sophie. Your maman and I are so very proud of you." She found her father's rich tones and French accent to be so very comforting. Sophie's throat ached with the effort of keeping her tears at bay.

He wouldn't see her. She kept reminding herself of that fact. They were taken into the interrogation area of the police station and then led into a dark room. The pane of glass, she was assured, was a one-way mirror. No one would see her. But he would know. Of course he'd know.

They brought five men into the other room, lining them up under numbers on the wall. She felt like he was staring at her. She cleared her throat. "It's number two."

"Miss Bellamy, you can take your time—"

She cut him off. "It's number two. That is Richard Devereaux. I have no doubts. Now, can I please go home?"

HER MOTHER WAS SCREAMING AT THE PROSECUTING ATTORNEY on the phone. Sophie didn't want to hear any more, but she couldn't seem to move. Kate Bellamy had one of those commanding voices that made grown men pay attention. She was a wonderful mother. Soft and sweet to her only child. But Sophie had seen her take someone to task before. She'd pitied every one of them up until today.

"What the hell do you mean, *not enough evidence?* You found the bloody man after he broke into my daughter's home and attacked her. You wouldn't even have the drug seizure if she hadn't called you!" She paused. "You know she didn't give him a key. This is a load of bollocks. This is all about getting a plea agreement and not paying for a trial. I can't believe you are dropping the other charges. He assaulted my daughter, and you are just casting that aside because a drug bust makes for better news! Don't want women to be afraid to come to London! Let's just cover up the assault, and you can all pat yourselves on the bloody back!"

Her mother slammed the phone down, angrier than Sophie had ever seen her. She took a few deep breaths. Sophie wiped a tear away and asked, "How long is his prison sentence?" *How long do I have to feel safe?*

I

ST. CLARE'S CHARITY MISSION, STATE OF
AMAZONAS, BRAZIL—TEN YEARS LATER

Antonio dove toward the shuttlecock, feeling the feathers brush his fingertips as he heard the children behind him moan and the children on the opposing team cheer. The children of St. Clare's learned *peteca* as soon as they could run, so it was no surprise he'd lost another round. It didn't help that he chose all of the least athletic children to be on his team. He looked up into the face of Emilio, one of the older boys, who wore a cheeky grin. "Emilio, you should take pity on an old man," he said in Portuguese. Emilio had always struggled with English.

Emilio said, "The médica is older than you, and she's playing better than you, too."

Antonio heard Doc Mary laugh, her Irish accent thick with fatigue. She said to Emilio, "I'm not sure whether to be insulted or flattered, lad." Antonio winked at her, wiping the sweat from his brow just before getting dog-piled by his young teammates. Cristiano squealed as Antonio grabbed him and tickled him. He was Doc Mary's little shadow, normally, but she'd told Antonio to pick Cristiano as his co-captain so he'd feel like he was special to someone else.

9

They walked to the dining hall, which serviced the abbey, hospital, and school. The smells were wafting out of the open windows. The cook, Gabriela, was a master of feeding many on a small budget and not sacrificing taste.

Antonio loved it here at the mission. The volunteer doctors came and went, with only a skeleton crew of nurses, doctors, and techs able to make St. Clare's their life's work. The sisters who inhabited the abbey were usually of two persuasions—medical or child care and education. There were a few here for administrative duties. The local staff included a kitchen of one, a caretaker, and security staff.

He watched Paolo in the garden, gathering squash for the kitchen. Henrico and Emilio were the two oldest children at the orphanage, and they also helped keep the grounds and learned essential building maintenance. Soon, the two boys were to leave for the Brazilian Army, and the thought made Antonio's heart squeeze. Antonio had seen these boys grow into young men. He turned to Mary. "So, Hans seems glad to be back." Her husband, Hans, had gone back to Ireland for the birth of his latest grandchild.

"He is. And we've been keeping a big secret, he and I. And the abbess, of course," she said. She was grinning like she indeed had a secret.

"Oh, yes? It's not my birthday. What is your secret, Medíca?" Mary opened the door as he looked up and saw something he was afraid he would never see again. Or someone, in this case.

A screeching woman ran at him while her husband laughed, shaking his head. Antonio said, "Santa Madre, I hope I'm not dreaming!" They were two doctors whom he'd said goodbye to almost two years ago, and he had genuinely feared he'd never see them again. They kept in touch, but it wasn't the same as seeing their faces every day. He filled his arms with this strong, soft woman. He'd been half in love with Dr. Izzy Collier not so long ago, but she'd fallen hard and unexpectedly for the Irishman, who now narrowed his eyes at him with displeasure.

Liam said, "Don't go lingering on that embrace, brother. I'm watching you."

Antonio swung her around just to antagonize the Irishman, then put her down and took a running start at Liam, grabbing the big bastard up in a bear hug. "It is good to see you, my brother."

The three of them just stared stupidly at each other, grinning with their hearts in their eyes. Then Antonio noticed two more people standing and watching the reunion with smiles on their faces. He didn't know them, but the resemblance was unmistakable. Liam looked like a leaner, sharper version of his father, and Antonio remembered Patrick O'Brien coming to St. Clare's last year. Patrick had his mother's auburn hair. "And you've brought us a midwife," he said with a bow. "Mr. and Mrs. O'Brien, I presume?"

They exchanged handshakes and Antonio said, "Liam always said you'd love this place. For the work we do, if not the weather and the wildlife. Signora, welcome to our humble hospital. You are greatly needed."

"Izzy told me you were a charmer." The woman smiled. "Meet my husband, Sean. He's my bodyguard and boy toy."

Antonio's friend Liam choked on his response. "Mam! Behave yourself. There are nuns running about."

This woman was just ending her fifties or maybe starting her sixties, but she was lovely and youthful looking. She had creamy, smooth skin and a sparkle in her eye. Antonio gave her a rakish grin. "Your husband is a lucky man to hold such a position." He watched her husband give his son a knowing look.

"Aye, Liam told me you were a flirt with the lasses," the man said. Sean O'Brien cut a commanding figure.

Antonio threw his head back and laughed, grabbing Liam for another hug. "We need you, brother. And our Izzy. The volunteers are coming in less frequently, and we haven't had a surgeon in four months. God has answered our prayers."

❦

ANTONIO WATCHED AS THE VISITING DOCTORS GOT reacquainted with the staff and children. They also met the new children. There were always new ones. Emilio and Henrico were elated to see Liam and Izzy, who would be here to see them off for basic training. His heart was full. He felt a presence at his side, and he turned to see Reverend Mother Faith sliding in beside him. "I do love a full house, lad."

The Irish nuns had started this mission over thirty years ago. The abbess was a complicated powerhouse of a woman. Antonio said, "Abbess, you look well. How was your checkup?"

"Sinus rhythm and all my own teeth." She smiled wryly.

"It's good to hear. And this full house of yours is an answer to many prayers, I think. You've been missing your countryman."

"Yes, and our Liam is transformed, isn't he? And he's gone from dodging his parents' calls to dragging them across the globe. Seamus can't recommend her enough. He suspects she might be a witch." At Antonio's gasp, she shrugged. "One of the good ones. He says she can coax the babe from the womb with her whispers. Then again, history has always painted powerful women as witches. Regardless, it's good to have her with us."

Her eyes lit on the young American surgeon with such love. "And our Izzy. I've prayed for this. For her. We needed a full-time surgeon. You are stretched to the point of breaking between the two hospitals."

"I would do more if I could. You all are the best thing in my life. You are my family," he said softly.

"Aye, but what of your family back home? Have you thought any more about what we've discussed?" the abbess asked, tilting her head.

Forgiveness. He had thought about it. He missed home, and he dreaded the thought of it at the same time. "I'll think about it, Reverend Mother."

"Yes, well there's thinkin' and then there's thinkin'," she said shamelessly. She had no problem poking at sore spots. It was the mental health clinician in her. She hadn't always been a nun.

"Has anyone ever told you that you are a pushy woman, Reverend Mother?" he asked dryly.

"Yes. It's a requirement for this job, as a matter of fact. I made full marks in being pushy. I suspect I may have met my match, however."

She motioned, and Antonio looked over just in time to see Sorcha O'Brien clout her son just behind the ear. He said, "I think I am going to love this woman."

❧ 2 ❧

PLUMPTON COLLEGE—EAST SUSSEX, ENGLAND

Sophie walked between the rows of vines at the college vineyard, enjoying the soft misting of late summer rain. Brighton was the sunny side of England, but it was still England. They got their share of rain. The grapes they grew here weren't the type that flourished in the arid climate of France or the Napa Valley. One worked with what one had.

She waved to her classmate, who was laboring under the scrutiny of the rootstock specialist and viticulture lecturer. Proficiency in identifying good rootstock was an extremely important skill in this field. After all, you reap what you sow. The next course was successful grafting, which had actually been her last final of spring semester. She'd worn a band around her head like some sort of eighties' jazzercise instructor while doing the painstaking work. It was a tough class with an even tougher professor. She knew her fellow student, Stanley, would ace it just as she had. He was bright and ambitious. Same ilk and all that. Still, the poor bugger looked so stressed right now. She gave him a sympathetic smile.

Sophie was working this summer, preparing for her final semester abroad. She was old to be an undergrad. At twenty-nine, she should have a doctorate by now, or at least full-time employment. She was going to school on a scholarship, but she still had bills to pay. She'd been working part-time on this campus for three years, two of them in the wine division. This summer, however, was a full-time gig. Her degree in Viticulture and Oenology required a semester-long internship. The program preferred a semester abroad, given the limited nature of English wine country. The major players in Sonoma and Napa had given preference to Californians. The need for all hands on deck after the fires was understandable. They didn't have time to break in some newbie who didn't know the soil or varietals as well.

French opportunities were even more grim. Centuries of bad blood aside, the French didn't consider England to be capable of making real wine. She'd thought her father's lineage would have carried some weight, and her ability to get by with the language, but no joy. So, Italy it was. Not quite Burgundy or Bordeaux, but she'd taken Italian and Latin in secondary school twelve years ago, and Italian again during her first attempt at college. She'd had a crush on a boy who was a foreign exchange student her last year of secondary school, and he'd helped her get high marks.

Italy might be middle of the road in wine quality, but they made a lot of it. And there was something about that accent. About the dark, bewitching eyes and silky, raven hair so common in the native Italians.

Sophie should have kept that handsome, young boy around instead of the one who followed. The man she'd let derail everything her second year of uni. So, here she was, pushing thirty, finally ready to graduate. She'd taken weekend-long extra credit courses to France and Germany, touring their world-class wine country. She hadn't made it to California, as the wildfires had devastated the agri-tourism and study-abroad programs and had wiped out entire estates. Plumpton's Viticulture and Oenology program had held a wine tasting in the great hall, paired with local chef creations. They'd collected two hundred fifty quid a plate and sent it to a wildfire relief fund, which aided the smaller vineyards with rebuilding. The wine culture was tight like that, even with the ingrained snobbery.

This internship was pretty low-key. Sophie couldn't get in with one of the Antinori estates or in the most coveted positions in Brunello, but she could work with low-key. Her host vineyard had just entered into the international student program. She'd be their first intern. She'd dug around a little. They'd won a lot of local awards twenty years back, but they couldn't produce the volume that the Antinoris and Ruffinos of the region could. And something had gone amiss around the 2014 vintage.

Sophie was anticipating some hard work and stress, but she loved a good challenge. She'd been very popular with her three flatmates. Four of them shared a two-bedroom flat, like a bunch of freshmen. But rent was very costly in Essex, given Brighton was a huge holiday destination. The reason she'd been popular was due to her attempts at learning all she could about Chianti in the last two months. If she didn't want to become a complete alcoholic and go broke, she had to share the bottles of wine. It was good to get the feedback, anyway. They were all in her field of study. Winos, one and all. Two in the viticulture program, and one training as a sommelier and headed for culinary school. She needed to learn as much as possible about the tier system, regions, and laws governing the Tuscan wine industry. Much like the French, they were very controlled with their wine standards. Little room for blending foreign grapes into their better wines. But the culture was an old one, and it was an exciting prospect. She'd be spending the next three months in Tuscany, right during the harvest.

Sophie walked into the staff office just as her mobile rang. She apologized to her colleague and answered it. The call was from London.

"Miss Bellamy, this is the London office of New Scotland Yard. I'm calling regarding a case that was prosecuted in 2011." Her stomach almost heaved up her tea. She sat down, suddenly finding that her legs wouldn't hold her weight.

"Yes?"

"It's our duty to inform you if there has been a change in status regarding your ... assailant's incarceration."

***

"Sophie, dear, put your head between your knees." The voice was gentle. Then it barked, "Stanley, get a cloth from the cupboard and run cold water over it."

Sophie was shaking so hard, she could barely stay on the chair. Her muscles were locked up like she was turning to stone. *No, no, no!* This couldn't be happening. Fourteen days. She had fourteen days.

***

Sophie opened the door to her apartment, just wanting to crawl into her bed and cry. Her three flatmates had other plans. The bottle of Italian sparkling wine gave a pop, and the three friends cheered. She'd texted them about the early departure for Italy, and obviously they'd thought it a good thing. They didn't know the why of it. Instead of feigning surprise and hugging them, she burst into tears.

Matt was the first one to her, a look of horror on his face. "Christ, love. What is the matter? We thought you were happy?" He hugged her, and she melted into his big body. He was quite a bit taller than she was, broad backed, and well fed. Perks of being a chef, no doubt. The other two descended on his heels. Gwen and Petra wrapped their arms around her and let her calm herself, then she was seated on the sofa. Matt sat to her right, Gwen on her left. Petra knelt before her, hands on her knees.

"Tell us." Her brown eyes and unruly, dark hair were a comforting sight. Her mother was Greek, so she had that unique blend of English features with Mediterranean coloring. Tears came down Sophie's face. "You're shaking, Sophie. What's happened?"

So, she told them. The worried looks on their faces confirmed that she'd been right to panic. This was bad. "He is released in two weeks. My name isn't on the lease, so you should be okay. Just be careful. Please, I couldn't bear it if something happened to one of you." She swiped a palm over her wet cheeks. "How could they possibly think it was okay to let him out early?"

"Psychopaths can be very charming if it's a means to an end," Gwen said, the psychiatry student turned viticulturist always offering a solid analysis.

"I'm going to miss your graduation. I'm so sorry," Sophie said.

"This is not your fault. We want you to be safe. Besides, I plan on putting my parents in your room when they visit. So, there's that." Gwen shrugged, grinning. It made Sophie smile. She loved her roommates.

Matt said, "I'll make sure no one walks home alone. We'll be okay, my darling. Just pack your bags and get the hell out of here. Did you call your mum?"

Sophie nodded. "Yes. I don't think he'd go to France, but my father has a hunting gun. He'd blow the bastard's head off if he came near my mum." She sighed. "I won't be able to write or anything. I mean, maybe we are overreacting. Maybe he's moved on to other things. Other ..."

Obsessions. She really hoped so.

ॐ

As it turned out, her parents were not content to let her stew in her own anxiety and fumble through a quick departure. When she looked through the peephole of the old door to her flat, she stifled a sob. "Mum! Papa!" She flung open the door and fell into their arms.

Getting her packed and ready took no time at all, and her father had rented an extra-large vehicle to haul her belongings to a storage unit. "Thank you, Papa. And you, Mum. You were just what I needed," she said softly. Afraid she would begin weeping like a child, Sophie cleared her throat. "You have to let me repay you. Since we'll be on airbeds and don't have to drive, I want to practice tonight. My roommates as well. I am going to lead you through a wine tasting. The Italian wines are going to be lower budget than the place I'll be staying, but it'll still be fun. So, let's get pissed tonight. A proper farewell."

Her father had been digging into his back seat while she spoke. He brandished two bottles. "It goes against my French nature to buy Italian wine, but these should be a nice treat, I think." Her face lit up. A treat indeed.

THEY'D BORROWED THE TASTING GLASSES FROM THE WINERY ON campus, and Sophie was excited to play at this with people she loved. A safe zone for her to practice her skills. "Mum, Papa, I'll be leading the tasting, and Matt will be offering up some advice for food pairing as our sommelier- in-training. There is water and bland table crackers if you need to cleanse your palate."

They made their way through the whites first. "We've all had the Pinot Grigio selections at the Sparr Market, so we are going to concentrate on some midrange selections, first from Tuscany and then from Piedmont." Sophie poured the Vernaccia di San Gimignano first, taking them through the tasting notes. "It is a dry, medium-bodied wine with fairly high acidity. What do you taste, Papa?" she asked in French. Putting the Frenchman on the spot was a good bit of fun.

Her father winked at her and took a sip, rolling the wine over his whole mouth. He said, "Citrus, apples ... pear, I think?"

She looked at Gwen. "Anything else?"

Gwen took a third sip. "Yes to all of those things. Score one for

France." She let the wine soak into her mouth. "Underripe pear more so than the sweet, ripe taste. And I'm getting almonds."

"Magnifico!" Sophie said, practicing her Italian. They tasted the Vermentino from Piedmont, then started with the reds by sampling a Nebbiolo. "Now, my father has decided to treat us and raise the bar a bit. This first selection is a wonderful Amarone della Valpolicella from Veneto. A 2016 that is a splurge bottle but won't put you in the workhouse." She took them through the full-bodied wine, pointing out the deep-garnet color and the plum, blueberries, and violet tasting notes.

Her mother, cheeky as ever, said, "I never understood the leather, bark, tobacco, and other such nonsense for notes. Do you really taste all that? And do we want it to taste like our handbags?" Sophie laughed because she was perfectly serious. Her mother tasted the wine. The rest was lost on her.

She smiled. "I love you, Mum."

They came to the star of the show. She couldn't believe her father had splurged on such a bottle. Her roommates' eyes bugged out when they saw the label. "Next is a wonderful Brunello di Montalcino from 2010 that is finally into its drinking window. Brunellos always taste perfectly wonderful, but the good ones should get better if you wait ten years and store them properly. This is not easy to get, so I'm not sure how he managed." She gave her father a sideways glance.

He gave a very French shrug. "I traded one of my good Burgundy vintages with another enthusiast. So, my retirement is still safe." They all laughed. Her father was such a charmer.

There was a collective moan when they all took that first, good sip. A properly aged Brunello was like sex in a glass. She'd only ever had a glass one other time.

"Which region is your vineyard?" Petra asked innocently. Sophie's face fell.

Sophie said, "I'm sorry. It's better that you don't know." She waved the grim looks away. "You'll hear all about it after I'm home.

For now, let's drink to my papa for this gorgeous bottle of wine. It's the perfect send-off."

THE RIVER THAMES
London, England

Sophie looked out at the black-and-grey water of the Thames and shivered, despite the warm evening. Her flight was at midnight. After the phone call from Scotland Yard, she'd immediately contacted the vineyard in Italy. They agreed to receive her early, as she'd require no extra wages for the time difference. Not that the wages were much. She'd spoken with her roommates because she had to talk to someone. Then her academic advisor, who'd blanched when she'd broken down, sobbing, and relayed her ugly tale. The abridged version, but the woman needed to understand that her whereabouts had to be classified.

Any trace of where she was going was taken out of her computer files until they figured out a way to secure their correspondence. After all, even madmen could be computer savvy. They could also be manipulative and conniving. The advisor could call the vineyard and check her progress without making a paper trail.

Sophie remembered her previous apartment here in the city. She'd shared a flat with a nursing student when she was nineteen. She received an occasional Christmas card from her, but that was it. Sophie was shocked every time one came. As much damage as he'd done to her relationships with other people, she was truly surprised Morgan had hung in there with her. She'd called her, of course. Morgan had been there during the worst of it. Morgan hadn't had to testify, which was good, but she still had a right to know.

Sophie looked out at the slow-churning blackness and she let herself cry just a little. She was glad her parents were back in Gordes, a beautiful, old village in Provence and her father's place of birth. When they'd retired, they decided to give up their home in

Richmond-Upon-Thames. They'd made a small fortune, having had the home through the housing boom, nigh on twenty-five years. Her father's retirement was modest, and this afforded them a comfortable, one-story in the Luberon Valley of Provence. Now they shopped the local markets together. Cooked all of their meals. Tended a gorgeous garden. They deserved it. They truly did. They'd tried numerous times to give her part of their profits from the London home. She'd refused, of course.

When Sophie was young, she'd had a full scholarship but lost it while recuperating. After that, she'd waited tables, then found a job at a wine shop in a posh part of London. That's when it all began. Where she'd learned about wine. Not the expensive stuff, but it had been enough to spark the fire in her. Her parents had always enjoyed a decent glass of wine at dinner. Her father was French, after all, but she'd barely taken notice, preferring a pint of bitter with her mates when she'd gone to the pub.

Her first attempt at university had been in horticulture and floriculture, something that had served her in the end because the classes on soil and minerals had crossed over. Now Sophie was headed to the slopes of Greve, a riverside valley in the heart of Chianti Classico that boasted some of the best wine in the world. Bravado? Maybe. But it was far away from England, and that's what she needed right now. She was suddenly grateful she'd decided to go abroad. Otherwise, her last semester could have been completely derailed. Again. She'd sleep in the barn with the donkey at this point. Didn't all Italian farms, orchards, and vineyards have at least one donkey?

Viti del Fiume
Greve, Italy

Catarina Rinalto smacked her stubborn partner on the rump, trying not to lose her temper. "I just fed you, you stubborn boy.

Move it." He was carrying some equipment for her, and he was currently trying to detour toward the kitchen garden.

Her father yelled from behind her. "You can take the ATV, little duck. We aren't so destitute as to go back to using a donkey. I don't know why we keep him."

"We keep him because he's part of the family. And he needs the exercise." Catarina urged him forward and waved as her grandfather spotted her from far into the vines. He still had eyes like a hawk.

Marco was on a conference call, as usual. He handled the business end but rarely got his hands dirty. He hated it here. Would he leave her as well, like their brother had?

Ten years. It was ten years since Antonio left. Sure, he sent emails, packages on Christmas, even called a couple times a year. But it wasn't enough. The gap just kept getting wider. They were strangers. And if no one else would do anything about it, Catarina was going to have to get creative. She smiled as she urged Fabio forward, wobbling with her gear strapped to either side of him. Perhaps her grandfather could help her with her brother? She did get her devious side from him, after all.

She came alongside her grandfather, sweating from pulling Fabio along with her pack. "Nonno, I need your help."

He wiped his own brow, dark from the sun. "I'll have to get my rifle, but it's about time you put that useless animal down."

"Nonno, don't say such things. He's a darling boy." Catarina petted Fabio's beautiful mane. Too beautiful for a scruffy mule. "It's about Antonio. He needs to come home."

Her grandfather said, "I've written to him, Paperotta." *Little duck.* She smirked at the endearment she'd never been able to shed.

"I was thinking of getting a bit more aggressive with my tactics," she said, giving him a sideways glance.

"You mean deceptive, I think. You are my granddaughter. Now, let's hear this plan of yours. It's about time we played dirty." Giuseppe Rinalto wasn't getting any younger, and his grandson needed to come home.

❦

CATARINA WALKED INTO THE OFFICE, SHEDDING HER DIRTY BOOTS at the door. "Marco, how was the meeting?"

"Productive," he hedged.

He could be such an asshole. Marco didn't necessarily want to run the family vineyard. They'd actually been struggling under his leadership. Not that he'd ever admit it. But her selfish mother had made both her father and brother take a vow just days before her death. She'd asked their father to tutor her firstborn to be the greatest winemaker in Italy, pinning both her father and her oldest brother to this commitment out of guilt.

Marco was petty when it came to vineyard business. As flighty as her mother had been, he was as clamped down and uptight. Two sides of the same coin because it was to the detriment of the family. Catarina had been a teenager, but she remembered. Antonio and Marco had been blind to her flaws. As had her father been. So, Marco wouldn't let her run the vineyard, even though he knew she should. It was pure, stupid male pride. And he might well destroy everything that had been built over a hundred years. Generations of winemakers at Viti del Fiume and one incompetent man at the helm could ruin it all. They were still paying for one of his bad decisions. It had started a ripple effect, making collectors less likely to pay premium prices. One year with bad reviews, and they were just now ready to reclaim their former glory. The two-year-old barrels were ready for blending, and it was going to be her greatest work.

"Prepare the guest room. The intern is coming early," Marco said.

Catarina jerked. "What intern? Which university?" she asked. "This is the first I've heard of this."

"Plumpton College," he said absently. "They have a good incentive to take students. I was lucky to get one. And I don't need to clear things through you, Catarina. All I need is clean sheets on the bed and some toiletries."

"Where the hell is Blumpton College? I've never heard of it. And you do need to talk to me. I help manage this place, whether you'll admit it or not. What sort of intern have you hired to be putting their paws on my vines?"

"Plumpton, with a *p*. It's in England. It's the best I could do with no previous history hiring interns. I tried to get someone local, but they'd already filled other positions. It's this English-woman or we wait until next semester. She's working for almost nothing. All we have to do is house her and pay her an embarrass-ingly low wage. She has very good references."

"You aren't hiring a nanny, Marco. This is a skilled profession. It takes much knowledge and instinct. What the hell does some Englishwoman know about wine?"

3

MILAN, ITALY

Sophie tipped the driver who dropped her off in front of the hostel in Milan. Her train left in the morning, which meant she had this evening to wait it out in the city. She'd take the train to Florence, then a bus to the city center in Greve in Chianti. Marcello Rinalto Jr. would collect her at the enoteca. Marcello ... what a name. She'd forgo trying to shag her boss, but the name brought forth visions of olive skin, a dark, silky mane, and lean muscles, honed by hours of working outdoors. She approached the clerk at the desk of the hostel. It was a simple, communal room for females. No co-eds at this place. Boys had their own room. The stern-looking Italian woman said, "Ciao, signorina. Nome?"

"Sophie Bellamy, signora. I'm afraid my Italian is poor, but I will try. You must be signora Fiore."

The woman's face softened. "Parli bene l'italiano, signorina. This way." She motioned to follow, but Sophie was pleased to find that she'd followed the conversation. She'd taken a refresher course her last semester, and it had paid off. Her Italian was rubbish, despite her hostess's kind words. But she could get by, and she knew that the host family in Tuscany did speak some English. Small favors.

Sophie dropped her bag in the locker, retrieving a change of clothing and some toiletries. She couldn't wait to see the city. She would head straight to the Duomo di Milano. It would be her only tour, as everything was closing in two hours. She rushed a quick washup, put on a pair of jeans and a T-shirt, and left for the cathedral. She'd realized her mistake about two blocks into her walk.

Milan—arguably the fashion capital of Europe—and she was wearing denims, track shoes, and a Plumpton College T-shirt. The day was warm, and she passed women dressed to the nines in silk, linen, good sunglasses, and great shoes. *Way to look like a tourist.* She was here to work, however. This was just a quick diversion. She'd worn the jeans and short sleeves because she'd read that Italian churches had a dress code. Nothing above the knee and no bare shoulders or chest. So, she'd forgone her tank top and cute shorts for something a twelve-year-old boy would wear to school.

Sophie passed shops, taking in the pretty dresses and leather goods. Maybe just a little shopping after the cathedral couldn't hurt. The only dress she'd packed looked like an oversize T-shirt. She cringed at the thought of her Birkenstocks being her only sandals. She'd been out of the dating scene for a couple years, once she'd gotten into her intense classes. At her age, the lads at the college were too young. One of the older students in her viticulture class had been interested, but she hadn't been comfortable with the age gap. She'd briefly considered using him for sex, because it had been even longer for that, but she wasn't comfortable with casual sex.

Sophie arrived at the front of the cathedral, giving them her three euro to enter. She took in the outside of the building first. It was enormous. The outdoor sculptures were so intricate, they looked as though they'd leap off their perches. Gargoyles guarded the structure, as did figures from religious history. At the tallest spire was the Virgin Mother, overlooking the city. She loved architecture and sculpture. She especially enjoyed lavish gardens with statuary incorporated into the flora. She couldn't wait to get inside, take the lift to the rooftop, and see the entire city.

Duomo di Milano
The Basilica of St. Mary

Sophie considered herself a connoisseur of cathedrals. She was English, after all. And French, come to think of it. Two countries that knew how to build a grand church. But she could see, now, why this church had taken six centuries to complete.

The stonework and marblework were true masterpieces. The art, the sculpture, and the glasswork all came together to make something that was sure to convince the biggest critic of God's existence. It was the largest in Italy because the one in the Vatican City was technically not part of Italy, but rather its own sovereign nation. This was the seat of the Archbishop of Milan, which would have been quite something when the world politics and the church were interwoven together much more tightly. It was so massive that when she looked up, she felt a wave of vertigo.

The open stonework and spires on the exterior of the church were impossibly intricate. What had these stone carvers been like, devoting their life to this church and responsible for the smallest details. And the stained glass, crafted long before modern tools and shortcuts made the process so much easier. It boggled the mind, really. And the gold Madonna ... whose privilege and responsibility had it been to sculpt her with such loving care?

Sophie ignored the other tourists and let her mind sweep her through the centuries. The statue of *St. Bartholomew Flayed* was eerie enough to cause a shiver to go through her. He wore his flayed skin as a cloak. The statue was disturbingly beautiful, with details that made you think about how he became a martyr.

She went to the chapel of San Giovanni Bono, or St. John the Good, the Archbishop of Milan in the mid-seventh century. She lit a candle for her parents, the best people she knew, and put a coin in the collection box. But it was the golden Madonna who drew her back. As she left the church and saw her again, she bowed her head. "Protect me from this evil. Protect everyone I love. I can't fight this on my own."

AFTER SPENDING AN HOUR IN THE CATHEDRAL, SOPHIE STEPPED into a few shops to see what Italian high fashion was like in comparison to the posh stores in London. The women working in the shops gave her dismissive glances, positive that she couldn't afford what they had to offer. They were right, of course. Eight-hundred-dollar shoes and off-the-shoulder blouses that cost more than her share of the rent. She needed, she decided, the Italian equivalent of Zara or H&M.

Sophie stopped at a food vendor for a small pizza, forgoing a sit-down restaurant. She sat on a bench in a less crowded piazza, eating the best thing she'd ever put in her mouth. Irregularly shaped and fired in a simple oven, it had bright-green olive oil, roasted garlic, and capers. She'd asked for anchovies on half. They'd looked at her strangely, as she wasn't sharing it with anyone. She'd explained, in broken Italian, that she'd never tried anchovies. So, they put the salty fish on a couple slices, placing basil leaves on the other part, along with slivers of prosciutto. Wise move, as she'd liked the anchovies, but the prosciutto and basil had been just the thing.

With a full belly, Sophie went back to the hostel where a different woman manned the desk. She was signora Fiore's daughter. Francesca was about forty, with dark hair and a beautiful smile. "The viticulturist? My mama told me about you. Off to Chianti? Your university experience was much more interesting than mine."

She led Sophie into the common area, opening a bottle of wine. She'd been studying Italian wines, but she hadn't tried them all. "Barbera d'Alba," she read as she tipped the label up. She held the glass up to the light. The color was dark and rich. The scent was bold and fruity with a hint of earth. When she tried the first sip, her brows shot up.

"It's good, no?" her host asked.

"Yes, excellent. Maybe I picked the wrong region," she said with a wink.

"Oh no, bella. Chianti Classico is the heart of Italy. The wine traditions go back centuries, and Tuscany is so very beautiful. I think you chose wisely."

"Your English is excellent. What did you study at university?"

"Tourism and hospitality. It's good to know English for this field. We have a lot of English, American, and Canadian visitors. Several a season from Australia as well. It has served me very well." Her accent was rich and lovely.

Sophie smiled and said in Italian, "Your language is beautiful, but we appreciate the effort." Or, rather, she thought that's what she'd said. Close enough, hopefully.

Francesca clapped. "Molto buona, Sophie!"

A shared bottle of wine later, Sophie padded to her room, gathered her toiletries, and used the communal loo to ready herself for bed. Head spinning just a bit, she fell into a rare, dreamless sleep.

SOPHIE GOT ON THE 5:40 A.M. TO FLORENCE, SUDDENLY WISHING she'd sprung for a first-class ticket. There were nineteen-year-olds leaning on their packs, smelling like they'd slept in their clothes. She managed to find a seat next to a petite German woman who smiled and left her to her coffee. She watched the city and suburban neighborhoods flash by, then they were in the stretch of country that led first to Bologna, then Florence. The landscape was beautiful, but she felt the pull of sleep as the jet lag and two hefty glasses of Barbera d'Alba started to back up on her.

Before she knew it, the train was stopping as her face slid on the cool glass of the window. The German woman exited the train at Bologna, and a large man took the seat instead. Australian by the sound of him.

His name was Peter, and he smiled warmly at her as he said, "So let me see if I've got this. Instead of listening to some bloke prattle on about statistics and pimp his facking, overpriced book out to his broke students, you're spending a semester in Italy drinking Chianti and working on your tan? I picked the wrong bloody path in life."

Sophie smiled at him. "Yes, but you'll likely get paid a decent wage. I'm working for room, board, and what would be considered slave wages in any part of England."

"Fair enough. My fiancée is meeting me in Florence. You should hang out with us. We'll grab some lunch, be drunk by teatime."

"I've got a bus ticket for Greve that leaves at ten. I wish I could, but I won't even have time to see the city. It's a tragedy, really. I'm going to rush from the train station to the bus station and skip one of the most beautiful cities in Europe. I've got to make that bus, though. My new boss is picking me up at the enoteca at eleven."

Peter said, "Tic-toc, mate. You're all business."

Sophie shrugged. "First impressions and all that. I'll make a point of coming back for a weekend once I get settled. Then I won't have to rush. I'd like to see Siena and Rome as well. Maybe Venice before I head back to England."

Peter put his hand over his heart. "Ah, Venice. Now that's a hell of a city. By then, you'll have met some sweet-talking Italian, and he'll tuck your hair behind your ear as you stare out over the Piazza San Marco."

Sophie barked out a laugh. "I doubt it. Where do you come up with this stuff?"

"My Tori reads a lot of romance novels. Some bloke is always tucking his lover's hair behind her ear. It's in the formula."

"And how do you know this?" she asked, eying him accusingly.

"Busted. I'm a closet romance reader. She leaves them in the dunny." He shrugged.

By the time they'd discussed Peter's upcoming nuptials and his fiancée's career in advertising, they were pulling up to the main station in Florence.

They stood, grabbing their bags. "Good luck with the wedding and have fun on your holiday. Don't forget to stand on the Ponte Vecchio and tuck her hair behind her ear," Sophie said, nudging him.

The man said, "Too right. And don't you forget to stop and smell the roses between all of the work. You never know who you'll meet or what you'll see."

৩৯৩

IT WAS ALMOST CRIMINAL, LEAVING FLORENCE WITHOUT EVEN seeing the Uffizi Gallery. Sophie looked out the window of the bus, and suddenly she was wide awake. They passed the rolling hills, and she saw rows of cypress trees, olive groves, and vines. So many rows of grape vines. She hadn't really let herself think too much about it, having left in such a hurry. She was extremely focused. The few holidays she took, she never really got excited until the week before.

Sophie spent the time leading up to a trip being practical. Laundry, passport, securing lodging. Then had to cancel and rebook since she'd left so abruptly. She was under such stress, she hadn't fully let the reality soak in. She was in Italy for at least the next seventeen weeks. She'd spend Christmas here as well, since her parents were going to spend Christmas at a friend's house in Bourgogne. Or, if the host family needed a break, she'd find somewhere else to go. The only place she knew she would not spend Christmas was England.

St. Clare's Charity Mission
Manaus, Brazil

Antonio waited at attention as the makeshift ambulance pulled into the rustic drive leading up to the mission's hospital. Izzy and a couple of nurses were next to him. Dr. O'Brien, or Izzy as they all called her, looked like she was ready for the race to start. He was tense. Sister Catherine, the only full-time midwife in the Order, waited stiffly as well. They'd brought the two patients from an indigenous village deep in the forest. They traveled by boat, in the floating clinic, because the roads didn't go that far back.

They opened the Land Cruiser and Antonio's Land Rover just as Paolo and Hans jumped out of the driver's seat. Doc Mary was hunched on the balls of her feet in the back of one ambulance, working an air bag that was attached to a trachea port.

"What has happened?" Antonio asked. "I know there was an accident." He noticed the nuns had exited their quarters. It was, after all, just past five in the morning. One of the tribal elders had agreed to keep a prepaid cell at the village. If an accident occurred, they sent a runner with the phone to a designated spot that had a signal. It was the only way they could be notified if they needed help. The problem was charging it, so they swapped the phone out once a week. Antonio saw the first patient, and a wave of dread washed over him.

Mary spoke in quick bursts. "A huge tree gave way after the river jumped the bank. It took out three huts. Three with major injuries. I left the rest of the staff at the village to patch up the others." She motioned to her patient as she bagged him, letting them gently remove him from the vehicle. Mary's briefing was quick and succinct. "Crushed trachea, possible head injury. Large splinter from the support beam pierced his abdomen. I think it nicked his liver. Abdomen is rigid and tender to the touch. Give him a full workup. It was a big, feckin' tree and he got the worst of it." She looked up at the row of praying sisters and said, "Sorry, Reverend Mother."

Antonio watched out of the corner of his eye as Paolo and Sean O'Brien slowly removed their precious cargo. Two patients, actually, not one. It was the pregnant woman from the village, whom Sorcha had been treating for gestational diabetes, and her toddler daughter. The little girl had a swollen lip, several lacerations, and an arm that looked like it was broken at both the radius and ulna. She was chalky and still, which told Antonio just how much pain she was experiencing. He'd just seen the child skipping around the village with her cousin.

That single X-ray machine was going to get a workout. The pregnant mother also looked as though she'd been thrashed about. She was breathing heavily, sweating, and it was obvious to all that she was having this baby today. Sister Catherine fell in step alongside Sorcha, who had been in the back of the ambulance with the two patients. "The child has a broken arm and requires some stitching along the thigh and at her temple. She also needs an assessment for a head injury. The mother took a branch and a ceiling beam across the hips and shoulders. She was on her side, so her abdomen didn't take the brunt of it. I'm worried, though. I need an ultrasound—stat."

Antonio yelled to another yellow-haired doctor. "Quinn, I need you to take the child. I'm taking this patient into surgery." Quinn was a pediatrician, and a damn good one. He was Irish, like many who volunteered. After all, St. Clare's had been founded by an order of Irish nuns.

Doc Mary yelled, "I lost his pulse!" Antonio wheeled him in as Mary started chest compressions. He readied the defibrillator.

"Clear!" The man's body surged. He'd come in unconscious, which didn't bode well. Still no pulse. "Come on, brother," he said in the Portuguese dialect of the area. "Again. Clear." Antonio shocked him again, and he felt a faint pulse. Mary worked efficiently, as did the surgical nurse, using all of the precious equipment they had on hand. He knew this man. He was in his middle years and respected for his hunting and building skills. He was strong. "Don't let go, my friend. Please, don't let go," he whispered.

Antonio could hear Sorcha behind the curtain, assessing the patient with the on-site OB-GYN. "Her blood sugar is in the basement. We need to stabilize her, assess her injuries, and as much as I hate this for her, I'm leaning toward a C-section." The doctor agreed. "I don't want to risk a spinal before we've fully assessed her. It'll have to be general anesthesia."

Sorcha must have checked her cervix because she said, "Scratch that plan. She's fully dilated and this baby is coming. Get that ultrasound in here and a fetal monitor!"

They worked on the woman, who was sobbing as she heard the screams of her other child. Their small radiology department had a new X-ray machine. Izzy poked her head into the O.R. "The little one is going to need surgery. Multiple fractures. Do you want to transfer her to the city hospital?"

Antonio shook his head. "No. She'll wait in pain for hours. Manage her pain and bring Sister Maria in to keep her calm. I don't want to separate her from her mother. Genoveva can take over her class, I think." Sister Maria ran the school at the *orfanato* next door. She was wonderful with small children. Genoveva, who was a previous resident of the *orfanato* and Quinn's daughter, could help mind the children while Sister Maria aided them here.

Antonio leaned down to his patient and said gently, "You're going to be a grandfather again, my brother. You must hold on." That's when he noticed Sean O'Brien and Hans Falk waiting on the sidelines with their hearts in their eyes. His patient wasn't much younger than the two men. Perhaps in his early fifties. Sean and Hans were lucky enough to have seen many grandchildren come into the world, but life was harsh in this dense and unforgiving forest.

It was as if the men felt his soul, struggling between staying and being pulled away. Sean O'Brien crossed himself as Hans whispered, *Hail Mary, full of grace, the Lord is with thee. ...*

But either God wasn't listening or He had other plans for this man beyond this life. He coded again, and this time, he left his daughter and grandchildren for good, or for now, depending on one's doctrine.

⚜

"The worst feeling in the world is the homesickness that comes over a man occasionally when he is at home." — E. W. Howe

ANTONIO SIPPED OUT OF HIS TEPID WATER BOTTLE, WATCHING the sun peek out from the warm, misting rain. The trees and vines were an explosion of color at midday, despite the rain. He'd moved from working on his patient to aiding with the setting of the child's arm. Two pins and a soft cast for now, and in three days, he'd come back with pilfered supplies from his posh, private hospital. They needed waterproof casting supplies in several bright colors befitting such a lovely, courageous, little girl. His heart hurt. Hearing the cries of the second grandchild had almost done him in because his patient would never meet the child. He'd moved beyond them for now. His jaw tightened with anger. There just never seemed to be enough time, enough equipment, enough room, or enough trained staff. He felt a presence approach from behind, robes swishing.

"Antonio, I thought I'd find you here. How is my lad?" Reverend Mother Faith's lilting Irish voice was like a songbird, mingling with the sounds of the forest. She always knew where to find him when he needed comfort. When he required space to think, he went to her garden or the abbey's chapel. But for comfort, he went to the play yard outside the school. He liked to watch the children, always lost in the oblivion of activity.

"Buongiorno, Abbess. How are the mother and child?" he asked.

"The child is nursing. We have the three of them in one room. Iara mourns her da. The children will be a comfort to her."

"Where is her husband?" Antonio asked.

"He's down with a malaria relapse. He was at his mother's house in the next village when the accident happened. His mother wanted the lass to rest before the child came, so she took over caring for him. We called in Raphael, even though it was his day off. Sean and Hans don't know the way to the village on their own, and Paolo has too much to do. They'll go with more supplies and Liam to help with the wounded."

The abbess seemed to ponder the situation. "I think we should monitor Iara's husband here so they can be near each other. The lass has a broken clavicle and some lacerations, and you know of the child. They're all beaten up, both in mind and body. Such a tragedy. We've had so much rain this season. More than usual. Apparently, the ground was so sodden that the tree just fell over, roots and all. The poor village is in shambles. All this wreckage in the wake of the fire last year. They'd only just finished the rebuilding." She shook her head. "I think they're due a respite from such tragedies." Antonio nodded absently. She asked, "When do you work at the hospital next?"

"Tomorrow," he replied, feeling so tired.

"And your sleep has been off. I can always tell when you haven't been sleeping. When you were younger, I suspected the clubs and a bit too much drink was to blame. But you've grown past all that. What troubles your sleep now, my son?"

"Sogni di casa, Madre," he said softly. *Dreams of home.*

"Home has many ghosts for you, I think. And did you know you've been speaking in Italian? I've pieced it together since it's similar to *Portoghese*, but I haven't heard it from you in quite some time. I mean, a bit here and there when you're trying to charm our Izzy, but not so naturally unaware. Do you think perhaps your mind is trying to tell your heart something, my boy?"

He raised a dark brow, knowing she'd tell him what she thought, regardless of his answer.

"That it's time to go home," she said simply. The abbess stood, but not before handing him a slip of paper. "A message from your sister. Apparently, she tried your mobile and the hospital, but you've had a busy morning."

It was in the neat, sweeping script of Sister Agatha. *Antonio, it is our grandfather. You must come home without delay. Catarina.*

🜲 4 🜲

GREVEN IN CHIANTI

**No matter how much cats fight, there always seem to be
plenty of kittens—*Abraham Lincoln***

T he enoteca had been easy enough to find. The bus dropped Sophie off across the Piazza from where she needed to meet the vineyard manager. She looked at her watch, wondering where he could be. Maybe she should explore a bit since she was already here.

Sophie went inside the enoteca to look at the local wines. She'd never heard of many of them, which was wonderful. It meant she couldn't get them in England. She suddenly wanted to try everything. There were Chianti Classicos, of course, and also some Super Tuscans—the rebels of the region who broke the Chianti standards by mixing foreign grapes above twenty percent, mostly French varietals like Merlot and Cabernet Sauvignon. It had certainly shaken up the region, and that was good. Traditional didn't mean it was a good wine. The makers of the Super Tuscans challenged the winemakers to return to quality, not quantity. She'd read all about the Super Tuscan rebellion while she'd been in school.

Sophie also found her host vineyard, displayed prominently on a table of its own. That was certainly a good sign. And that made her look at her watch. Hmm ... maybe she should call. She walked out to the sidewalk, looking again for her new boss. Marcello, however, had been a no-show. In his place, a stunning, young woman peeled up to the sidewalk, speaking half in English and half in Italian. She was olive-skinned, but pale and ruby-lipped. Her hair fell in a dark, thick cascade down her back. She'd have been at home on any Milan runway. However, she wore Timberland work boots, dust-covered, skinny jeans, and a tight NASA T-shirt.

"Oh, signorina, I'm so sorry. My stupid brother planned some sort of conference call and told me to pick you up about ten minutes too late. I had to leave the vines in this"—she waved her hands up and down her body—"condition to come for you. What you must think of us. It's totally unprofessional. I could beat him bloody." Then Catarina grabbed Sophie and kissed both cheeks. Sophie almost dropped her oversize purse.

"It's no bother, signorina, I promise. I've only just arrived. The bus was running late." A lie, but it seemed to ease the woman's embarrassment a tinge. Sophie cringed at the stunning woman's appraising gaze. She probably looked a right mess. She wasn't an elegant traveler. She'd worn a smart outfit for first impressions, but a train, cab, and bus ride later, she was a bit wrinkled and unkempt.

"You are unexpected," the woman said. "I was expecting some young university student."

"Yes, well, I'm a bit of a late bloomer." Christ, she wasn't that old. She thought she was rather passable for pushing thirty.

"You misunderstand. You are bellissima, Ms. Bellamy. It is so good to arrive to find someone my own age."

There was no way this fresh-faced, sexy, young woman was pushing thirty, but she'd take it. She gave her a cheeky grin. "Please, do go on."

Catarina smiled. "Your hair is quite something. It's not brown, blonde, or red. It's like the amber honey that the wild bees make. Marco is going to be sorry he failed to keep his appointment."

Catarina smiled inwardly because if she had her way, both her brothers might be competing for this Englishwoman. She was more interested in Sophie Bellamy's mind, however. She'd read the woman's application and letters of reference. She was particularly good at assessing rootstock and also had some aptitude with marketing. For once, she had to admit that she'd torn into Marcello prematurely. This woman might actually be an asset. She'd have to see. *Keep an open mind.* She took the woman's bag from the sidewalk and put it in the trunk of her car.

Sophie climbed into the buttery, leather seat and grabbed the armrest as Catarina Rinalto drove toward the vineyard like a bat out of hell. By the time they arrived, she was ready to lose the pizza slice she'd had on the way to the bus station. Sophie had been warned about the roads and drivers in Italy, but honestly, she drove like a madwoman. An old, tanned man stood by the drive with a huge smile on his face. A younger, handsome devil stood next to him. This must be the *I can't be bothered to come fetch you myself* Marcello Rinalto and maybe his grandfather? The website did boast of three generations living together on the vineyard.

"I see you've had a taste of my sister's driving. Welcome, signorina Bellamy, to Viti del Fiume. River Vines or Vines from the River, depending on who's trying to win the argument." He glanced at his grandfather, who gave a dismissive snort.

"Thank you, signor. You must call me Sophie," she said graciously.

"Yes, indeed. You've met Catarina. This is Giuseppe, my grandfather. My father will be along shortly. He's also called Marcello. We often name our first sons after their fathers or grandfathers. I'll answer to Marco if you get confused. But come now, you must be tired. I'll show you—" Catarina cut him off before he could put her in the guest chamber next to his room.

"The pool house, yes. It's all ready." Catarina smiled. It wasn't ready, not by half, but she could put it to rights in mere minutes with some open windows and fresh linens.

Her grandfather said, "That's Antonio's space."

Catarina gave him a silencing look and said innocently, "Yes, but it's well appointed, and Antonio hasn't used it for years. She'll have privacy and her own kitchen. It's perfect." She turned to Sophie and said, "Although, we'd prefer that you take your meals with the family. My grandmother is the best cook in Italy."

"High praise, indeed, but you mustn't put anyone out. I don't need anything but a clean bed. I'll be working nonstop leading up to the harvest, and I can survive on pot noodles. Don't feel like …"

A soft, feminine voice came from behind them. "Pot noodle? I've not heard of these noodles." They all turned to see the matriarch of the house, standing and listening.

"And this is my grandmother, Magdalena." When Catarina clarified what pot noodles were—a glue-like substance put into the shape of a noodle that tasted like wet crackers with bouillon powder poured over them—the elderly woman crossed herself as if it was the worst sort of blasphemy. "I will feed you, signorina. You don't need to eat the glue."

They were still laughing when they reached the pool. Sophie whistled through her teeth. "If I sent pictures to my classmates, they'd be jousting to get this internship next term." Catarina had ordered her brother away at the pool gate, not wanting him to see that she'd lied about having the apartment ready.

Their father had employed a housekeeper for the household ever since Marcello and Antonio had been boys. Her grandmother protested, of course, and for a time after their mother's death, Magdalena had done a lot of the work herself and made Catarina do her fair share as well. Now, Catarina absolutely refused to clean up after the men in her house. She kept her own rooms clean, and she helped her grandmother with dinner. However, she'd put her father and Marcello on notice that if they didn't start doing the washing up afterward, and do their own laundry and change their own bed linens, no one would eat another home-cooked meal. She'd even threatened to move into her own place. At that bit of heresy, her father had demanded that Marcello start pulling his weight with the everyday cleanup.

Her grandmother had been scandalized, but Catarina had to stand up for them both. Her grandmother was old school, but she just couldn't take care of this large household anymore, and Catarina had to work. Thus, she'd hired another housekeeper twice a week. Now her grandmother just doted on her grandfather, as was her pleasure to do. And in turn, he rubbed her feet, brought her coffee, and found her reading glasses for her. The system worked. And the pool house was kept clean and tidy, but it hadn't had linens put on the bed in years and the appliances weren't plugged in.

Catarina smiled, seeing the cool, serene swimming pool through fresh eyes. "Yes, it's nice after a long day with the vines."

"You speak of them like they're your children. The vines, I mean," Sophie said.

"They are. They're our children and our great-great-grandparents'. Some of our vines have been going for several generations, some we planted a few years ago. And like a family, we take care of them and they take care of us."

"I love that. Truly, it's a beautiful way of looking at it. I'm so happy to be here, Catarina. And I must confess, your English is so much better than I could have dreamed. Everyone seems to have some degree of aptitude, and I appreciate it. I did take a condensed, intense Italian refresher course, so I can follow you, but I'm afraid I can't speak it as well. You'll have to be patient."

Catarina shrugged and said, "We'll all help you. The best way to learn Italian is to come to Italy and hang out with a bunch of Italians. You'll learn in no time." Her accent was as beautiful as her face. When they went into the pool house, she said, "I'm sorry it's so compact. More of an apartment than a house. There are only two small bedrooms."

But Sophie's eyes were on the picture window. It overlooked the beautiful, sloping land and the valley below. And the acres and acres of vines. "Oh my. Catarina, why don't you live here?"

Catarina was under a cupboard, plugging in the refrigerator. "I've got my own view, and it keeps me closer to my grandparents and father. My brother and I have to be ... present? Is that the word?"

"Yes, that's it. I understand. My parents retired to France. My grandparents are gone on both sides. I lost them too early. My parents are very fit, thankfully. They're both runners. I just still worry with them living so far away from me."

"Bellamy, this is a French name?" Catarina asked.

"Yes, my father's family moved to England when he was a teenager until he was through university. His father transferred for work and moved on, but my father had already met my mum and he stayed. They were college sweethearts. Now Papa is retired, and they live the good life in the Luberon Valley."

"Did they live in Blumpton?" She said the word as if it were a bad smell.

Sophie laughed. "Plumpton, and no. They were on the posh edge of London. I went to Plumpton later. It's near Brighton in Essex. It's more rural, which makes it a good spot for growing things."

"What is posh?" Catarina asked.

"Um ... it's just nicer, like upper middle class," Sophie said, because rich or fancy seemed a sort of tacky way of putting it. Her family was neither rich nor fancy, and she didn't want to misrepresent her situation. "But my flat in Essex was about this size, and there were four of us living in it."

"All girls? How many bathrooms?" Catarina looked intrigued.

"One bath and one water closet. And it was three women and one man. He was a chef, though, so we were willing to make allowances. He's training to be a sommelier at the college."

Catarina's smile was conspiratorial when she said, "Do yourself a favor, Sophie. Don't mention that small fact to my grandmother. The male roommate confession would have her dragging you to mass."

"I rather enjoy mass, actually," said Sophie. And she did. Her father was a Catholic and she'd been brought up that way. Her mother's Anglican sensibilities were placated once a month. She'd traded one of her days with the vicar per month for Sunday brunch at her favorite posh restaurant. Marriage, her parents told her, was about compromise.

Catarina gave her a dry look. "So, you like going to mass, do you? That's good. My grandmother goes every day and it's all in Latin."

"Mum's the word on the male roommate. Got it," Sophie said quickly.

"Just help me get your bed ready, and I'll let you get settled," Catarina said as she led her to the room with the bigger windows. They began spreading the sheets as Catarina eyed her speculatively. "I had a fight with my brother when I found out he hired you."

Sophie paused, mid spread. "Oh. I'm not sure how to respond to that. Any reason or just sibling power struggles? I'm an only child, but I know it's a thing."

"I couldn't imagine why on earth he'd hired a woman from England instead of someone more familiar with the ..." She motioned out the window.

"Terroir?" Sophie offered.

Catarina had the decency to look sheepish. "Exactly. I'm sorry. I'm protective of my family and this vineyard. This is our livelihood and our way of life. It has been this way for so many generations. My brother hasn't impressed me with his management. He's more business oriented. He spends hours poring over these spreadsheets and making conference calls, but despite the fact that he's never lived away from this land, he can't even graft with any proficiency. His palate is ..." She seemed to catch herself and blushed. "I shouldn't speak of him like this. He's a good man and he's your boss. What you must think of me."

"I understand. Honestly, I'm of the opinion that some of the nose and palate talent is pure genetics. My mum is rubbish. She can tell if I used too much baking powder in my cakes but can't tell a Pinot Grigio from a Sauvignon Blanc. My father is French, so there's that. Obviously, he saved me from a life of drinking crap wine." Sophie winked, trying to put Catarina at ease. "I think what you are trying to tell me is that if I'm in the office, I'm working for Marcello. If I'm in the vineyard, I'm working for you." She met her eyes and they were kind as she said, "And learning from you, I hope. I worked and studied at the college vineyard and helped produce some pretty impressive wine, considering the limitations. I also toured some wonderful vineyards in France and Germany. But I don't have to point out that reading something in a book or taking a tour isn't the same as getting your hands dirty. I'd like to take some soil samples, if you don't mind. I mean, I'd like a tour and a tasting first, but then I'd like to get my hands on your dirt and your roots. I know I can learn a lot from you. And I swear to you, Catarina, I will respect your vines and your home."

MANAUS, BRAZIL

Antonio and Izzy sat next to each other in some waiting room chairs. They'd just done a cesarean on a woman from the neighboring village, all while setting her broken wrist and tending to a cut on her scalp. She'd been thrown to the ground. She wasn't, however, pointing the finger at her assailant. They all knew, of course. "Just one hit," Izzy said. "If the abbess would just let me hit him once."

Antonio smiled. "And one kick in the ass." They both grumbled with laughter. The only excuse for the inappropriate mirth was fatigue. The wife-beater piece of shit was down the hall, waiting to see his wife and child. Sorcha was making him wait, hoping he'd sober up.

Speaking of the Irish midwife, they both perked up as she walked into the hallway, standing before him like a giant among women. Her petite stature didn't signify that she was to be feared, and the rousing of her ire to be avoided, if you knew what was good for you. Or so it was told by all who knew and loved her. Liam O'Brien, Sorcha's son and the infectious disease specialist, came into the room. He sat next to Antonio while mumbling, "And here we go."

The bastard actually had a bag of popcorn. Antonio dug into the bag, munching alongside his friend as they watched.

Sorcha smacked the sleeping man upside the skull. "Get up, ye wee bowsie! You have a daughter, in case you were wonderin'. Drink this cuppa tea and go wash out your gob. Ye smell like the pub floor. And don't go looking at me with that long face. Everyone knows what ye did!"

By this time, Sean had discreetly come within striking distance, but not interfering. He'd let her vent her spleen on the little weasel. Liam and Antonio were laughing so hard, the tears were squirting out of their eyes. It wasn't the least bit funny, really. They saw this now and again. An abused woman with marks on her skin and old breaks that hadn't healed correctly. Something about Sorcha O'Brien just made everyone watch in awe. She answered to no one, and she was pissed.

Antonio wiped his eyes. "I do love Irish women."

The voice came from behind them, a melodious lilt despite her age. "We are collectively flattered. Now, this isn't a spectator sport," Reverend Mother Faith said just as Sorcha O'Brien cut loose with more colorful, Irish slang. The abbess coughed, trying and failing to cover her laugh. "Well then, best let her tire herself out."

Liam said, "That's what my da always says. It's the Mullen blood. Right awful tempers, the lot of them."

"You'll have to tell me, someday, how a family from County

Cork ended up in Belfast. But for now, I need Antonio. The children are ready to say goodbye."

Antonio's heart lurched. "It won't be forever. I shouldn't be gone long." And it seemed more like he was telling himself this assurance, not them.

"Don't put a time limit on it, brother. We've got your back," Izzy said. "If I have to extend, I will."

⁂

Antonio handed the keys to his friend Liam. "You can use it as often as you like. The pool boy has keys to the gate, so he shouldn't need anyone here while he works. The housekeeper comes every other Tuesday. She has a key and she comes early."

Liam smirked. "And when does the royal ass wiper come?"

Antonio took a swipe at him, which Liam dodged. "I've got four brothers and a hell-spawned sister. You're going to have to be quicker than that. But I'm kidding. I know you're busy. You need them for this big of a place."

Antonio shrugged. "They kind of came with the house. I didn't have the heart to put them out of work. My housekeeper would be overjoyed if you made a mess or asked her to cook. I'm rarely here, and I usually eat at the hospital or St. Clare's." He embraced Liam. "I appreciate this. Take care of everyone."

"I will. Go to your family, Antonio. It's been too long. I, of all people, can tell you that hiding from your troubles rarely works. I don't know why you've stayed away from your home in Italy for so long, but there are obviously people there who love you. Don't worry about the hospital, and I'll keep an eye on Faith." Their beloved Reverend Mother Faith had a heart condition, a fact that worried them all a great deal.

Antonio remembered when Liam had come to St. Clare's. He wasn't sure, initially, why Liam seemed so dark and brooding, but the Irishman had suffered his own tragedies. Suffering and loss that made Antonio's seem less, somehow. He exhaled. "I just hope my grandfather hangs on until I get there. My sister was vague, but it seems grim. She wouldn't have ordered me home otherwise."

Viti del Fiume
Greve in Chianti, Italy

Sophie marveled at the physical stamina of the men beside her. They'd just come in from the vineyard and were now moving barrels of wine from rack to floor. There was a litter of kittens and a mother cat, who was beside herself. She'd nestled behind the barrels in order to give birth. Now that the four kittens were born, she couldn't manage to get them all out unassisted.

Sophie's first glimpse of the vineyard's cave was exciting. The cellars were built right into the side of a hill, underground and perfectly dark and eerie. It was equipped with modern climate control, obviously a recent addition, but it was the perfect setting for her first wine tasting. That, however, was going to have to wait. Momma cat had derailed their plans quickly. She'd met Giuseppe earlier, but the older Marcello had joined them when he'd heard about the new intern and the fate of his favorite cat.

Marcello Sr. said, "They keep the mice and rats out of my cellars. My dog helps, but they're clumsy. Cats are *abile* and *agile*." Cunning and agile. "I've been waiting for this litter. My neighbors will buy them when they are ready to leave their mother." He knelt down and gently took the two smallest off the teat. He handed them to Sophie, then gave the other two to Catarina. Then, with such gentleness that it made Sophie's throat tighten, he picked up a distraught Calendula. He crooned in his native tongue, "There you go, my girl. You are sore. Don't be angry with me. You can't keep them there. See this nice bed I've made for you and your babes."

"They're so small," Sophie whispered as they mewed and whined for their mother. "What does her name mean?"

Catarina said, "Marigold. See the mark on her side?"

She was white, with a few tabby markings. And sure enough, the orange one on her side resembled a flower. The man set the cat on her side and motioned for them to bring the little ones. Once reunited, they rooted and latched both for sustenance and comfort. Then Marcello carried them like royalty up to the main house.

"He loves that damn cat," Catarina said.

"You can tell a lot about a man by the way he treats fragile things," Sophie said. She knew this well.

Giuseppe came behind them, wiping his brow with a handkerchief. "You should listen to her. She's a wise one," he said indulgently. "Now for some wine."

⚜

***"I cook with wine, sometimes I even add it to the food." —
W.C. Fields***

SOPHIE WALKED THE SLOPES OF THE VINEYARD, ENJOYING THE simple glass of the neighbor's table wine. Apparently, neighboring vineyards traded their house wine if they were on good terms. They'd refused to give her a sneak peek at their own wines. The tasting was postponed until tomorrow because they'd spent a good hour putting the barrels and bottles back to rights. It was delicate work, handling good wine. Marcello must really love that cat.

The weather was warm and dry with a little breeze rolling over the land. "You are smiling." She'd almost forgotten Catarina was next to her.

Sophie said, "Yes, I was just ... at peace. It's so beautiful here. I needed this. I can't wait to get to work, but this peace, this is what I needed. I got some news before I left. Something disturbing. It's why I came early. And I just realized that ever since I got off the bus in Greve, I haven't thought about it once."

"And you don't have to think about it now. Come, *mi amica*. You and I will be friends. And sometime, you can tell me of this disturbance. But now, we have peace and food. *La cena* should be ready. And a word of advice. Pace yourself. My nonna thinks they've been starving you and feeding you glue at that college. She's going to make it her mission to fatten you up a bit."

Sophie smiled at that. She was hardly skinny. "Challenge accepted. My calorie counter is officially broken. I can drop the stones when I go back home."

An hour later, Sophie was halfway through the *secondi*, or the meat course as the English would call it. The fourth course. A full, traditional meal had nine courses, including the coffee and liquor at the end. This was a casual, family meal, so there were only six courses. They'd forgone the salad, fruit and cheeses, and coffee. But they'd never skip dessert. She was delighted to see a bottle of their award-winning Vin Santo brought to the table with some biscotti-type cookies for dipping. She'd read about this tradition, but she hadn't been able to find any Vin Santo in Essex. It was a very Italian thing that hadn't caught on with the rest of the world.

Marco tipped the bottle's label toward her. "We have this, or I can get some limoncello for you and pour it over some gelato."

"As amazing as that sounds, I'd be honored to sample your Vin Santo. Thank you. This has been wonderful. I promise I won't impose on you every night," Sophie said.

"While you stay here, you are family. Family eats together," Marcello Sr. said. It warmed her. She'd lived away from her parents for almost a year, and she missed this. She'd been an only child, so big family dinners were rare after her grandparents were gone, but her family always had dinner together when they all lived under the same roof. She looked at Magdalena, the matriarch of this wonderful homestead. She was small and compact, with silver hair that she kept coiled at her neck. Her face was smooth and soft looking, but she had the deep lines of a woman who'd had a happy and active life. She had dark-brown, kind eyes. They all did, as a matter of fact. They had the lush coloring of the people of this region. Olive skin, dark hair, and warm, chocolate eyes. Catarina was tall for an average Italian woman, so far as she'd seen. It just made her more stunning. More noticeable.

Sophie said, "Thank you, Marcello. And thank you, Magdalena. This was a truly gorgeous meal."

Catarina said, "So, tell us about your life in England. I know you have roommates and faculty advisors. We've heard from them in your letters of recommendation. But we know nothing of you out of school. Your parents are in France now. Is your mother trying to marry you off to a Frenchman?"

"Oh, it's come up. I'm going to be thirty this November. Tick-tock," Sophie said as she pointed to her smartwatch. The older people looked confused. A language issue, no doubt. Sarcasm was harder to interpret. Catarina spoke in Italian, and Sophie understood *il bebè* and something about tired eggs. "Jesus wept," she muttered under her breath. Only Marco caught it, and he almost spit out his wine-soaked cookie.

SOPHIE DODGED SOME QUESTIONS ABOUT HER "LIFE" IN ENGLAND. Other than that little game of chess, she'd had an absolutely beautiful day. She'd seen several of the grape varietals they grew on the property. Chianti Classico contained no white grapes by law, but there was a compact area that grew Trebbiano grapes for their Vin Santo. There was also a small section where they grew the Sangiovese grapes for a different version of Vin Santo. Most were made of white grapes, but a few select vineyards used their precious Sangiovese to make a rosé version of Vin Santo known as *Occhio di Pernice. Eye of the partridge.*

Giuseppe had proudly told Sophie that this year, they'd make this in a limited quantity. Apparently, Marco, who often stayed in the office, had done the artwork for a very special label. This wine, unlike the others, was aged in smaller barrels and had to age for three years. Sophie wanted to fly back three years from now just to taste it. She was curious to see the drying room. She wanted to watch the entire process because it was so native to this area. And it really had been delicious soaked into those little biscotti.

SOPHIE HAD WASHED UP AFTER THE TOUR OF THE VINEYARD, BUT she was dying for a swim and a hot shower. When she looked at the time, she knew the swim was not going to happen. The shower was heavenly to behold, however, and she planned to linger under the hot sprays. Traveling made her stiff in the joints.

The hand-painted, ceramic tiles were done in the local style—grapes and olive trees and rolling hills. Like a fresco, but not. Vibrant and inviting. The water pressure was strong, which was perfect. Outdoor work made for a tight back and shoulders. She'd come in from dinner and immediately stripped down to her skin, sniffing the scented soap Catarina had given her. Something floral and herbal. Then she sighed as the warm water washed away any thoughts of her troubles back home.

5

How often have I lain beneath rain on a strange roof, thinking of home— *William C. Faulkner*

Thirty-two hours, four plane changes, and a five-hour drive later, Antonio was as prickly as a boar. He'd forgotten just how atrocious Italian drivers behaved, but he needed a car for however long he'd be here. He'd sold his long ago. All he wanted now was a shower and a bed. He shut the lights off as soon as he entered the drive. He'd sent an email to his sister, giving his general travel plans, but he didn't want a big family reunion right now. He'd also caught an earlier flight just out of pure luck.

Antonio was feeling off. This was harder than he'd expected. *Bullshit.* He'd known exactly how hard this would be. Hence the ten-year gap. He was caught in a cycle of anger, uncertainty, and guilt. He parked by the pool house, unsure what condition he'd find it. He hardly cared. He'd spent more than one night on the grounds of St. Clare's, checking under his bunk for deadly spiders and other such creatures. Thin mattresses and thinner pillows, no air conditioning, under a mosquito net. His family's dusty pool house wasn't going to be a hardship.

He opened the gate door around the pool, expecting it to squeak. It had been like a burglar alarm for him, sneaking in late after the clubs as a youth. At least until he'd caught on and greased it up with olive oil. It didn't squeak, however. Small favors.

Antonio looked at the gleaming pool and paused. He was stiff from traveling and wired from too much caffeine. Maybe just a quick dip to knock off the cobwebs. He stripped down to his skin because he'd been the only one to ever use the pool when he was a young man. At least this late at night. He'd missed this small pool. It was different than his pool in Brazil.

Antonio slid into the cool water and sighed. It's funny because he rarely used his pool at home. He worked a lot, falling into an exhausted sleep almost every night. He hoped his grandmother or sister didn't catch him bare-assed. He didn't even own swimming trunks. He lived alone and he swam alone. And the few women he'd had a chance to swim with didn't mind the lack of swimwear. It had been so long in that regard that he could barely remember the interludes.

He glided through the water, diving under to feel the peaceful silence of being fully immersed. The lighting was low. Just landscape lights and the lights that lit from underwater. When he came up out of the water, he listened. The bugs and the occasional Egyptian Nightjar or tawny owl were all you heard in this part of the country. At least at night. Antonio lived and worked in the city, and St. Clare's was in the dense forest. Nothing like this gentle symphony that he'd missed so much. In Brazil, the rainforest was humming with life all day and night. It had its own appeal, but just now, he felt the hum of his homeland through the smells and sounds he'd almost forgotten about. He floated on his back, leaving his feet to dangle just beneath the surface. It was a clear, beautiful summer evening. There was no jungle canopy to cover the night sky.

Antonio enjoyed the weightlessness for a few more minutes,

then got out of the water. He looked in the outdoor cupboard, finding freshly laundered towels. Maybe someone was using the pool. He dried his body off and put the towel around his waist while he used another to dry his hair. It was as long as he'd ever grown it, just touching his shoulders. His grandfather might pop up out of his sickbed and grab the shears when he saw him. He also needed a shave. He was always clean-shaven because he was a surgeon. The mask and goggles fit snugger when he didn't have facial hair, and he felt it was more hygienic. He was three-quarters Italian by blood, so it would take him a week, at the most, to start a healthy beard.

Once he wasn't dripping, Antonio walked over to the gate and retrieved his luggage. He couldn't wait for a hot shower.

Sophie stirred, hearing what she thought was slushing water. She turned over in the soft bed, warm and content. She'd taken her valerian root, hoping to get on a regular sleep schedule for the work week to come. She briefly considered getting up but drifted back into oblivion before she could act on the halfhearted impulse.

Antonio used the key from his long-ago set of estate keys. The lock didn't stick, which was surprising. What had he expected, really? That the family would miss him so much they'd let the place go fallow? He left the door open, letting the fresh air seep into the place. He was surprised at the lack of musty odor. They really had maintained the place. Catarina hadn't mentioned anyone was staying here, and if his brother had moved in, there were two bedrooms.

He walked toward his old bedroom, wanting to wake up to the rolling hills of Viti del Fiume ... his home ... or was it? After all, he was thirty-six years old. Antonio had been away for a decade. This was a guesthouse now. Funny how he recognized every line, every doorway, every window. The moon was glowing over the vines and his heart pressed in on itself, making his chest and throat ache. The windows were open, which surprised him. He smelled a hint of citrus as the herbs and the lemon orchard came in on the breeze.

Maybe he should have come earlier in the day so that his family could greet him properly. Antonio rolled the suitcase into the living space, then went into the bedroom to see if there were linens on the bed. He started to flip the light on when he saw her. Sprawled out on the bed with no covers was a woman. She was in a tank top and panties, and he knew by the long, spread-out hair that it wasn't his sister. Thank God. It had been ten years, but he knew it wasn't Catarina. This woman was smaller and curvier than his sister. He shook himself, realizing what this would look like if she woke. She might be a cousin or his brother's girlfriend. He knew nothing of his family's life anymore. The slight motion must have sent a ripple through the room because in three heartbeats, she came off the bed with her fists, elbows, and knees swinging.

Sophie sounded like a feral beast, growling as she tried to claw at his face. He whipped her around and pinned her flat against the wall. He realized he was speaking in Portuguese and switched to Italian. "Basta!" The little she-devil actually headbutted him, and he backed away, howling and swearing.

"No, it's not enough! You will have to kill me, you pervert! I hope you're into necrophilia!" Sophie couldn't reach the door, but he was backing out anyway. She soared out of the doorway with a lamp over her head. He jumped out of the way as she stumbled over the coffee table. He'd done enough self-defense with the teenagers at St. Clare's to know when someone thought they were fighting for their life. Hans and Raphael's voices came back to him. *Keep fighting until you can get away or disable your attacker.* And in this scenario, he was the attacker. Or at least she thought so. Then it struck him that she was speaking in English.

"I'm sorry. I'm leaving. Don't be afraid. I'm going to turn on the light. Please, this is my home," Antonio said. Jesus, what a mess.

Sophie couldn't hear him. She was breathing like a wild animal, and when he turned on the light, her face was absolutely frantic. She took in the towel around his waist, as he was nearly naked. Thank God it was still covering his business end. One look at his half-naked form and she screamed. Blood was oozing from his brow, and she had a red blotch forming on her forehead where she'd head-butted him. He backed out the door just as he heard people coming from the main house. She screamed again as he backed up ... right off the edge of the pool.

◌⁙◌

SOPHIE THOUGHT, *NO, NO, NO. THIS IS NOT HAPPENING*. ON SOME level, she registered that this was not a ghost from her past come to harm her again. He was, however, some sort of burglar or rapist. Maybe someone who worked at the vineyard who knew she was out here alone. She didn't really know these people after all.

When the bastard went into the pool, she was half ready to throw something electric in there to electrocute him. That's when Marco and Marcello piled in through the gate. Behind them came Catarina, Giuseppe, and finally Magdalena. Sophie was alarmed to see that Giuseppe had a shotgun and Marcello had a hatchet.

It was Magdalena who spoke first. She was smiling. Why was she smiling? "Antonio! Mi coniglio! Mi bebè!"

Relief and irritation flickered through the rest of the crowd, then they all took in the state of their guest. Catarina walked toward Sophie. She was backed against the pillar, a lamp in her hand. And was that a bump on her head? "Antonio, did you hit her?"

Antonio was getting out of the pool after his father had given him another towel. He'd lost the one around his waist in the plunge. "No, I didn't hit her. She headbutted me." He wiped blood from his brow, suddenly feeling like a complete rotter—an Irish slang term that he'd picked up from Liam and Seamus, and Sister Catherine, but he'd never tell the abbess this. "She beat the hell out of me, to be honest. I'm sorry, signorina. Forgive me." But Sophie wasn't hearing him. Jesus, she was terrified. But he saw a flicker of reason start to penetrate. She looked at Catarina as his sister took the lamp out of her hands. He cursed, causing Nonna to cross herself.

Marco asked, "What the hell are you doing here? Why didn't you pick up the phone before just showing up? You scared her half to death. I want to hit you with a lamp!"

But Antonio ignored him as his grandmother walked to the young woman and took her into her small, frail arms. Like she'd done to him and his siblings, time and again. There were many types of healers. He had a flash of Sorcha O'Brien, the midwife at St. Clare's, taking one of the injured children in her arms in just this way. He said again, "I'm so sorry, miss."

His sister gritted her teeth at him. "Would you please pick a language, Antonio? You are giving everyone whiplash!" That's when Antonio realized he'd been slipping in and out of Portuguese. Surely they could give him a bit of a break. He'd been in Brazil for a decade, and now he found himself speaking to an Englishwoman while standing poolside in his Tuscan home. He was getting a little case of whiplash himself.

Antonio spoke in English, and spoke only to the woman. "I'm just going to get my suitcase and put on some pants. Please, signorina, forgive me. This was my space at one time. I wouldn't have … it doesn't matter. I'm sorry. And I'm leaving. I will stay on the couch tonight and …"

Catarina said dryly, "I have a room for you, Antonio. Next to Marco's. I think you should just get dressed and go to bed."

Sophie finally spoke. "Antonio? Your brother?" Her voice was shaking, and Antonio wanted to hit himself with a lamp.

Sophie remembered the grandfather saying, *That's Antonio's space.* Some sort of reasonable explanation started forming in her mind. "I'm okay. I'll take the spare room. If I'd known you were coming, I wouldn't have used your cottage. I just saw you standing over the bed in the dark," she said defensively. She really had cleaned his clock, and now she had an aching head. She was rather proud of herself, though. That was some proper Chuck Norris shit she'd done. Her father would be proud. "I'll just get some of my things and move to the house."

Marco cursed again. Magdalena crossed herself again. Marcello Sr. shot Marco a chiding glare. "You are all distressing your nonna." Then Marcello said, in his sternest fatherly tone, "Everyone go into the house but Catarina and Sophie. Go now. I'll speak with you later."

Antonio was already wheeling his suitcase away. He said, "Catarina, once I get dressed, I need to look at that bump on her head."

"You can speak directly to your attacker, thank you." She was curt and blushing like mad because she was, after all, in her underwear. Nonna was wrapping a towel around her waist as she said it. "I'm fine. I don't need you pawing me again!"

"Pawing you? I'm a doctor. And I never pawed you. I subdued you because you were coming at me like an angry jaguar. I'm sorry I scared you, but you look intelligent enough to understand that letting a concussion go out of pure despeito is ridícula." Sophie flinched at his tone, but her chin went up at the insult. She'd understood his meaning well enough.

His sister walked by, visibly put out with him. "Pick a language, you buffoon. You've lost your manners in your travels, dear brother." She said it in English, knowing that in her new friend's state, she'd have trouble processing anything other than her native tongue. "We all speak English until our new intern isn't scared of the family anymore."

❦

ANTONIO TOOK TURNS BEING HUGGED BY HIS NONNA, WHO'D decided to cry. As if he didn't feel bad enough. Then being chastised by his brother, and finally being kissed on both cheeks by his grandfather. He was surprised. They were so much older looking. Marcello was thirty-eight years old and greying at the temples. He was still unmarried, like him, and living at the family home. They were both broken a bit in that regard. His grandmother's hair was thinner. He knew this because her bun was smaller. It had been a great, bulging mass of black hair that had threads of silver streaking through it. Now it was all silver, and her face had lost some of its fleshiness. She was in her seventies, after all. He looked at his grandfather more closely. He'd expected him to be bedridden. He looked hearty and well. He was older, but he was still somewhat muscular, like the body of a person who did physical work. Like a man who spent his days running a vineyard and orchard. "You look well, Nonno. If I didn't know better, I'd say you appeared in excellent health." Yes, very healthy. But he couldn't assume. Some sicknesses you couldn't see.

Antonio's father walked in, putting his shotgun behind the cupboard that was used for such things as raincoats and mittens. He looked tired. But then again, everyone was in their night clothes. He felt so damn stupid. "Padre." He nodded awkwardly. At one time, he'd only been *Papa*. His beloved papa.

"Good evening, my son." Antonio's throat felt thick. He had missed hearing his native tongue and missed the deep, fluid voice of his father. A thought that caused a great deal of conflict in him. Marcello said, "It's been ... too long. Despite the action of this evening, it is so good of you to come home."

Antonio's words were clipped. How strange it was to feel like Italian wasn't his native tongue anymore. "I came to see Nonno." He blushed and added, "And Nonna. Catarina called me." He paused because it was none of his father's business why he'd come. "I'll arrange a pensione in town in the morning."

Nonna waved her hands. "You will not stay in some stranger's house when we have plenty of room."

"Nonna, I scared that poor woman half to death. I won't make her ..." The screen door opened behind him and cut off his train of thought. The little fiend who had bashed his brow with her forehead was standing there defiantly. She was wearing a sweatshirt with some college name on it and a pair of running shorts.

"I can very well speak for myself. No one needs to leave. It was a misunderstanding. I know that now," said Sophie. He was surprised that she'd followed the conversation. She still looked wary of him, and the sight twisted his guts.

Antonio said in English, "I can't apologize enough. I'm jet-lagged. I just wanted a swim and to crash," he said.

"Crash? What crash?" Nonna said behind him.

Catarina explained, "It's an expression. It means to fall asleep very hard."

Nonna's English was labored, but her brow was stern and her meaning clear. "Why he no just say fall asleep? What are they teaching him in that country? Why the nuns not teach him to speak clearly?" Like he was a boy who had been sent off to Catholic boarding school. Antonio felt ten years old. He knew his ears were getting red and was glad for the long hair.

And as if she'd read his thoughts, she continued. "And why the Irish nuns no cut his hair? They don't have scissors?" That actually made the young woman smile, and Antonio got the impression she was trying not to laugh. Well, then. He supposed that was progress, even if it was at his expense.

Antonio said, "Anyway, I'm sorry. I don't want you to be uncomfortable. I can get a room in town."

"I'll move out of the pool house," Sophie said plainly. "It's your space."

Marco said, "It hasn't been his space since he walked out on this family ten years ago and never looked back." Sophie saw pain flickering in both the men's eyes. Pain and resentment.

"I'm not looking to get into a family debate. I can take the bedroom down the hall," Sophie suggested.

"Next to Marco's room? I don't think so. You'll stay in the pool house. You are settled and I won't be here long. Please, I insist. Now come, if you would allow it. I want to look at your head."

Antonio motioned to the sofa, and she went. She hadn't liked the idea, but brains won out over ego.

He dug in his bag for a little penlight and knelt down in front of her. "You didn't break the skin."

"I didn't break my skin, you mean," she said as she gestured toward his brow with her eyes. She had the most beautiful hair color. Not quite brown, or at least not all brown. It was fair, like spun bronze and copper. And her eyes were green and blue. He saw them up close as he had her follow the light with her eyes. "You are leaking." She was right. He felt the blood forming another drip down his temple.

"Does your head hurt, signorina?" he asked.

"Does yours, signor?" She was in a pissy mood to be sure, which told him she was in pain and not going to admit it. He switched off the light.

"Are you like this with all doctors, or just the ones you take for a burglar? It's a simple enough question, miss. Are you in pain?"

She ground her jaw, giving the response begrudgingly. "A bit."

"Dizzy?"

"No, and I'm not nauseated. I don't have a concussion. Now who is going to assess you?" she asked, lifting a brow. Her words were clipped, and she was almost embarrassed. She sounded like an uptight, stereotypical Englishwoman, the lessons in clear diction having been drilled into her since birth.

No sooner had she said that than Magdalena sat down next to her with an ice pack. Then she started cleaning Antonio's brow. He hissed at the alcohol swab. His nonna said, "No stitches," as she put a small Band-Aid on the wound. "You'll live. Just keep it clean." She handed him another ice pack. He took it and saw one side of his patient's mouth twitch with humor.

"Well, she keeps you humble, Doctor Rinalto," Sophie said.

"You may call me Antonio. And you are miss?"

"It's just Sophie. Sophie Bellamy."

"You shouldn't headbutt an attacker, Sophie. You could have just as easily knocked yourself out, and then you'd have been helpless. That stuff only works in the movies," Antonio said.

"It worked on you," Sophie replied, and he could feel her temper rising. His father coughed, and he knew it was to stifle a laugh.

Antonio said simply, "Yes, but I wasn't trying to attack you. I was attempting to subdue my attacker. If I'd been really trying to attack you ..." He stopped and shook his head. "I'm not going to argue with you. I forgot I'm supposed to be contrite in this situation." Then he turned to Marco, who had a smirk on his face. "An English intern at an Italian vineyard? How long have we been taking interns?"

"We aren't doing anything. This isn't your business or your home," he said with unnecessary bitterness.

"Basta, Marco! Your brother has been serving Christ and the Holy Church. You should welcome him home," Marcello said.

Sophie shouted, "Oh my God, I headbutted a priest?" *Can priests be doctors?* Yes. After all, there were nuns who were nurses. She'd headbutted a man of the cloth. *Jesus wept.* Mortified at the thought, she wore a horror-stricken look on her face. Catarina started laughing so hard, she was actually doubled over. Then Giuseppe, and so on. It rippled through the family as Marcello translated what she'd said to Magdalena. Even Marco had lost the sour look of disapproval and was chuckling deep in his chest.

Sophie knew her face was bright red. "I'm guessing you aren't priest material?" Sophie said with a smile. The first smile he'd seen from her. It was a lovely sight.

Antonio said, "I am most certainly not," although it had seemed like it sometimes, over the last year or more. He hadn't had a woman in that long, and he had to get a rein on his response to this pretty, little Englishwoman right now. If she was an intern, she was probably younger than his little sister. He really was a rotter.

Sophie stood at the same time he did. He towered over her. She looked at his sire and Giuseppe and realized that his height must have come from his mother's side. She hadn't wanted to ask about Catarina and Marco's mother. There was a solitary picture of her in the flower of her youth. She'd been stunning. So had he. The whole family was beautiful, but this man was like the Roman God of hot men. She sort of wished, now that she wasn't fighting for her life, that she could have gotten a more thorough look at him in that towel. She just stared up at him dumbly, realizing they had matching ice packs.

Sophie walked toward the door. "I'll make you a deal, Antonio. The one with the biggest shiner tomorrow has to take the smaller accommodations."

"Shouldn't it be the other way around?" Antonio asked, grinning like an idiot.

"No way. This is the animal kingdom. Might is right." She turned and walked out, listening to the rumble of laughter from the family.

⚜

ANTONIO STOOD OUT ON THE BACK PATIO, OVERLOOKING THE kitchen garden and small olive grove. He reached down and plucked some oregano from the border. He rolled his hands together, spreading the strong scent into his skin. His grandfather came out, and Catarina was next to him. "I'm sorry, Antonio. Truly. I thought you were coming in tomorrow."

"I caught an early flight. What I can't figure out is why no one else knew I was coming. I mean, it's not like I left on good terms. You could have warned them."

Catarina said, "I never understood that, Antonio. Why do you say this? What bad terms preceded your departure?" They were speaking in Italian now. They'd slipped into Italian as soon as Sophie had gone to bed.

"You lied to me," Antonio said, changing the subject. He turned to his grandfather. "You were in on this, I suppose? Because if you are in poor health, then I'm James Bond."

"Ah, I like the James Bond," Giuseppe said.

"Nonno, Catarina," he said with a warning tone.

"We didn't lie. He's old. Look at him." Catarina waved a hand toward him. "He has high blood pressure and a suspicious mole on his neck," she explained.

Giuseppe pulled his shirt collar to the side to show him the mole, trying to look like an ailing, frail, old man. And he was failing at it. "You two should be ashamed. I have responsibilities!" Antonio blurted.

Catarina shot back. "I'm not ashamed. Nonna gets more frail every year. They both do. Surely you see it. People die unexpectedly in their seventies all the time. A bad flu or a stroke. You left us, Antonio. You said two years, but you never came home. You forgot us!" Catarina wiped her angry tears away. "The vineyard is struggling, and Papa keeps hoping Marco is going to get his act together. He won't see that Marco hates this place. He stays with us out of duty. He never looked for other employment, never traveled, never did anything. He graduated from business school and stayed at the vineyard. I haven't seen him pick up a sketch pad in fifteen years."

"None of that is my fault. You all have to live your own lives. My life is in Manaus. My work is there. It's not just my work at the private hospital. St. Clare's needs me, and I need them. We are our own sort of family. But I still love you, Catarina. You can come stay with me any time you like. I've told you this. I just couldn't stay here after …" Antonio pulled his sister to him. "I'm sorry, little duck. I should have come home sooner. I just thought I would come when I was ready, but I never felt ready." Even now, the sight of this place caused his chest to tighten. "I'm exhausted. I will sleep in the spare room for now." He kissed his sister's head, then he hugged his nonno. "Then we will talk more."

When he walked into the house, his father stood quiet and still in the kitchen doorway. He just nodded at him and went to his grandmother. He wasn't ready for more. "You look beautiful, Nonna. I've missed you." He bent down and took her little body in his arms. Even now, her arms wrapped around him and he felt safe and protected.

"Voglio molto bene, Antonio," she whispered.

SLEEP ELUDED SOPHIE. SHE'D RECOVERED FROM THE ALTERCATION with the good doctor. She actually felt guilty that she'd hurt him. She'd also felt a smidge of pride that she'd sent him scurrying out of the house. Going ass over teakettle into the pool had been the bonus round.

When she finally fell asleep, she had nightmares. Horrible visions of being choked. She woke up gasping and burst into tears. Finally. She'd held them back last night, but now in the early morning, she gave herself permission to let them go. The incident with Antonio Rinalto had been a misunderstanding. She knew that. But it had triggered a lot of long-buried anxiety that had to find a way out.

ANTONIO STROLLED THE GARDEN PATH BETWEEN THE SWIMMING pool and the orchard, wanting to walk among the vines that he'd missed deep in his soul. He hadn't acknowledged his need to come home, but now that he was here, he was glad his sister and the abbess had pushed him. He thought about the young woman staying in the pool house. Sleeping in his bed. She was a pretty thing. Not the exotic beauty of South America or the native beauty of an Italian woman. It was a quiet sort of loveliness that was not appreciated on the cover of a magazine. He, however, appreciated it more than he should.

As he walked by the window, Antonio averted his gaze. One

usually had to keep the windows open this time of year. There wasn't an AC unit in the pool house unless something had changed in ten years. Just ceiling fans and the wind that God saw fit to push through the windows. He was used to it, having spent more than one night at St. Clare's when he wanted to monitor a patient. An Englishwoman, however, might not be acclimated.

Antonio tried to push thoughts of her out of his mind and listen to the sounds that came with the sunrise. A chorus of bugs and birds. Work would begin soon, and he would lose this solitude. Then he heard her. He stopped in his tracks. *She is weeping.* It wasn't loud, but he heard it just the same. Sniffling and that stuttering noise of someone who was trying and failing to stop the flow of tears. He briefly considered knocking but decided against it. Had he made her cry? Was she sorry she'd come? Was she afraid? *Damn it.* Why the hell hadn't Catarina told him someone was sleeping in there? And why on earth, of all the places they could have acquired an intern, would Marcello bring some Englishwoman onto the staff?

Catarina was right. Marcello was mismanaging the vineyard. He'd also been more than a little unwelcoming to Antonio. Marcello had no right to feel put out. This was still Antonio's grandfather's home. Antonio was still in this family, even if he'd been gone for many years. He'd sent cards and an occasional gift over the years. It wasn't like he'd just disappeared. *Who are you trying to convince? Them or yourself?* He walked more briskly, away from his inner guilt and the sounds of a woman crying.

There was a foggy mist that was settled over the ground as dawn drew closer. Antonio ambled through the vines, felt the leaves and grapes in his fingers, smelled the soil. Something shifted in his chest, then loosened. Despite the trickery at the hands of his sister and Giuseppe, it felt good to be home. He looped around the row of grapes, making his way back up toward the house. He had just passed the pool when a screech came from the house, then a door slamming. Sophie Bellamy came running out of the house like a bat out of hell.

St. Michael defend us. What now? "What is it?" Antonio shouted.

She skidded to a halt, then she pointed. "There's a bloody scorpion on my bloody duvet!"

Antonio put his hands up, ready to placate her. She shot a finger up and pointed. "Don't you dare laugh or say something patronizing, or I swear to God I will headbutt you again."

He said calmly, "It's not the same type of scorpion that you're thinking about. They are harmless. Well, not totally. They will sting you, but it's more like a wasp sting."

"Yes, well, if I get stung by a wasp or bee and my EpiPen is nowhere around, tell my parents to sprinkle my ashes in the bloody rose garden." She said it through her teeth. It was amusing until he absorbed what she said.

"Did it sting you?" Antonio grabbed her by the shoulders and started looking her up and down. "Where is your pen?"

"No, it didn't sting me. I don't know if I'm allergic, and I don't want to find out. Now go kill the damned thing and call an exterminator!"

He stifled a grin. "An exterminator?"

"Yes, like pest control."

"Well, my dear Miss Bellamy—"

"Sophie," she said.

"Okay, Sophie. This is the country, not London. If you keep your door closed, they shouldn't bother you." Then he looked at the house. "Ah, no screens. You are missing your first line of defense for bees, bats, bugs, and scorpions."

"Bats!"

"You don't have bats in Britain?" Antonio asked.

She sighed. "Yes, okay. Screens. But for now, go kill that little fiend before it hides somewhere." He saw a shudder go through her, then she remembered her manners. "Please."

Sophie followed him, peering around his body like it was a tiger and not a small nuisance. Antonio said, "Last time I came into my cottage, you beat me bloody. You can't kill a small thing such as this?" He pointed at it, and it actually reared its tail up in a Hollywood-worthy performance.

She jerked in surprise. "Jesus, that thing is hideous."

"Remind me to tell you about Goliath spiders. And wandering spiders. And bullet ants," he said. "I have to check my home daily, or the housekeeper does it."

"A housekeeper, eh? Must be nice," she said. Then Sophie observed as he took a cup from the kitchen and then a plate. Antonio walked slowly, put the cup sideways on the bed, and backed the little creature into the cup while it bounced its stinging tail off the plate. Then he brought them together and went outside. She watched as he proceeded to the olive grove and let the little guy go. She was not far behind him when he turned, his dark eyes tranquil. He just lifted a shoulder. "She was brave. And she was trying to find a meal for her babies."

"You can't possibly know she has a nest of babies. I call bluff," Sophie said with an indulgent smile. It was rather sweet. She'd have smashed the thing to kingdom come if she wasn't such a bloody coward.

"I *can* know that. Her abdomen is full of them. She's fat with child. She'll give birth and carry the scorplings around on her back until they're old enough to walk on their own."

"And then I'll have a hundred in my bedroom?" she said, but not with any real irritation.

He looked at her with tired eyes at that moment. "The world has too many parents who don't care for their children. And I witness enough death. This was an easy one to prevent." He turned to see the fat, little scorpion going under the scrub beneath an olive tree. "Go, Mama. Don't scare the poor Englishwoman."

"I'd have thought they would lay eggs like spiders," she said, ignoring the poke at her expense.

"They're sort of inside, but they come out the old-fashioned way. A lot of them. So, keep that door closed. They won't be helpless forever." Antonio turned on her. "Now, tell me what the rationale was for your career choice, given you'd be safer from bees with an indoor job."

"If you tell me why an Italian doctor is living in South America," she shot back. She was getting rather good at this. She hadn't had a good verbal sparring partner in a while.

"How do you know I live ..." he asked.

Sophie snorted. "The Discovery Channel. *The Deadly Amazon: Season 2.* Bullet ants and wandering spiders and that Godzilla spider." She shuddered. "And to answer your question, because I like it. I love the whole thing. The vines, the grapes, the soil, and, of course, the vino."

Antonio smirked, stifling a laugh. "It's Goliath spider not Godzilla." He seemed to take in her face, as if trying to look into her mind. "Hmm ... I think my brother has finally lost his mind. What university do you attend?"

"Plumpton College in Essex. And before you make a crack insinuating this foreigner couldn't possibly know anything about wine, remember the headbutt. Nice shiner, by the way. I'm going to go get dressed for work in my amazing, two-bedroom pool house." Sophie was in yoga pants and a big T-shirt, and she stretched like a cat. "Comfortable bed, too." She heard a begrudging rumble of laughter behind her as she left.

Antonio walked to the main house, finding his family trying to pretend they hadn't been watching through the window. "Buongiorno. Where is Padre? The pool house has no screens. I just removed a scorpion from the Englishwoman's bedding. She was not pleased."

Marco said, "How should I know? He's probably already in the cave. Ask Nicolas." Nicolas was the groundskeeper. "He's in the front, trimming the hedge."

Catarina rolled her eyes. That lord-of-the-manor routine Marco was playing at in front of Antonio was getting old fast. "They're in the storage area. As well you know, Marco, since that's where you and I put them in winter."

Antonio stole a piece of the fresh pastry his grandmother was leaving to cool. He bounced it between his hands. "It's still hot, Antonio. And get a plate."

But he'd already risked scorching his mouth on the flakey, sweet goodness. He moaned. "Gorgeous, Nonna. So fresh. Thank you. I've been eating Brazilian food for so long, I forgot about these pastries of yours."

"Do they feed you in that godforsaken place?" she asked resentfully.

"Oh yes. Not so well at the hospital, but at the mission, no one goes hungry. I think you'd like it. Lots of children. God has not forsaken them. God is in all things," he said, "but especially at St. Clare's." Antonio was surprised at how easily he'd slipped back into Italian. Mostly. He slipped up with a Portuguese hybrid every now and again.

"Since when did you become a good, God-fearing man?" Marco asked. Antonio didn't miss the snideness in his brother's words.

Antonio answered calmly, albeit a bit sadly. "Since when did you become so full of anger, my brother?" He didn't have the heart to fight with his brother this morning and looked away. "I'll go get those screens."

His grandfather rose from his seat. "I'll help you."

6

Antonio walked alongside his grandfather, who was wiping his brow from the exertion of putting the screens on all of the windows. He said, "If you have some rolled screening, I can patch the two holes." For now, he'd taped over them. The affected windows were off the bathroom and kitchenette, so of little consequence, but he was trying to break the silence. His grandfather ignored him.

Instead, he said, "Please, Antonio. Try to be kind to your father. His life hasn't been without its own trials. You've changed, little rabbit. You aren't so quick to anger. You're a man. I believe you can find this kindness in your heart if you try."

"I was a man when I left," Antonio had to point out. "I was almost twenty-six."

"Yes, yes. But you were a hurt boy, too. A hurt son," he said. "Please, for me and your nonna, be kind. You don't know everything. No one truly knows everything that goes on in a marriage. But he loved your mother and he loves his children. Family is important, and I won't always be around to play referee."

Antonio's jaw was tight. He hadn't even noticed when Catarina approached. She said, "I agree. It's time to let some things go, Antonio. Even if you go back. I mean, when you go back, do it with a lighter heart." She sighed. "We lost her, too, Antonio. Marco and I lost our mother, too."

That hit him right in the gut. He was a horrible brother. "I know, my sweet. I'm sorry I stayed away. I'm sorry I wasn't here for you." She leaned into him, giving him a nudge. Antonio swung his arm around her shoulders and kissed her head. "I'll try. I promise to try."

It wasn't so easy. He knew things Catarina didn't. He'd been his mother's confidante. Since he was a young boy, she'd always come to him for a hug ... for a simple understanding and acceptance that can only come from a son. He missed her. Being in Italy reminded him of her. This place did as well, a little. It hadn't been their home when he was a small child. They'd lived in town in a small house, but for some reason, when he was barely school age, they'd moved in with his grandparents. His mother had never truly fit in here, even though his grandparents loved her like their own daughter. *It was my father's way of controlling her.* They'd kept an eye on her while he went out and did as he pleased. And for some reason, his grandmother Martha and his grandpa hadn't had a problem with their son-in-law.

Antonio shook himself. Changing the subject, he said, "I have to go into town for a few things. Can I do anything for you while I'm there?"

Catarina said, "Yes! Take Sophie with you, if she's okay with it. She said she needs to go to the *supermercato*."

Behind them, Marco said, "I was just getting ready to drive her. You need not bother."

"Bother with what?" There was an awkward pause when they all turned around to see Sophie standing there with her handbag.

Catarina talked over both men. "Antonio needs to go into town. He's going to take you to the supermarket, if that's okay."

Sophie shrugged shyly. "All right, then. Marco, there's no reason for you to make a special trip. Thank you both. I'd like to drive back, just to try my hand at driving."

Antonio said, "Great, I'm ready if you are."

Marco's frown said exactly what he thought of the idea without him uttering a word. Catarina said to him, "Now you don't have an excuse for not helping in the cave."

"Why can't Antonio help?" he asked to their backs.

"Is that the Antonio whom you rudely reminded that this wasn't his business or his home? It's time you started pulling your weight, Marco. You can't just do video conferences and power lunches if you are going to succeed in the wine business. You have to get your hands dirty." Catarina said to Antonio, "Turn that rental car in, brother dear. We have enough cars to spare." She threw her keys at Sophie, who caught them easily. "And you can practice driving by following him to the rental company. Don't look at me like that, Antonio. I know you're a successful surgeon, but it's wasteful to spend the money. Besides, Sophie will like the Ferrari."

Both Sophie and Antonio's mouths dropped. Then they looked at Marco and Giuseppe, who were suppressing grins. Sophie smiled. "You're kidding, too, right?" She looked at the key with the FIAT emblem on it.

Catarina winked. "Yes, but it's a Spider. The top is already down."

"Very nice. You don't have to ask me twice," Sophie said with a smile.

Antonio gave his sister a chiding look. "Thank you for the loaner. I'll take care of it."

He turned and gave Sophie his attention. The full force of him hit her like a punch to the gut. He was quite simply gorgeous. Silky, black hair to his shoulders, olive skin that was tanned, but still more fair than his brother or father. The tan was probably from living in South America because she thought he'd normally look very much like his sister. Marco was more Mediterranean looking. A little shorter than Antonio, more deep-olive skin. For someone who stayed inside at his computer, she wondered why his coloring was so different. Genetics were interesting. She followed Antonio as he walked toward his rental and the garage. "I'll just follow closely and not bother with GPS. I'm ready now, if you are."

Antonio watched in the rearview mirror as Sophie got comfortable with his sister's little Fiat. She was lovely. Neither short nor tall, fair-skinned, blue-green eyes, and at first glance, rather ordinary looking. But she wasn't ordinary. She was natural and untainted by time or artifice. He thought about what she'd said earlier in the day. He needed a pharmacy. He'd kept up his license to practice in Italy. It had been required by the Brazilian government for his work visa.

❧

ANTONIO TURNED THE CAR RENTAL IN WITH LITTLE ISSUE, THEN walked out to the car park to find Sophie waiting by his sister's car. "How was the drive?"

Sophie replied, "It rides very smoothly. I'm a bit wind-blown."

"Do you want the top up, then?" He moved to do so and she waved him off.

"No way. I've never had a convertible. They're not overly practical in the UK," she said. "Probably less so in the rainforest."

"Yes, my work often involves four-wheel capability," Antonio said. Before she could ask questions, he got into the driver's seat and buckled up. "We have a few choices for shopping. If you tell me what you need, I can steer you in the right direction. We have a butcher, a co-op that my family belongs to ... or at least they did. Although, you have access to our kitchen garden and orchard. Please don't be shy about taking what you need."

"I think the Carrefour supermarket is best. I'll venture out to the specialty shops after I've stocked the essentials. You can drop me off if you have errands."

"Just the farmacia," he said. "And my nonna needs a few things.

I'll drop you off and then meet back up once I'm finished." He noticed she was battling with her hair in her face, the wind whipping it into her mouth and eyes.

"I don't have your mobile number," Sophie said.

"Don't worry, signorina. I'll find you." And he would. She would stick out in this small village, even with the occasional tourist group. He noticed she was simply dressed. Trainers, shorts, and a cotton shirt. Not fussy, but showing shapely legs, womanly hips, and toned arms. She had long hair that she kept tied up, but the multi-hued, butterscotch-and-honey highlights made it much lighter than that of the local girls.

He went into the farmacia, showing his credentials to the pharmacist. He recognized the old man behind the counter. "Antonio Rinalto. I'd given you up for dead."

Antonio smiled at the old man. "Not yet. It's good to see you, Lorenzo. How is your family?"

The man answered, "My daughter is single, if you are looking. My wife died last year."

"I'm sorry, old friend." A stab of panic went through him. Lorenzo's wife had been younger than both his grandparents.

The man said simply, "Yes, well, I was hoping to go first, but now she waits for me. What do you need today?"

Antonio told him, then thought of something else. He went to the aisle where the hair accessories were kept and bought some simple hair ties that were a little darker than his passenger's hair. He paid what he thought was rather too much for the pharmaceuticals, then started back for the supermarket.

After getting his nonna's yeast and bread flour, he went to locate the sparkling water. That's where he found her. "Is that French mineral water?" he asked accusingly.

"Does it matter?" She shrugged.

"It does. This"—he pulled a bottle of water off the shelf—"is a little closer to home."

"Well, it's cheaper as well. I'll take two, signor," Sophie said smartly. He handed her a second, plucking the French stuff out of her trolley.

Antonio looked as though he smelled something bad. "Next, you'll be buying Greek olive oil and Spanish wine."

"No, no," she said. "I'm going to shamelessly mooch a bit of that from your family for the next few months."

"You'll stay through the harvest?" he asked as they walked toward the cashier.

"That is the plan. Then I will graduate. I have no plans afterward, other than seeking employment," she said absently.

Antonio thought that was rather vague. "Will you stay in England?"

She sighed almost sadly. "I don't think I can."

Sophie let him think it was due to lack of job opportunities. He didn't need to know the real reason. The thought of it made her skin prickle. He started putting her groceries with his. "No, you must keep them separate," she said.

"Catarina told me to buy your groceries. She didn't have time to properly stock the pool house." Lie. Total, shameless lie. But Antonio knew how little interns were paid in most professions.

"She doesn't have to do that. No supervisor pays for their intern's shampoo!" she said as she placed the items onto the belt.

"This is going to take all day if you don't stop moving things," Antonio said with a grin. He was rather enjoying himself. "Your internship terms included room and board. Food is part of your boarding." He took the toiletries. "There. You can buy your own shampoo if you're going to be stubborn about it."

The cashier was a middle-aged woman. She said to him in Italian, "If she doesn't want you, I'll certainly take you." Antonio winked at her.

As they made their way to the car, Sophie asked, "What did she say? I didn't catch all of it. She was mumbling."

"She said the bread was on special," Antonio replied a little too smoothly.

"She did not. I didn't catch it all, but I know the word for bread," she said. "You aren't going to tell me, are you?"

"No. Now, you take the keys and pop the boot, please?"

"Your English is very good, and I noticed something." Sophie continued. "You use British slang terms. I mean, not slang so much as informal speech. British or maybe Irish?"

"I work with both and some Americans, and the occasional French or Australian," he said as he loaded the completely insufficient trunk space. "You'll have to hold the bread and eggs and ..." He took out a package of chocolate biscuits. "We wouldn't want these to get crushed or melt." Antonio motioned to the chocolate-covered biscuits. "My nonna would have a fit, by the way. She'd make it her mission to stuff you to bursting with her pastries and cookies."

"Don't tell her! She does enough. I should be cooking for her. These are her golden years," she said so sweetly that it made Antonio's heart squeeze. It was such a nice saying. *Golden years*. Precious because there were so few years left. A time to rest.

"Do you cook for your grandmothers?" Antonio asked.

Sophie sighed and said, "I lost my grandparents too early. In their sixties and early seventies. My parents are in their fifties and would never eat my cooking."

"Catarina told me your parents live in France. How did that come about? Bellamy is a French name, or at least Norman."

She smiled at that. "My father is French by birth. My mother's parents almost had a heart attack. The British never forget a grudge. They couldn't understand why she couldn't just settle down with some perfectly respectable Englishman. But they are really happy in the country. They have a big garden and a little country house and they enjoy ..." Sophie was trying to find the words.

"La dolce vita," he said softly. "The sweet life."

"Exactly," she said.

Antonio said wryly, "What I can't figure out is why, if your

79

parents refuse to eat your cooking, you'd inflict it on my poor nonna?"

A laugh escaped her. "Touche, Dottore."

He said, "I have an English grandmother. My mother was half English. I seem to remember my grandmother telling me that her parents were rather put out for the same reason. But my grandmother knows her own mind, and her mind was set on the dashing Italian man she'd met on holiday."

Antonio started the car, then seemed to remember something. He dug inside a shopping bag and pulled out something that shocked Sophie. Shocking due to the simple thoughtfulness. He blushed as she gave him what was probably a sappy look. He said, "Put the rest in the glove compartment for Catarina. She's always losing those things ... or at least she used to lose them."

"Thanks for this. Truly. I wear them in the field, but I didn't think about it this morning. I wasn't expecting a convertible."

Antonio shrugged, feeling awkward about her gratitude. "It's nothing. And your hair looks very pretty down."

He was actually blushing, so she changed the subject. "How long were you away?" she asked as she tied her hair up in a messy bun.

"Probably too long," he said. He remembered how young the pharmacist's wife had been. How young Sophie's grandparents had been when she lost them. And what about Catarina? She'd been a girl and was a woman now. He'd missed it. "Yes, too long," he repeated absently.

Sophie had so many questions, but she knew somehow that this was not the time to ask them. Instead, she changed the subject. "So, aside from the aforementioned bats, scorpions, and spiders, what else do I need to worry about?" she asked.

"There are only a couple of spiders you need to be concerned about. We do have a breed of tarantula and black widow. Wild boar and wolves are the predators we worry about in this area. They prey on animals, and the boar will rip through the vines and devastate parts of the vineyard if they come across it. There will likely be a hunting party soon. As the grapes ripen and the scent carries, there are more concerns about the boar."

He drove over a bridge, and Sophie noticed a creek bed. "What is this? A creek off the Fiume Greve?"

Antonio smiled. "That is the Fiume Greve. It runs through the town, then right along the edge of our estate."

Sophie thought about the Thames that ran through London. "That's not a river, that is a creek. Creek would be kind to its ego. That is a babbling brook."

"How dare you insult our mighty Fiume Greve!" he said with feigned insult. Then he shrugged. "You think about your big river in London. I lived on the Amazonas. We imagine a river has to be wide and flowing. This river dries up like this in the summer. This is an arid region, and it has been an exceptionally dry season. When the rainy season comes, it will flow and look a bit less pitiful. It's fed by the springs and torrents of this area, and everything depends on the rainfall. It's okay because too much rain isn't good for the grapes. I think we are going to have a beautiful harvest. The grapes look *magnifico*."

"I think you're right. Tell me about your wine. Which is your best? What notes—" Sophie was cut off when he threw his head back and laughed.

"Oh no. You are on your own, bella. I'm giving nothing away before your tasting. You have to prove you have the"—he looked for the correct English term—"chops for this work. This isn't Essex." Antonio's tone was joking, but she bristled at the implication. She'd been fishing for intel, yes, but the insinuation that she didn't know enough to pass muster gave her the scratch.

"Just because I'm English doesn't mean I can't analyze and judge wine. I've traveled extensively in France's best wine regions. Spaghetti red isn't going to be a challenge." Sophie grabbed the dash as he hit the brakes. His face went from kidding to very dark. Had she just called her host vineyard's vintage a spaghetti red? Not a compliment in this business. She was an idiot.

"If that is what you think of Italian wine, then why don't you pack your bags and head to France, signorina? You are smugly sitting in some of the oldest wine country on the planet, dating back to Ancient Rome and even older. If you want to survive this internship with your professional integrity intact, I'd keep those types of comments to yourself."

His English was good, but his accent had grown much thicker. Sophie sighed, knowing she'd said something terribly insulting and snobbish. And inaccurate, of course. It had been a cheap shot. She just couldn't get on a good foot with this man. So, she took the high ground and let her maturity and good breeding take control of her mouth. "You started it," she said pissily.

He continued driving up the hill, and she thought she saw the corners of his mouth twitch upward.

❧

"Quickly, bring me a beaker of wine, so that I may wet my mind and say something clever." — Aristophanes

MARCO SAID, "I DON'T SEE WHY YOU THINK IT'S YOUR PLACE TO attend this tasting. She's a student, and we will be assessing her for her advising professor. We don't need you there flirting with her and distracting her."

Antonio chuckled at that. "Flirting? She's a college student. I don't make advances at twenty-two-year-olds."

"Actually," Catarina said, "she is almost thirty. I couldn't believe it when I met her and then read her file. Her skin is flawless."

"Would you stay out of this?" Marco said, instantly knowing it was a mistake. Catarina put her hands on her hips. Her mouth started flying so fast, he hoped to hell Sophie didn't hear her from the pool house. Her Italian was passable, and his sister was not even trying to be quiet.

"You listen here, you arrogant, stupid jackass. You can't even begin to compare your skill in the tasting room to mine. You have the palette of a buffoon, the instincts of a toddler, and it is you who would be flirting with her and a distraction!" Catarina then turned to Antonio. "I don't need your help. I have Papa and Nonno. However, you haven't tasted your birthright in ten years, so it's time to see if you've lost your stuff. I could use some fresh perspective. We are losing money!" She looked accusingly at Marco. "Be in the cave in fifteen minutes. I'm going to go see if Sophie needs anything.

⚜

A STORY IN FIVE GLASSES. THIS WAS A TEST, SOPHIE KNEW. EACH of them had five glasses that were numbered, more so that they knew they were all drinking the same thing at the same time. Antonio hadn't said anything about the spaghetti red comment. She owed him an apology. One just had to walk the estate, inspect the facility and equipment, and speak with the family to know that they took winemaking very seriously. And this wasn't the type of wine-making countryside that made crap. This was the home of the black rooster. Chianti Classico was a small region within Chianti that made exceptional wine. They had their own DOCG. The tier system had strict standards and rules. Other than the Brunellos that came out of Montalcino, Chianti Classico was some of the best wine in Italy. And Greve was the centuries-old epicenter. This vineyard was several generations old, and she hoped to God she didn't make an idiot out of herself. Sophie stole a glance at Antonio, who just smirked at her, still keeping silent.

Antonio was trying not to laugh. The Englishwoman was so tense, she looked like she was going to crack. He knew she'd be nervous he'd tell his family what she'd said about Italian wine.

STACEY REYNOLDS

Spaghetti red was cheap, substandard table wine that was sold abroad. He had a feeling she was getting ready to eat her words. The smells coming out of the glasses were making his mouth water. He hadn't had his family's wine in so long. Antonio said, "You've really modernized some of the equipment. I can't believe Nonno agreed to it." He smiled at his grandfather.

Giuseppe said, "Our Catarina is very knowledgeable." Then he said, as an afterthought, "And our Marco has a good business sense."

His sister stayed quiet, not wanting to bring Sophie into the family squabbles. He was glad. "Well, I have missed our wine. Who is going to lead the tasting?"

Before either could volunteer, Marcello cleared his throat from behind them. He took a seat next to Antonio, across from Sophie, and said, "I will."

Well, then. Antonio tensed at the closeness, then said simply, "As you wish, Padre."

"How are the kittens?" Sophie asked, knowing he'd been checking the mother's health and weighing the little ones.

"Bene, Sophie. Growing well."

She noticed his dog was in attendance as well. She stayed with him constantly, but Sophie loved dogs. She had to remember to carry some treats in her pocket. She wasn't above bribery. She noticed something interesting. The dog put her head up into Antonio's seeking palm, letting him dote on her. Then she laid her head in his lap.

Catarina had been watching as well. "I think she missed you."

Sophie spoke before thinking about it. "She must be getting up in years. How old was she when you left?" she asked.

"She was two. She'd just had her first litter. The puppies were in demand," Antonio said as he stroked her head. "Have you bred her again?" He didn't direct the question to his father, and Sophie felt that tension between them again.

Marcello replied, "Two more litters. Then we let her have her rest. People overbreed sometimes, for the money. But I didn't do it for the money. And when she had trouble with the second birth, I had her spayed, just in case the scoundrel down the road thought to take liberties with my beloved girl." Sophie smiled as she watched the aging man speak so sweetly to the dog, rubbing her chest. Antonio didn't tense this time, as if the dog was a conduit for tender feelings that they wouldn't normally allow between them.

"She's a Spini. A Spinone Italiano. She's sweet and mild. She's good with children, although we don't get them here very often."

Sophie thought about that. Three children in their twenties and thirties. None married. No children. *That's odd.*

"Okay, bellisima, it is time to taste our wine. I can't wait. Now, what can you tell me about this first one?"

It was Catarina who spoke. "Nothing. What can you tell us about the first one?" And so it began.

Sophie took a sip, swirling it over her whole mouth and tongue. It was bold. "Dark fruit, leather."

Antonio, she noticed, took his time, taking more than one sip. Then he gave her a dry look. "Use your mouth, not your reading glasses. You can get that out of any magazine. What kind of dark fruit?"

Marcello said, "I thought I was running this tasting." But he smiled at his son, pride showing on his face.

Sophie loved a challenge. "You cut me off, Medíco. Give me a minute," she said saucily. She took another sip, rolling it around her mouth. "Sour cherries, leather, herbs. Maybe thyme or something more peppery? It's very good. Is this your Annata?"

Marcello smiled. "Very good. It's our 2017. It was in traditional barrels for twelve months."

Sophie cocked her head with her eyes closed, as if not wanting to distract from the tasting. "It's not all Sangviovese. I'm not completely familiar with the grape varietals you might blend in, but if I had to guess, I'd say Cabernet Sauvignon and something else. Something that smooths it out a bit."

She'd raised some brows. "What? I mean, Zinfandels are peppery, but I know that's not it. Give me a hint here, people."

Marcello gave a nod. "You're right. The blend is 15 percent Cabernet and the final 5 is Canaiolo Nero. It's milder, a little brighter. When we harvest next month, I'll show you where our blending grapes are planted. We have Colorino grapes as well. They add a bolder, juicier, red fruit taste."

Sophie hung on the older man's every word. He was normally quiet and reserved, but when he talked about his grapes, his eyes came alive. His voice was richer.

"Okay, so not too shabby on that one. What do we have next?" she asked cockily.

Marcello gestured to the next glass. Sophie noticed that Antonio took a hearty sip and gave a small smile as he swallowed. She tilted the glass. "The color isn't as refined." She smelled it, getting her nose into the glass, nice and deep. "It's young, floral, and fruity. It smells nice. Like summer."

Sophie took a sip, then her eyes lifted. "Definitely young, but really rather nice. Is this your house wine? A table wine? It's Sangiovese, but it's light. I think you've played with this blend, maybe not a classico. It's very mellow."

Giuseppe raised his arms and said, "Sfuso!"

Sophie smiled. "I haven't heard of that varietal."

Antonio took another sip, closing his eyes. It wasn't a complex wine, but it reminded him of less complicated times. Of his youth before everything got so hard. He said, almost sounding like an instructor, "Sfuso means unpackaged. Or, in this case, loose. This is Viti del Fiume's *loose wine*. It's a very Italian thing. Our everyday wine that comes loose out of the barrel. Every vineyard has their own sfuso. Neighbors who don't make wine for sale still make sfuso. If they don't, they trade. Like the goat herder up the slope, for example. He trades a jug of sfuso for some cheese. It's not about tasting notes and points in some magazine. It's about family and community and—"

"La vita dolce?" she said, remembering a previous conversation.

He smiled at that, then gave his siblings a warm look. "Exactly. The sweet life and easier days."

Sophie said, "Well, I don't know about anyone else's estate, but your sfuso is a gorgeous, simple wine." She cleared her throat, suddenly missing her parents. "So, what is next?" She picked up the glass, immediately catching a disappointing whiff. She kept her face steady, twirling the wine.

Marco said, "I don't remember this," and Catarina talked over him.

"Please, I'm dying to know what you think."

"It's dry but fruity. There's a stronger tartness." Astringent and almost apple cider vinegar, but she didn't say that. Sophie sipped. She smiled, but it was strained. How was she going to handle this? She couldn't believe this below-mediocre table wine had passed muster. Then she narrowed her eyes on Antonio. He was grinning as he left his glass where it was and continued to drink the sfuso. One corner of her mouth went up. "Touché," she said under her breath. His eyes held mischief, then he winked. The smug bastard winked at her.

She straightened, meeting Marcello's eyes. "This isn't one of your wines. Someone with your reputation wouldn't create or serve something this ordinary. This is wicker basket, pizza parlour—"

Antonio interrupted, all seriousness. "Spaghetti red?" he asked innocently. Her throat closed up.

Catarina laughed. "I'm sorry we tricked you. For some reason, Antonio dug out Nonna's cooking wine. He's trying to tease you, I think."

So, he hadn't told them. Her challenging stare turned into something softer, something grateful. She nodded at him, in silent thanks, then said to Catarina, "He's going to pay for that somehow."

Marcello's belly grumbled with laughter, and Giuseppe looked confused, tilting his head at Antonio. "I will never understand the young," he said. "In my day, I'd have tried to kiss her. You're trying to poison her." And at that, Antonio turned almost as scarlet as the awful spaghetti red.

The last two glasses were two different vintages from their Riserva stores. One was good, the other was great. She thought about the differences. There was definitely less finesse with the one glass. And she thought perhaps they'd mixed in another varietal. "May I ask you, what year is this one?"

Antonio shook his head. "It's not our normal quality. I'd like to know as well."

"It's the 2014," Catarina said grimly. "We had an early frost and lost some of the grapes." She sighed, smiling tightly. "The decision was made to blend the full 20 percent allowed with Corolino grapes. They'd been less affected by the frost. Normally, our Riservas are all Sangiovese. If we add anything, it's 5 percent Merlot if the tannins are too sharp." She shook her head. "Instead of making less wine, we compromised quality for keeping our production numbers steady. It was a mistake. We haven't had to make the choice since then, but we learned a painful lesson. We are still recovering. It was the first year in eighty years that we didn't place in the local rankings. We are small, and we rely heavily on local sales and tourists."

Antonio was shooting looks between his father and brother. Sophie cringed inwardly, knowing that she'd opened up an old wound. Hurt pride and defensiveness flowed off of Marco. She said brightly, "Well, everyone has an off year. In America, one of the major California vineyards had a tank go awry. They pumped over forty thousand gallons of wine into the local river. It was an environmental nightmare. Yet, if you go into any wine store or supermarket in most American towns, you'll find that vineyard's wine on the shelf. Everyone has bad years. Thankfully, this glass"—she lifted the last of the glasses she'd tasted—"is absolutely magnifico."

Giuseppe clapped his hand. "Yes, signorina. It is a very special vino. I think it will be one of our best. A carefully picked blend of our finest Sangiovese grapes."

"I'd love to take a walk to each part of the estate where you chose the grapes," Sophie said. "I know the terroir varies, even on single estates, and you have slope differences. Areas that have more sun exposure. I would like to take soil samples and rootstock samples. Part of my internship will be grafting and judging rootstock."

Catarina said, "We'll do more than that. We'll give you a bit of ground to see if your grafts take. I mean, you'll be long gone by the time it bears any fruit, but it might be interesting to see what you create."

Antonio watched Sophie's face light up. Some women wanted jewels. He'd met a few of them in his day. Some wanted fine dining and exotic holidays. Some just wanted sex. This strange, impish, little English girl wanted dirt.

THE MEN LAGGED BEHIND AS THEY TOOK AN EVENING STROLL. Antonio had missed this. Long walks after the evening meals. There were fewer natural predators in Tuscany than where he lived, mosquitos being the most dangerous in Brazil. They carried deadly diseases and liked to hunt at night. This past week was the first in ten years that he hadn't slept under a mosquito net. The air was not thick with humidity. Even the sounds were different. He watched his sister walk arm in arm with his nonna, and he was surprised to find himself close to tears.

His grandfather stirred beside him, putting a hand on his shoulder. His nonno had always been able to read him. Antonio's voice was hoarse. "How is her health? Is she well?" He knew more about Reverend Mother Faith's health than his own flesh and blood.

Giuseppe answered thoughtfully, as if he made a study of his wife's health. "She's in good health. She needs longer naps, now. She eats less. But she's still up with the sun and making caffè."

"And you, Nonno? How are you really?" Antonio knew he'd lose them someday, but he wasn't ready. He'd never be ready.

"I'm old, Antonio. Just an old man who has lived a good life. None of us can say when our Father will call us home. I don't fret over such things. I have a good son. I have wonderful grandchildren. If I go first, my Magdalena will be in good hands. And my vines will be passed on to another generation ... if any of you jugheads will get married and make my son a grandpapa."

Antonio couldn't tell if his grandfather was trying to impart a life lesson right now, or if he was just evading his real question. He was suddenly glad they were speaking in Italian because Catarina was laughing and Ms. Sophie Bellamy was utterly confused.

"I didn't catch all that. I thought you were going to speak in English around me?" Sophie said with only a tiny bit of annoyance.

Catarina answered before Antonio did. "And I thought I told you that the only way you'd become proficient in Italian was to hang around a bunch of Italians."

"Hmm ... too right," Sophie said with a smirk. "Still, it would be nice to have an interpreter until I get the hang of it. Besides," she said, gesturing toward Antonio, "he's speaking some sort of pig Latin."

Antonio laughed. Marcello asked, "What does Latin have to do with swine?"

Antonio ignored him. "I'm sorry, Ms. Bellamy. I can curse in Gaelic if that helps."

She smiled. "Your Irish nuns, then?"

"Occasionally, but no. Irish doctors and nurses. They do have a way with the spoken word. Very witty and a lion's share of sarcasm, a language in which, it appears, you are fluent."

"Absolutely," Sophie said, "and with eight ounces of wine in my system, I get funnier by the moment."

"But there were five glasses, not four," Antonio said, just to goad her.

"Are you referring to that swill you swiped from your nonna's cupboard? I didn't let more than a minor sip of that rubbish cross this palette," she said. "I may be a woefully ignorant English viticulturist, but life is decidedly too short to drink piss wine."

Sophie realized that Catarina was translating the entire exchange in Magdalena's ear. With her last comment, Magdalena threw her head back and let out a girlish laugh. She looked at Antonio, and his face was full of love.

Antonio's heart swelled at the sound of his nonna's laughter. When was the last time he'd heard his grandmother really laugh? And why on earth had he stayed away so long?

Sophie gave Antonio a small smile and his eyes returned the gesture. Those eyes. Warm, butterscotch-colored eyes with impossibly thick, long lashes. She almost shook herself, turning before she blushed in front of the arrogant man.

THEY HAD A WONDERFUL MEAL PLANNED FOR THAT EVENING, AND Sophie was surprised to see Marco and Marcello in the outdoor kitchen. They were grilling three of the largest steaks she'd ever seen. Huge T-bone steaks that were four times as big as any she'd ever seen. "We trade our sfuso with the local cattle ranch," Marco said. "Olive oil, salt, pepper, and some herbs. Eight minutes on each side." He kissed his fingertips. "Bistecca alla Fiorentina. It's the regional dish of this area." Florentine-style steak and smelling heavenly. "They are almost finished."

Sophie noticed they were eating outdoors tonight. "I'll just go see if Magdalena needs any help."

She smelled something wonderful upon entering the house. Sophie put her head over the pot on the stove. Sautéing greens and another pan with the white beans, which were a staple in Tuscan cooking. Olive oil and herbs seemed to be a common theme in every dish. She picked up the jar of olive oil. "Is this from your trees?"

Catarina replied, "Yes. Nonna has a press in the outbuilding. Her trees make wonderful oil."

Sophie watched Magdalena zest a lemon over the greens after she'd put them in a serving dish. Her mouth was watering. Antonio was sitting at the dining room table, finishing up some other sort of project. "First aid kits?" she asked.

"Yes, medical kits. Anything I think they might need in the field. One in each truck, one in the cave, one near the equipment, and one for the house." Antonio worked as he talked. "We have one near the pool already," he added.

"That's very thoughtful," Sophie said, and meaning it.

"They are my family. And the workers who come in for the harvest and the year-round workers ... they are an extension of that family. They are our responsibility." Antonio lowered his voice and added, "And I ordered a mobile defibrillator."

Her face softened. "Ten years absent makes your mind see things that others will not," she said. In other words, the grandparents had aged.

"Yes, and I make a good living. It's not so expensive where I live. And I'm so busy, I hardly have time to use any of my salary for extra things. Medical care is not right down the road when you make your living in the countryside. I just want them to have these things. Sometimes you don't have fifteen minutes to wait when a critical incident happens."

They were called to dinner outside, and Sophie helped carry dishes from the kitchen. The steaks were very rare, which was fine with her. Catarina smiled when she said as much. Catarina said, "I never understood your country's need to cook meat to death. How can you taste it?"

Giuseppe raised his glass, and a piece of beef on his fork, and said something in Italian. Antonio saw that Sophie hadn't caught the meaning. He translated, "A good marriage. The beef and the wine of this region, it's a good pairing." He remembered something. He said, "Oh, I believe someone called for you. You'll have to ask Nonna, although her English is less proficient, so I'm not sure how much she can tell you."

"So, it was a call from England?" Sophie asked. Her face blanched. "What is the date?" she inquired anxiously. Her heart started pounding.

"What's the matter, Sophie?" Antonio asked. Then he stood. "You've gone pale." He took her wrist and immediately started timing her pulse. "Sit down."

She shook him off and said, "I'm okay. It's jet lag. Um ... could you just tell me the date? I'm just a little fuzzy right now."

7

Something was wrong. Antonio had good instincts about people. He read them fairly easily, especially when they were concealing something. People often hid things from doctors. Something had rattled Sophie, and she was trying just a little too hard to act like everything was fine. He saw the stress in her body, and he could tell that his grandmother noticed it as well. She'd periodically reach across the table and pat Sophie's hand, as if to comfort her.

Once dinner was over, Sophie excused herself. "If you're sure I can't help with the washing up, I have some notes to write up. I also need to return a phone call." She walked quickly to her little house, needing privacy and to retrieve her mobile, which she left on the charger in her bedroom.

Her hands shook as she thumbed through her contacts to find her roommate's phone number. "Matt? What is wrong? Something has happened, hasn't it?"

Matt sighed, clearing his throat. "I got a call from a Donald Radcliffe."

"Donald Radcliffe? I don't know a ..." She paused, something like cement coursing through her body, starting at her head and going down to her feet. "Morgan's husband?"

Morgan, her old roommate from London. "What's happened?"

"Someone beat her almost to death. She went missing for about ten hours. They found her half in and half out of the river, left for dead."

"Oh my God, no!" She swallowed a sob. "Is she dead?"

"No, she's alive. They've induced a coma. She has several broken bones and some ..." She heard him swallow hard. "She has some cigar burns. She was tortured. Sophie, she said your name. It's all she could manage. She was in so much pain, they are keeping her under. She needs extensive surgery. She has a ruptured spleen and other injuries. I'm so sorry, my love. I think this may not have been random. It's been two days since they ..."

He didn't need to finish. *Since they released him from prison.* She'd told Morgan. She'd tried to make sure she was prepared and warned, but Morgan had a life. A career. She couldn't just disappear. She and her husband had been trying for a baby. "Oh, God. She wasn't pregnant, was she?" Sophie screamed.

"I don't think so. Her husband actually mentioned it, that he was glad she hadn't been pregnant. He doesn't blame you, sweetheart. He knows everything and he doesn't blame you. He thinks the bastard was trying to find out where you were."

"Oh, God. I should have changed my name. I made sure to use a burner phone. I never signed any leases, but I applied to the college with my real name. I just thought when they gave him thirty years, they bloody well meant thirty years. It's only been ten! Why the buggering hell would they let him out! He's a violent maniac!"

"But he wasn't convicted on that, love. He was convicted on a weapons charge and for selling drugs. They didn't prosecute him for what he'd done to you. That's what I don't understand."

She'd told them the story, but not the why of it. "They told me it was very hard to prove. At least enough for a conviction. They arrested him for violating a court order, then found the drugs and weapon on him and in his apartment. That was a solid case, so they dropped the rest."

"I'm afraid, Sophie. We all are," he said.

"I'm so sorry I put you in this position," she said, her voice tight with grief. "Poor Morgan. Oh, God!"

"We aren't afraid for us, you dolt. We're afraid for you! And your parents. I called them first. I didn't want to wait, and I didn't have your new mobile. I'm going to delete this call. I don't want an Italian number coming up in my contacts, even if it is a burner mobile." She'd only given it to her parents. It was an Italian burner phone she'd picked up in Milan. "I thought you'd want to know. Scotland Yard apparently said their hands are tied. She didn't identify him as her attacker and now she can't. At least not for now."

"They should have never let him out!" she screamed.

"Yeah, that's another thing. They couldn't believe it, either. They are wondering if he's got friends in low places. The officer said something like, *Prison is an excellent place to make new contacts.* Like the bloke was connected or something. Don't worry, Sophie. We don't know where you are. I mean, he can't search all of Italy even if he knew where to start looking. He'd never think to look abroad."

"I wouldn't be too sure about that. Now, this has to be costing you a fortune. I have a question for you. If you didn't have my mobile and I didn't give you my whereabouts, how did you call the house?"

"I think that may have been your father. I didn't call you, love. You better phone him next. They are out of their heads, as you can imagine."

"I will. Thank you, Matt."

Matt asked, "How is the internship going? A vineyard in Tuscany is a dream job. Is your host family nice?"

"They are wonderful. And instead of a room in the basement, they put me in their pool house. Two bedrooms with a view of the vineyard."

"Shut the fuck up! You're taking a piss," he said.

She laughed. "I'm not. Tell the girls I miss them. I need to call my parents. I love you all."

"We love you, too. And Sophie ... be careful. I mean, he's not going to come to Italy, but just watch your back."

She said, "I know. Believe me."

The call to her parents didn't go quite so well. Her mother was beside herself. Her father was ready to commit murder. She nearly broke down when they talked about Morgan. When she rang off, she just sat on her bed. And for the second time in as many days, she broke down, crying.

Antonio walked toward the pool house, wearing a pair of his brother's swim trunks and an old T-shirt. He'd ask Sophie first, of course. This was her space right now, and it was a courtesy they'd all extend to her. And no more skinny-dipping, for obvious reasons. He approached the house, walking around the pool. Then he heard it. She was crying again. This was different, though. No mere sniffles. She was crying in great, racking sobs. Jesus.

He turned around, going quickly back to the house. When Antonio entered the kitchen, his sister was sipping a glass of wine, talking to Marco. "I need you, Catarina. Now. It's Sophie."

"Is she all right?" She started walking toward the door.

"I don't think so. She is crying inside the house like the world is ending. This is the second time I've heard her, but she's much worse this time. I think she could use a friend."

Catarina backed up, grabbed the remains of the bottle, and marched toward the house. She knocked on the door, and it took a while for Sophie to appear. She was a mess. Catarina walked in, set down the bottle and glass, and opened her arms. Sophie burst into tears.

STACEY REYNOLDS

"I SHOULDN'T BE BOTHERING YOU WITH THIS. IT'S SO unprofessional. Please, Antonio shouldn't have said anything."

Catarina knelt down in front of her, taking both her hands. "Did some bastardo break your heart? Don't waste your tears, amica. You are young and beautiful."

Sophie shook her head. How could she explain? How could she tell such an ugly tale? She barely knew this woman. And Antonio had heard her crying. Bloody open windows. She felt so stupid. "It's not that. I didn't get dumped or anything. Jesus, you'd really need to go on more than a couple of dates and actually like someone in order to get dumped! It's so much worse, Catarina."

Catarina said, "You don't have to tell me, but I wish you would. Are you in some kind of trouble? Please, Sophie. Let us help you."

"I can't get into it. I mean, I just can't right now. What I can tell you is that ten years ago, I started seeing someone. It didn't last long. A couple weeks. Maybe three dates. I tried to end it. Something was off with him. I felt it pretty early on. By our second date, I started feeling uneasy. When I told him I didn't want to see him anymore, he didn't take it well. It was as if he had this long, intense love affair built up in his mind that never really happened. He started following me and calling the apartment. He threatened my roommate over the phone. He'd show up in the middle of the night. I began staying with my parents on the weekends."

Catarina held her hands tightly and had moved next to her on the couch. Sophie took a deep, cleansing breath. "He went to prison for something else. It's a long story, but I thought I was rid of him. Right before I came here, I got a call from Scotland Yard. The courts were releasing him after serving half his sentence. I left early, before he got out."

"That's why you asked to come early?" Catarina inquired.

Sophie just nodded. Then she started to tear up again. She got to the awful conclusion of her story. She told her about Morgan. Catarina's face blanched.

"Oh my God, Sophie. Did he ever hurt you?" she asked.

98

Sophie looked away. "It was just a lot of harassment. Scary stuff. Threats and showing up in public places, bothering me at home. He always seemed to know where I was. I was so stressed that I dropped out of school. That's why I'm pushing thirty and finally finishing my degree."

Catarina didn't believe her. She was hiding something. She'd evaded her question. She wasn't going to press her, though. This was pretty serious trauma. "I think we should talk to the family and the staff. We want you to feel safe here."

"No! Oh Jesus, Catarina. Don't tell them. I'm so ashamed. I let this happen on some level. I obviously didn't set boundaries early enough. I let him manipulate me."

"This is not your fault. I won't hear another word about it. Why does the woman always blame herself? And if he was willing to brutalize your friend in order to find you, we are going to need help."

"He can't find me. I never signed a lease in Essex. I don't even have a contracted mobile phone. Just burners. I've been careful. And Morgan didn't know where I lived after London or where I was going."

Catarina seemed unsure. She exhaled. "If anything changes, or if you get any new information, I need you to promise me you will come to me. My family won't let anything happen to you. My papa will want to know if we need to take precautions. Promise me, Sophie."

"I promise." She took a shaky breath and Catarina kissed her cheek. Then she got up and went into the kitchen to get another wineglass.

MARCO ASKED IMPATIENTLY, "WHY ARE THEY TAKING SO LONG?"

"It could be personal. She's here with no friends or family and she might not be forthcoming. Just let Catarina handle it."

Marco dipped his toe in the pool. "I have not had a swim in probably two years."

Antonio stopped, frozen in place. "I'm sorry, did you say two years? You used to love to swim. Remember our pool parties?"

Marco smirked. "Three children who are related don't make a party."

"So you say. I called it a pool party, and I will still call it a pool party. Nonna would bring out cocoa and biscotti," he said, smiling at the memories.

"She still makes biscotti on Sundays," Marco said with a smile.

"Go get your trunks on, brother. We need to lighten this mood a bit." He tilted his head. "I mean, unless you're out of shape from pushing all of that paper. You don't want to make a poor showing," Antonio said with a grin.

"I am not out of shape. I still have my road bike, you arrogant, little shit. I could swim circles around you."

"Big talk, fratello. Big talk."

❦

CATARINA AND SOPHIE BOTH PAUSED MID-SIP AT THE SOUND OF raucous laughter coming from outside. And splashing. Lots of splashing. Catarina smiled and said, "It seems my stupid brothers are getting along better."

Sophie actually blushed. The thought of those two gorgeous brothers outside her door in swimsuits made her want to jump out of her seat so she could gawk through the window. They both stood, and Catarina led the way out the door.

They saw Antonio, but she was sure she'd heard two voices. Catarina asked, "Where's Marco?" But no sooner had she asked the question than Marco shot out from the changing area and scooped his sister up in his arms. "Pool party!" they bellowed. And in they went, with Catarina fully dressed. They'd been speaking in Italian, but Sophie quickly sorted out the translation.

Sophie's laugh was loud and unladylike as she eyed the siblings hitting the water. Antonio watched her, and his heart tightened behind his ribs. He could tell she'd been crying, which made her face, lit up with laughter, all the sweeter to behold. He got out of the pool slowly, the water running off his body as he pushed his hair back. He saw her eyes flare and heard her voice hitch. He wasn't sure whether he wanted to carry her into the pool or right into the pool house to the bedroom. She had a simple, tender sort of beauty that made his body hum and his heart sing.

Sophie put her hands up, realizing she'd been too busy gawking at his fine body. He was only a few feet away. "Oh no, Medíco. What happened to *first do no harm?*"

He cocked a brow. "I won't leave any permanent damage. Pool party means everyone swims."

"I'm a guest. You wouldn't," she said with a little more certainty than she actually felt.

"I would. I've pushed my elderly grandfather into this pool. A little girl like you is child's play."

"I can't swim. Never learned." She lied.

Marco yelled, "She's lying. She was on her school swim team. Team captain."

Antonio made a *tisk-tisk* sound and said, "You should be ashamed of yourself, belissima. Telling lies so easily."

She darted for the door of the house, squealing as he looped his arm around her waist. Catarina and Marco yelled, "Pool party!" Just as he went sailing through the air, Sophie tucked tight against his chest. Her squeals came to a crescendo just as she hit the water.

AFTER JUDGING CANNONBALL TECHNIQUES AND ONE GAME OF Marco Polo, Sophie reflected that she hadn't had this much fun in years. She smiled as she saw Giuseppe carrying a tray of drinks and

Magdalena bringing a plate of biscuits. Giuseppe pointed at Antonio. "Don't even think about it, cattivo."

Sophie said, "I don't know that word."

Antonio winked at her and explained, "It means naughty."

She said, "So you were called it often, obviously." Then she splashed him in the face.

Antonio dunked under the water just as it would have hit him, grabbed her foot, and she went in ass over teakettle. She scowled as she took a towel from Magdalena. Sophie growled at him and pointed. "Cattivo!" Then she went to fetch a cup of cocoa and a biscotti, ignoring the rumbles of rich laughter behind her.

His eyes roamed over her body appreciatively, before he thought to control the impulse. Her clothes clung to her. She'd changed into pajama bottoms and a tight, little T-shirt before he'd thrown her into the pool. She was lushly curved through the hips. Even more so than he'd imagined. Antonio shook himself, diverting his gaze. He didn't want her to think he was some creeper. Marco hissed through his teeth. "Wow."

"Would you two behave," Catarina said on a whisper. "She's had a rough night."

They all sat around the table, shivering, even though the night was warm. The cocoa was just the thing. Magdalena said, "They are big bambinos. I never get any great-grandchildren like this!" But her eyes were warm as she took in her three grandkids. Together again, finally.

Sophie had shared her deepest and darkest secret with Catarina tonight, and Antonio had overheard her crying like a mental patient. So, she felt entitled to some reciprocal prying. "Why haven't any of you gotten married?"

Antonio said, "I'm too busy. She's too picky." He cocked his head. "Marco was the ladies' man. Why haven't you tied the knot with some village girl yet, brother?"

Catarina, Magdalena, and Giuseppe all froze, and Antonio

watched his brother actually wince. "Um ... I'm sorry. I was kidding. What did I say?"

Catarina tried to change the subject, but Marco spoke over her. "He may as well know. I have nothing to hide." He looked at Antonio and said, "I was married. For three years. I'm not anymore." Then he got up, kissed their nonna, and left toward the house.

Antonio just sat there, stunned into silence. Then he said, "Jesus, I'm sorry. I didn't know."

"Well, that's what happens when you don't come home for ten years," Catarina said. And her tone wasn't accusatory or snarky. It was a little sad.

Sophie cleared her throat. "Well, I need a hot shower and some dry clothes." She gave Antonio a chiding look. He winked at her—again. And when he smiled, he had dimples. Of course he did. Every rogue in every romance novel she'd ever read had a face like a masculine, beautiful angel and they'd all had dimples.

Catarina got up and hugged her. She said, "I'm always here to talk, Sophie. And if you get too scared out here, I'll come and stay in the other bedroom. But you have to talk to me. Don't suffer needlessly."

She said the words softly, but she could see Antonio's shoulders stiffen, his smile gone. He narrowed his eyes. He walked closer, putting his T-shirt over his head as he approached. "What has happened? And don't lie to me, I heard you crying. Why would you be afraid?"

"Don't be nosey, Antonio. She's okay. She needed a friend, just like you said," Catarina admonished lightly. Like she was trying to downplay whatever had disturbed Sophie. But Antonio didn't think Sophie was the type of woman prone to theatrics. Neither was Catarina. Women and their damn secrets.

So, that's how she knew to come out and check on me. Antonio thought she needed a friend. She inwardly recoiled with embarrassment, feeling her cheeks heat. "I'm okay. Thank you, Antonio. I mean, not for throwing me into the pool, but ..."

"But you had fun?" he offered.

Sophie gave him another chiding look. "Maybe," she said, "but the Rinalto offspring have a peculiar way of inviting someone to a party." She thought about the thrill of being flush against his chest as they soared through the air. She met his eyes and saw awareness, like he knew what she was thinking. She cleared her throat for no reason, other than to assure she didn't come out sounding breathy and infatuated. She lifted her chin, and in her best Queen's English said, "Good night, everyone."

❧ 8 ❧

Antonio performed health screenings on the group of workers who would be helping the vineyard during the harvest. He hadn't given the hospital or the mission a return date. He had so much personal time accumulated, he could afford to stay for this season's harvest. Being back at Viti del Fiume was kind of exciting. The wine, the people, and the traditions had all shaped his childhood. He was surprised to see that Catarina had brought the harvest process out of the Dark Ages. They still hand-harvested, but they had good machinery for destemming, sorting, and pressing.

As Antonio worked, trying to help the family prepare for the upcoming *Vendemmia*, the grape harvest, he was always tuned in to the Englishwoman who worked side by side with his family. After lunch, he'd volunteered to drive her out to the area where they grew the other varietals. Actually, his nonno had suggested it, but he'd quickly agreed. Sophie wanted to see the French Cabernet Sauvignon and French Merlot grapes, which were grown in two plots about a kilometer northeast of the house. She needed to take soil samples and get samples of the rootstock. Then she'd check the Colorino vines and take pictures and more samples.

As he stood in the kitchen, stealing bites from his grandmother's soup pot, he felt her come into the room. Antonio knew it was her before he even turned around. The sight of her slammed into him like a kick to the chest. She was, hands down, the most adorable thing he'd ever laid eyes on. She had piles of hair bound on top of her head, a pale-yellow visor, overalls, a long-sleeved T-shirt, and a pair of work boots. He didn't think they made work boots that small. Her little feet were even adorable. She came beside him, thoroughly washing her hands. He handed her a towel before she could even ask. "Thank you," Sophie said. He caught her gaze, holding her in place with it. Then he reached up and thumbed her earlobe.

Antonio said, "You got a bit overzealous with the sunscreen, I think."

He waited for the pink blush to hit her cheeks and ears, and he was rewarded when it happened. "Yes, well, I don't have your genetics. I look like a proper lobster bake if I'm not careful."

"Good, I'm glad to hear it. Despite my tan, I never leave the house without sunscreen. When you are as close to the equator as I am, you have to be cautious. We are constantly chasing the children, trying to keep them covered."

Sophie's heart sank. "You have children? I thought you said you'd never been married."

"Sorry, I forget sometimes that we don't really know each other. What I meant to say was the children at St. Clare's. It's a charity mission run by the Irish nuns. It's not just an abbey and a hospital, it's an orphanage."

Sophie put her hand to her heart. "Oh, my. How many children? Can they be adopted?"

And Antonio's eyes crinkled and a warm smile shone on his face. As they sat at the table, eating his grandmother's ribollita and panzanella, he talked about his favorite place and favorite people on

Earth—the motley crew of missionaries, nurses, doctors, gardeners, security guards, and, of course, the children. He kept filling Sophie's water glass, loving how she looked him in the eyes, her genuine interest apparent. His family hadn't asked him much about St. Clare's. He felt, for a time, like he and Sophie were the only ones in the room. But they weren't. When he looked up, wondering why no one else had come to lunch, he noticed that his father and grandfather had been listening. His father's eyes were misty, a thing that took Antonio aback. His father never cried.

ANTONIO LOVED SEEING HIS ITALIAN HOME THROUGH FRESH eyes. His passenger couldn't decide which way to look. They tested the soil in several different areas of the vineyard, and Sophie took samples of a few of the Sangiovese roots. After they were done, he escorted her to the oldest vines at Viti del Fiume. She walked around the plants, and when she talked, she did it at a whisper.

"They're not asleep," he said, teasing her.

"Let's hope not," she said. Then she watched him pick a couple of grapes from the vine. He wanted to feed one to her, but he figured that might not go over too well. They were bursting with flavor, even though they had at least two more weeks to go. Sophie said, "This is wonderful. I never imagined it would be this beautiful." They were up on the high grounds of the estate, and he motioned for her to walk with him.

"We'll be very busy before too long, and you won't get to see this," Antonio said as he took her hand.

Sophie's heart was beating so hard, she was sure he could hear it. There was no demand to the simple gesture, and yet an electric thrill sparked up her arm and straight through to her belly. She tempered these thoughts, however. Antonio Rinalto was a six-foot, gorgeous slice of heaven. But Italians were more affectionate. The male relatives kissed each other and hugged way more than the average English person. They talked closer, used their hands more. Catarina walked arm in arm with her father and did the same with Sophie. They just touched more. Still, this was nice. It had been a while since someone had held her hand. They walked into a patch of forest and she stiffened just a bit. Antonio felt it.

"I'm sorry," he said, letting go of her hand. "I didn't think. Are you uncomfortable with this, cara mia?" He shook his head. "You don't know me, and I start dragging you into the woods. Cristo, I'm sorry."

He almost turned around when Sophie surprised him, and herself. She took his hand and said,

"Show me."

Antonio was trying to be a gentleman, but those simple two words shot straight down from his chest to his cock. He inhaled harshly at the contact. "Are you sure?" *Because I'm not. I'm starting to get scared myself.* He hadn't felt such an immediate attraction since ... well, since Izzy, and that had been a brief infatuation. He'd valued her friendship and Liam's too much to press the matter and compete for her affections. She'd not been *the one*. This, though ... this was magic.

"I'm sure. I'm okay. Just a little jittery today. Too much of that gorgeous coffee your grandmother makes."

"Yes, the old way is best. The coffee in Brazil might be better, though, but don't you dare tell her I said that." He squeezed her hand.

Sophie nudged him and said, "You didn't tell her about my spaghetti red jibe, so I owe you one."

Antonio laughed, really laughed, where it met his eyes. "And do you still hold Italian wine in such low esteem?" he asked as they walked. She smiled at that.

"Not at all. All of the true Viti del Fiume wine was wonderful. Even the new wine. The *sfuso*. And the last one ... well, that is something special. I think in a couple of months, you may have a Gran Selezione contender."

"You're biased. We have you set up in a pool house instead of with three hots and a cot like some interns get," Antonio said with a smile.

Sophie barked out a laugh. "Where did you hear that term? It sounds like a very American thing to say."

"My friend Hans at the mission. He is a retired US Marine. He's an endless wealth of colorful sayings and expletives. Some of them I won't repeat."

"Those are the ones you absolutely must repeat. Between the Irish slang and the military expletives, peppered with my English wit, you'll be the most clever Italian on the planet."

The woods opened up, and before Antonio could reply, she gasped. "Oh, Antonio." Her words were soft, and it did funny things to him. Right under the ribs. "What are they? They look like spring flowers, but it's September." Looking over a meadow, which was surrounded by the indigenous forest, the sloping ground was covered in small, blue-violet-colored flowers. She bent, looking at the blossom. "It has a burst of orange in the center. What are they?"

"They are saffron crocuses. I couldn't show you our beautiful poppies. Those bloom in spring. And the sunflowers peaked last month. This is our autumn glory," he said as he looked over the rolling carpet of flowers.

"Thank you for this," she said. Sophie closed her eyes, listening and smelling, wanting to absorb this place with all of her senses. "Is it wrong that I want to roll in this like a dog?"

Antonio answered her by turning, sitting, and reclining. She laughed and did the same. She sighed. "This is a good minute." He gave her a questioning look, like it was an odd thing to say. She shrugged. "Sometimes you have bad weeks, bad months, or even bad years. It's those times you have to take your joy minute by minute, isolate a single moment that is truly beautiful."

"That is a wonderful philosophy, and I'm going to hold on to it," he said. Then he took his phone out. He lifted it, and Sophie moved her head next to him. They took a completely silly picture because it looked like Antonio was wearing flowers in his hair. "Now I can look back at this minute when things are difficult."

She smiled and tears pricked her eyes. Sophie glanced at him and he'd put the phone down. He was just ... watching her. "You have your own demons, I think. I'll send you a copy. You'll be making your crappy English wine, surrounded by inferior males, and you'll sigh and look at our picture. Ah, that handsome devil, Antonio, with the flowers in his hair. What has become of him?"

Sophie socked him in the ribs. "And so humble." She knew he'd been trying to lighten the mood, which made her adore him even more. He rolled onto his side, and his eyes were full of something. She wasn't sure what, but he seemed, for all the world, like he wanted to kiss her. Then his gaze shifted to just behind her. He moved so fast, she just squealed. He was up on his feet and jerking her off her back. "What the hell just happened?"

Antonio was shaking. He was so stupid. His mind had been focused on laying her down in this bed of flowers and taking her mouth. "I'm sorry." He pointed and she looked behind her. Two honey bees were drifting over the area where her head had been resting.

Sophie said, "Oh, well. Yes, I suppose that wasn't a wise impulse. Thank you."

"Where is your EpiPen?"

She patted her pocket. "It's in my bag in the truck."

Antonio sighed. "Close, but not close enough. I'll try to find some sort of pouch that is easy to strap to your waist. I want it on you or close to you at all times." When he'd seen that bee near her head, he'd had a few not-so-great minutes doing a flashback slideshow in his mind.

Sophie shook herself. "You don't have to do that. I usually keep it on me. I was just ... distracted."

Antonio rather liked being her distraction. He bent and picked a crocus. "I don't think they'll miss just one." He tucked it behind her ear. He looked down at this unlikely addition to the vineyard staff and felt a pang of affection so deep that it surprised him. He couldn't resist rubbing his fingers over her cheek and jaw. "Bellisima," he said softly. Then he turned and walked her back to the truck.

She stopped when they got to the vehicle. "I could feel you shaking. I'm sorry," Sophie said.

"No, I'm sorry. I handled you pretty roughly, I think. It's just"—he exhaled—"anyway, I'll try to find a good solution to you carrying that pen on you while you work. If we have a particularly hot day, we'll rig up a small cooler. It's supposed to stay at room temperature or it spoils the medication."

Sophie sat in the passenger seat. She turned to him as he started the truck and said, "It's just what? You said 'It's just' and then you changed the subject."

"Persistent," he said. "Yes, well, I just remembered some difficult situations. The Amazonas is full of toxic creatures, and sometimes we weren't near a hospital when we had to deal with them."

"I thought you said you worked at two hospitals? Is the one at St. Clare's as primitive as all that?" she asked.

Antonio was surprised she remembered the name of the mission. Pleasantly so. He said, "St. Clare's is humble and underfunded, but it is fully equipped. I'm referring to our trips into the forest. We have a mobile unit, like a large van, and also a riverboat. A sort of floating clinic that gets us to the tribes that live in the remote areas of the rainforest. They need medical care that their medicine man can't manage. And sometimes they require a midwife if there is a complicated pregnancy. We also record disease patterns, or our infectious disease specialist does. We vaccinate those who will accept it. I've seen advanced sepsis from snake bites. The Fer-de-lance pit viper's bite begins to rot a limb within minutes." He looked at his hands, as if remembering something. "And the children sometimes take walks to the next village to see their friends. One of my older bambinas was bitten by a tree viper. The little bastards hide in the trees and blend in, and they wait. She almost died. She was special, and it may very well have killed me to lose her."

"You said *was*. Is she gone?" Sophie was almost afraid to ask.

"Yes, but to a good place. It's a long story worth telling, but maybe later. Anyway, the snake bites can end a life in a couple minutes. And then there were the wandering spider bites I've seen over the years." Antonio shook himself. "Watching someone die from anaphylaxis or a venomous bite is something that sticks with you. So, when I saw the bee around you, I just panicked a bit. I'd rather handle you a bit harshly than need to use that EpiPen. Again, I'm sorry."

"Don't apologize. I was caught up in the moment, and I didn't even consider the risk of getting stung. I've watched documentaries about the deadly rainforest, but it's not the same as dealing with it in person every day." Sophie paused then asked, "What is her name? This older bambina?"

His face softened. "Her name is Genoveva. She lives in Ireland with her father now. I miss her. We all do."

Sophie was humbled by this man. By all accounts, he looked like a well-off, dashing, young doctor. With those looks and his sharp mind, he could go anywhere and have anyone. Yet, for ten years, he lived in a foreign country and worked as a medical missionary. "You are quite a surprise, Antonio." She swallowed hard, wondering why all the good ones were taken. He wasn't married, but he was committed elsewhere. She shook herself. "As for missing your Genoveva, you'll definitely need to take a trip to Ireland. It's a beautiful place. One of my grandparents was from the North. She grew up in a small village on the Antrim Coast. We went all over Ireland, though. It's one of those places that sticks with you." Sophie looked around her at the gentle slopes of Viti del Fiume, and farther to the valley. The quietly beating heart of Tuscany. "Like this place," because she knew this place was going to stick with her as well. It had only been a week, and she was hooked.

Her words pierced Antonio's heart. At one time, this place had been his whole world. A safe haven and happy home until he'd lost his mother. Then it was too painful. He couldn't stay. His grief and anger were all he could see or feel. He said, "St. Clare's has healed a lot of wounds for me. I hope our home might do the same for you."

Antonio thought of the tears. Of the anxiety and dread he'd seen in her eyes. All after a couple of phone calls. She'd come a month early, according to Catarina. He knew her tears didn't come from Italy. They came from England. He impulsively reached across the bench seat and took her hand. "I am glad I came home in time to meet you, Sophie."

Her voice was suddenly hoarse. "I'm glad as well. I feel happy here. Happy and safe."

Antonio's warmth was invaded by a spear of cold foreboding. Happy and safe would imply that she had, at one point, felt unsafe.

He didn't want to spoil those happy minutes lying among the wildflowers or that *almost* kiss that had his toes curling. He wouldn't ask. Not now. But eventually, he must. Almost kiss ... Jesus, it had been so long since he'd been kissed—really kissed—by a woman who wanted more than sex or a doctor's salary. He thought he'd like being kissed by Sophie. That her kiss had the potential to be his very best minute.

SOPHIE SHOWERED AFTER HER DAY OF DIGGING IN THE DIRT. SHE couldn't wipe the stupid smile off her face. As she'd stripped down for her shower, she took a good look at her clothing. Jesus wept. Overalls and shitkickers. Nothing says sexy like a pair of droopy, bibbed trousers and sensible shoes. She could swear he'd almost kissed her. Twice.

She wasn't going to think about it. Nope. And if she took a little more care with her hair and wore her cute shorts to dinner, it was completely a coincidence.

❦ 9 ❦

Catarina discreetly looked at Sophie. She'd done her hair and was wearing lipstick. And those shorts were easily the cutest thing she'd seen out of Sophie's suitcase. All because she'd spent the afternoon with Antonio. It was definitely time for some matchmaking. She watched Marco as he stared at her freshly shaven legs. He was too old for her, of course. Ten years her senior and kind of grouchy. But Antonio needed a reason to stay, and Sophie needed someone to heal her. To make her feel loved and safe. Catarina could kiss her grandfather. It had been a stroke of genius having Antonio drive her around. He'd even taken her up the slope to see the old vines. She tuned into Sophie's conversation with Nonna.

Magdalena said in broken English, "The ribollita and panzanella are of this place."

Sophie smiled. "And they are made from day-old bread and left-overs? It's like the French dish, *cassoulet*."

Nonna smirked. "No French kitchen can make this. It is of this place. Our oil, our tomato. The basilico that grows in our Tuscan soil. You test the soil today. You see." As if that was all there was to say on the matter.

Sophie said, "Yes, I understand. Or I'm starting to understand." Then she said in Italian, "I saw your crocus sativus today."

Magdalena threw her hands up in celebration. For the flowers or for Sophie's improving Italian, she wasn't sure. "Yes, the croco." Then she showed Sophie the dried saffron included in her spice cabinet.

Sophie said, "You'll have to show me how to use that, Magdalena. I'd like to learn how to cook. I get by, but your cooking is magnifico. I'll never want to leave."

Antonio had been listening to the conversation, getting knowing looks from his sister. He watched his grandmother cup Sophie's face in her palms and kiss her. She said, "You call me Nonna, little flower." He knew that all of Sophie's grandparents were gone, and this hit him in the chest. He thought about her hair against the violet-colored flowers, its honey hues blending in more with the saffron and the sunshine. Now she was showing a splendid amount of thigh, and he cursed that blasted bee to hell. It would have been a perfect spot for their first kiss. Because there would be a first. And many after, if he had his way.

Catarina surprised everyone at dinner by making an announcement. "I must go to Firenze. I want to go before the harvest, and time is short. There are some *enotecas* I would like to visit in person. I want to see how they are shelving our wine and maybe arrange some tastings. It will be good for the vineyard." Their tastings were sporadic, and her father usually handled them. Tourists would drop in to sample the different wines and enjoy a snack plate of cheeses with bread. He also let them sample their precious and limited supply of olive oil. "I want to cultivate better relationships, and maybe find a few more shops to carry our Riserva. Sophie should come with me."

Sophie's soup spoon froze halfway to her mouth. "Really? Can you spare me at the vineyard? I mean, I'd love to see that aspect of the industry, but ..."

Catarina shot Marco a look, daring him to interfere. He raised his hands, surrendering without an argument. Catarina said, "The seasonal workers start coming in this weekend. They can spare you. It's time you saw our beautiful city." She turned. "Antonio, didn't you say you wanted to check in with the University Hospital?"

Her eyes bore into his, willing him to play along. Without batting an eye, he said, "Yes, I did. I was going to try to secure a donation for the mission. Some surgical equipment we are lacking. Thank you, *sorella*. When will we leave?"

"Tomorrow. I think three nights should cover it. I'll take care of the arrangements," she said.

Antonio smiled and said, "That's fine, as long as it's clear that I am driving."

The whole family rumbled with laughter. Sophie cleared her throat, remembering the ride from town in Catarina's little sports car. "Yes, quite."

❧

OF COURSE, ANTONIO CORNERED HIS SISTER AFTER DINNER, AWAY from prying ears. "Have you gone mad? Marco looked like his head was going to pop off when you included me. Why drag me into it?"

"Marco likes to remind me that he is the one who runs this vineyard. He takes pride in doing a job he hates, all for the sake of the family. The dutiful martyr. So, he can run it. I need a break and so does Sophie. And you, brother, are on vacation. This place is not your job. So, why not? It's been ages since I took even a short holiday." She grabbed his hands. "And I want to hang out with my long-lost brother. I was a girl when you left. Take this time with me."

Antonio narrowed his eyes at her. She was right, of course, but there was one thing that didn't make sense. "Then why bring Sophie?"

He said the words just as Sophie had rounded the corner. Her face blanched and Antonio's stomach dropped. Her Italian was improving by the day. Perfect. There's no way she wasn't going to take this out of context. *Why bring Sophie?* Damn.

Sophie raised her thumb, pointing behind her. "Magdalena wanted me to fetch you to the terrace. She has some ... um ... gelato. I'm sorry to interrupt." She fled back to the terrace, making her excuses. She was going to take this stupid makeup off and get in bed. She was tired, and she had a good book waiting.

Catarina slapped Antonio on the arm. "Sei un coglione!" *You are an idiot.* Yes, he was. He walked calmly but quickly to the terrace, just to find Sophie all but sprinting for the pool house. Dammit.

His grandmother shoved a gelato in his hand. "Two, please. Sophie needs to try this. I'm sure it's wonderful." His grandmother made her own gelato from the lemon trees and the Sicilian pistachios she bought at the marketplace. Tonight, it was the lemon. She handed him another bowl, and then he left for the garden path. He heard his sister calling him an idiot under her breath. Again.

Antonio went through the pool gate just as the door closed. He approached, dreading this and needing it at the same time. He couldn't let Sophie think he didn't want her to come with them. Quite the opposite.

He had to knock three times before she answered. "Sophie, I know you're not asleep. You haven't had time to fall asleep," he said through the door.

Sophie came to the door and opened it, painting a smile on her face that made him want to shake her. "I brought you some dessert," he said calmly. He could feel his ears turning red.

She exhaled. "Thank you. I'll put it in the freezer. I'm just headed to bed."

Antonio walked in uninvited, feeling bold and more than a little unsettled. "You need to eat this fresh. This is summer in a bowl. Do you want to sit in here or out by the pool?"

"You're very pushy," she said.

"You are angry," he replied as a gentle retort.

"Not at all. Why would I be angry?" she said, knowing with growing dread that he'd never believe it.

"Bollocks," he said.

Sophie put her hands on her hips. "You certainly have picked up some multi-cultural sarcasm, haven't you? I'm not angry." She was angry. Angry because she'd dressed to impress as much as possible from her farm style-chic clothing. Like an idiot. And it was obvious his sister was angling to play matchmaker, and he was having none of it.

"What you heard, it was out of context. I want you to come to Florence. Catarina had said something about—"

"It doesn't matter. I can see Florence after the harvest. I'm not a slave here. I can take some time to sightsee. I don't need an escort."

"You aren't listening. You are just assuming you know the situation and being stubborn. Christ, deliver me from stubborn women. My life is full of them," Antonio said.

"Strong, not stubborn. Perhaps there's a translation issue. It doesn't matter. There is plenty of work here for a lowly intern. I should work on blending this weekend, anyway. I am not a part of this family or even a guest. I won't be joining you. Now, please excuse me."

Antonio set both bowls down on the end table, then met her eyes with such a look, she took a step backward. He said, "You think I don't want you to go with us? You are partially right. As much as it shames me to ditch my only sister, I'd do it in a heartbeat if I could get you alone for three days. Florence is a city for lovers. Sensual art, beautiful music. Leather that was made to caress bare skin. I'd like to show you everything. My sister wants us to get to know each other again. She was still a young girl when I left. But she also wants to show her new friend this very special part of Italy. I'm not going to ditch her and neither are you."

Sophie stood, frozen, trying to get the picture of Antonio peeling a leather skirt off her body and spreading her thighs out of her mind. She was supposed to get angry that he'd just forbidden her to bail on the trip, but all she could think about was skin and leather and his darkly stubbled jaw.

Antonio felt the shift in her. What was an embarrassed blush turned slightly pinker as the flush of arousal battled for dominance. She was magnificent. She'd washed her face, which was an odd thing to do instead of answering the door. He closed the distance slowly, not wanting to bully her. He touched her face, and that pang of affection and yearning spread tightly through his chest and up into his throat. "Your skin is like cream." Antonio thumbed over her lips, now absent of lipstick. "The lipstick was lovely, but these are perfect and pink. They don't need adornment." He wanted to kiss her, and he felt her breathing speed up. His heart was going like mad. "Please, bella. Let me show you Italy."

She closed her eyes and swiftly backed away. Like she'd known what was on his mind just then. She gave a curt nod. "Okay, I'll go. For Catarina. And for work."

He gave her a sad, crooked grin. Like he'd won, but actually lost. "Ciao, Sophie. I'll see you in the morning."

ANTONIO WAS RESTLESS, NOT READY FOR BED. IT WAS GETTING late, and his head was fuzzy from the wine. His tolerance for alcohol had sorely diminished since he'd been here last. None of them were drunks. Wine was just a part of this culture. It was in their blood. They drank a small amount with dinner and drank for the art of it. In pursuit of perfection.

He looked out over the rolling slopes that had defined his childhood. Before college and medical school when he'd only visited home, having already pulled away a little. When he was a boy, it was different. He played with the other children, hopping cattle fences and cutting through orchards to go to each other's houses. They'd been fed, by all the mothers and grandmothers, fresh bread and olives, lemonade, and a bowl of soup at lunchtime. When they were older, they'd steal into the caves of their family vineyards, helping themselves to the *sfuso*. Just in time to get caught by someone's papa and getting a swat for their troubles.

Antonio smiled at all of this and something more. His youth had been full of her ... and him. His parents. His mother, so lovely and lithe. Like she'd been touched by the fairies. Not the creatures of Italian folklore, all witches and elves and goblins who dwelled in the forest. More like the fae that occupied the myths of the Celtic lands. Ethereal, magical, and beautiful. Something almost wild and untamed. They'd play hide-and-seek in the vineyard. She'd even pull his father into it. He'd seemed such a devoted husband back then.

"Come, Marcello. See if we can catch these wild beasts we've made."

The night had been full of squeals and laughter. Two boys who knew, without a doubt, that they were loved. And parents who, from the outside, seemed happy together. Their home had lost some of that magic. It happened slowly. His mother would stay abed some days. He'd hear her crying.

"What is the matter, Mama?" he asked. His mother smiled sadly.
"Your father and I had a disagreement. But you mustn't be angry with him.
He tries. He just asks too much some days."

Antonio realized he was crying. He leaned his back against an old olive tree. One of their oldest. Its trunk twisted, like sinewy muscle tissue, leaning sideways so far that it almost made a chair. A wild tree, unlike the lines of neatly pruned trees that stood in rows in their beloved olive grove. Why had he come here? To Italy? He could have called to check on his grandfather. Nonno wouldn't have lied outright to him if he'd called. Catarina may have, the little shit, but not Nonno. The simple answer was that it was time. He missed this place. He'd missed a huge part of everyone's lives. Marco had been married, and it had ended in an annulment after three years. And his brother hurt over it. He was a selfish bastard. Had Catarina ever been in love? She was old enough, of course. Not that they'd had a particularly good example set for them.

"Why does my son weep?" the voice asked in Italian.

When he'd returned home, it had been strange. Ten years of English and different Portuguese dialects had changed his brain, but he'd fallen back into it so easily, his native tongue. He wiped his face angrily. "Old ghosts. You should know all about that."

"You cry for her. I understand. I miss her every day," his father said in his low, steady voice. Like he actually meant the words.

Antonio snorted. "You miss the idea of her. You liked having a pretty wife to come home to and to show off to your friends. Too bad you couldn't stay home."

His father flinched at his words. "Antonio, you don't understand. It's not all you imagine. She and I—"

"Spare me the speech about people growing apart and not having their needs met. And don't even think about placing any of the blame on her." He was spitting mad, now, wanting his father to hurt like she had hurt. "You drove her away. Slowly, every day, you drove her away. She was so sad by the end, she had no one to talk to but me. She felt like a prisoner here. Trapped with a man who didn't love her, surrounded by his family."

"I would not disparage your mother," he said simply. And that was all he was going to offer.

"Whatever happened to her? Your mistress? That's assuming you only had one," Antonio spat. "Don't worry. I never told Catarina. I'm not sure if Marco knows. I've kept your dirty little secret."

His father showed the first flash of anger. "You don't know anything! You think you do, and I'll let you have that delusion to hold on to if you need to hate someone. But you don't know! Not really. And let us get one thing clear. I was faithful to my wife from the day I met her until the day she died, wrapped around that damn tree." Marcello grunted in frustration and just walked away from Antonio, not giving him a chance to debate the point.

Liar. But there was a niggling part of his brain that had seen the hurt and offense in his father's eyes. The sincerity. He dismissed it. His father had always been a convincing actor.

From the other direction, Antonio heard motion. He said, "You never could walk quietly, little duck." She appeared in the moonlight, and he saw the disappointment on her face. "Jesus, Catarina. How much did you hear?"

Catarina said, "*Basta.* Don't look so crestfallen, darling brother. I'd heard it all before."

His eyes shot to hers. "From whom? I never told anyone. Mama begged me not to tell anyone."

She laughed, and it seemed such an inappropriate response. This wasn't the least bit funny. And he also heard a sort of bitterness that made him want to weep. His little sister. He'd abandoned her to this mess of a family. "Who, Catarina? Was it Marco?"

"No, I don't think she told him. Though I can't be sure. She did love to go on about her misery. But Marco was her first and best. She may not have sullied his world with all of this."

"How can you speak of her so coldly?" Antonio asked. "She was your mother." He was astonished by the anger he saw in her eyes. Anger toward their mother instead of their father.

"And he is your papa!" she said, pointing in the direction their father had left. Then she took a breath and calmed down. She was calmer than he felt. "And should a mother speak of such things to her twelve-year-old daughter? A daughter who loved her papa with her whole heart?"

Antonio said softly, "Twelve?" That gave him pause. Good God. "Oh, Catarina."

"It doesn't matter. None of it matters now. I stayed through the worst of it. The loss of my girlhood at the hands of my selfish mother. The loss of her because despite what you are thinking right now, I loved our mother with my whole heart as well. I grieved with my family. You were in Milan, drinking and womanizing and becoming fabulous. Then you were gone. So don't come here expecting everyone to ruminate with you, Antonio. Your ghosts are your own to bury."

Catarina wasn't even angry. She spoke to him not like a petulant teenager, but like a woman who knew her own mind. She was very strong, and despite her cutting words, he was proud of her. She said, "Now, get to bed if you are going to do the driving. Let's forget all of this for a while and plan for a wonderful holiday." She'd come closer as she spoke, then she hugged him. Antonio squeezed her to him, not knowing what to say. Not knowing where to start with her. He was letting his resentment of his father taint his time at Viti del Fiume, his time with her, and if he was honest, his time with Marco.

His brother had taken on a lot when he'd agreed to run the family business. He'd spend this time with Catarina, but then he owed his brother his full attention, and his understanding. Did he really hate it here? Why the hell didn't he just let Catarina run things? She'd been born to do this. He hated to think, despite the advances in this traditional society, that his father was making his decisions based on the fact that Catarina was a woman. It was the worst sort of backward thinking.

Antonio had seen women excel in medicine, watched the abbess of St. Clare's gut out her future in the middle of the jungle, seen tribal mothers command respect within the hierarchy of the indigenous tribes. Was this village life really so isolating and traditional that it wasn't giving his sister an even shake? The thought incensed him. Look at Sophie. She was an intern, yet she seemed to have an instinct for this business that far exceeded Marco's. He knew he had no right to insert himself in this. He'd walked away ten years ago. But he was a part of this family, albeit on the outside looking in. Maybe his perspective was needed. After all, Viti del Fiume was part of his heritage, and maybe someday, part of his legacy. Antonio hadn't given up hope altogether of having a family. Children who might visit this place and have their own ties to it. That made him think about his brother again. What happened to end his marriage so quickly and with no children? Who had the woman been?

He shook his head, knowing it was indeed time to go to bed. He certainly wasn't going to let Catarina drive them into Florence. Absolutely not.

⚜

ANTONIO WAS FINISHING LOADING HIS TOILETRY KIT BEFORE their trip when Marco came into their shared bathroom. He handed Antonio the keys to the car they'd be taking, then turned to leave. Antonio followed him out and said, "Come, Marco. Talk to me while I finish."

Marco looked unsure, which made Antonio sad. They'd been close once. Marco came into his room and sat on the chair while he watched Antonio pack a small bag. Antonio asked, "Are you sure you won't join us?"

Marco waved a hand. "Catarina is right. I should be here in case we get busy with the tourists. This is our big tourism time. It will give you two time to catch up. And a chance to flirt with my intern." Antonio looked at him sharply, but he had a knowing grin that just made Antonio laugh.

"I suppose there is that," Antonio said with a self-deprecating shrug. "She's a lovely woman, but that's not the only reason. I missed the last of Catarina's childhood. I missed many things. I'd like to ..." He shook his head. "I don't know what I want. I know I deserve your anger. I've been selfish."

His brother just picked at his shoe, not commenting. Antonio said, "I'm sorry, Marco. About your wife. I'm sorry you went through that and I wasn't here."

"And what would you have done, Antonio? Saved my marriage?" he asked, looking tired.

"Gotten you drunk and laid after the papers were signed, of course." He looked at him as if to say, *Duh*. That produced a real laugh. Marco didn't laugh enough.

"You won't ask because you don't want to appear nosey. So, I will offer the story freely. I made the same mistake many village boys make. I married a city girl. Someone fashionable and beautiful whom I met at a wine competition. She liked the look of me. Liked me in her bed, well enough. Then we married." He gave a bitter smile. "Let's just say Viti del Fiume wasn't her idea of home. She was from Milan. She wanted to live there, or in Florence, and visit the vineyard now and again. She liked telling her friends that she married into an old wine family in Tuscany. And I think she thought she'd wear me down and we'd eventually move. But I couldn't leave here. This is my home, and I was needed. I offered to live in town near the marketplace, but that wasn't quite urban enough for her."

The tale hit Antonio right in the gut. "You are a good man, Marco. Better than me. I'm sorry it happened. She didn't deserve your love. I hope you know that."

"A year of therapy, and yes. I know that now. She was very beautiful and sophisticated. I was infatuated. Infatuation isn't love. You can fill in the blanks. She cheated. More than once. I'll tolerate a lot, but I don't share. Someone's wife got my number. That's how I found out. Then I took her phone while she was asleep. The rest was in there. Texts to two different men in two different cities. I was a fool."

"Jesus, I'm sorry. Maybe I should take you out now, retroactively. I think I could get you drunk and laid in Florence."

Another laugh, and Antonio was happy to see the smile on his brother's face. He'd gotten through the worst of it already, it seemed. Marco said, "I'll take a raincheck. Just keep our sister out of trouble."

Antonio smiled. "I think I can handle that job, at least."

Marco got up from the chair and said, "Have fun. It's good to have you home." And before Marco could get away, Antonio pulled him into a real hug.

"I love you, Marco. I've missed you."

⚜ 10 ⚜

Antonio chuckled at Catarina's face when she saw the vehicle they were taking into the city. "I'm not cramming Sophie into one of those sports cars. Besides, Nonna never drives it. Whoever thought the woman needed a car? She doesn't drive!"

"It was Marco's sixtieth wedding anniversary gift. Nonno likes the trucks, so it kind of sits in the garage. Papa takes it out occasionally, but you know him. He likes his old Iveco. He never goes anywhere other than town, anyway."

"He still drives that 1993 Iveco?" Antonio asked, laughing as he got into the comfortable seat of the sensible Alpha Romeo.

"It still runs." Catarina shrugged, as if that explained everything. "And he's nostalgic. Remember how we'd pile in the back with Mama and Nonno? Papa would drive and Nonna would ride up front."

Antonio smiled, his throat suddenly thick with emotion. "We are ignoring Sophie and speaking in Italian. I'm sorry, Sophie."

Sophie had been quiet up until this point, barely following the conversation. She was pleased to find that she'd gotten the gist of everything, however. She said in English, "I've been keeping up. And you don't have to take a bigger car on my account. You should see the atrocity I drive at home. I've got an old Twingo, which stalls out at very inopportune times."

Antonio frowned. "You should have a reliable car, Sophie. It's not safe."

Sophie smirked. "Yes, well it's silly of me. College is so inexpensive, and my summer job at the high-yielding, wildly successful English vineyard keeps me in the lap of luxury. I should purchase a Land Rover for my graduation present to myself." Catarina stifled her laugh. "And what does the poor, underpaid surgeon drive where the cost of living is half what it is in England?"

Antonio's mouth was tight. He was an overprivileged idiot, but he didn't need it pointed out. He worked hard. Catarina flipped her hair. "Yes, Antonio. What does my dear brother drive?"

He sighed, knowing they both had a bone in their teeth. "I drive a Land Rover." Catarina cracked off a laugh, and Sophie's smug, crooked grin grated his pride. "It doubles as a backup ambulance when I'm at the mission. And I bought it used," he said.

Sophie suddenly felt like a rotter for teasing him. "I'm sorry. I shouldn't tease you. You make us all look bad. You're a bloody saint compared to the rest of us disreputable winos." She winked at Catarina.

Catarina gave his shoulder a squeeze. "She's right, brother. I've missed you, but I'm so proud of you. Truly. Everyone is."

"Marco isn't." He said the words before he could take them back. "I'm sorry, Sophie. You don't need our family drama ruining our road trip. Catarina, where are we staying?"

"It overlooks the Arno, but it's modest, I'm afraid." She looked at Sophie, whose body eased with relief.

Sophie asked, "How much is my room? I can either pay you or the clerk."

"We are all in one room, I'm afraid. It is a triple with a

communal bathroom down the hall. One double bed and two twins. It's all I could find this last minute. It is tourist season. And you don't owe anything. This is business." She looked sheepish. "Well, partially business. I'm going to need you as my spy."

"No one will expect a pasty Englishwoman to be anything but a tourist, eh?" Sophie said wryly.

"You are not pasty," Antonio chided. He looked at his sister, who didn't understand the term. He gave her the equivalent in Italian.

Catarina looked askance. "Basta! You have lovely, creamy skin. Like my grandmother Martha when she was young. Those shorts didn't hide many secrets last night." Sophie blushed, noticing Antonio's eyes in the mirror. Her blush deepened. "She's blushing, Antonio. We must stop teasing her."

"I wasn't teasing her," he pointed out.

"Like you didn't notice the shorts. Marco's eyes almost popped out of his head." Then a thought occurred to her. "Sophie! We must go shopping! Florence has wonderful shopping!"

"She just admitted to driving a Twingo," Antonio jibed. "She might not want to go shopping. At least until Marco writes her first paycheck."

"That will be a while. I'm not getting paid for this first month. I came early, remember?" She looked at Catarina, who knew the reason why. "I did allot some funds for souvenirs, however. I might be able to splurge if I really like something. I would like to find my roommates and parents something at the very least, if shipping isn't too dear."

"You can just take it home in your bag." Catarina waved.

Dread hit Sophie right in the stomach. How was she going to go home if Richard was still at large? Because she was positive he'd been the one who beat Morgan and left her for dead. Her breathing started speeding up as she realized just what deep shit she was in. What if he went to France? She pictured Morgan on the riverbank, pale and cold. Battered and barely alive. She clawed at her collar, wanting to rip her blouse off. It was too tight. Everything was too tight! She heard Catarina's voice, but she couldn't get enough air in her lungs.

Suddenly, the door came open, and Antonio yanked her out. He asked, "What is it? Are you stung? Where is your pen?" Tears pricked her eyes. An EpiPen wasn't going to fix this. She shook her head. "No, I'm okay." A lie even to her own ears. Her parents. Her roommates. What if Morgan died?

Catarina came beside her, removing her from Antonio's grip. "Easy, Sophie. Breathe with me, bella." She turned to Antonio. "Get some water." It was more to busy him so he didn't stab her with an EpiPen.

Antonio was relieved she hadn't been stung. They were on a country road, nowhere near a hospital. But the look on Sophie's face chilled him to the bone. Fear. She was having a panic attack. He poured the icy water on the clean handkerchief his grandfather kept in the glove box. Thank God for the elderly. No one carried hankies under the age of seventy. He put it on her neck, then started rubbing circles on her back. "Easy, *mia cara*. That's it." He nodded, encouraging his sister to keep slowing down the breathing. He could tell right when she came back to herself.

Sophie said, "I'm so sorry. I haven't ..." She shook her head, her body still trembling. "I haven't had a panic attack in years." Eight years, to be exact. It had taken almost two years for them to stop.

"What triggered it, Sophie? Can you tell me?" Antonio's voice was so gentle, and suddenly she was ashamed. She felt weak and stupid. This was written all over her face, and he said, "None of that, *cara*. They are very common." He was taking her pulse, satisfied that her heart rate was coming down.

"I hate them. They make me feel weak," Sophie said to no one in particular.

"Do you think I'm weak?" Catarina asked.

"Of course not," she answered.

Catarina said, "I got panic attacks for over a year after my mother died. The doctor told my father I was a hysterical teenager." Antonio jerked at her words. "Papa snatched him by his stupid, white coat and shoved him into a gurney. Then he found me another doctor."

Sophie grabbed her, hugging her tightly. "Thank you." *For not making me feel alone. For not making me feel weak.* She closed her eyes, took a deep breath, and smiled. "I'm okay, I swear. Let's get this blasted holiday started."

Antonio decided to let it go. Asking what the trigger had been might just start the damn cycle over again. Instead, he focused on an issue he could solve. "Marco will pay you for this time. You are working. You are getting paid." He'd pay her out of his own money if he had to do it.

"Did you know she wasn't being paid for an entire month? She's worked every day since she got here."

"No, I didn't," Catarina said softly.

"I offered this. I needed to get out of England quickly, and this was a good solution for me. If you've budgeted for an intern for one semester, you shouldn't have to pay me out of charity. I'm working for room and board. You are feeding me every day. I will not hear of it, Catarina. Just respect the agreement I made with your brother. Discussion is over." As she was talking, Catarina was typing something on her phone.

"Apparently not," Catarina said, looking up from her phone. "He sent the funds to your account yesterday. He agreed to that arrangement just to appease you."

Sophie sighed. "He didn't have to do that."

Antonio said something before his sister made some cutting remark. "Marco is a good man. And he wasn't always so stern. I feel bad for leaving him behind. He always loved going to the Uffizi Gallery. He's an artist. Did you know that?"

Sophie was surprised. He seemed so ... businesslike. Catarina said softly, "He was. He doesn't paint anymore. He wanted to be an

Art History professor. He does what he does out of duty. It's an eldest child's burden, I suppose."

Antonio said, "He's still an artist. It is in the soul. It doesn't go away, even if you choose a different career. I have a doctor friend who comes from a long line of musicians. He didn't stop being a musician just because he went to medical school. You should encourage him to paint, Catarina. We all should."

Sophie asked, "So, is it to be the Uffizi first?"

Catarina said, "It is to be a cappuccino on the benches near the Duomo. If we hurry, that is. If not, it will be an espresso. I know you British like your cappuccino all day long, but we have rules about this sort of thing."

"I read that in my tour guidebook. What if I want tea?" she asked, just to goad her.

Catarina smirked. "Oh, yes. We have lovely tea. It's a special grape tea. Fermented grape juice tea that is served at room temperature, but I think you'll like it." Sophie laughed as they continued on their journey. All troubles temporarily forgotten.

FIRENZE, ITALY

Antonio tipped his face up to the sun while Catarina sipped her espresso. He was trying not to watch as Sophie licked her gelato cone, and the effort was damn near killing him. His sister had already caught him once.

Sophie said, "This is why you are thin and I'm not. This is the best thing I've ever eaten. Well, except for literally everything Magdalena makes."

"I'm not thin. I'm tall. At least by Italian standards. And you put the gelato in all the right places. That's all that really matters. Wouldn't you agree, Antonio?"

He gave a non-committal grunt, not engaging in this sort of

conversation with his sister. Sophie asked, "Do you have to go to the hospital?"

He said, "I have an appointment the day we leave. We'll drive there. It's not easily accessed on foot from where we are staying. So, what should we do? The gallery? The Duomo and Baptistry?"

Sophie said, "I'll order tickets for those things tomorrow. Let's work first."

"You are working. I'm on holiday," he said, grinning.

Sophie looked around her. "Where is the Straw Market? I've heard the prices are better."

"Excellent idea. We can grab an easy lunch after we look around. Catarina, when did you want to visit the *enotecas*? Are there any on the way?" Antonio took out a map.

"I don't need a map, brother. Put that away before you embarrass me," she said in Italian. "We can go to the enoteca after we do some sightseeing. There is one that is close to the market."

They began walking, and Sophie's head swiveled back and forth, taking in the churches, the fountains, the sculpture, the vendors, just ... everything. Her smile was so big, Antonio finally got a good look at her perfectly straight, white teeth. She was wearing jeans and an elbow-length top, but he wanted to see her in a dress. She was so pretty. Her honey-and-copper highlighted hair was in a loose braid over her shoulder. She was wearing sunglasses, which was good, but also a pity. She had lovely eyes. They walked around the Straw Market, looking at cheap, leather goods, hats, scarves, and random clothing.

Catarina was teaching Sophie. "This leather, it's not so good. For a cute bag or something, it's fine, but not so much for the clothing. We will go to the Ponte Vecchio tomorrow to a leather goods place I know that makes beautiful gloves, and another that makes clothing. That's where the gold trade is as well. It's carefully regulated in Italy so that you know its authentic Italian gold."

Sophie bought a large scarf. "I can tie it around my waist and legs like a sarong, in case I want to wear shorts tomorrow. I am positively melting in these jeans." But Catarina had already found something much better. Sophie's eyes bugged out. "I can't wear that. It is beautiful, but not on me. I mean, you'd be gorgeous in it."

It was a slip of a dress, and Antonio would much rather see it on Sophie. He took the dress, crooking his finger at her. The clothing booth had a curtained area just big enough to change clothes. "No, no. I can just tie this over my legs. It'll be fine," Sophie said, lifting the scarf.

He leaned in, his lips touching her ear. "Coward." Then he held the dress out to her. "When in Rome ..."

She came out, wearing her old clothes. "Didn't it fit?" Catarina asked. "I thought for sure it was your size."

"It fit, and it's very nice, but I'm really okay with this." She held up her scarf again, like an idiot. "Let's look at the straw hats. I need one for the vineyard." She put the dress back on the rack, and Catarina walked over to look at the straw hats with her.

Catarina peered over her shoulder just in time to see her brother buying the dress. "Good boy, Antonio," she murmured.

Once the shopping was over, Antonio pulled his two companions to the entrance of the Nuovo Mercato. Sophie smiled at the sight of children and adults alike, fawning over the sculpture. It was a large, rather intimidating-looking boar. The nose was shiny, having lost its patina. She immediately saw why. Everyone who passed it stretched an arm into the fountain to give the boar's nose a rub. Others would put a coin in its mouth. Antonio walked around it, and at some point, he'd taken Sophie's hand. "You put your hand in his mouth, maybe leaving a coin, but it's not necessary. Wish to return to Florence as you do it, lest he bite your fingers."

Sophie laughed until she got a look from both Antonio and Catarina that said they were completely serious. "So, put a coin in his mouth and wish to come back to Florence? Then rub his nose for good measure?"

"Yes, watch me." Catarina showed her what to do and she

repeated her actions. Catarina said, "Now you are guaranteed good fortune and to return to Florence."

Florence was so much bigger than she'd imagined. The four quarters were teaming with life and action. Medieval churches nestled around the corner from modern businesses and slick, glass windows, the contrast of the new and very old architecture managing to work together. She couldn't wait to sightsee tomorrow.

Antonio brought her out of her head and back into the conversation. "I thought we could see the cathedrals tomorrow, then the Uffizi. Before we drive back, I want to take you up above the city to Fiesole. There is a church up there that is almost a thousand years old. *Cattedrale di San Romolo*," he said, and the words rolling off his tongue were enough to curl Sophie's toes. He tried to speak mostly in English with her, which she appreciated.

She repeated it in English. "The Cathedral of St. Romulus. It's in my guidebook. I'd love to see it." Antonio's face warmed. And he found that he rather liked escorting Sophie around the city.

Catarina interrupted, clearing her throat. "There are Etruscan ruins up there as well. We'll go in the morning. What time is your appointment at the hospital, Antonio?"

"Le due," he said absently. "Plenty of time. Now, let's find somewhere to eat before I expire from hunger."

❧

Sophie wasn't sure what she'd been expecting, but their idea of lunch was better than anything she could have imagined. The Mercato Centrale was a vast expanse of open-air market stalls. Cured meats, fresh bread, vegetables, and olives. So many olives. She watched in amusement as Antonio bought a large loaf of bread, asking the clerk to slice it open. She saw him and Catarina run to all of the different food stalls, adding to this exquisite sandwich. It was loaded with sun-dried and roasted vegetables, cheeses and meats, and some sort of olive spread. "Find something different that looks good. We'll eat anything. Just get enough to share. Catarina eats like a sumo wrestler," Antonio said.

Sophie laughed. It was like a game. And the prize was going to be eating themselves sick. She stopped at a pizza stand and picked out a wood-fired pizza, hot out of the stone oven. Then she saw some sort of ravioli with shaved truffles over a cream sauce. The caloric intake of this meal was spiraling out of control as she passed the salads and soups without a second glance.

She slid in next to Catarina as Antonio uncorked a bottle of Vernaccia di San Gimignano, a lesser known, very Tuscan varietal. He poured the wine into the everyday, stemless, juice-style glass that Sophie noticed Marcello favored. Her eyes widened. "Is that octopus?"

Catarina smiled. "Yes, grilled to perfection. It's the only place I'll eat it. And I see you've been ensnared by Nicola's ravioli." They split up the food, and when Sophie held up her portioned slice of sandwich, she had to pause. It was huge.

Sophie said, "I need some strategy tips. I don't think I can get this whole thing in my mouth." Then she paused, closing her eyes as Catarina barked out a laugh. "I suppose I walked into that one." But then she glanced at Antonio and he wasn't laughing. He was looking at her mouth.

Antonio averted his gaze and downed the glass of wine in two gulps. Then, fortified, he picked up his portion of the sandwich. "Use both hands, press in to squeeze it together, but don't do it too hard or it will spill out the sides. Tip your head and go in at an angle."

Catarina was laughing at her brother now. "You've really put some thought into this."

"Sì, I have." He returned his attention to Sophie. "You want to get every ingredient into every bite. This is all about the technique." He took a huge bite, oil glossing his lips as he chewed. Sophie tried next, and Antonio's face glowed with mirth. She looked like a baby bear trying to fit an entire king salmon in her mouth. Her chin was dripping with olive oil, and instead of being embarrassed, she moaned around the biteful of sandwich. She looked at Catarina, who had a tentacle hanging out of her mouth. She almost spit her food out. Antonio said, "You two need to get out more."

🦋 11 🦋

SAN LORENZO QUARTER, FIRENZE

Catarina grabbed Antonio before he walked inside the wine store. "Wait, we are going to send Sophie in alone. Sophie, do you think your Italian is good enough to get by?"

"Of course. What do you want me to say?" she asked.

Catarina said, "I'm not sure if she'll recognize me, so I will hold back for a few minutes. Just go in and start looking around. If she asks you what you want, just tell her you'd like to see the Chianti Classico Riservas she has to offer."

Antonio understood. "You want to see how she handles a tourist and what she is going to offer her. And you want Sophie to look at the shelving of our wines."

"Sì. Our sales are almost zero for the last six months since this woman started working here. I want to know what has changed."

Sophie walked into the enoteca and was surprised to see the woman behind the desk was thumbing through her phone. Not even a hello. She approached. "Ciao, signora." The woman looked up and put her phone down. Sophie did as Catarina had instructed, and the woman took her to the large section of Chianti Classico wines. There was a prominent display of a well-known vineyard.

She searched, but she couldn't find Viti del Fiume's Riserva anywhere on the shelf. Hmm. "Is this everything you stock?"

"Yes. We've rearranged a bit. This is the 2016 Riserva from our most popular vineyard."

She smiled politely. "Yes, I know it well. I can get a lot of these in England. Do you have some of the smaller family vineyard selections?"

That's when Catarina and Antonio entered. Catarina said, "Sì, Sophie. I am wondering the same thing."

❦

THE WOMAN RUNNING THE SHOP WAS A RECENTLY HIRED manager and, after some prodding, it was obvious that she'd been the one to rearrange the store in order to push the big players in the Tuscan wine production. They did find two bottles of their wine after thoroughly looking, but it had been shoved to the back behind a display, along with some other very good varietals from neighboring vineyards. Small, single-estate vineyards. Sophie wondered if this woman was getting some extra profits, or if the markup was just better on the larger vineyards.

She was stifling a laugh as Catarina humored this woman's lies. She said, "I completely understand. So, you won't mind if we do a tasting today."

The woman's jaw went slack. "Today, as in right now?"

Catarina smiled wolfishly. "Great idea. We will do it now. We'll catch the tourists who haven't gone home for *riposo*," Catarina said, leaving no room for the woman to say that they were closed during that time. Sophie knew the shops often closed in Italy for a sort of siesta, which they called *riposo*. Catarina continued. "Now, if you'll please go to the back storage and get all of the cases of wine we had delivered that aren't on the shelf, I'll alter the sign in the front of the store."

Antonio just stood back and watched his sister in action. Jesus, she was a force. She always had been. He'd known that she had an instinct for making wine. She was gifted with a good palate as well. Very good, in fact. But this was a side of her he hadn't seen. Savvy. A businesswoman. Why his father wasn't letting her run the vineyard was a mystery.

Sophie turned to him and said, "Antonio should do the tasting."

He'd love to, in private, no wine needed. "Why me?" he asked.

Sophie looked at Catarina. "There are a lot of tourists. Female tourists."

Catarina smiled at that. Sophie turned back to Antonio. "You know, because of all this," she said, motioning up and down his person.

His jaw dropped. He was trying to look offended, and failing. He glanced at his sister and said, "You'd exploit your poor brother for financial gain?"

Catarina said, "We put up with it all the time. You can—"

Sophie offered, "Take one for the team?"

Catarina said, "Exactly."

Antonio remembered a fundraiser for the *orfanato* in Brazil. His friend Izzy had set up a kissing booth, and he was the head kisser in charge. Now his own sister was pimping him out for financial gain. He just shook his head, resigned to his fate.

THE QUEUE WRAPPED AROUND THE BLOCK FOR THE TASTING. There was something about a line forming that drew people's attention. Then passersby had to peek into the store. Just about every female from age fifteen to eighty-five headed right for the end of the line, the teenagers getting in line just for a better look at Antonio, wine be damned.

Sophie watched as Antonio led the tasting, six people at a time. Catarina kept the line moving, assisting Antonio with opening bottles and filling splashes of wine into the small glasses. The manager of the shop rang up the orders between washing glasses. Antonio could speak English very well, but he was laying the accent on thick as the women, and a few stray men, swooned as he spoke. He was also very good at pulling out the tasting notes. Their Riserva was excellent—as good as anything in the shop—and even better than most, if she was honest. They poured it sparingly, as it was more costly.

The Chianti Classico, however, sold by the armfuls. They dropped the price one euro for the tasting, a portion that would come out of the shop's pocket. Another command from Catarina, this time not as pleasantly demanded. How many sales had this woman cost them? If the owner wanted to argue the point, Catarina would certainly explain to the family that owned the shop what the new manager had been up to. She'd also tell some of the other vineyards. She didn't get any resistance after that little threat.

Sophie talked to the tourists in line. She knew French and English, which got her pretty far with the crowd in front of her. She knew enough Italian to get by with the others. There was a group of Swedish women who only had eyes for Antonio, however. She laughed as they raked their eyes over him.

He whispered, "You two owe me for this. I'm starting to feel dirty and cheap." But he wasn't just there for show. He was smart. He knew wine. He'd explain the five *S*s when tasting wine. *See*, where you'd evaluate the color range as you tilted the glass. *Swirl*, to aerate the wine, opening up the aroma and flavors. *Sniff, sip, and savor.* The women focused intently on his mouth, and how could she blame them?

Sophie said, "Man candy sells, Medíco. What can I say?" His eyes flared with heat. He loved the way she said medíco because her BBC English accent was almost prim. Yet her words were witty and just a bit suggestive.

After two hours, they'd sold every bottle of Chianti Classico and three cases of the Riserva. The customers had also taken pamphlets about Viti del Fiume, promising to come visit the vineyard. Sophie had a feeling they were going to get bombarded with female tourists. They'd harnessed the crowds of tourists who were trying to find something that was open during the rest period between lunch and evening. Before they left, Sophie helped Catarina and the store manager move not just their wine, but the wine of the small, neighboring vineyards onto a more visible shelf. Sophie left some pamphlets on the tasting table and a display of their best Riserva.

As they left, Sophie said, "You are a she-wolf, my friend. That was brilliant. I can't wait to tell your father and grandfather what you did here today. You sold almost fifty bottles of wine in two hours."

"We did it, not just me. I couldn't have done this without you both. We are an excellent team. Now, let us get some gelato before my drunk brother falls asleep."

"I am not drunk. I took small sips." But he was comfortably tipsy. Maybe more gelato wasn't such a bad idea.

They found Catarina's favorite place. Sophie ordered a cone with chestnut gelato. Antonio got the chocolate orange, and Catarina got one scoop of zabaglione and one of cannella. It was a local favorite consisting of cream, sweet wine, and cinnamon. When Antonio went to take a bite of Sophie's cone, she couldn't resist. She quickly dabbed his nose with it, much to Catarina's delight. He wiped it off, eyeing her playfully. "Paybacks, my dear Sophie, are the sweetest treat." Then he captured her wrist and licked her cone. Not a mouthing bite, like a civilized person, but an actual lick. It was then that she saw it. Something feral that would cause a well-to-do medical student from a comfortable family to go seeking adventure in the dangerous jungles of South America. He was magnificent, and way too much man for her.

Sophie had watched him today, flirting outrageously with all of the customers. For a while, he'd held one woman's child. An American whose husband was in the US Navy. He was at sea, and she'd come from Naples to Florence with her friends. Not willing to leave her baby, she'd strapped the little girl on her chest and taken her along. Sophie kind of liked that. And Antonio had been something worth watching as he cooed and nibbled on the baby girl's fat, little hands. Her ovaries were working overtime, watching him tend to a baby.

He'd known just how to soothe her, rocking her and whispering as the mother tried their wine. *Come to our family vineyard. My nonna would love to have a little one in the house again. It's been too long. She'll take care with this sweet girl, and you can explore our beautiful vineyard.* And the woman and her friends melted. They would come, she knew. And he was right. Nonna would spoil the baby with attention and give this woman a little time with her girlfriends. And she'd tell her husband all about Viti del Fiume when he returned.

Sophie narrowed her eyes at Antonio, moving her cone away from him. "That was more than a bite. You'll have to buy me another in a couple of hours. I'll be weak with hunger again."

Antonio smiled at this beautiful, enchanting Englishwoman. He liked that she ate like a real person instead of picking at her food. She wasn't afraid of hard work, either. She had toned limbs and a flat stomach. He wondered if she had that delicious swell below her navel. That slight curve that hinted at the paradise that lay within her depths.

His imaginings were interrupted by his sister's voice. "Where to next? Back to the hotel? They'd have opened our room by now, and I, for one, would like to change. There's another enoteca nearby that I need to check. Our numbers are good, so it won't take long. My suspicions about the other place were correct, however."

Antonio smoothed a palm over his sister's dark hair. "You were brilliant today, Catarina. I'm so very proud of my *paperotta*." Catarina nudged him.

She said, "I'm too old for such names."

Sophie watched their interactions and was envious. She was an only child. "What does it mean?" she asked. "I've heard your family call you this."

"Paperotta means little duck. It's a *termini affettuosi*," Catarina said, knowing Sophie liked learning the Italian term for things. "A term of endearment. They called Antonio *coniglietto* when he was small. *Coniglio* as he grew. Little rabbit because once he had his mind set to something, he was fast. My mother couldn't catch him, apparently." Her face grew shrouded, and Sophie felt Antonio stiffen. They never talked about their mother. There was a story there, but she wasn't going to open a wound on a perfectly beautiful day.

Sophie asked, "And why did they call you little duck?"

Antonio smiled, as he'd picked the name. "She liked to follow me around. I was always her favorite." His sister swiped at him and he laughed. "Even in diapers."

"I waddled! Go ahead and say it. And I had rounded legs," she said, and Sophie didn't understand.

"All babies have pudgy, little thighs, I think," Sophie said mildly.

Antonio shook his head. "Not rounded so much. Bowed legs. It happens with some children when they walk early. They have the frog legs that turn out at the knees when they are infants. The legs straighten out as they grow, but when they walk early, there's still a bow there sometimes. As you can see, she's perfect now." He said it indulgently. "But she had a pronounced waddle." He rose and scrunched up his face, and she could picture it in her mind. He bowed his legs and waved his arms erratically, trying to catch an invisible target. "She hated being left behind. She'd come waddling through the vines, giving chase in her little ruffles." Sophie was laughing, and then so was Catarina. He made quite a spectacle of himself to onlookers, and he didn't seem to care. "She'd make it far enough to where we either had to take her with us or walk back up to the house and give her to an adult."

"I was so cute, they couldn't leave me behind most of the time, unless they were going to do something they couldn't handle with a baby on their backs," Catarina said.

"Climbing the turkey oaks or going to a neighboring farm," added Antonio.

"I always wanted siblings. I envied my friends with four or five brothers and sisters. You're lucky," Sophie said wistfully. Her heart warmed as Antonio pulled his sister in with one arm and kissed her forehead.

"I've missed you, little duck," Antonio said.

And Sophie was surprised to see his eyes had misted. He was so masculine. Muscled and broad-shouldered and tall, compared to many of the local men she'd seen here. Beautiful, exotic-looking men, but he was something different. His English blood, maybe, because she knew his other grandmother was tall. But he was kind and gentle. A healer. She was going to have to guard her heart, so rusty from lack of use. They existed in a bubble here. His life was in Brazil and hers was in England. An affair would be inappropriate. Falling for him would be a self-inflicted wound. And she wasn't sure England could be her home anymore. Maybe she could settle in France? Or try finding something in America.

"You look very serious, Sophie." Antonio's voice was soft. "Where did you go?"

She shook herself. "Sorry, just … thinking. It's nothing." They'd started walking. He looped an arm around her neck, now having both women pulled tight against his sides.

"Well stop, *bellisma*. Just be here today. The rest will catch up to us soon enough." She looked up at him, then, into his golden-brown eyes. He had a disarming smile, which gave her a flash of dimple. He was beautiful to look at, to be sure, but he was also funny and sensitive. He loved his family, although some past hurt had wounded this family enough to fracture it. Sophie suddenly missed her parents. She swallowed, staving off the tears that bubbled up.

Her voice was hoarse. "Deal."

Antonio looked at her, his face changing. *She's afraid.* And the thought of it made him ill. He pulled her in closer, more of a protective embrace than a passionate one. No woman should have to be afraid.

❧

"THIS IS BEAUTIFUL, CATARINA. I REALLY DO WANT TO PAY MY share. It's not right for me to holiday at your expense."

"You worked today. You are an employee. And this hotel would have been the same cost if it had just been the two of us."

Antonio was rifling through his small bag. "Why don't they call it a *pensione* anymore? I remember this part of the city and these places. They were pensione. Family run and intimate."

Catarina said, "The government. They love to dip their hands in everything."

Sophie chuffed her agreement. "Yes, we have the same problem in the UK."

"They reclassified them and made the owners conform to more rules, but Italians are stubborn. It's still the same charm and principle. They just had to build a few more bathrooms, add more fire extinguishers, and other things. Some of the owners couldn't afford the changes and had to sell, but most found a way to stay afloat," she said.

Antonio pulled out some stylish jeans and a black T-shirt. He had black, leather boots as well. "I'm going to go to the men's communal bath. I'll give you two some privacy." He left without a backward glance.

Sophie turned to her suitcase and stopped. She'd opened it, but what she saw hadn't been there fifteen minutes ago. It was the dress she'd left on the rack at the Straw Market. "Catarina, you shouldn't have done this."

Catarina gave a casual shrug, hiding the thrill that she felt. She enjoyed watching her brother's tender heart start to slip under Sophie's spell. Sophie really didn't know how pretty she was, or how absolutely brilliant. Antonio didn't simply feel lust for this woman,

Catarina knew. She'd seen lust before, many times. She hadn't seen Antonio for many years, but some things a woman just knew. *Catarina, you shouldn't have done this.* She answered simply, "I didn't."

ANTONIO CHANGED INTO HIS CLEAN CLOTHES, WANTING TO WIPE his skin down and give his sister and Sophie some time to themselves. He thought maybe the two women each needed a friend, Catarina because she'd sequestered herself with the aging family instead of getting a place of her own. Sophie was another story. She did have friends, but she never seemed to mention much about her life in England. Something was off about her. Off and almost sad.

He walked down to the lobby, where the proprietor had set out some biscotti next to a carafe of coffee. He poured two cups, after downing one quickly, then he took three cookies. When his sister answered the door, she gave him a knowing look. She took the two cups of coffee, and he set the plate of biscotti on the dresser. When he turned around, he almost swallowed his own tongue. Sophie wore the slip dress like a goddess. Flowers in pale pinks and neutrals adorned the top, thin straps coming down to the portion that covered her creamy, small breasts. Below the bottom of her breasts, the dress was black, with smaller flowers of the same colors. It flowed over her belly and hips, flaring just a bit at the knee. Her hair was down. She usually wore it up, but it was wavy and spilling over her shoulders like honey and butterscotch. He just stared at her stupidly.

Sophie said, "Thank you. Your sister insisted I wear it. It's very ..." *Slinky, tight, revealing.* It was feminine and not any of those things. Not really. She just didn't wear dresses very often, and when she did, they were like overgrown T-shirts or bulky sweater dresses. Something for church. She was extremely fair, and she wasn't used to showing bare shoulders and the flesh between her breasts, unless she wore a swimsuit.

"I knew you'd look beautiful in it. You should have bought it at the market. I'm glad you didn't, though. It's nice to get treated by someone else every once in a while."

She walked to the window, looking over the Arno. "You've already done that." She motioned out the window. *"A Room with a View."* She could tell he wasn't following. "It's a book about a young English girl who goes to Florence for the first time. Her aunt insists that for her first time, she must have a room with a view of the Arno."

Antonio looked at Catarina, and it was obvious she'd read the book as well. His sister clapped her hands in front of her, grinning. He said, "And so you have it. Now, I've made reservations for dinner at eight. What shall we do until then? Sophie, you've never been here. We are at your service," he said with a small bow.

Sophie said, "I think I'd like to see some of the sculpture and architecture, if that's okay."

Catarina said, "The best place to do that is right outside the Uffizi Gallery. Neptune's Fountain, Perseus, and Medusa. That's a wonderful idea. Antonio, where are we going to dinner?"

"The same area, near the gallery. Do you need to rest?" They both grabbed their bags, and Sophie was a little embarrassed that she didn't have the shoes or bag to go with her pretty, new dress. But as Ferragamos weren't in the budget, she got by with a pair of basic sandals and her small, leather satchel. She grabbed the scarf she'd bought, feeling the need to have something on her shoulders.

Antonio took it from her and, with a practiced hand, draped it over her shoulders like a whisper. Sophie felt his nearness to her bones. "I just want something in case we go into a church. I'm afraid I'm not accustomed to dressing up. I'm an overgrown college kid who has to wash the dirt from her fingernails."

He said, "You are a gifted viticulturalist, according to my sister. You are similar, I think. Tomboys. It wasn't long before she was joining us in the turkey oaks. She's a country girl at heart."

They strolled into the setting sun, the evening warm and breezy.

After walking for about twenty minutes, they turned the corner into the beautiful stone piazza that was full of world-famous sculpture. They wandered around, taking photos of each other.

Antonio bristled as he watched the men ogle his sister and Sophie. It was stupid, of course. His sister was well old enough to attract male attention, but it wasn't just her. Their eyes roamed over Sophie, her hair spilling over her back and shoulders. Her pale throat and her soft hips. He hadn't felt like this in a long time. Not since ... He hated thinking about Liam's wife like that. He'd had a brief infatuation with her before she'd become involved with Liam, but she'd become one of his dearest friends after her feelings were clear and he'd swiftly quit pursuing her. And if he was completely honest with himself, she'd never stirred this sort of yearning in him. Something deep in his chest that said, *Mine*. He'd heard the O'Briens speak of such things, but he hadn't really understood until now.

Sophie couldn't be his, of course. They were both on such different paths. An ocean away once his time in Italy was done. And she wouldn't stay past winter. A semester abroad, and then back to her life. Either in England or France, most likely. The men in his family were broken when it came to women. Not his grandfather, of course, but his father. His brother. Himself. Three adult children and none married. No grandchildren. He wanted all of these things. A wife and children and a happy home to fill with love. He just hadn't ever made it stick with his previous romantic entanglements. Never fallen head over heels for a woman. As he watched Sophie pretend to be Perseus, his sister pretending to be Medusa's severed head, he laughed. It was almost a sob. He snapped a photo, shaking his head. Timing was everything, and in this instance, it was fatally flawed.

SOPHIE BRUSHED HER TEETH IN THE COMMUNAL WOMEN'S bathroom. Dinner had been wonderful. She was so comfortable with Catarina, like they'd always been friends. Not just colleagues, but heart sisters. And then there was Antonio. She saw the heat in his eyes when he looked at her. A surprising thing that stirred her deep in her belly. Made her blood warm at a time when she thought attraction of any kind was dead to her.

After everything with Richard had concluded, after the trial and the depositions, she'd eventually tried to date again. If you could call it that. She hadn't been intimate with Richard. They'd barely known each other. Afterward, she'd taken a couple of men to her bed. Shallow sexual encounters that weren't meaningful but gave her a sense of control again. She hadn't even really enjoyed it all that much. That's what happened when you tried sex with someone whom you didn't really take the time to get to know. Bad choices, but she'd been in a dark place. Since then, she hadn't dated or had any flings. Her dry spell was like the Sahara, stretching over an eight-year period. She was shaken out of memory lane by a knock at the bathroom door.

Catarina's lovely voice spoke to her through the cracks. "I need to go out. I'll be back in a couple of hours. A friend of mine from school is meeting me at her hotel lounge."

Dread washed over Sophie. Alone in the hotel room with Antonio, she asked, "Catarina, do you have to do it tonight?"

"Sophie, my brother would never try anything on you. I'll be back by midnight." Catarina was walking away and down the stairs when Sophie opened the door. "Ciao!"

ANTONIO CAME OUT OF THE MEN'S BATHROOM, COMING FACE-TO-face with Sophie in her pajamas. She looked wary. "What is it?" he asked. Maybe she'd had another phone call because she looked rattled.

"Um ... your sister went out." Her cheeks blushed a deep pink, and Antonio was definitely going to kill his sister. Sophie obviously wasn't comfortable.

"I'd get another room but there aren't any available. Maybe I could just wait in the lobby until she gets home. I'll take my book." He didn't want to, of course. He was exhausted. But he also wanted Sophie to feel safe.

"No! I'm sorry, that's not necessary. We are both adults. I have a male flatmate. I'm more than capable of co-ed living."

"But you thought my sister would be here. Listen, I'm not sure what you've been dealing with, but I want you to feel safe." He opened the door to their room, letting her go in ahead of him.

Sophie went silently and sat on her bed. "It's not that. I mean, I can distinguish between this and ... that."

She met his eyes and saw compassion there in the golden depths. The healer. She wondered what he must be like in his own arena. Antonio said, "I'd like to help, mia cara, even if it's just to talk. I'm not a woman, but I've seen a great many things. Human suffering and tragedy. Some hurts are not so easy to sew up. Some wounds need other things my hands can't do. But I've learned to listen." Sophie closed her eyes, close to tears.

She said, "Could we just lie down and turn off the lights?"

If he was disappointed, he didn't show it. Antonio had learned a lot from the nuns. Silence wasn't always a bad thing. He could give her peace. She suddenly looked so small, in a college T-shirt and baggy pajama bottoms that had cats on them. He walked over and turned off the lights, listening as she climbed under the covers. He did the same and offered, *"Boa noite, Sophie."*

Sophie's heart settled at the sound of his words. He never pushed. "Did you know you're speaking in Portuguese?"

He shook his head in the dark. "Sorry, it's difficult to transition. When I'm speaking with my family, I can go back to Italian, but I'm just ... thinking about home."

"You don't think of Tuscany as your home?" she asked. There was no accusation in her tone.

"I do, but I'm grown now. I planted my roots elsewhere. Brazil is my home, and although I am having a wonderful time here, it calls to me. I'm pulled toward my work. To the children and the sisters. I am needed. They gave me this time because I wished to come home. It has been too long. Catarina is grown. My brother was married and that marriage ended. I wasn't here. I'm feeling conflicted, and when my head and heart are at war, I cling to the familiar."

His words were touching. He was opening himself up to her in the absence of his sister. It was a gift. "I think I'd like to see your Brazil someday. Bugs and snakes and all."

He laughed, and it swirled like music in the dark of the room. Streetlights glowed through the window, and she saw his shadowed form tremble with laughter. Sophie felt the sudden urge to cry. She took a deep breath, calming herself. Then she spoke.

"When I was nineteen, I met a man. He was older than me. At the time, he told me he was twenty-two, but he was actually twenty-seven. It was a silly lie, but the start of many more."

Antonio barely breathed. He didn't want to startle her into silence. She continued. "I dated him for a couple of weeks. Two dates and some phone calls. He was persistent. He wanted to see me during the week. I'd tell him I had a test or that I had plans with friends, and he'd just worm his way into my evening, uninvited. I was trying, gently, to give him the push. It was smothering, and after two dates, some red flags were raising. I told him I couldn't see him anymore.

"It didn't help that I'd found a pretty sizable stash of marijuana in his bathroom storage. I grabbed a clean hand towel out of the airing cupboard. The whole stack came with it, falling to the floor. It was behind it, though, and hidden from plain view. It was packaged individually, like he was selling it. That's when I broke it off. I didn't tell him why, but when he used the bathroom that evening, he came out and I could tell he knew. I mean, you think ... pot. It's no big deal. But it wasn't a joint in his drawer. It was a lot. Packaged like you see in the movies. Things were already strained, and I wasn't going to date a drug dealer, even if it was just marijuana."

She paused, and Antonio couldn't stay silent. "You did the right thing, Sophie."

That seemed to urge her to continue. "He was angry when I broke it off. He said he didn't accept it. He scared me. The look on his face ... it was possessive and a bit frantic. He wouldn't let me leave until I told him that I'd start screaming. He lived in a pretty crappy flat, thin walls. He finally let me go after I said, 'Do you really want the cops showing up here?' Then I looked at the bathroom door. His face turned to ice, and I was truly afraid of him. I left, and I thought that was the end of it. But he started following me. He'd text me at all hours. He sent me flowers and candy, for God's sake!"

She was angry now, so angry. "It gradually escalated until I finally got the police involved. He'd cut my cable so I couldn't have access to the Internet. He'd show up outside my classroom door during a test, walking slowly by the door's window so I could see him. He harassed my roommate. Got me fired from my part-time job."

Antonio asked, "Did you press charges? I mean, I'm not judging your choices. I know it's a hard step."

"I tried, but stalking is really difficult to prove. You have to show a pattern of behavior. You need witnesses. It's not like in the movies." Her voice grew hoarse. "It only made it worse. And one night, when I was home alone, he broke in." Tears started spilling into her hairline, but she'd gone down this road with him and she wasn't going to stop. "I haven't told your sister all of it. He didn't rape me. I'm glad for that. But he was over me, hand over my mouth, pressing me into the mattress. He told me he was going to rape me. He pinned me down and touched me. I fought, though.

He was a big guy, heavy. But I fought. He didn't rape me," she said again.

Antonio's voice was tight. "He sexually assaulted you, even if he didn't rape you. No one should touch you without your permission."

"He had a pair of scissors. I didn't understand. I was afraid he was going to stab me, but he cut my hair. He took something from me to keep. I'd made enough noise that the neighbor next door was banging on the wall. It was a young, single mother, but she had called the police. He stroked my face." The bile rose in her throat. "Then he ran out." She stayed still as her grave jaw clenched, until she regained her composure. "The police caught up with him within a few hours. He had drugs on him. Then they raided his apartment. He'd been dealing weed and ecstasy. They found my hair. It was ... on the bureau next to his bed."

Sophie heard Antonio make a sound, like he was choking on some sort of emotion. He said, "If he was here in front of me, I'd kill him. I'm not a violent man, but sometimes jail isn't enough for certain types of men." And it sounded like he'd met his own monsters, or at least their victims. She was comforted by his anger, not afraid of it.

"The prosecutor dropped the assault charges because I'd dated him and he told them I gave him a key. I didn't, of course. But it was a bargaining chip to get him to plead guilty to drug possession and intent to sell, and they charged him with possessing an illegal weapon. The type of prosecution that the BBC would eat up. No one wants to hear about a man who copped an illegal feel. It's too commonplace. And he'd put a question in their mind about how he got into the apartment and how involved we were. He'd stolen the spare key from our kitchen. Mine and Morgan's. She was my college roommate back then."

The thought of her old flatmate broke something in her and she started to cry, her breath stuttering as she stifled her sobs. Antonio got up and turned on a side table lamp. Then he was on the floor, holding her hand. He didn't pull her to him or invade her space. He just took her free hand as she lay with the other arm draped over her eyes. Then she told him. She told him the rest. Why she'd come early. What he'd done to her old flatmate. The measures she'd taken over the last ten years to make herself as hidden as she could be while still living her life. He'd threatened her many times, and she knew he'd meant them.

Sophie said, "He cut her hair like he did mine. He kept a piece. Her husband saw it missing when they'd cleaned her up at the hospital. The bastard beat her, interrogated her, and threw her in the river to die." Her chest heaved with the pain of it. She'd often wondered if he was a budding serial rapist or even a murderer. Poor Morgan. Had he touched her? There was no evidence of rape, but there were other ways to violate a person.

She cried into her arm, trying to hide from the questions in her own mind. Sophie said, "I don't think he'd be able to find me or my parents. I mean, he's an ex-convict with no job. But the officer from Scotland Yard seemed to think I should worry. That he'd made connections in prison. I'm worried about my flatmates. My current ones, I mean. And I'm worried about my parents. What if he finds them in France? And Morgan is still in a coma. I'm scared to even call for an update." Sophie hadn't disappeared completely. She'd taken scholarships, had credit cards. She used a post office box, but still. No one could disappear in England. If he had connections, he could trace her to Essex. He could find her parents, even if he didn't find her.

Antonio interrupted her wild imaginings. "I'm glad you told me, mia cara. And I'm not going to tell you that you are worrying for no reason. If he does find you here, you'll be protected. My family will not let anything happen to you."

"I thought of leaving, but where would I go?" Sophie finally looked at him. "My lease ended, and I stored my goods. But you can never really disappear anymore. The Internet is everywhere. I have a little money, but I can't just leave my life and my family! I'm afraid to go back. It's irrational on some level, I know. I wake up some-times, feeling his weight on me." Her breath stuttered.

Antonio just rubbed the top of her hand, lulling her into calm. "Right now, you are in the safest place you could be. Next week, the vineyard will start paying you in cash. I have to tell my grandfather. Not everything, because this is not my story to tell, but we need to tell the family some of it if we are to keep everyone safe. I'm surprised Catarina didn't."

"I asked her not to tell anyone. She said if anything else happened, that we'd have to tell your father. I was just ashamed. How could I share such an ugly story?"

"You shared it with me." He said the words softly and she choked on a sob. He just rubbed her hair back from her face. "You have nothing to be ashamed of, Sophie. Nothing. And Viti del Fiume can be your sanctuary. You are good at what you do. You are a natural. And right now, you are safe to learn and grow and fall in love with Italy. This *bastardo* cannot take this from you. You won't let him."

Sophie smiled sadly, wiping her tears. "I'm sorry to put all of this on you. We were having so much fun."

"And we will have more fun. This truth is a weight that you can put down now. Tomorrow, you will see Florence, a city known for rebirth. You are lighter now. Can you feel it? In your chest? Breathe, Sophie." His voice was hypnotic. "And feel how light your chest is now." She did take a deep breath. "My mother used to ask me to play with her hair, to help her find peace and to sleep. May I touch your hair, Sophie? We can see if it does the same."

Sophie felt the exhaustion press into her. Her mother played with her hair in the evenings, even now that she was grown. She'd always done it. And when she gave herself over to the consistent, undemanding strokes of Antonio's gentle hands, she fell into the abyss of a dreamless sleep.

❦ 12 ❦

Antonio hadn't mentioned anything to his sister about what had happened the night before. He wasn't sure if his sister had given them privacy, hoping to ignite some sort of entanglement between them. Or maybe she'd been honest, having met a friend. He didn't pry because she was a grown woman. And if she hadn't disappeared for those couple of hours, he'd never been able to really talk to Sophie. He closed his eyes, and her voice came back to him. *He was a big guy, heavy. But I fought.*

He pushed the thoughts away, just watching her. She stood before Botticelli's *La Primavera*, staring at *The Three Graces*. Their elegant hands, their pale skin. Then he looked at the other art from the Lippi and Botticelli collections. *The Birth of Venus.* Venus was depicted nude, born from a shell and emerging like a flower from the sea. Her hair covered her woman's sex, but she was undeniably sensual. She was indeed the goddess of love. Wavy, fair hair that caressed her body and the very wind itself. Her small, perfect breasts. Her delicate face. And he suddenly knew why he found Sophie so beautiful. It seemed he and the famous painter had an

eye for this particular female form. Serene, with innocent eyes and
a soft, quiet beauty. Lush curves through the hips and the swell of
her belly that were just made for a man's hands. Her breasts that
weren't large or curvy, but high and round and indescribably
perfect.

Antonio had seen enough of Sophie to know these things about
her, even in her conservative style of dress. He'd seen her hair down
and blowing in the breeze. She looked at him, then, and he knew
that everything on his mind was showing in his eyes. Not lust or
leering gazes. Not that. She saw adoration. And probably the
yearning he felt deep in his soul. She looked sad, as if wondering the
same thing. Why couldn't she fit into his life? Why couldn't he fit
into hers?

※

THE REST OF THE SHORT HOLIDAY WENT BY IN A BLUR. THEY
visited the Duomo Cathedral and Baptistry. They climbed the
tower to look over the city. Then Antonio took the car to the large,
nearby hospital to meet with the Chief of Staff. He was attempting
to secure a donation for St. Clare's. Nothing extravagant, but necessary things. They offered him a job, as they were in need of trauma
surgeons. He didn't even consider it. Well, maybe for a minute. The
thought of keeping Sophie here, near his family. She could find
work here easily. But he couldn't think that way. He couldn't leave
St. Clare's. He had a house, a life, friends. They were more of a
family to him than his own family, and he couldn't be ashamed of
that. He was no saint, but God brought him to Brazil. To heal him
and to help him learn what it really meant to be a healer himself.

Antonio drove to the front of the hotel, just as Catarina was
rolling her suitcase out the front door. Sophie had her backpack
and was again wearing her sensible shorts. She'd bought souvenirs
that were tucked safely in his bag. Beautiful gloves for her mother, a
religious icon for her father. She'd also bought one for his nonna. St.

Martha, the patron saint of cooks and homemakers. His grandmother undoubtedly had something representing this little-known saint, but she didn't have one from Sophie. And people mattered to Nonna. Sophie mattered. In a short time, she'd enchanted the entirety of Viti del Fiume.

Unlike the sunny day when they'd arrived in Florence, it was grey today and began sprinkling a few minutes out of the city. It was good, these short and intermittent showers. Good for the animals and flora of these rolling hills. Harvesting would start soon, so too much rain wouldn't be good. He was happy as he drove into the city center of Greve to see that they'd had very little rain. And the vines in the distance were the right color to signal harvest time.

As they finally pulled into the dirt drive that led to his family home, Antonio wasn't surprised to see several trucks and men milling around. The harvest workers were here at last, mostly local men who needed extra work and some migrant workers who would find lodging nearby at a campground. He'd checked with his brother when he'd done the physicals, making sure that everyone was being paid a fair wage. His grandfather was a fair man, but he wasn't running the vineyard right now. Marcello and Giuseppe were training Marco to take over.

They unloaded their baggage, and he watched as Sophie humped her stuff to the pool house. He followed her with his bag, as he had her souvenirs. He didn't go in, even though she'd seen him and left the door open. Antonio opened his suitcase on the pool's dining table, pulling out her treasures. Then he heard her screech. Not a terrorized scream, but a yelp of surprise that could mean another scorpion. He hurried in to find a woman standing in the kitchen.

"Hello, my dear boy. Were you going to come to the continent and ignore me altogether?" Then the woman smiled and he stifled a little sob.

"Buongiorno, Grandmother." She opened her arms and he went to her. Sophie was watching with fascination as he took the tall, slim woman in his arms like she was a priceless treasure. She was striking, with straight, silver hair that came down to her shoulders in an elegant sweep. She had amber-colored eyes and a regal way about her. Antonio turned. "I'm sorry. Grandmother, this is Sophie. She's the intern. My father should have told you. She's staying in the pool house. Sophie, this is my grandmother, Dr. Martha Wellington."

Sophie looked truly horrified, which gave him the absurd urge to laugh. His grandmother had an intimidating air about her. Sophie said, "Oh no, Dr. Wellington. I can move to the main house. I'll find room, and it's no bother. I insist you take the house. Antonio, you have the spare bedroom. I can sleep with Catarina, maybe?"

"You insist, do you?" Martha said, brow raised. Antonio almost laughed until she turned the look on him. He could swear he heard Sophie gulp. Then his grandmother smiled, clapped her hands together, and laughed her light, musical laugh. "That look always did work on you, my dear. And there is a spare bedroom, Sophie darling. It's right here." She pointed to the bedroom. "Surely I don't need the whole house to myself. If you don't mind sharing, neither do I. It'll be the English stronghold," she said with a smirk.

"Are you sure, ma'am? I really don't mind—"

"I've begun unpacking and will be perfectly comfortable." Martha shrugged. "Bob's your uncle." She put her hands out, deciding the matter settled. "Now, Antonio, my love, let me look at you. A doctor in his own right. And a missionary. I dare say you are making us all look bad. Do you have a woman tucked away in Brazil? Don't blush, darling. I need to know these things. I have made it my mission to become a great-grandmother before I die, and you three are completely failing me."

Sophie choked on a laugh. "I'm just going to go see if Marco needs me in the vineyard. Harvest time and all that. Good day, Dr. Wellington."

"Retired, and please do call me Martha. I feel like I'm back at the teaching hospital getting ready to quiz you."

Sophie's face softened. She liked this woman. English wit aside, Antonio looked a little bit like her. It wasn't anything obvious. The long bones, chiseled face, the golden eyes. "Martha it is."

Antonio watched her go, his heart full of something that must have shown on his face. His grandmother said, "Are you sure you don't want to share the cottage with her? She's a beauty."

He gave his grandmother a chiding look. "You were always the naughtier of my two grandmothers." He hugged her again. "I'm sorry I missed your retirement."

She said, "It was time. I was too old to keep up with technology. I liked talking to my patients."

"You'd like St. Clare's. Not the private hospital, but the one at the mission. We are on a skeleton crew with outdated equipment and cast-offs, but it is wonderful. I wish you could see it."

"I wish I could as well. Maybe I will yet," she said, but not with a tone that would convince either of them. "Come, let's walk down and see what they are up to at the cave. It's still my favorite part of the estate. It's like a creepy, old catacomb in some ghastly castle, but a treasure trove hidden in the mountain. I need a glass of your father's sfuso and a chat with my grandsons."

Martha took his arm as they slowly walked through the vines. Her back was still straight. She was thinner, though. "Who called you?" Antonio asked.

She replied wryly, "Not you, apparently. Your father called me."

"I'm surprised you still talk to him. Do you come often?" She stiffened.

She said, "Why on earth would I stop talking to him? He is my son-in-law. A widower, but still my family. And your siblings needed me after your mother died. I will always come when I'm needed."

Antonio bit down, grinding his teeth a bit. He wasn't going to interfere if his grandmother came here and felt welcome. It would serve his father right if he told her exactly why she shouldn't want to talk to him. But that would hurt the rest of the family ... and her. And what was done was done.

⟡

DINNER WAS A RAUCOUS AFFAIR, WITH GIUSEPPE AND MARTHA telling stories about Italy in the fifties and sixties. Martha said, "Out of the frying pan and into the fire. Your grandfather, that is to say, your other grandfather, was a forward-thinking man. His mother could not understand why he couldn't have married a nice Italian woman instead of the pale giantess he'd met in the city. When they found out I'd come to Italy to do my residency, they tried to talk your grandfather out of marrying me. Apparently, I would make a terrible mother." She paused. "Perhaps they were right. I worked a lot, which was very uncommon. Your grandfather was a gifted psychiatrist and a wonderful father. He ran his practice out of our home and managed to keep an eye on your mother. At least when she was young."

It was a shock hearing someone speak of his mother so freely. Antonio looked at his sister, and her face was distant. His brother just stared into his plate. But the infuriating thing was the look on his father's face. He wore a warm smile as he looked at Grandmother Martha. Marcello said, "She was a beautiful girl, wasn't she?"

Antonio cut off the conversation. "Grandmother is a retired obstetrician," he said to Sophie. "She was the first female Chief of Obstetrics and Gynecology at her hospital."

Sophie smiled and raised her brows. She stumbled through the words in Italian, which caused a wave of delight to go through the room. She didn't want to exclude Nonna, who was, for once, content to sit at the table and talk. She said, "That's quite something to be proud of, Martha. It must have been very rewarding work."

"It was. And a miraculous field to be a part of as the modern technology and advances in medicine have taken women's medicine out of the Dark Ages. I was there when all three of these children were born." She beamed as she looked at them. "Italy was still very traditional. They were still making the sign of the fig to ward against the evil eye."

Nonna chuckled, the way grandmothers did. The sound, round and sweet, and just a little deeper than a young woman's laugh. She said in Italian, "And the English, still putting a knife under the bed."

Sophie wasn't sure she heard her correctly. Nonna said in English, slowly and deliberately, "To cut the pain."

The group laughed, even Antonio, who was uncommonly tense. After dinner, he left. Sophie watched the door, wondering where he'd gone. Next to her, the clear, steady voice of her countryman, or woman, in this instance, came low in her ear. "He's having a hard time, love. He's been gone a long time. His anger has been dormant. Now he tries to reconcile what he's made truth in his mind with the reality that he's faced with today. I won't go into it. It's a long story. But I know about pain in its many forms. He won't talk to us right now, but he might draw comfort from a friend. One who isn't a part of this particular theater."

Sophie met her gaze, wondering what to say. "I don't know what I could do. I'm a stranger."

Martha just smiled. "Are you, now? I think not. Go, my dear. See where my grandson has gone to lick his wounds."

THE MOON WAS FULL AND BRIGHT, AND SOPHIE HAD NO NEED OF a flashlight. Despite the time, over an hour after sunset, she could see over the rolling vines. She started her search in the orchard, but he wasn't among the citrus trees where the lemon scent wafted over the night air. She made her way downhill, among the olive trees. The trees weren't ready for harvest, but she knew this was the time that the sun and water were important, as the olives were beginning to produce more oil. She plucked an olive and found it to be rigid and smooth. It was still a vibrant green, as she'd seen in the daytime. She licked it, testing. Knowing, really, but she did it anyway. She scraped her teeth into the flesh, not going deep and avoiding the pit. The astringent feel and the overwhelming bitterness attacked her like a vice to the jaw. She made a gurgling sound, her entire body shuddering. She spit it out, shaking her head. That's when she heard him. He was laughing. A real laugh, rich and deep.

She looked into the night air, seeing him perched on the large tree on the outskirts of the olive grove. Antonio said, "You aren't supposed to eat them raw, mia cara."

Her jaw unclenched itself, and instead, her throat was thick with longing. Mia cara ... *my darling.*

Sophie shrugged. "I know. I'd heard they were unbearably awful right off the tree."

"And this made you want to eat a raw one that is two months from ripening?" His grin was warm and appreciative.

"Of course. You read something, but sometimes one has to experience it for one's self. It's like the sign that says, *Beware! Don't touch!*"

Antonio shook his head, chuckling deep in his belly. "And such a sign would make a young Sophie immediately desperate to touch it?"

"And not a young Antonio? I find there are two types—the type who eat the olive, and the type who wait for someone to offer it during dinner. You didn't strike me as a coward. Not the young lad who took off for the Amazon with his doctor bag in his hand."

Antonio said, "Guilty. We dared each other when I was five and Marco was eight. He knew already, of course. He'd done this particular trick with the neighbor kids and cousins. So, I tried it. I wasn't going to be the soft child who wouldn't rise to the challenge. As a matter of fact, my older brother had to intervene at times. The boys to the west, from the big goat farm, would dare me to jump off the high branch of some turkey oak or let a scorpion sting me.

Marco didn't want to explain why he'd stood by and let his thick-headed brother kill himself."

"Or maybe, and humor me with the absurdity, just maybe Marco loved you. Still does love you. And you are very lucky indeed."

Antonio thought about that. "Maybe, yes. And then when I was ten, we got our sister. Trouble from the time she could roll over. She was definitely the type to ignore the *do not touch* sign."

It was Sophie's time to laugh. "I had no doubt whatsoever." She walked closer. "You seemed tense at dinner, like something was on your mind." She noticed his glass of wine and raised a brow. "You've been into the sfuso."

"Have a sip to rinse that olive off your tongue," he said. She took it and sipped, then she put space between them, keeping his glass. "I said a sip. You have to come closer if we are going to share."

Sophie turned, her eyes soft. "You don't have to talk to me. I just thought you could use some company." She stretched an arm out, offering the wine back to him. He stood, his face coming into the moonlight. There were solar lights spread along the path that led to the cave and the processing barn. It wasn't a lot of light, but enough to see the tight lines of his beautiful face. He downed the wine in one gulp and tossed the stemless glass to the ground. "I'm not good company right now, Sophie. If you aren't prepared for what is on my mind, you should go back up to the house."

"Friends don't need you to be good company. They just stay, even when it's hard." She said the words like she knew what she was talking about.

She was right. His friends at St. Clare's were the type who stayed. Even when it was hard. "Is that what we are, Sophie?" Because he wasn't feeling like a friend right now. He had a consuming need to get inside her. To run his hands over her hips, kiss the pale column of her throat. To kiss his way down and taste her between her thighs. To feel her come against his mouth. To spill himself inside her. He knew this was all showing on his face.

Sophie's breath was fast and shallow. When had he gotten this close? But then she looked at his mouth and he moaned deep in his throat, threading a hand into her hair. He used the other hand to pull the tie out of her hair, unraveling the braid. Antonio hovered over her, their mouths almost touching. "Sophie," he said. And it was a plea. He felt her rise up on her toes and close the distance. Her kiss was soft and sweet. A caress. He trembled, but he let her explore, so gently. Like she didn't want to break him. Or maybe herself. He tilted his head finally and pulled her body to his. He slanted his mouth over hers, kissing her deeply, alternating sips as he tasted her lips. She made little noises, tiny moans and gasps in the space between them. And into his mouth.

Sophie was breathless and overwhelmed. She thought she'd been kissed before, but never like this. Skill mixed with a wild recklessness that he was keeping a tight rein on. His arousal was a thick rope on her belly as she dug her nails into his shoulders. She could do this for him. Be his comfort. Be what he needed. He didn't want to talk, but this he wanted.

Antonio broke the kiss. "Sophie, I want you. But if you don't—"

She interrupted. "I know what you need. You don't have to say anything. I can be this for you." When she said the words, it took a second, then he stiffened. He leaned back, taking in her face. He looked almost shocked.

He said, "Is that what you think this is? Me trying to ... escape from my worries? Do you really think I'd use you like that?" He put distance between their hips, but he didn't let her go. Antonio gazed into her eyes. "You can't believe that I'd just want you for you? Because what is going on in that house right now is the furthest thing from my mind." He kissed her temple, her eyes, her cheeks. But he didn't take her mouth again. "I think about you every night, Sophie. I lie there, wanting you. And in the morning, I wonder if you're awake already. I wonder if something woke you or scared you during the night. I think of you down in the vines, working with my nonno. Wondering if you've had enough water. Wondering if you need a break. Wanting to curl up and rest with you. Feel your sweet breath and heartbeat against my skin. I always want you, mia cara, but until you feel that fact completely, this can't happen. I wouldn't come to you as a diversion, no matter what kind of pain I was in. You are more than that."

Sophie rubbed her hands down his face, tears starting to pool. "Why couldn't we have met when our lives weren't so committed to other things? I want you, Antonio. But I know what a fling feels like. I'm not proud of that, but I do. And I don't think I could be that or do that with you. I don't think I could stop myself from wanting more."

Antonio thought about his friend Liam. The trials and pain that had been a part of his joining with Izzy. It hadn't been a fling. It had been a slow growing, hard, wonderful thing. He looked down at Sophie and thought, maybe, he felt something like that starting between them. "Then we take this slow, Sophie. I won't hurt you. I couldn't do that." *But you could very well leave me in pieces.*

He kissed her, then, warm and deep. She opened to him, letting him explore her mouth. Her nipples brushed against him and he sought them out, running his hands up her ribs to rub thumbs over the underside of her breast.

They both heard it at the same time. Sticks snapping. Marcello's dog came off the porch, racing toward the orchard as Antonio heard someone break into a dead run. He didn't think, he just ran. But it was hard with no lights. He saw a figure, fast and sure, through the property. He was fast, but the person had been at least a hundred feet away when they'd begun and had a head start. The dog whizzed past him, but he reached a small, dark car on one of the side roads adjacent to his father's property. He didn't get in the driver's side, but in the passenger side. The car was halfway down the road to the turnoff when Antonio met up with the dog. The car had almost run her over. "Vieni, Dolce!" She growled one more time for good measure, then came to him. "You are a good girl. A good watch dog," Antonio said as he stroked her head absently, just watching the lights disappear.

Sophie came to the road, gasping for breath, short legs and too much food working against her. Antonio was crooning to the dog in Italian. She wanted to kiss them both, for some reason. Someone had been on the property who did not want to be seen. Someone who had been watching them.

❧ 1 3 ❧

Sophie sat at the large table, Nonna on one side and Catarina on the other. They both held her hands, but it was Antonio who kept her grounded. He knew it all and hadn't shied away from it. He sought out her eyes every few seconds, as if to reassure her from across the table. The person on the property could have been anyone. A teenager or a competitor from another vineyard. An old worker who was scoping out the property for something to steal. But they hadn't caught them in the cave or in the processing barn where the equipment was kept. He'd been closer to the house and he'd been watching them.

Sophie needed to call the agent from Scotland Yard. He had her number. And he was the only one who knew where she lived in England. But for right now, they had to tell the family what was going on. She should have done it when Morgan was attacked, and it was time to stop being ashamed about something that was not her fault.

She spoke in English, trusting Antonio to interpret all the finer nuances in Italian. Broken, subpar language skills were not what was required. She skimmed over the assault in her apartment. She didn't lie, exactly, because they needed to understand how dangerous he was. But she couldn't bring herself to give a detailed account. And no one pushed her.

When Antonio had finished telling them about Richard's early release, Morgan's attack, and why they were concerned about someone being on the property, Nonna's hand was so tight on hers that she was afraid to look at her. Marcello, Marco, and Giuseppe were tight-jawed and stoic. Would they send her away? She wouldn't blame them one bit. How could she? She was nothing to them. Their family meant everything to them. She needed to call her parents again. She didn't realize she was hyperventilating until Antonio was in front of her, having turned her chair. "Breathe, mia cara. Look at my face."

Sophie did, and it grounded her. She took in steadying breaths, her eyes not leaving his face. He was taking her pulse. Wait, no. Martha was taking her pulse. She was suddenly so ashamed, which was a stupid, useless emotion. But when her tears came, it was Marcello who took her out of the seat. He treated her like she was made of glass and he held her. "You are not alone," he said in his deep, richly accented voice.

The sight of his father holding Sophie did something to Antonio. Something stirred in his chest. Protectiveness and something else unexpected. A deep affection for his father. He'd been angry for so long, he'd forgotten what it was like. Forgotten that this man had once been everything to him. His beloved papa. He shook himself, turning away.

His grandmother came next to him. "He's a good man, Antonio. Better than you know." It's all she said, then she went to the kitchen to help Nonna pour everyone a ration of their good brandy.

ANTONIO SAT BACK AT THE TABLE, LISTENING TO HIS FATHER AND grandfather speak as if they were going to war. The men were pissed, and it renewed the righteous anger that had flowed through him that night in Florence when Sophie had told him everything. She was on the phone with her parents now. They would call her roommates. Tomorrow, she would contact the victims' assistance officer at Scotland Yard to see what could be learned about the man who had been released early from prison. She'd covered her tracks with good cause. Because of Antonio's experience with drug dealers in Brazil, he knew it was often a complicated network. There was a hierarchy of rotten bastards at this man's disposal, if he'd continued his illicit activity while inside the prison. Hadn't the officer told Sophie the man had made connections while incarcerated? If so, why would they let him go?

Marcello said, "I have three shotguns and two rifles. We have enough of a staff at our disposal that we can stand guard in shifts."

Antonio stiffened. So did his brother. Marco spoke first. "Do you think that's necessary? Is it perhaps a bit premature? Maybe we should call the police, but guns?"

Marcello pointed a finger into the table. "We had someone on our land, watching our family. Even if it has nothing to do with this man who hurt Sophie, someone is coming into our home. They are lurking that close to the house. Watching us. Our women. Sì! I think it is necessary."

Giuseppe said, "He's right. Our local men can be trusted with a weapon. We are in the hunting club with two of them. We don't need to tell them all of it. Sophie is entitled to some privacy in this matter. This is hard for a woman to share ... this ugly business. If we have two men take a shift every night after sunset, until perhaps five in the morning, that should be enough."

"And women. I can handle a shotgun as well as my brothers," Catarina said.

Giuseppe started shaking his head. But she found an unlikely ally. Marco said, "She's right. We will be worn thin as it is. And she is as good a shot as any man in this room. Well, except for you, Nonno. No one can outshoot you."

Catarina nodded. "And I can beat you all on foot."

Antonio said, "All but me, little duck. I hate the idea of this, Catarina. This man targets women. But I've known some very tough women in my time away. Women I wouldn't want to come across in a dark alley if their blood was up. So, I agree. We should put her in the rotation, Padre, and I think we should move Sophie into the house."

"Was anyone going to ask Sophie?" The voice came from behind them. Sophie stared, arms crossed. "Why are you having a meeting about me without me?"

Antonio almost said it was a family meeting, just to shut her up, but he wouldn't do that to her. "I'm sorry. You were on the phone, and we just started talking." Sort of the truth.

"I didn't hear anything before Catarina started talking. What's this about guns?" They'd been speaking in Italian, of course, and she hadn't followed most of it.

They told her. Sophie wasn't comfortable with guns. France and England were as strict as Italy with gun control, if not more so. Her father had one gun, but he'd never taken her shooting. She'd never asked. "If you teach me, I'd like to take my share of the shifts."

Catarina said in English, "You are a foreigner. You cannot be caught with a weapon, Sophie, and there isn't time for enough lessons to make you proficient. You are here to learn the wine business. Let us handle security. This may not have anything to do with you. This may be a competitor or some locals up to mischief."

Antonio thought this argument was sound, and it was better coming from Catarina. Sophie would think it was due to her gender and naught else. Sophie couldn't argue. However, she said, "If you need to move Martha into the house, that's one thing, but I'm not going to move. If someone is after me, better they just come into the pool house and not endanger Nonna or Martha or anyone else. You're right. This may be simple paranoia, but I am better off on my own out there if it is Richard or one of his associates."

Antonio couldn't countenance this logic. He could hardly

believe her words. "Sophie, that is the most ridiculous thing I've ever heard."

"Why, exactly? I'm not family. I'm an intern. By all rights, you should send me packing for this mess. I'm sure as hell not going to put your family in more danger by placing myself inside the house. I should go get a room at the local hostel. I can call tomorrow, in fact."

Antonio stood, the chair screeching and nearly tipping with the force of his anger. "You are not staying in the local hostel. You don't even have a car. And if you insist on staying out in the pool house, then I stay out in the pool house." He silenced his family with a sharp look. "There are two rooms. Grandmother Martha moves into the guest room tonight." He walked out past a stunned Sophie. Catarina and Marco were trying not to start laughing.

Giuseppe clapped his hands together once. "A good plan. I'll speak with the men in the morning. I think we've scared them off for tonight. Catarina, you can help your grandmother move her things."

Marco and Marcello narrowed their eyes at him. When Marco left, Marcello said under his breath, "You don't have to look so pleased about it, old man."

☙❧

ANTONIO REALLY HADN'T THOUGHT THIS THROUGH. HIS NONNA would likely hit the ceiling when she figured out what they were doing. But she was in bed now, and Martha was packing up her belongings to move into this room. He threw a few things in a bag, figuring he'd get the rest later. Then he changed the sheets on the bed so his grandmother had fresh ones. His brother came to the door, and he was readying himself for an earful.

"If I was a few years younger, I'd have given you a run for your money with this woman," Marco said. And for once, there was no bitterness in his tone.

Antonio's eyes darted to his. "That's not what this is about."

"I know, but you have to admit it's got potential. I'm glad you are doing it. She's independent, but wounded, I think. She needs to feel safe while she's here. She needs to be safe while she's here. They all do. They don't know what it is to be a man. The natural instinct to protect."

"They understand when it's a child, though. That's a different sort of instinct, but it's even stronger," Antonio said, thinking about all of the women he knew at the mission.

"You are different, brother. You've seen a great many things, I think." He sounded almost sad about it.

Antonio sat on the bed, really looking at him. "Why do you stay here when you want other things, Marco?" Marco bristled. "I'm not trying to hurt you by saying that. I really want to know. You don't seem to have any sort of passion for this business. For your family, yes. For wine, I don't think so."

Marco said, "Papa wants me here. And Mama wanted this. It was her dying wish."

"What do you mean her dying wish? She was killed on impact! How do you know what her dying wish was?" Antonio was suddenly angry, and he wondered what his father had said to Marco. Marco came closer, sitting next to him on the bed.

"Keep your voice down, Antonio. Listen to me," he murmured. "Mama told me that if anything ever happened to her, she wanted me to take over the vineyard like my father and his father. That it was my birthright. Granted, Catarina was a young girl when she said this, but she did say it. She told Papa this same thing. A few days before she died, she said it! They argued about something and she made him promise."

"So he says." Antonio knew how bitter he sounded and he hated it. He'd never seen himself as a bitter man.

"Basta! You have no right to treat Papa this way. He raised our sister by himself for years and managed this vineyard for Nonno. Even before she died, he did all of these things. Mama had problems, Antonio. How could you not see it? You were a grown man and a doctor! How did you not see it?"

"Her difficulties lie squarely at our father's feet," Antonio said, not expanding on the statement.

"You are wrong, Antonio." It wasn't Marco who said that, but his grandmother. His mother's mother. "And don't tell me that I don't understand the situation. You remember your mother through a boy's eyes, not a man's. And you don't know as much as you think you do." Antonio looked at his grandmother and his father beside her. Marcello seemed stricken with hurt and a bone-deep sorrow.

Marcello said, "Martha, please. Let this go. You must be tired, and Antonio has prepared the bed for you."

Martha sighed. "I am tired. We all are. But I will have my say in this matter. Not tonight, given the stress of the evening, but I will be heard."

Marcello motioned to his sons. "Come now. Tomorrow is a big day for the vineyard. We will be packed with locals and tourists. Let us all get some rest."

SOPHIE COULD HEAR HIM MUTTERING TO HIMSELF, SLAMMING drawers. Really, this was too much. She steeled her spine and walked to his open door. "Antonio, I don't see how you could possibly be upset with me. And if you didn't want to stay here, why the bloody hell did you ask? No, that's not the right word, is it? You demanded to stay in this house."

Antonio glanced up at her, and she was taken aback by the look in his eyes. Anger, yes, but hurt and frustration. And she knew something else had upset him. Something that had nothing to do with her. "Let's go sit down. Leave this for now," she said a little more calmly.

They sat in the living space, a glass of wine in each of their hands. Sophie was acquiring a taste for this local tradition. This loose wine that was neither valuable nor complex. She let the fresh fruitiness of the new wine roll into every corner of her mouth. Someday she'd be somewhere else. She'd be able to buy a bottle of good Chianti Classico at any decent wine store. But this taste would linger in her memory, and she wouldn't be able to reproduce the feeling of connection that it offered. Both with the land and the family.

"What are you thinking about right now?" Antonio had calmed, and his gaze was curious. His head tilted in question.

She looked at the glass, wondering if he'd understand. So, she told him. He nodded, a sad smile on his face. "I understand. I've spent ten years away from this place. And our good, bottled wine has always lingered in my memory. Our distribution is limited to Italy and to the tourists who take it from here to their own land. But this"—he looked at his glass as she had—"this tastes of home. Simple pleasures are often the sweetest to recall."

"I'm ruined, of course. How am I going to go back to Essex wine?" They both laughed and Sophie said, "That's not to say I'm not proud of my education. It's a good program. The only one in the UK. I am a fortunate woman, and I learned a lot about fermentation. I even studied under a master brewer who made local ale. Not for a grade, but for the curiosity of it. I toured the areas in Germany, between a wine-soaked adventure down the Rhine to the schnapps distilleries. That was a good bit of fun. It's an old tradition, and Germans do love to get foxed. The language barrier was a little more difficult. I know French and can get by in Italian, but Germany required a close relationship with an interpreter."

Antonio smiled as he listened, content to let her lead the conversation. He finally said, "There are two liqueurs in Brazil. Not particularly world renowned, but the locals like it. One is made from sugar cane, spices, citrus, and honey. The other one I've tried is made of catuaba. Its origins lie with the indigenous tribes. I learned about it because of the plant that is used. It's considered medicinal."

This piqued her interest. "So, what is catuaba?"

"It's a native plant. It has a good dose of caffeine and it's added to red wine. It's sweet. The locals like it over ice. It's not very good."

"So why do they like it?" she asked with a laugh. His wolfish grin was something new. He was devastating in any form, but this was something else altogether.

"It's considered to be an aphrodisiac. Never having needed such potions, I rarely partake." And that comment lit her up like a Christmas tree. Sophie hummed with awareness, having almost forgotten this feeling. New attraction and sizzling chemistry. Come to think of it, she may have never felt this. Not really. Seduction not just of the body, but of the mind ... and the heart. Antonio was a good man. Better than anyone she knew, other than her father.

Sophie smiled weakly, clearing her throat. "I don't doubt it." Her male English friends were nothing like this man. He didn't pursue her, but he had an innate sensuality that called to her. A fact that caused her great inconvenience because the situation was impossible. Dr. Antonio Rinalto wasn't the fling type. He was the keeping type. A man who could make your life beautiful. Adventurous, smart, and loyal, despite his issues with his father.

"You were upset when you came in tonight. If you'd let me, I would like to be a friend to you, Antonio. The way you've been to me. I don't pretend to know all that has transpired, but it's obvious there is an old rift between you and your father. As I'm not family, maybe I can offer you something."

Antonio took a sip, looking away. "It's nothing. It doesn't matter. None of it matters anymore."

"If it hurts you, then it matters." Her words were calm and soft, but he felt pushed. He downed his wine in one final gulp, suddenly ready for another subject. Any other subject than this. He got up and went to the kitchen, rinsing out his glass and putting it in the dishwasher.

"Tell me about your roommates." Antonio was trying to lighten the mood, take an interest in her life in England, but it just made her face adjust to something a little bit less than he was used to. Her back straight.

She said, "I see." Sophie took her empty glass, passing him as he came back into the living room. She did as he did, rinsing her glass and not meeting his eyes. "It's late. I'll see you in the morning." Antonio wished she'd been the least bit pissy. Some overreaction or dramatic exit that could help him paint her in a lesser light. But she didn't. She gave him a tight smile, allowing him wide berth as she passed him again, going toward her bedroom. "I'll shower in the morning. Just let me brush my teeth and the lav is yours."

"Sophie, wait. What did I say?" He knew, bastard that he was. But he was going to mess this up royally. He couldn't seem to stop himself.

"It doesn't matter." She repeated the words he'd spoken to her, and it chafed.

"If it hurts you, then it matters." He said her words back to her. Two could play at this.

"Apparently not. Good night, Antonio." His blood was heating up, his anger coming forth, even though it didn't have anything to do with her. It was just that some secrets became so old and rank, it was hard to let go of them. He wanted to shake her. To tell her to let it go. Not to push. He wanted to do more than shake her. The thought of those kisses in the orchard had him hard within seconds. Sophie sensed it somehow and met his eyes. She pointed at him. "You know what? Screw that. I am pissed at you. Because I opened a vein in that hotel room in Florence, which is not something I do often. I told you more than I even told my own mum. More than I told Catarina. All I wanted was to help you. To give you even a little bit of the comfort that you so selflessly gave to me. But obviously, this isn't that kind of relationship. I want to be a friend to you. And I'm so bloody desperate for some sort of connection, I missed the signs."

THE LAST SIP OF WINE

Antonio took her arm, pulling her close. "What signs? What the hell are you speaking of?"

Sophie lifted her chin. "The signs that I probably made an idiot of myself in Florence. That this"—she motioned back and forth between them—"this is about lust. You want a quick shag before you head back to Brazil. I felt it in that orchard. Christ, you are aroused right now. I can see that you're hard and ready to bend me over that table. And I would undoubtedly enjoy the ride, Dr. Rinalto. But I left quick, meaningless shags behind a long time ago. I'd rather do without if it's all the same to you." She sounded so English, even to her own ears, that it seemed completely at odds with the crass words coming out of her mouth.

He drew her hard against him. "You are right. I am hard. I'm hard every time I think of you. Anytime we are near each other and no one is around. I won't apologize for wanting you. But you are wrong about the rest. I care for you, Sophie. Too much. Enough to make me sad before anything has even started. I care and I want to protect you. And I want to hunt down that bastard who hurt you and beat him to death with my bare hands." His accent was thickened with anger, and it ignited something fierce and unwise inside her. He bent his face, nose-to-nose with her, and said, "And yes, I'd love to bend you over and sink my cock into you. I'd love to drop down to my knees right now and kiss you long and deep between your thighs." She swayed, her eyes glazing over. "But I won't use you. That's not why I'm sleeping out here."

Antonio forced himself to let her go. He saw her throat working, fighting her desire and tears. She turned, silently, and her legs were wobbly. He cursed, then said the words so fast that she barely had time to process them. "My father is responsible for my mother's death." She jerked, turning to meet his eyes.

"Jesus wept. Antonio, I ..."

He said, "You don't believe it. No one would. He seemed like the perfect husband. But he cheated on her. I saw him holding her one evening. Holding her and whispering to her. The woman he was involved with, I mean. She lives a few villages over. And my mother knew. I didn't tell her about seeing them together, but she knew and told me everything a few nights before she died."

Sophie couldn't even imagine it. He'd been a young man, still in medical school when she died. "I'm sorry, Antonio. And you're right. I can't imagine it of Marcello. But I didn't know him back then, and I didn't know your mother. I'm not going to pass judgement on any of it. But how did that lead to your mother's death? Oh, God. Did she commit suicide?"

He shook his head. "No, I don't think so. I don't think she did it on purpose. She was upset. They'd had a fight, and she left the house in her little sports car."

Sophie put her arms around him. He shook in her arms and buried his face in her neck. "She loved to go for drives. She said it helped her clear her head. But she was reckless that night. I was outside when I heard the engine roaring up the road. I looked down to the road. You know how winding it is. She was going so fast. Too fast. I saw the whole thing. Her losing control and crashing into a fence. I watched her clip a tree, and that caused the car to flip. She was in a convertible."

She squeezed him harder. "I'm so sorry. Oh, love. I'm so very sorry."

"By the time I got there, it was too late. She died on impact. I tried, Sophie. I tried to bring her back, but her whole body was broken and so was her heart. I couldn't save her! Jesus, I couldn't save my own mother!"

Antonio didn't cry. He just gave her the story in stops and starts. Then he separated their bodies. His eyes were dry, and somehow that made her even sadder. "I don't think Marco knows. Catarina does know, or she thinks she does. She was young, though. I don't know." He ran his hands through his hair. "And I doubt my grandparents know. I mean, maybe my grandfather knows a little, but it would kill my grandmother. Martha knows something. Or she thinks she does."

"You keep saying that—that they think they know—as if you're the only one with the whole picture."

He nodded, "Yes, so?"

"And maybe they are thinking the same thing. Maybe no one has the full picture. I mean, no one other than your father. Have you talked to him?"

Antonio laughed, but it was an angry snort. Nothing gleeful. "He said he was faithful to my mother from the time he wed her until the day she died."

"Okay." Sophie wasn't sure what to say after that. She said, finally, "What does Catarina say?"

"She doubts my mother's account. She confided in Catarina at a tender age. I wish she hadn't. It's too much for a young girl to carry."

"It's too much for a son to carry as well," Sophie said. "I'm sorry. I can see you are angry at me for saying that. I just wonder why she'd speak of such things to her children? Why not one of her mates? Or her mother? Even the parish priest. But a teenage girl?"

Antonio shook it off. "I had been living in the city. I was here for the weekend. After the funeral, I stayed away. I came to get some belongings six months later, then I left for Brazil not long after that. It was wrong, though. To punish the rest of the family because of my anger toward mio padre." He'd been slipping in and out of Italian, and she knew he was exhausted.

Sophie took his face in her hands. "You need sleep." She kissed his mouth briefly. Just a peck, but it made him lean toward her, their foreheads together. She left him then, closing the bathroom door behind her.

❧ 14 ❧

"Here with a Loaf of Bread beneath the Bough, A Flask of Wine, a Book of Verse—and Thou Beside me singing in the Wilderness—And Wilderness is Paradise enow." — The Rubáiyát of Omar Khayyám, by Omar Khayyám

Sophie was introduced to every worker. It was nice to see a business that still took the time to look people in the eye. To thank them for their hard work. Some of the younger men watched her. She was a novelty among all of the dark-haired men in the crowd. There were even some women who helped with the harvesting and operated some of the machinery. They eyed her suspiciously, and their gazes lingered appreciatively over both the Rinalto sons, and a good share also on their father. A widower with good looks and family money.

Marcello smiled as he looked out over the rolling hills of his vineyard. "They come every year. I pay fairly, and they are loyal. It's hard to get enough help if you are starting from scratch. See that family just there with the young teenage sons? They have harvested these grapes for four generations. They own a small parcel of land to the south of ours about fifteen kilometers. They have sheep. But this is extra income for them, and they come together. As soon as one of them turns sixteen, they are allowed to join the ranks."

"You must be a good man to inspire such loyalty," Sophie said. But Marcello saw a question in her eyes, and his face fell just a small bit. Barely noticeable, but she saw it.

He replied, "I have always tried to be loyal. I wasn't the best of men, but I always tried. I still try." She wanted to weep. She saw the same depth of pain in his eyes as she saw in Antonio's. But where Antonio's was turned outward, Marcello's was turned inward.

Sophie said, "Don't stop trying. It's never a lost cause if you keep trying." And there was a not-so-hidden understanding between them.

Antonio watched as the statue of Saint Vincent, the patron saint of winemakers, was brought to a place of honor by his brother. The priest said a prayer for a favorable harvest and prosperity for good people. Little did he know that at sunrise, the workers had come to their garden and his grandfather had also paid his respects to Bacchus, the Roman god of wine and fertility. He was along the garden wall, which enclosed the kitchen garden and exited out into the vineyard. It was a tradition, meant for luck. His grandfather was a good Catholic. But they'd always done this, for generations, and he wasn't going to stop now.

The place looked so festive. Even the donkey was decorated. He couldn't believe Fabio was still alive. He had aged, but he was still tolerant of the children. They stroked him and fed him carrots while the adults spoke of the harvest and the wine that would come from their efforts. It was a good year for the grapes, and they were all excited.

Sophie watched the men as they rolled out great, giant tubs. Worn wood that had seen decades of use. *Pigiatura*, the stomping of the grapes. It wasn't done at most vineyards anymore, but Marcello explained that they used the lesser grapes for this ritual, making their table wine and sfuso for personal consumption. She remembered the old, American television show, *I Love Lucy*. There was an episode where she and her best mate, Ethel, did this very thing. It was funny in the physical comedic nature of such shows. Now, as she watched Marco and Giuseppe wash the feet of Magdalena and Catarina, her throat thickened with emotion. It wasn't funny. It was very special. "It's a beautiful tradition, Marcello." Her accent was clipped, even to her own ears. The curse of the English-born. Reserve to the point of pain when emotions ran high and there was a crowd about.

Marcello said, "I used to do this for my wife. It's a sign of respect. An act of humility. The women bear the fruit of the bloodline, as our vines bear the fruit of our other legacy."

Just as Sophie was ready to speak, someone tapped her on the shoulder. Antonio stood behind her and motioned. "You are our guest of honor," he said. "Sit, please." There was a third chair and bin of water.

She shook her head and said, "This is for the family. I don't want to intrude."

Marcello urged her forward. "It's tradition, you see?" He pointed to a fourth chair she hadn't noticed. He went to it, kneeling to wash Martha's feet, his mother-in-law, though his wife had been in her grave almost eleven years. Antonio gently but insistently put his hands to her shoulder. "Sit, bellisima. You think entirely too much. Is the thought of mucking around in squashed fruit offending your English sense of propriety?"

Sophie stiffened, but he went on. "Look at Grandmother Martha. She has done this before, and she didn't perish from the shame." He was teasing her and she turned her face up to him, raising a brow that likely made her look even more British. He leaned down, his mouth hovering just above hers. "Tell me you aren't dying to get into that vat of grapes and squish your pretty, little feet in there." His accent was like rich chocolate.

Antonio was so close, she felt the desire swirl in her belly, even with all these people around. She'd show him her sense of propriety. She raised her mouth as she said, "Maybe I just want to see you on your knees before me, Medíco." She fed her breath into his mouth, her nearness letting her mouth just faintly graze his. A split second and then gone.

His eyes were feral. "Don't worry, *mia Sophie*. You will." Two could play at this game. She knew not what she provoked. He would be on his knees. Soon. Her sex pulled tight against his mouth. And he couldn't wait. He knelt in front of her, and the gentle caress of his hands on her feet seemed even more personal than a kiss. Antonio said, "Don't think I didn't notice that you've shamelessly stolen my dog." Marcello had insisted they keep the dog in the pool house, wanting the security. He also gave Antonio one of the shotguns.

Sophie smiled and said, "It's not my fault she wants to sleep with me. She made her choice." And she had. The dog had begun following her around with a renewed spring in her step, happy to have a new playmate. Dolcetto was seated on the ground next to her, watching Antonio. Sophie put a palm on her warm head, reassuring her. Trying to get the image of Antonio's head buried between her thighs out of her mind.

The musicians were local men whom Giuseppe hired every year for the last twenty years. And as Antonio lifted her off the chair, she squeaked to the delight of the visitors and workers. Open to the public, the tourists already had their phones out, snapping pictures. The women were placed in the tub, and Sophie saw the love between Giuseppe and Magdalena, the sibling silliness between Marco and Catarina, and the mutual fondness and respect between Marcello and Martha.

Antonio smelled so good. He was warm, and he smelled like shaving soap and his own unique maleness. The only couple involved here were his grandparents, and she wondered at the four others, all unmarried. Marcello and Marco hadn't remarried, and

Catarina and Antonio were unattached. It was odd, and she met Antonio's eyes as he took in the unlikely group as well. Then he stared down at her and placed her gently into the grapes. Now she knew why Catarina had told her to wear shorts.

Nonna began swaying to the music like a girl. There was an accordion, a guitar, a mandolin, and a tambourine. Then one of the men started to sing a rolling, beautiful melody. Sophie joined in, feeling hopelessly awkward. Catarina was laughing and Martha was lost in the moment, closing her eyes as she stepped and pranced. Sophie was an Englishwoman who'd fallen in love with an Italian man. She'd also fallen in love with Italy.

Antonio watched them all, and he felt the tears prick his eyes. His sister had been fifteen the last time he'd seen them bring in the harvest. Just old enough to take part in the squashing of the grapes. Now she was sure and confident, not minding the crowd's attentions. His grandmothers had both aged, but they were healthy and light on their feet. Then there was Sophie. He could tell she felt like she didn't belong, but then Nonna took her hand and they joined with the other two. The four strong women circling the tub, juice kicking up on their legs and clothing. And the giggles, so sweet and pure. He remembered his mother doing this, and then he couldn't stop the single tear that fell as he recalled her bright, golden eyes. Just like Martha's. Just like his. And her broad smile lit up the room. There had been sad times, but there had been such good ones as well.

The tourists were eating it up, snapping pictures and taking videos as these beautiful women danced the bountiful harvest into the loving arms of his family. Transforming what nature had given them into one of the oldest and most glorious drinks in existence. Something Christ Himself had partaken in.

His grandfather placed a ring of grape leaves and autumn foliage on his Magdalena's head. The matriarch of this family and the vineyard. A queen of sorts. Giuseppe beamed at her, and Antonio wiped another tear away. What was it like to have such a love? He'd seen

THE LAST SIP OF WINE

it, of course, with other couples. With Liam and Izzy and even Liam's parents. With Hans and Mary at the mission. He'd seen it but never had the good fortune to find it. He looked at Sophie again. A sprite of a woman. Thick, coppery hair coiled at her neck. Fair-skinned with her soft, blue-green eyes. She met his eyes, and a blush creeped up her neck and to her cheeks. He gave her a gentle, encouraging smile. "You are doing fine, mia cara. You are lovely."

He saw the hard swallow, and her blush deepened. It pleased him to make her so flustered. Her blushes were beautiful. She was so strong sometimes, but just now, she'd needed a gentle nudge. The song ended and a tarantella number was next. Fast and intense. And the women sped up their feet, their faces flushing with exertion. That's when he saw his grandmother watching something, distracted. His grandfather was sitting on a stool, head down and resting on one fist. He was pale. Antonio got to him at the same time as his father. The song ended, and Marco distracted the crowd with some sort of speech. Then it was over. The tourists went to the tasting area, lining up to try their last bottled vintage. And the rest of the family was at Giuseppe's side.

⚜

"HIS BLOOD PRESSURE IS LOW AND HIS HEART IS RAPID," ANTONIO spoke to his grandmother Martha, who was covered in grape mush.

She was remarkably calm. "Let's get him over to the truck, love. I'll drive him to the house and get changed. Too much sun, perhaps."

Antonio looked at her, narrowing his eyes. Catarina had the good sense to say, "The man lives in the sun. The day Giuseppe Rinalto swoons from too much sun is the day I leave Italy to join the circus. Antonio, what is wrong with him?"

"I'll drive them both up to the house with Nonna, Catarina. Why don't you get cleaned up at the pool house with Sophie?"

"Don't send me off like a child, brother. I'll walk up and take a short shower. Then I want some answers."

Their grandfather was on his feet now. "Stop fussing," he said. "I'm very good. I'm just old. You are like two hens pecking at me. Antonio, stay down here with your brother." He looked at Marcello, who was stock-still, like he was afraid to speak. "You, too, my son. Go and finish the celebration. I'll see you soon."

Antonio ground his jaw, his instincts firing off as he watched his grandmother Martha. She was not meeting his eyes. "I'll see you both soon." She finally glanced at him, nodding and turning to help Nonna to the truck. He put Giuseppe in after her.

He turned to see Sophie beside him. "You think something is wrong, don't you?" she said as she watched the truck drive toward the house. Worry etched the lines of her pretty face. She had grape juice in her hair.

"You should go get cleaned up before the fruit flies think to make you a meal," Antonio said. But then something caught his attention. His father was talking to someone. A woman. The floor dropped out of his stomach. It was her. It had been ten years, but he knew her. Catarina and Sophie's eyes followed his.

Catarina asked, "Antonio, what is wrong? Why are you looking at Papa like that?" But before she could figure it out, he was walking toward them with purpose. His father's brow creased as Antonio butted into their conversation.

"You have a lot of nerve having her here. Especially with Grandmother visiting." The woman's eyes seemed to take in his features, but his words drew her up short.

Marcello said, "Antonio, you are being unforgivably rude. This is Rosina. She's a friend of this family."

"I know exactly who she is, in case you've forgotten," Antonio said bitterly.

Catarina took him by the arm. "Stop it, Antonio. You are wrong about this. Just leave it alone before you open up something you can't close again!" She hissed the words.

He looked at her, suddenly angry. "You would defend these two? After what Mother told you?"

"What Mother told me was bullshit. Pardon my frankness, Rosina. But it is, Antonio. You don't know what you are talking about."

"I have done nothing to this family to deserve such treatment. I remember you, Antonio. It's been a long time, but I remember you. You have the look of your mama." She tried to soften her words. To soften him.

"Don't speak of my mother," he said. "If it weren't for the two of you carrying on under her nose, she'd probably still be alive."

"Antonio! Basta!" Marcello was angry now. "I'm sorry, Rosina," he muttered.

But the woman's eyes were tearing up. "Is that what you think? That your father and I were ... lovers? You can't be serious!" She looked at Marcello. "Why would he think this? Does anyone else believe this nonsense?" Marcello's jaw was tight. "Explain, Marcello! Why would anyone think such a thing?"

"I saw the two of you! He was holding you!" Antonio said.

Catarina stood in front of him. "You are wrong, Antonio. Now let's go check on Nonno."

But they were beyond salvaging the situation. This collision would happen. Marcello's words were quiet but clipped with anger. "You saw nothing! You saw a friend comforting another friend. I've known this woman since we were in diapers."

Something flickered in the woman's face. Realization and understanding. "You think we were lovers because of that night I was crying in the garden?"

"Tell him." They turned around in unison to see Martha standing there. "Nonna forgot her bag. It has Giuseppe's pills in it. He is resting. Why don't we all go up to the house? The tour group is leaving." They were indeed leaving. Marco was walking them to the car park. She looked at Marcello and said, "You can't protect them from this anymore. It's time, Marcello."

Sophie said, "I'll clean up here. I'll wash the glasses and lock up the buildings. Go, Antonio. This is family business. Tell Marco I've got this. This is intern work." She got in front of Antonio. "Take a breath, Antonio. Please just let go of this anger, for Nonna and Nonno. Let your family talk this out and then go check on him." She squeezed his biceps. "I'll see you tonight."

❧

ANTONIO WATCHED HIS GRANDMOTHER MAKE A POT OF TEA AND he wanted to start screaming. He checked on his grandfather, but he and Nonna were curled up together, taking a nap. He didn't have the heart to wake either of them. Especially given the ugliness that was getting ready to go down.

Martha came into the parlor carrying a tea tray. He shook his head quickly, not wanting tea. Not wanting the civility of it all. She put the tray down on the table and said, "Sit, Antonio. Everyone needs to be seated before we have this conversation. It's long overdue."

Antonio had always been a good boy. Obedient to a fault. He sat, and he noticed with some distress that his sister was pale. Too pale. He took her hand. She whispered, "Why couldn't you leave it alone?"

Martha said, "Marcello has been too loyal, too much of a good man to tell you the whole of it. Of what happened with your mother. Not just the day she died, but from the beginning. So, I suppose I must."

Marcello said, "This isn't necessary, Martha. Please, I beg you. Let them have their ..."

Martha gave a distinctively British snort. "Their what, Marcello? Their delusion? And at what cost? You'd rather have your son think you were a philanderer than to hear the truth about their mother, who has been dead for ten years? Well, I won't have it. She was my daughter, and I loved her above all else, but she would not want this."

Antonio bristled. He spoke in Italian, as she'd understand. And he wanted to make damn sure that his father's mistress understood every word as well. "I know what I saw, Grandmother. And I know what my mother told me." He pointed and shouted, "These two were having an affair! He and Mama fought the day she died. Over HER!"

Rosina's face blanched. "You're wrong, Antonio. Your father and I are distant cousins and childhood friends. He's like a brother to me. Why would your mother say such a thing?"

Antonio jerked, as if she'd hit him. *Cousins?* Like a blow to the head, it left him reeling. Although, distant cousins could marry in Italy. In many cultures, actually. Suddenly, he remembered his father's words, claiming that he'd been faithful to his wife until the day she died. He put his head in his hands, suddenly feeling sick. His brother broke the silence. Marco said, "I don't understand any of this, Papa. Why does Antonio think you were unfaithful to our mama?" And he sounded so young just then. So much younger than his years.

Martha answered, "Your mother was unwell. Surely you could see that, Antonio. You are a doctor. You were a grown man when she died. And I don't mean physically unwell. Your mother had mental difficulties. She refused to seek treatment as a young woman, but when she had Marco, we convinced her to be medicated and see a therapist." She cleared her throat.

Catarina said, "Mama told me the same thing, Antonio. But I knew things you didn't. Things I wish I didn't know. And I knew she was lying. At least, I thought she was at the time. I think it was deeper than that, though. I think she may have been delusional. You didn't live with us while you were in medical school, but I saw the deterioration."

Finally, Marcello sighed and said, "She stopped taking her

medication, and a degree of paranoia had always been part of her mental problems. Not always, but when she was off her meds, certainly. Then she renewed an old acquaintance, from before we were married. He was Rosina's husband." Antonio watched a shudder go through the woman. "When you saw us in the garden, Rosina was upset. Her husband wasn't a good man. He tried to rekindle a relationship with your mother, and I truly believe she rebuffed his attempts to seduce her again. But there was a small part of her that thought she was still in love with him. A sort of hold he had on her. He'd bother her from time to time, but with her off her medications, she was more susceptible to his mind games."

Rosina spoke then. "He strung your mother along while we were engaged. He could be very charismatic, and your mother was very young. Too young and barely out of the schoolroom." Her words were painful. "I'm sorry for it. She suffered disappointment because our families had arranged our marriage. Matteo and I got along very well, actually. I was happy about the match. I thought he was happy as well. But he was having a relationship with Margarite almost the entire time leading up to the wedding. Margarite was devastated to find out that he would go through with the marriage. She confronted me. I'm afraid I wasn't very kind to her. Our families knew each other, and we came to a sort of peace later, thanks to Marcello. But when I first discovered the deception, I said some unkind things. I blamed her, even though it was he who was to blame. It's a small community, and the gossip would shame both our families. Then she was marrying your father soon after, and I let the matter rest. I did what was expected of me." She gave a small shrug. "She wasn't his last indiscretion, but he never forgot her. He was obsessed with her. He hated your father."

Antonio looked at his father and asked, "Why did you marry her so quickly?"

He blushed. "We'd been seeing each other for about a month. I didn't know about Matteo until right before the wedding. It was over by then. It hurt me, but I loved her. I like to think she loved me a little as well. And after we were married, she grew to love me. We were happy." He looked at all of his children. "We were happy. I know you remember this. She loved me!" He put a fist to his chest. "A man knows this. He feels it. He sees it in his lover's eyes. Your mother and I were happy." He started to tear up, and Catarina pulled away from Antonio to go to him. She hugged him, and for once, he just sank into the comfort. He'd been strong for so long, held these secrets for so long, it was like he'd just worn himself out.

Marco's voice was hoarse. "I remember when it changed. She was different. She cried a lot. I mean, she'd always had her down-times. Times when she'd stay in bed or be extra emotional. Especially when she was pregnant with these two." He motioned to his siblings.

Martha spoke then. "She had to alter her medication during her pregnancies. The safer medication wasn't as effective. She had side effects. It wasn't until Catarina was about fifteen that she went off them completely. Against her doctor's orders, of course."

Marcello said, "Matteo was coming around again, when I was traveling. He told her that I was trying to control her with the medication. That there was nothing wrong with her other than unhappiness. That's when she went off of them. She started having spells about a week later. Bad bouts of depression, and she would rant. She was paranoid and accused me of cheating. Maybe he told her that I was bedding his wife so she'd be easier to prey upon. But I never did, Antonio. I never even looked at other women. I loved your mother."

Catarina said, "I remember. And I remember the man coming to the house. I was hiding in the big turkey oak. I heard them talking."

Marcello blanched and said, "She wasn't herself, my sweet girl. Please, don't dwell on it. Whatever you heard, just forget about it."

STACEY REYNOLDS

Antonio asked, "What did you hear? I mean, that's what this is about, right? No more secrets?" And as soon as Antonio said the words, he regretted it. His sister's face crumpled, and her father pulled her to him.

"What is this, little duck?" Marcello crooned. "It can't be that bad. Antonio, we don't need—"

"She had his child! Me! She had me and I was his child!" She began to sob and Antonio jumped out of his seat.

"No! She wouldn't do that," Antonio said. "Did she say this or did he?"

She wiped her eyes and said, "He did, but does it matter? Obviously, they'd been together. He thought I was his. It must have still been going on for over a decade!"

Marcello said, "You are my daughter, Catarina. I don't know how the hell you came to think otherwise, but your mother and I planned her pregnancy. We went to Venice on a long weekend. I know exactly when you were conceived. Pardon me, everyone. This is so private, but I will not have you believing you were another man's child. And even if you were, it wouldn't have mattered. I love all of my children equally. And if I'd adopted you, I would still love you the same. But I know when we made you. And she was not unfaithful. You were a conscious choice, even though your brothers were much older. We wanted you. Do you understand?"

A niggling fear crept up Antonio's spine. A quick marriage. She had been seeing this Matteo man and his father at the same time. Jesus. He wasn't going to say it. No fucking way. But then Marco made a noise deep in his throat. A tight sort of ticking. Marco said, "Because you weren't the child he was talking about. That's right, isn't it father?"

The look of betrayal on Marco's face was something that would haunt Antonio until he died. He had done this. He'd pushed, even though everyone had warned him. Marco continued. "Isn't that right, Father? Grandmother? Because this Matteo person broke it

194

off abruptly, and our mother hurried to marry another man. She was pregnant, and he turned her away."

Marcello stood and walked to him. He sat next to him and took his hand in his. "You are my son. You are all my children. All three of you."

"It's a simple question, Papa. Was my mother pregnant when you married her? And don't lie to me. You said I came early, but that was a lie. Don't lie to me again." Marco's words were bitter, and Antonio wasn't sure who he was angrier with—Margarite, Marcello, or this Matteo, who had ruined all their lives.

"I can't answer that because I don't know if she was pregnant right before or after the wedding. Your mother and I"—he rubbed his upper lip, blushing scarlet—"we were together before we were married. Afterward, I insisted we marry. I loved her. I'd been infatuated with her for years. She was so alive and beautiful. And we'd been seeing each other for a month. I felt like the luckiest man in the world once I really got to know her. She was smart and funny. When we lost our heads to passion one night, I insisted we marry. I wanted to marry her, though. It wasn't out of duty, but because I truly wanted her to be my wife. And she said yes. She seemed genuinely happy to marry me. I don't question anything other than that." He met each of their eyes.

"We had many good years together and three beautiful children. The last year was difficult, and I blame myself for letting her leave in that car after our argument. I knew she was feeling reckless. I should have stopped her. I'm so sorry I didn't stop her." His voice broke. "You lost your mother and it was my fault." He turned to Antonio. "When you blamed me, it was for the wrong reasons, but I knew you were right. I was responsible. She wasn't capable of taking good care of herself. It was my job to protect her, even if it was from herself."

But Marco wasn't to be distracted by this confession. "Why did she make you promise to pass the vineyard to me? Was she afraid you'd cast me out if she died? Because I wasn't your real son?"

"Basta, Marco! You are my son. You are named for your father. Marcello Antonio Rinalto, my son!" He gave Marco's hands a squeeze and said the words with such confidence, as if forcing everyone in that room to believe him.

Marco said sadly, "But you don't really know, do you? You don't seem the sort of man to seduce a young woman, Papa. It was she who seduced you. She knew she was pregnant, and she wanted to pin it on another man, to pass me off as yours."

Martha interrupted. "That's enough of that. The truth is, there's a small chance that the idiot formerly known as Matteo is your sire. But I was there at her doctor appointments. I saw her ultrasounds. I knew her due date. You did come early. And she conceived the same month your parents were married. Short of a paternity test on a dead man, we will never know."

Marco said, "But we could test. We could test myself and Father."

Marcello's body tensed. "I will not agree to that. Never. It doesn't matter. You are mine, Marco. My first, beloved child. I loved you from the moment I felt you move inside your mother's belly. You made us a family." He pulled Marco to him, and they both wept. Everyone did.

Then Catarina said weakly, "I think I was afraid the reason you didn't let me run the vineyard was because I wasn't yours." She seemed to be coming out of a horrible dream, confused and a little relieved. "I wouldn't even admit it to myself, but I think that was my fear. And I'm so sorry I took us down this road. I'm sorry I've made Marco question all of this. I'm so sorry."

Marcello pulled her to him, joining their hands, and pressed a kiss to her forehead. She and Marco looked at each other, and Marco said to his father, "You need to release yourself from that promise you made to her. As do I. You should let Catarina run the vineyard, Papa. She was born to do this. I don't know what I was supposed to do with my life, but so far, I feel like I haven't done it. I think I should start preparing her to take over and then

I will just ... help. I'll help on the business end until I figure it out."

Antonio watched the exchange and suddenly felt like a stranger. He also felt like a villain. At one time, he'd loved his father so much. Worshipped him. Then it all came crashing down because of a few careless words from his mother. And a misunderstanding that had been completely innocent. "I should go." His voice was hoarse with shame. "I'll go. I'm sorry ... for everything. I'm sorry I hurt you, all of you." Antonio stood. "And I am so sorry to you, Rosina. I was unforgivably cruel to you."

She stood, taking his face in her hands. Rosina had tears in her eyes. "Matteo was a cruel man. Once the polish wore off, he was not so charismatic. He was a monster. He wanted my family's money. The night I found out about your mother, I tried to end the engagement." Her voice was weak as she continued. "He forced himself on me." She looked at Marcello, who gasped with shock. Martha covered her mouth. "I'm not completely sure, but that may have happened with Margarite as well. But she was young, and he'd convinced her she'd wanted him. That she'd teased him. And he had a way of making you believe things. She didn't know anything of real love until your father took her into his home and loved her."

Then Rosina faced Marco and knelt in front of him. "He never gave me a child. I had myself checked. There's nothing wrong with me that they could find. I believe I was fertile. He still blamed me, but I think it was he who was infertile." She put her hands on his shoulders and kissed his cheek. "Matteo was a cruel, heartless man, and I see nothing of him in you." Rosina turned his body toward Marcello. "This is your father. Your true and only papa. Don't you ever doubt it." She spun around and reached for Antonio's hand. "Come, Antonio. Come and hold your family. You've been apart for too long."

He went, and when he knelt down to take Rosina's place on the floor, he choked on his grief. The lost years where he'd hated his father for no good reason had all been a terrible mistake. He should

STACEY REYNOLDS

have believed in his father. He should have helped his mama. He should have seen she was having problems. He'd ruined everything. "Papa," he croaked. "Oh, God. Papa, please forgive me."

⚜

ANTONIO TURNED TO LEAVE THE HOUSE AND HIS GRANDMOTHER stopped him. "I loved your mother. She was my only child. I tried to help her. So did your grandfather. But her true salvation was Marcello and then you three children. She was happy. She wasn't ever completely stable, but she loved you all, including your father. I hope you find comfort in that." She kissed his face. "Go to bed, love. Or go see that woman of yours. I'll check in on Giuseppe. He's going to be fine."

"She's not my woman, Grandmother."

"Well, she should be. Jesus, Antonio. When I met your grandfather, I set out to have him or die trying. You make everything too difficult."

⚜

SOPHIE WASN'T IN THE POOL HOUSE, AND ANTONIO HATED THAT she was still working. How long had they all been talking? An hour? It seemed a lot longer than that. The workers had all gone, but he saw her hauling the juice from the ceremony in large jugs into the processing building. Suddenly, he couldn't get to her fast enough. He doubled his pace, coming into the building just as she put the jug on one of the tables. She was a mess, wearing Wellingtons and shorts, grape juice and skins sloshed all over her legs and down her front. She stopped short, taking in his face.

She said, "Oh, Antonio. You are in such pain. Tell me what to do."

He crossed the room in two steps, pulling her to him. She was small and soft, curving into his body. She let out a little sigh into his

198

mouth as he kissed her. Suddenly, his hands were everywhere. Stroking, kneading, pulling. She actually climbed him, her legs going around his waist as she took his tongue into her mouth. He pressed his hands under her ass, fitting her snug against his cock. She broke the kiss and made a sound that had him ready to rip her clothes off. He backed her to a table, not caring that it was spattered with grapes and sticky residue. Then he was over her, pinning her hands to the table. She was warm and sticky, and her hair was tangled on both their faces. It was perfect. He moaned as he ground his hips against her. "Il mia," he whispered.

She murmured soothing words to him, the emotion behind them sinking into his skin. "I'm here, Antonio." The desperation gave way to soulful, languorous kisses. The kind that made a man want to weep. He let her wrists go, moving his hands to either side of her face. Resting on his elbows so he could take his time. She was sweet and soft as she rose to meet his mouth. She slid his shirt up and over, and he did the same, their warm chests coming together. She made little noises as he buried his face in her neck. "I need you," he said against her neck. "Not as a distraction. I need YOU. Please, tell me if you don't want this."

She cupped his head through his dark mane. "I need you, too. Desperately, Antonio. I want to be close to you." He kissed along her jawline.

"Thank God," he said in a rush, and her tummy rumbled with laughter. He smoothed his hands over her body, nipping and tasting her collarbones, her chest, and the soft skin just at the swell of her breast. "You are covered in sweetness, but I need more." He started to work the fly of her shorts and her breathing sped up. He took her mouth as she moaned because he slid his hand inside her panties without preamble. Right into her silky heat. "Look at me, Sophie. Look at me while I touch you. Let me see those beautiful eyes."

She met the strokes of his hand with her hips, starting to come against his hand. "Antonio, I can't ..."

"Don't wait, amore. Show me. Let me watch you." That did it. She cried out as he expertly circled the pad of his finger right where she needed him, gliding along her slick sex. He stayed with her, until she was limp and dazed. Then he slid first her boots and then her shorts off. She bowed off the table as he put his mouth where his hand had been. "Ancora. I want more, Sophie. Again." He slid his hands up the backs of her sticky thighs, resting her feet on his shoulders as she threaded both hands in his hair. When she started the second climax, she moved her hips at her own rhythm, sliding her sex on his tongue. He wanted to sink himself into her, right here. Maybe flip her over and fuck her hard from behind, but he managed to remember where they were. Almost. He would have this first. Have her taste on his lips as she came. He clamped his hands on both thighs as he spread her wide, sucking hard as she shattered into a thousand pieces.

Sophie was completely undone as Antonio slipped his tongue along her sex. His thick, silky hair was in her hands and on her spread thighs and belly. She felt the tightening in her womb just as he drew a long, intense pull on her sex. Like he was drinking her in. She could feel the rush of moisture and heat release as she started to contract. She could hear her own moans but she couldn't control herself. She looked down just as he moaned against her flesh. His gaze was hot and demanding, and she flew apart in a white, hot explosion.

She looked half dead when he rose to his feet. She watched as he rubbed a thumb at the bottom of his lip, then drew it into his mouth to savor what had happened. He looked devilish, and she was having a hard time remembering why she'd had reservations about this. Whatever the outcome, she wasn't going to regret this for a second.

Antonio pulled her off the table, sliding his shirt over her head. "This one is clean, at least. I'll meet you in the house. I'll be right behind you." He brushed his knuckles over her face, then he slid his hand in her hair, cupping the back of her head. He leaned down and said, "If you'll have me, I want to be inside you, Sophie. I'm insane with the need for it. Will you take me inside you?"

"I will," she said without hesitation.

Sophie slid her boots on and made her way up to the back entrance of the pool house without being seen. Her legs were trembling, making her steps jerky and unsure. Her body was on fire. She stripped and was in the shower in under a minute, not waiting for it to warm up. Her nipples pebbled under the cool spray, and a thrill shot through her as she heard him come inside the house.

Then he was opening the shower door, joining her just in time for the warm water. Antonio lavished attention on her, soaping a body sponge and washing her limbs, her breasts, her back, and ass. All while he stopped for kisses. Sophie would likely live to regret this. They would both regret it when they separated, but she'd be a fool to turn away from this sort of passion. Something she'd never felt with anyone.

Antonio wrapped her in a towel, and that's when she got a good look at him. He was well muscled. Long-boned and beautiful. He had a dusting of dark hair over his chest and legs. His thick sex was hard and ready, reaching for her. "You're magnificent, Antonio." She feathered touches over his chest and shoulders, getting to know the feel of him. He let her have her way, tensing as she came nearer to his arousal.

His voice was hoarse and thick with the stress of his restraint. "If you touch that, it's going to go off like a cannon, Sophie. It's been a long time."

She cocked her head, believing him, but at the same time, baffled at the idea of all this man sitting idle and unexplored. Sophie said, "It's been even longer for me, I'd wager."

Antonio touched his mouth softly to hers, murmuring something in Italian she wasn't following. His accent was thick with desire. He lifted her, taking her out of the bathroom and into her bedroom. When he laid her on the bed, he opened her towel. He swayed as he closed his eyes. She was pink from the warm water and swollen from his attentions. He hovered above her. "Like a Botticelli. Perfect breasts with pink tips. Fair skin. Miles of soft, wavy hair." He kissed her between her breasts. "You are so beautiful, Sophie." Antonio reacquainted himself with the feel of her. With his hands and his mouth. His lazy kisses and sumptuous licks. Her body trembled and rolled against his mouth, her hips rocking. He felt her sex tighten around his fingers. He came up fast, fitting the ridge of his cock against her, then he rolled a condom over himself. She wrapped her hand around him and guided him there, answering the doubts she saw in his eyes.

"Come to me, Antonio. I need you."

He took his time, not wanting to hurt her. But his golden-brown eyes never left her. "Il mia. Il mia," Antonio whispered as he pushed farther into her. Then when he couldn't control himself anymore, he gathered her hips in one arm and thrust until their bodies fused. Sophie closed her eyes at the invasion, gasping for breath. He was big, and she tried to adjust around him. He held her there, seated deep in her body. She knew he wouldn't move until she opened her eyes. Until she was ready.

Antonio was ready to come. Sophie was so tight, and he was trying not to hurt her. Her hips were off the mattress, and as he looked between them, her nipples grazed his chest. Her harsh breathing made her body pull at him. Then she opened her eyes. Her blue-green gaze and her flushed mouth. Sophie was the picture of female arousal. He pulled back, then thrust slowly into her. Her hips jerked against him as she whimpered. He slid his hand down over her ass and farther, feeling the slick desire where they were joined. How he stretched her, taut and swollen around him. He filled her, over and over again, until her breathing stuttered.

He knew he was speaking nonsense, but the words poured out of him like a lovesick fool. He sensed just when she started to slip over the edge. Antonio thrust harder, deeper, and faster until he felt her surrender. "Look at me, Sophie. Show me." He could hear their bodies slapping together as he pulled her harder against him, seeking a place so deep that she'd be marked as his forever. "I feel you. I feel it starting. You are pulsing around my cock." His words undid her. She arched and cried out, gripping him so hard, he thought he'd die from the joining. He came hard. It seemed to go on and on as he watched her climax. Felt his own orgasm surge up to the surface to meet her, ripping through him like a tidal wave.

Sophie couldn't move. Antonio was poised on his elbows, trying not to squash her. But it didn't matter. She was completely ruined. He was breathing against her neck. Then he was kissing her—her eyes, her cheeks, her chin, her mouth. He pulled out of her, and she missed the strong presence of him. He was still hard as he slid the condom off and put it in the bin next to the bed. Then the kisses started all over again.

ANTONIO MADE HER STAY IN BED. SHE HEARD HIM IN THE kitchen, putting together a lovers' feast. When he returned, it was with a carafe of the loose wine, two glasses, and a platter of meats, cheeses, marinated artichokes, olives, and a loaf of crusty bread. "To get your strength back," he said with a devilish grin. He was utterly comfortable in his nakedness. They nibbled and fed each other, then she saw his cock stirring. He was trying to ignore it, talking with her about the olive harvest. At least until she moved the tray to the nightstand and kissed him.

He took her hips, ready to flip her, but Sophie pinned his hands with hers. He groaned as she grasped his mouth. Then, while never breaking eye contact, she kissed her way down his body. His cock was at full salute now, and he bowed off the bed when she took him in her mouth. Antonio let her have her way for a bit, greedily observing as she pleasured him, pulling her hair up and off her face so he could watch her, unobstructed. But he couldn't keep it up. He wanted to feel himself inside her. In one swift motion, he pulled her astride him. He let her ride the ridge of him while he slipped another condom on himself. Then he guided her down where she wanted to be.

Sophie ran her fingers through his thick, silky hair, kissing him with gentle thoroughness that was uniquely womanly. The kind that could bring him to his knees if he hadn't already been beneath her. He was at her mercy, his eyes glazed over as she made love to him. He gripped her close, his ear coming to rest just at her heartbeat, and he let go, shaking and trembling against her.

❧ 15 ❧

*"Every season hath its pleasure; Spring may boast her flowery
prime, Yet the vineyard's ruby treasuries Brighten Autumn's
sob'rer time."* — *Thomas Moore*

"I have to get up and go to work. The picking starts in earnest
this morning." Sophie was curled into Antonio like a kitten,
breathing in the smell of his skin with her lips just at his
pulse. He rumbled with suppressed laughter against her ear.
"What's so amusing?" she asked.

"You sound like such a proper Englishwoman. But you are a
scandalous vixen in bed." Antonio kissed her pursed mouth, taking
a thumb and pressing it along the crease between her brows. "You
don't like being a vixen?"

"I just don't think I've ever been considered one," she said with
a begrudging smile. "Not that I've slept around much, but still."

"I'm glad no one else knows, and that you saved all of that pent-
up woman for me." Antonio paused, treading carefully but too
curious to stay silent. "You said it had been much longer for you.
How long?" he asked, not sure why he even wanted to know.

"Somewhere around eight years, give or take a month." Sophie shrugged.

Antonio stilled against her. When she tried to get up, he noticed she was blushing. He pulled her down so he could see her face. He cupped the back of her head, threading a hand in her hair. He searched her face for something, then said simply, "Thank you, Sophie. Last night was beautiful. And it was a gift because you obviously don't give yourself lightly."

"I don't, that's true. And it seems, neither do you," she said.

"Don't paint me in such an innocent light. I came at you like a barbarian last night." His cock stirred at the thought of her on that table. Grape juice coating her skin. Her arousal coating his tongue. He could tell she was thinking about it as well, her cheeks flushed with some sort of emotion. He cleared his throat and said, "It's true. I've been without companionship for a couple years. But I wasn't always so noble. I had my wild oats to sow. That's what you call it, right?"

Sophie smiled. "Yes, sowing your wild oats. Now, you've kept me long enough. I can't lie around all day, enjoying your charms. I am a lowly intern, after all."

The sun was just cresting the horizon, and Antonio suddenly felt guilty for the shadows under her eyes. He'd had her four times throughout the night. She had to be tired ... and sore.

"Let me run a bath for you. It's the least I can do, given the night we had. I hope you aren't too tender?"

"Don't worry, love. Some things are worth the discomfort. A bath would be wasted on me as I don't have time to linger over it. I'll have a quick shower and be off. Do come down and help. But first ... maybe check on your grandfather? I'm anxious for word."

His face stiffened. Yes, that was just what he had planned. His family had a lot of explaining to do.

Antonio came into the kitchen just as his grandfather was starting his breakfast. His nonna was busy washing dishes. He looked at what she'd prepared and frowned. "What are you eating?"

It was Martha who answered. "You don't recognize porridge when you see it?"

"I don't think I've ever seen oatmeal in this house," Antonio said.

His grandfather was pretending, and failing, to enjoy it. Bananas, oatmeal, and some sort of tea. He picked up the cup, sniffing it. Ginger tea? The clinically bland diet raised a red flag.

"Is it nausea or loose bowels?" Antonio asked.

His grandfather put his spoon down with a clang. "This is not table talk."

"We are beyond niceties. Tell me, Nonno. You called for me to come home because you were ill. You let me believe it was a ruse to get me here. But you are ill, aren't you?"

Their collective faces caused the floor to go wavy. He sat just as his grandmother did. "Please, tell me."

Catarina and Marcello came in just as he asked. His eyes were grave, and they stopped in their tracks. "What is this?" Marcello asked.

At the same time, Catarina asked, "Tell you what?" She said this just as Marco came into the kitchen. Apparently, no one knew. Well, wasn't this going to be a party.

They all sat, then, looking at Giuseppe and then at Martha. They wanted the answers, and at the same time, they didn't. "You have him on a bland diet. Is it cancer? He's not doing chemo. He doesn't ever leave the property. What is it, Martha? Nonno? We are all here. You are keeping something from everyone."

His brother spoke then. "He did go somewhere. While you were in Florence."

Antonio digested this news, jaw working. "But you haven't been back. So, it's oral medications, not an IV." He looked at his grandmother. She just nodded. Then he glanced at his father. Marcello

Rinalto was one of the strongest men he'd ever known. Yet he trembled. Antonio peered at Catarina, who was also staring not at Giuseppe, but at their father. Giuseppe got up from his chair and walked to his son. "Don't worry, my Marcello. This is why I didn't want you to know. I didn't want to worry you."

"Papa," he croaked. And that's when Catarina lost the reins on her emotions. Nonna held her, and she wept. But Antonio couldn't take his eyes off his father. He sounded like a small boy. A son, not a father. A child who needed his papa. His eyes pricked with tears and he looked at his brother, then back at his father. Jesus. Not now. He'd just come home. He couldn't lose one of them.

It took a while for everyone to settle, but they did. Nonna seemed to be at peace, now holding Giuseppe's hand. Giuseppe said, "It's in the lung."

Marco said, "You have never smoked. Not even a cigar or pipe. This can't be."

Antonio said, "There are other types of lung cancer. Other causes." His voice was strained with the effort of not weeping.

Martha was trying to put on a brave face, raising her chin. "When your grandfather was a young lad, he worked on a large farm for extra money. They used some pesticides that were very toxic. Specifically in the orchards and olive groves. These are chemicals that are now banned in Europe. The way he's told it to me, he'd be covered in the stuff and would have to go change clothes partway through the day. They didn't wear any protective equipment back then, other than a scarf over their mouth and nose and maybe a hat. We are talking about almost sixty years ago. It's very possible that this long-term exposure is the culprit. Cancer statistics are lower in this part of the world. He has a good diet and is very strong for his age. I know this is a blow, but we are hopeful. He is getting treatment."

"Any lymph node involvement?" Antonio asked, retreating to doctor mode in order to protect himself from a complete meltdown.

Martha said, "We don't think so. They biopsied three, which are closest to the tumor. It is a single tumor in the upper part of his right lung. The lymph node biopsy is a precaution, and we are waiting on the results. If there is involvement, they caught it early. This round of chemo will likely cause him some intestinal discomfort. Perhaps some other difficulties. He may be a bit weaker. I can stay to help. I know you won't be here long, Antonio."

"I will be here as long as I'm needed," he said with absolute certainty. "Is surgery an option?"

"Perhaps, once they shrink the tumor. He'll also start radiation at the local hospital. The concern is his age. It's an intrusive procedure, and the chemo will weaken him. We just have to wait and see how he responds. He's physically more like a sixty-year-old man than an eighty-year-old. Good genes and all that. His prognosis is good," she said, looking them all in the eye. And they believed her. Still, Marcello was destroyed.

Giuseppe took his son's face in his hands and kissed both cheeks. "Do not weep for me. I'm not going anywhere."

Antonio saw Giuseppe settled in his bed, insisting he save his strength. "If you are feeling better in a couple of hours, and you've kept your breakfast down, then one of us will be up to get you. For now, humor your family and rest a bit more." He sat for a few minutes, watching the steady rise and fall of his chest. Someday he'd lose his father. Nonna and Martha. Someday he'd lose Reverend Mother Faith, who was like another parent to him. He wasn't ready. He was fortunate, at his age, to have living grandparents. He knew this. But he wasn't ready to lose any of them.

ANTONIO WALKED DOWN TO THE AREA OF THE VINEYARD WHERE they were harvesting the first Sangiovese grapes. His family preferred to pick them by hand. The workers were efficient, and he laughed when he saw his brother. "Are those cutoff track pants? You?"

Marco smiled. "You don't think I'm going to wear my designer clothing, do you? Pick up a scalpel and get to work, Dottore."

Antonio selected a hooked harvest knife and grinned. "Was that a joke, Marco?" He gave a tsk-tsk. "Raggedy clothes, goofing off. Next, you'll be womanizing."

"I'll leave the Cassanova work to you, brother," he said as he motioned down the row of vines. Sophie was working hard, her bin almost full. "I hope you don't mind. I told her about Nonno. She asked."

Antonio shook his head. "Of course not. Bad news is bad news, no matter who tells it."

"You really like her, don't you?" Marco's voice held not one trace of bitterness. "She's a good person. Pretty, too. And everyone loves her."

"She is a wonderful person. But our lives ..." He shook his head. "They pull us in two very different directions."

Marco gave him a dry look. "Whatever you say, Antonio. Just don't let Nonna see you two making eyes at each other. You are staying in the same little house. Nonna will call a priest by sunset."

"Nonna isn't as clueless as you two think," Catarina said from behind them. "She didn't bat an eye at the sleeping arrangements. Just be careful, Antonio. Sophie has been through a lot. Speaking of which, we have a good rotation scheduled to patrol the property. It's on the desk inside the processing building."

Antonio went to examine the schedule, letting the harvest wait a moment. He was still surprised when he noticed the new equipment. Catarina saw his eyes comb over the setup. She said, "We still harvest by hand. Still have the old tractors because Nonno refuses to use the new sort with the computers. But I took him and Papa to one of the neighboring vineyards and showed them the machine that removes all of the stems. I still believe in sorting the berries by hand, but I had them install that conveyor. It's much faster, and the workers love the improvements." They walked out of the room and into the maceration vats, where the fermentation started. The juice from yesterday was already fermenting in a stainless-steel vat, making the sfuso. There were empty, French oak barrels waiting to be filled with the better wine and separated into the regular Chianti Classico and Riserva. One group would be aged for twelve to eighteen months, the other for two years.

Antonio said, "Marco was right. You were born to do this, Catarina. I'm proud of my baby sister."

"I'm proud of your baby sister as well," she said, nudging him. "Now, here is the schedule. You're on for tonight, so take a nap today. You look like you've been up all night." She eyed him from the side. "So does Sophie. Don't break my intern, Antonio."

"Hush, now. You aren't supposed to talk like that. You are my little duck," he said.

"Not so little anymore," Catarina replied. "And I wish someone looked at me the way that you look at her. It's not a fling, I think. You really care for her, don't you?" Antonio stayed silent. She sighed. "Make it work, Antonio. Haven't you learned anything from all of this misery? Take your happiness when you can get it and hold it close. With both hands! Papa has been alone for ten years because he feels guilty. But this wasn't his fault. It wasn't anyone's fault. I used to blame Mama." She swallowed hard, her voice shaking. "It was wrong of me. She was ill in a way that maybe a child couldn't understand. I didn't know everything. But I get it, now. It was a stupid, careless accident that happened to a woman who just felt things more intensely. When she was happy," she said with a smile and closed her eyes, as if picturing her mother in front of her. "When she was happy, she was amazing to be around. She glowed so brightly. She showed her love to her family and made the whole world seem magical. Do you remember those times?"

Antonio's throat was working, trying to fight the tears that always tried to come when he thought about his mother. He laughed with a hitch deep in his throat. "Yes, I remember."

"I think that's how Papa remembers her. And she did love him. I know that. It may not have been the traditional sort of love, but Papa is one of those men whom you can't help but love. She may have married him for different reasons, but she fell in love with him. She didn't stand a chance. He's like Nonno. And he's like you."

Antonio finally let a tear escape. The thought of losing his nonno made his chest crack open. He said, "I can't lose anyone. I wasted so much time. I can't lose Nonno."

Catarina said nothing. Probably because she felt the same way. That perhaps they were downplaying the illness for the family. What would they do without Giuseppe?

❧ 16 ❧

The harvesting continued throughout the week, and Sophie soaked in the experience with the fervor of a new recruit. She'd taken part in the harvest process at the college, but it really couldn't compare to life at Viti del Fiume. Generations of Rinaltos had worked this land, analyzing each portion of the vineyard as the grapes became ready to pick. The local Colorino and Canaiolo Nero, and the French Cabernet Sauvignon and Merlot grapes, each ripened a bit differently. The real magic was when the Sangiovese grapes were picked. The lifeblood of Chianti Classico, and the rock on which this vineyard was built. Their Chianti Classico Riserva was purely a blend of their best Sangiovese yield. Some old vines that went back generations while others were from newer plants. After the harvest and processing of the new wine, there would be the blending from the wine that had been aging in the barrels for two years. They would be picking and choosing the perfect combination of grapes that would make or break their reputation.

They'd begun analyzing this year's fruit in mid-September. And as they got closer, they began testing the Ph, the acidity, and the weightiness of the berries.

They tasted the berries, Marcello explaining to her what they were looking for in the fruit. The smile on his face the day the grapes were ready was priceless. Sophie loved this place and this family. And she admired them for how much they loved what they did.

Antonio was an ever-present distraction. He was there daily, working with the family to refresh his memory and to learn the new equipment. He was a doctor first, and had volunteered at a vaccination clinic in town a few days earlier, but he was making his way back to this place. Reconnecting with his father in a way that warmed her heart. It made her miss her own father. Giuseppe was doing better. They'd managed the nausea, and he came out a couple hours a day to supervise and to charm the tourists with his wine-tasting lectures. These three generations of Rinalto men were quite something, and she hoped with all her heart that they continued these traditions. Sophie turned to Catarina, who was putting a large basket of grapes into the destemming machine. "Are you seeing anyone, Catarina?"

Catarina stopped and asked, "What brings this on? Why do you ask?"

Sophie looked over the vineyard, thinking for a moment about how she wanted to answer. "Someone has to continue this, Catarina. It's too special to let it die out. It sounds old fashioned, I know, but I see this place and three generations of Rinaltos. None of you are married. No children. I know you're still young, but I'd like to think that someday you'll be showing your sons and daughters how to run this place. That Marco will find love again and bring his children up around here."

"And what about Antonio?" Catarina asked with a smirk.

The words stuck in Sophie's throat, but she said, "He's through the hardest part. He came home. And I think with some of these old hurts put to rest, he'll open his heart to someone. Maybe some

Brazilian doctor will earn his love, and he'll bring his children here to visit."

"A Brazilian doctor? That's not who I had in mind." Catarina gave her a side glance. "I was thinking of an English viticulturist."

Sophie blushed. "I'm not such a fool as all that, my dear. I know he cares for me, but we are heading in two different directions. He'll be back in Brazil. And once my crisis has passed, I'll be somewhere else. Somewhere that needs my particular set of skills."

"Someplace like Viti del Fiume?" Catarina said softly.

Sophie shook herself and said, "It was a nosey thing to ask. I'm sorry."

Catarina finally answered, "I'm not seeing anyone. There have been a few who've come and gone, but no one whom I couldn't do without. The person I marry will be someone I can't do without."

And therein lies the rub. Sophie couldn't imagine doing without Antonio. Without any of them. But they needed an intern, not a permanent fixture. Antonio's calling was an ocean away, in the middle of the rainforest. "You should open yourself up, Catarina. You deserve to be loved. We all deserve to be loved."

SOPHIE'S BROW WAS FURROWED AS SHE SPOKE ON THE PHONE, trying again and failing to get ahold of the detective at Scotland Yard. She was sure he'd given her this number. It sounded like him on the voicemail, but he never returned her call. She looked at her watch again. Everyone was taking a midday riposo.

She walked toward the spot where the wild saffron grew, hoping to check the progress. They'd just begun harvesting. A group of nuns came to the spot with volunteers. Marcello told the group of pious women that if they picked what remained, after the family had harvested a small amount for their shop, they could take the saffron and sell it for their missionary work. He made the donation every year and asked them to pray for the soul of his beloved

Margarite. It had to be thousands of euros worth of saffron, and Sophie thought it was a wonderful tribute to a woman who'd blossomed brightly for a short time and was taken away too soon. She heard some rustling in the vines behind her and thought perhaps it was the dog. She'd taken to following Sophie around, as she was sleeping at the foot of her bed almost every night.

Sophie was disappointed when she came to the crocus field, having expected to find the nuns working in their more practical, lightweight habits. Their equipment was still there, but they were nowhere to be found. She knew they took breaks throughout the day in order to take refreshment and say prayers, but she didn't hear them anywhere. Sister Maria Agatha was coming today, and she'd promised to buy some of the abbey's honey. She saw three jars next to some gardening gloves and a bucket. The sticky note said *Sophie*. She took the euro out of her shorts pocket, figuring she'd leave the money inside the gloves. She reached into her back pocket for the pen and small pad of paper she always carried with her. *Damn.* She'd changed clothes and showered at lunchtime, after getting grape juice all over her jeans. She hadn't transferred the stuff out of her pockets.

She bent over, intending to just leave the money poking out a bit with the sticky note on it when she heard someone approach. She didn't have time to turn around before someone charged her from behind. It knocked the wind out of her when someone twice her size landed on her. But it only rattled her for a second, then she started to fight. And scream like the devil was after her.

Antonio heard the sound just as he and his father were cresting the slope where they'd been doing the day's picking. Antonio took off, Dolce and his father not far behind him. "Sophie!" He ran toward the noise, and Dolce went ahead of him. He heard her snarl and then heard a wail from someone who wasn't Sophie. The dog yelped and Sophie screamed.

Antonio broke through the trees into the crocus field just as a man was running. Sophie yelled, "Go! I'm okay!" So, he did. He ran faster than he'd ever run. And suddenly, he was thankful for those teenagers at St. Clare's who had persuaded him to train with them before they left for boot camp. This little bastard in front of him didn't stand a chance. He was limping just a bit, and his arm was leaking from a bite wound. Bravo, Dolce.

He tackled the man just before he reached the road. A car was sitting idle, but he never made it. Antonio flipped him on his back and punched him right in the mouth. He should have been watching the man's hands. He sliced at Antonio just as he dodged it, but he nicked his flesh between his shoulder and neck. The knife did more damage to his shirt, thankfully, but Antonio knew when to live to fight another day. This man was panicked and willing to kill. The fact that he had a knife meant Antonio needed to go check on Sophie instead of getting another stab wound. He jumped off the man and watched as he ran to the car, just as he knew he would. That's when Antonio snapped three photos in rapid succession, getting partials of the man, the car, and the license plate.

SOPHIE WAS BRUISED, WITH A NASTY SET OF MARKS AROUND HER wrist and neck. She hadn't recognized the man, but she was pretty sure he hadn't been trying to kill her. He hadn't used the knife until Dolce had come out of the woods. The stab wound sustained by the dog wasn't serious. No more serious than the several hunks the dog had taken out of her attacker. The dog was in her lap now. She shouldn't have told Antonio to go after him. He had a knife, for God's sake! She hadn't realized it until she'd gotten a good look at Dolce's wound. Hopefully, Marcello caught up with them.

She saw the sisters coming back to their work, and Sister Maria Agatha ran to her to see what was amiss. "She protected me," Sophie said as she ran a palm over the dog's head. Sophie was shaking, the adrenaline working its way through her system. One of the other sisters brought their first aid kit and began tending to the dog's wound. Sophie was feeling wobbly, but she started to get to her feet, not thinking as she put her hands down into the nest of flowers she'd trampled. That's when she felt the small legs curl around her fingertip just before the burning sting happened. "Ow! Oh, Jesus. Sister Mari ..." her breath started coming fast. One of the nuns came to her side. "Bee s-s-s-sting. I'm a-a-allergic!" The last coherent thought she experienced before the panic kicked in was that she'd left her emergency epinephrine in the jeans that were now tossed on the bathroom floor.

❦

ANTONIO AND MARCELLO JOGGED BACK TO THE CROCUS FIELD, more concerned about the dog and Sophie than calling the police. It could take an hour for the local police to show up. Antonio came into the field from the opposite side, surprised to see the Sisters of St. Francis scurrying around, one running for help in the opposite direction. Oh, God. Maybe he had stabbed Sophie. Antonio ran to the group of nuns. One was holding Sophie's head, trying to calm her, and the other was searching her pockets. Another was looking through the first aid kit they always carried. "Marcello! Where is her EpiPen?" the nun asked in rapid Italian. All of the blood drained from Antonio's head. Sophie was barely getting air. "It's not in her pockets, signor! Does she have an EpiPen?" she asked in her sternest nun voice.

Antonio didn't wait. After a brief check of her pockets himself, he scooped her up and he ran. Marcello was calling an ambulance. Antonio could hear him in the background as he ran for the truck. That was the closest one. He had the EpiPens in key locations on the property. In the cave, in the work truck, in the pool house, and in the main house. She usually carried one on her. *Dammit! Why didn't she have it with her?*

"Hang on, my love. Please, God. Hang on!" But her color was off, with a blue tinge. He opened her eyelid and the pupil constricted, but he wasn't sure she was breathing. He could see the truck ahead. "Catarina! The glove box! An EpiPen!" He screamed the words in Italian, then again in English.

It was Martha who got there first. Antonio dropped to the ground in front of the truck just as she came out of the cab. She took the cap off and handed it to him. Martha lifted Sophie's shorts to expose her outer thigh. He stabbed and plunged the epinephrine into her system. Marcello came in, winded, but continuing to give emergency services the information. "Get another pen! It's in the office bathroom!" He pointed to the grape processing building. "Come on, Sophie, please. Please, amore. Don't leave me." He rocked her back and forth, his palm on her chest. Antonio felt it the moment some air started making it into her lungs. "That's it, Sophie. Breathe with me, my darling." He was speaking English now. He saw that the blue tinge of her lips and skin was starting to lessen. He shuddered with relief. He could hear his sister crying. It was Marco who handed him the second EpiPen. Antonio looked at his grandmother. "Tell me when it's been ten minutes." Then to his sister he said, "Catarina, help me find the stinger. I don't think the nuns took it out."

It didn't take long. Sophie's hand was grotesquely swollen. Antonio used a plastic card from his wallet and scraped the stinger away. It was a honey bee, the end of the stinger fleshy and glistening with venom. It was likely still pulsating, pumping venom into her. "I need ice on this. Call the house and tell Nonna I need lots of ice." He was like a general, assigning jobs and giving orders. No one seemed to mind.

Marcello said, "It's going to be about fifteen minutes for the ambulance." He and Marco helped Antonio lift her into the bed of the truck where Catarina was waiting to cradle her head. Antonio got in beside her, as did Marcello. Then Martha got into the cab and Marco drove them to the house.

Antonio said, "Her pulse is erratic. It's most likely due to the drugs. We are probably going to have to give her another dose before they get here. Just help me keep her calm." Antonio realized he was crying when the drops fell onto Sophie's shirt. He didn't have time to cry, and he wiped them away angrily. When the tears stopped, he said to Martha, "I need your stethoscope." He'd seen her using it on his grandfather. "We are going to put her on the sofa and out of the sun until the ambulance gets here."

The men eased her off the bed of the truck, and she began thrashing and moaning. "I know, baby. It hurts like the devil." The venom and the epinephrine were pounding through her system. Not to mention the fact that she'd been attacked about five minutes prior to the sting. Her adrenaline and heart rate had probably already been through the roof even before the sting. "Call the police. I have pictures of the car and maybe of the man. Did someone get Dolce?"

Marco said, "I sent one of the men to fetch her. She's okay. The sisters took care of her." An order of St. Francis, patron saint of animals. How fitting.

Antonio carried Sophie against his chest, whispering gentle words until he could settle her on the sofa. His voice seemed to ease her. Martha said, "It's been ten minutes. Let's get some vitals."

She took her blood pressure on the opposite arm from the sting while Nonna brought ice packs. Martha said, "It's eighty over fifty-nine. Too low." Nonna crossed herself, then began to pray.

Antonio listened to her breathing. "It's shallow. Jesus, she's barely getting enough." He had to remind himself to breathe. He couldn't lose her. Her face was tense and still. Like all she could expend any energy for was that next labored breath. He'd read her employment file. She'd only had an incident like this once, and she'd been a child. She didn't remember much of it, but she was going to remember this. Her eyes had been frantic before she'd closed them.

Martha said, "Give it another minute. Let's see if she settles down. If she's breathing, we don't want to go in with another shot too quickly. If it slows down at all, then you give her the shot." She took Sophie's hand. "Brave lass. Just be easy. Breathe, Sophie. Steady and calm." Her voice was so solid, and it seemed to calm Sophie. Antonio would have liked to have seen his grandmother in the delivery room, taking care of laboring mothers. He took her other hand.

"I'm glad you're here, Grandmother," he said softly.

It was just after the second shot that they heard the siren. The ambulance made good time by Italian countryside standards, as it was during *riposo*. This made for less traffic. Antonio rode in the ambulance, watching as they started an IV drip and prepared to give her more epinephrine as she needed it. Her skin was cold and her face was swollen. The sight of her made him want to start weeping again. Now he knew why doctors didn't treat family.

They replaced the ice pack on her hand with one of their own, and slowly her vitals began to stabilize. Marcello would speak with the polizia, then send them to the hospital to get statements and take pictures of Sophie's injuries. His father had already texted him, as the officers had arrived just as the ambulance was leaving for the closest hospital. As soon as she was stable, Antonio would have her transferred into Florence, where the hospitals were better. Right now, however, closer was better. His father texted him again, letting him know that the polizia would be meeting the ambulance.

SOPHIE STARTED TO COME AROUND IN DEGREES, HEARING THE wailing of the ambulance. *Thank God. Oh, thank you, God, for letting them find me.* She didn't remember much after the sting. The last clear thing she remembered was ... She jerked. Her throat was hoarse as she tried to speak. Then Antonio was above her. Pain filled his eyes. "You're okay, mi amore. You are going to be just fine." Her face felt puffy, and she wondered just how bad she looked. The paramedic was checking the bruises along her wrists and neck. She heard Antonio speak to him in Italian. Something like, *It wasn't me*. And, *polizia*.

Sophie started to cry then. She couldn't help it. She'd almost died. Some people had luck in spades. She had the kind of luck that made her sit on a bee after someone assaulted her. Flashes of the altercation came back to her, and she thrashed her head back and forth. The flight or fight instinct renewed itself in her mind. Antonio whispered to her, like one would soothe a child, "It's okay, mi amore. It's over. The police are coming. This is going to be okay. Please, my love. Calm down. Mind your IV." Sophie looked at her bad hand and made a gasping sound. Then Antonio readjusted the ice pack while she looked at the IV in the other hand. She probably needed whatever they were giving her, and she made herself calm down. She looked into his warm, loving eyes and they grounded her. She breathed with him, nodding. She was alive. She was going to be okay.

AFTER INTERROGATING THE DOCTOR ON DUTY, ANTONIO decided not to have Sophie transferred. The college had provided her with insurance, but the bill was still going to be sizeable. They called her parents, once they had a free moment, and had to talk them out of coming there on the next train.

Her father asked, "What the hell are the police doing? Have they found this man? I bet that son of a bitch, Richard, had something to do with this. Drug dealers always have a network of unsavory people. I've been trying to call the officer at Scotland Yard Headquarters, but I haven't been able to get anyone. I'm going to fly to London tomorrow and start making some inquiries."

"Be careful, signor. I agree, it's time to involve them and perhaps Interpol. Tell Sophie's mama that she is being very well taken care of. The polizia will come back this morning, now that the restriction in her throat has gone down and she's more able to speak. She's starting to remember everything."

"Why the hell didn't she have her EpiPen?" He sounded like a father who had lectured his child ad nauseam.

"She had to change her clothing. Harvest time is messy work. I believe it was in her discarded pants."

"So, how did you manage to give her two doses of epinephrine so quickly?" her father asked.

This was going to be a telling confession, but he wouldn't lie to the man. "When I found out she was allergic to bees, I obtained four more pens to place in strategic parts of the property. It's a large estate, and I didn't want to take any chances. We used the two from the farm truck and the pressing shed. We keep first aid kits in the same place."

Her father paused, making Antonio a little uncomfortable. "That had to be over a thousand euro. I would like to reimburse you, but I suspect you would not take the money."

"No, signor, I wouldn't."

He could still hear the rural French accent despite the decades he'd lived in England. "You saved my little girl, Dr. Rinalto. She's my beating heart. Her mother's sun and moon." His voice cracked. "I owe you more than I can ever repay."

"You owe me nothing. I care for Sophie. I promise you that this will not happen again. We've been patrolling at night, but this was in the middle of the day. During our riposo. A siesta of sorts. This man chose his moment. And according to Sophie, he wasn't trying to kill her. He was trying to take her." He heard the man curse. "This is what they need to focus on at your end. Where is this Richard? Is he accounted for by his parole officer? And how in the hell did he find out she was here?"

Sophie's father said, "I'm going to tell you something, but you can't tell my daughter. You must promise me."

"Yes, I promise." Antonio almost didn't want to hear it.

"Someone broke into our home. They went through my desk,

our bedroom bureaus. They took a laptop and my wife's tablet. Thankfully, it is an old one that I haven't used for several years. I changed my passwords for everything. I can't think of any way we could have given her away. We've been careful. It happened yesterday while we were in Avignon for the day."

"Then it wasn't you. I chased someone off the property almost ten days ago. They are getting their information from someone else."

"You said they. Who is involved in this?"

"I don't know, but Sophie said the man was Italian. I thought so due to the look of him, but she confirmed it. It seems this petty drug dealer has made friends with people of influence. People with a broader reach."

"Maybe it's unrelated, but I don't think so. There is virtually no crime in this part of France. Please, Dr. Rinalto. Watch over my girl. I'd tell her to come stay with us, but she would never do it. She is too close to finishing her education."

"We will watch over her. I promise you. And now that the local police are involved, I think we will see them around the area more often. Good evening, sir. And I will tell her to call you when she's doing better."

⚜

ANTONIO STARED DOWN AT THE SLEEPING WOMAN, HIS HEART clenching in spasms. She was extremely fortunate. This very well could have killed her. If this had happened while she was alone that far from her medication, it would have killed her. It had only taken about three minutes for her to completely stop breathing. They'd given her Benadryl and anti-inflammatories in addition to the medications for anaphylaxis. The swelling in her arm and hand was still significant, but her face just faintly puffy.

Sophie opened her eyes, confused. She looked around the room, then seemed to settle as the memory of what happened came back to her. She'd spoken to the police briefly, but he hadn't really been able to talk to her before she'd passed out again. Antonio said, "I called your parents. Your father's number was in your contacts."

She put her hand to her forehead. "Thank you. I'm sure they are beside themselves. Hopefully, they aren't on a train headed to Italy?"

"No, but your father is flying to London tomorrow. Don't look so surprised, Sophie. You are his daughter. And he has not been able to get ahold of the police contact that you gave him. Maybe it is just a bad number. An old one, perhaps."

"Does he really need to fly there? It seems a bit extreme," she said.

"It's not. Sometimes you have to show up and make a little trouble in order to get results. They are releasing you in a couple hours, when they are through with their rounds and can come check on you one more time."

"Have you called the vineyard?" she asked.

"They've called every fifteen minutes. They are tag-teaming." Sophie just smiled at that, and he could tell she was drifting off again. He wasn't going to keep her talking. She'd been through trauma in more than one way today, and her body needed to rest. She looked frail in her hospital johnny. Antonio wanted to gather her into his arms and feel her beating heart. Feel the steady rhythm of her breathing. Watching her face go blue had brought back several traumatic memories. First of his mother, broken and still after being ejected from her car. Then, of a little girl at the orfanato in Brazil. She'd been bitten by a green tree python. It's often a fatal bite. The venom worked its deadly magic within minutes. One had been lost, the other saved. He didn't want to think about living in a world where Sophie didn't exist anymore.

Antonio hadn't known her long, but he cared deeply for her. She was smart and lovely, and she touched a part of him that had been sleeping for so long that he wasn't sure he even remembered it. He'd known a fair share of women in his thirty-six years, but he didn't think any of them had ever affected him so deeply. Not even close, actually.

He touched her sweet face, understanding perhaps a little what it must have been like for his father to lose his mother. They'd still been fairly young. She'd been in her late forties. Him, not much older. They should have had another thirty or forty years together. Antonio wondered, as he stroked Sophie's soft hair, what she'd look like at Nonna's age. He shook the foolish thought aside. As much as this woman stirred his blood, their lives were too different to sustain anything long term. A fact that made him suddenly very sad.

❧ 17 ❧

Sophie was out of bed. Again. The hospital had released Sophie after a period of observation. Antonio had inspected the entire cottage, looking for random spiders, scorpions, and any sort of bee or wasp that had wandered in through an open door. He inspected the screens, reinforcing a few gaps and outright replacing the screens on a few that were a bit tattered. She slept at first, the antihistamines making her groggy. Her arm and hand were still swollen, but the facial swelling had been minimal and had gone away. Just a small puffiness at her lips and eyes was all that remained.

She wouldn't stay in bed, though. Sophie was the type that couldn't stay sedentary for very long. She went to the dresser to get clothes and saw it. Her EpiPen. It had been in her shorts, in the bathroom hamper, but Antonio had cleaned up. Magdalena was doing her laundry, and he'd placed it on the dresser. She didn't understand.

Antonio was irritated that she was up and out of bed, but that wasn't her problem. "Is this still full?" she asked, wondering why he hadn't thrown it away.

He looked up from his work on the last screen. "It is." That's all he said.

She was irritable. Antihistamines gave her headaches. "If this is still full, what did you inject into me when it happened?" She could see his jaw tighten. He cracked his neck, weighing his response.

"I used the epinephrine pens I bought at the farmacia."

"Pens? As in more than one? What ... do you have them stashed everywhere?" He didn't answer her, so she said, "Antonio, look at me!"

He did, and his eyes were full of something she couldn't pin down. He snapped, "Yes! I had them stashed everywhere. I bought four, in case we needed them. Sometimes one isn't enough. Sometimes irresponsible interns leave their personal medication on their bathroom floor."

She bristled, which seemed to irritate him even more. "Do you have any idea what could have happened to you? We are in the country. We have limited first responders and a terrible response time! If you hadn't had two doctors here ..." He ground his teeth. "I had to give you two shots. That one dose wouldn't have been enough, even if you'd had your pen with you. By the time the ambulance got here, you could very well have been dead. As it happens, you didn't have it on you and you were isolated up in the saffron meadow. You WOULD have died."

"Why are you so angry with me?" she screamed. "Do you think I don't know that? Do you think I wasn't scared half out of my mind? Do you know what it's like to slowly stop breathing? This after having some man pin me down and choke me into submission?" She was shrieking now. She knew it.

His eyes misted and his voice broke. "I've seen people die from anaphylaxis. I've watched people die in my arms. You were blue, Sophie. You weren't breathing, and I had to run to the truck for the first dose. You weren't breathing. I thought I was going to watch you die!"

She let out a sob, and he closed the distance between them. He pulled her close, saying, "I'm sorry, amore. God, I am so sorry. I'm being a bastard."

"I'm sorry, too." She put her hands on his shoulder as he kissed her softly. Then she stopped, pulling away. "What is this?" She ran a thumb over what looked like three stitches at the strip of flesh where his neck met his shoulder. Right over his trapezius muscle. "What is this?" she asked again, looking at him hard. "Oh, Jesus. Antonio, did that man cut you?"

He just nodded. "It's not bad."

"A couple inches higher and he could have cut an artery, Antonio!" She was shrieking again. "And he cut Dolce. That son of a bitch stabbed my dog! Who the hell was that man?"

Antonio thought it unwise to point out that Dolce was, in fact, his dog. "The polizia are looking for him. He is a petty drug dealer. I got a picture of his license plate. What do you remember, Sophie? Because he didn't cut you."

"No, but he choked me. I think he wanted to scare me enough so that I would submit. He wanted me to come with him," she said. He'd wanted her alive. "He found me. Richard is behind this. I know it."

"I think you're right. We will have to see what your father finds out. I scanned the police report for him to take to the London police. If he's here, he's likely breaking his parole restrictions. They need to access Interpol so that he can be arrested in another country. Your father is supposed to call tonight. He won't call the house. He'll call my phone."

Her shoulders slumped, and she leaned into his chest to put her forehead at his breast. "It hardly matters, Antonio. If this is his doing, and I think that it is, he already knows where I am. I need to leave. I don't know how he has been able to find me here, but I must leave."

Antonio put his arm around her. "You aren't going anywhere, Sophie. I've learned a few things in Amazonas. There is safety in numbers."

SOPHIE SORTED THE ALREADY-PICKED GRAPES AS THEY WENT BY on the conveyor. She wasn't much help. Her good hand was clumsy due to the edema. But she got to know a couple of the local women, practicing her Italian and making them laugh. She had her arm in a sling, ice packs used periodically to try hastening her recovery. She was surprised to hear singing coming from outside. She went out to find the source, hearing another two voices joining the sweet tenor voice.

Sophie weaved her way through the vines until she found them. She covered her mouth, stifling a grin. Giuseppe was reclining in a lawn chair, wearing a big hat to shade him from the sun. Marcello was next to him. And they were both drunk. The two men were singing some sort of Italian opera, and Giuseppe was scolding both of his grandsons, trying to get them to sing along. They did, although the only one with any real flair for music was Giuseppe.

Antonio was taking his blood pressure, shaking his head as he weakly joined in. Giuseppe ended the number by taking off his hat, putting it over his heart, and belting out the final bars. He was the only one who knew she was watching, and he gave a small sort of bow in her direction. Sophie clapped vigorously. "Bravo! Bravo!" Antonio and Marco blushed matching shades of scarlet, but Marcello just smiled and nodded at her.

Then Giuseppe said, with a slight slur to his words, "Buongiorno, bellisima. How is the sorting going?"

"It's slow with this thing, but it's going," she said in English as she held her useless hand up from the sling. "Giuseppe, I didn't know you could sing. You've been keeping secrets, I think."

The oldest Rinalto man just winked at her. Antonio said, "And he's had quite enough wine. He's on medication. Right, Nonno?"

Giuseppe gave a non-committal shrug, more to appease Antonio than to promise anything. Everything was interrupted by a

230

shrill from Antonio's mobile. He answered it, looking up into Sophie's face. "Your papa."

THEY SAT IN A CIRCLE, LISTENING AS SOPHIE'S FATHER POURED out the details of what he'd learned. The long and short of it was that there was no such officer at their precinct in London, or in the whole of Scotland Yard. Richard Devereaux had been released three months ago. Whoever called Sophie wasn't a police officer.

Dread washed over her. "The officer in charge of such matters should have told you this four months ago, through the Victim's Advocacy Department. The woman in charge of that department ..."

He paused and Sophie said, "Just come out with it, Father."

"She's missing. She skipped town with her daughter. She was a single mother. She left a letter of resignation, pulled her daughter from her primary school, and left no forwarding address. They've had to put an officer in the position temporarily until they replace her. So apparently, you fell through the cracks, the main reason being he was never actually convicted of assaulting you. There was a note in the file, but ..." He paused, not finishing the thought. "So, I'm working on tracking the officer down. Maybe she has information."

"She was scared. That's why she left. Which means they either threatened her and she fled, or she told them my mobile contact and then fled afterward. And I was stupid enough to give someone my information over the phone and blindly believe they were the police. But I didn't say where I was going, exactly. I just said I was doing an internship abroad." Sophie sounded disgusted with herself. "What about the number I've been calling?"

"They are working on it. There's something else, Sophie. Did you tell the man which college you were attending?"

"Um ... I don't know. I mean, yes. It came up. His daughter was looking at schools, or so he said. I guess that was a lie as well. I didn't tell him where the vineyard was, though. And there's no way to tie me to my roommates. I'm not on the lease and I paid cash. The only person who knew which vineyard I was going to was my advisor. She wiped the information from her files. All she has is a flash drive so she could save everything. No emails or anything. She was supposed to call but—"

"But she hasn't," her father said solemnly. "I'm sorry, Sophie." He paused. "Jesus, I don't know how to tell you this. She's dead."

◈

"Sophie, wait! Stop packing!" The infernal woman had her suitcase opened on the large coffee table in the sitting room. She'd shed her sling and was walking back and forth from her room with clothing. She wasn't listening. Wasn't hearing him.

She said, "She told him where I was! And then he killed her anyway. Just like he almost did to Morgan. He dumped her in the fucking river, Antonio!"

"I know, Sophie. Jesus, I am so sorry. But you can't just leave, *mi amore*. You have to stay where we can protect you."

He was so calm that it was making her more mental. "I will not stay here and put your family at risk." They heard a car door. She turned to see a white car with the word *Polizia* written across the side.

◈

They'd found the man who had attacked her in the crocus field by using the snapshot of the vehicle. They'd arrested him and pressed the little bastard all night until he caved. He'd been so jonesed, he'd have told them anything in order to get loose and have access to his stash of narcotics. All they'd done is put him in the sick bay of the regional jail, having a doctor to monitor his detox.

Antonio worked as her interpreter with the police officer, as the man's words seemed to merge together in a sea of confusion. Panic did that to a person. Antonio said, "He's a drug dealer. Small stuff, but his supplier has international dealings. All throughout Europe. This Richard Devereaux has put out the word with his English suppliers, and his connections in Italy, that you stole from him. Two kilograms of cocaine and eight hundred thousand euro. He's offering to split the money with whomever brings you to him alive."

He asked the officer in Italian, "What is to keep them from just interrogating her and taking it all?"

Antonio's face blanched when the officer said, "He has strong connections. He took over the drug trade in a major British prison. They won't cross him."

Sophie said, "I don't have any money! I don't have any drugs! I barely knew him, and the police seized his stash. He was dealing marijuana and ecstasy. No cocaine or anything else on that level."

"Right, but that wouldn't get him what he wants. He likely told them he was a major dealer and that you were his ... consort." It was the only word Antonio could think of that might not make her hit the ceiling.

She lifted her chin. "I have to go."

❦

Marcello yelled, "Basta! Enough, all of you." They'd been arguing for at least a half hour straight. "We will send Nonna to my sister's home in Siena. That's the end of it, Mama. Catarina will go with you."

Catarina shot back. "The hell I will go with her. I am staying. I can shoot as well as any of you."

"We have more than enough fire power," Antonio said. "With the neighboring men coming to help, we don't need anyone else to stand guard."

His sister showed her teeth, like an angry wolf. "We are in the middle of our best harvest in two decades. I am not going anywhere. Grandmother Martha can take Nonna."

Martha said, "I can. She's right, Marcello. You can't very well bring in this harvest and watch over our Sophie without her. And well you know it. Now, I'll take Magdalena tomorrow, which I hesitate to do. You'll likely starve without her. Do any of you know how to turn on the bloody cooker?"

꩜

SOPHIE LEFT WITH ANTONIO ON HER HEELS. "YOU SHOULDN'T have to send her away. No one should have to deal with this. I did this to your family." Her eyes were blurred with angry tears. She walked into the house, letting the door almost hit Antonio.

He ground his jaw, trying to be the reasonable one in this relationship. "They already know where you are. If you leave, they'll come after us like they did your advisor. It's better that we close ranks around you and see this through, Sophie." He hated separating his grandparents—it rarely happened—but Nonno was not going to be put out to pasture due to illness or age, and the men in this family would not take his pride from him. Even at his age, he went on the hunts when there was a wild boar sighting. He was deadly with the Benelli rifle he'd been gifted for his eightieth birthday. He wasn't bad with a shotgun, either. Antonio knew they could protect her better if they stuck together. At least until the harvest was done.

She was packing again. Jesus, this woman was single-minded. He turned her body to him. "Stop packing your goddamn clothes, Sophie! You aren't thinking!"

"He killed her! He killed her, Antonio! I didn't know her well, but she was a good person. And I'll bet he took a piece of her hair. Do you want to see Catarina washed up in the Arno? Dead with a piece of her hair missing?" Sophie was bordering on hysteria, her eyes wild with fear.

"We have to stick together. And if they've found you, they won't need to press anyone for information. Do you understand? It will make it worse if you leave."

She did, but she didn't want to understand it. She wanted to run. She wanted to kill that son of a bitch with her bare hands. "That man cut you. He was just a petty dealer trying to get the payoff. If Richard comes here ..." She shook her head. "Thank God he can't find my parents."

Antonio's face flickered. He covered it up, but she'd seen it. "What aren't you telling me?" She looked ready to do violence and beat it out of him. She was on a hair trigger.

He sighed, knowing she had the right to this information, despite what her father thought. "I want you to know that I'm breaking a confidence by telling you this. Your father won't thank me for it." He closed his eyes, hating that he was breaking a promise to her father. Antonio said, "Someone broke into their house. They took your father's laptop, some other things. Not a proper burglary, though. They left valuables." He hastened to reassure her, "No one was home. They have an alarm system now, and the French police are patrolling there more often."

The rage boiled up so quickly in her that she just shook, then she screamed. Not a scared scream. It was born of a fierce, unholy anger. She wanted Richard Devereaux dead. Antonio let her do it. Let her have her anger, which she appreciated even through the fog of her fury. Marcello burst through the door and Antonio waved him off. He hesitantly exited, closing the door softly. She said, "I have to go."

Antonio closed her suitcase. "The police are watching the house. We are armed better than most families in Italy. They may be old shotguns, but they work just fine. You are safe here and you aren't leaving. If I have to tie you to that bed, I will."

She slammed her fists into his chest, and he barely moved. "Don't you understand? He'll find out. He'll find out that I love you and he'll try to take you from me! He'll try to take you all from me!"

She hadn't meant to say it, but it was out there. She tried to walk away and he stopped her.

He had her face in his hands. "What did you say?"

Sophie was so angry, she wanted to hit him. She wasn't really angry with him, but he was there and she wanted to lash out. She screamed, "I said I love you!" She yelled the words at him like an accusation. "I love you, you boorish, arrogant, bullying"—she searched for the word—"Italian!"

She pulled away from him. "Which is just one of several reasons why I am the biggest idiot on the face of the earth! An Italian doctor who lives on the bloody Amazon who could have anyone he wanted." She stopped as she watched what he was doing. He threw the bolt on the door. His eyes were aflame with need.

Antonio reached her in one long step. Her blush told him that she hadn't meant to say it. Not first, at least. Maybe not ever. *She loves me.* He took her mouth, silencing her protests. Then he had her up on the countertop of the kitchen, stripping off her pants in one fast motion. "Say it again," he said against her mouth. "Say it again, Sophie." He crooned the words in Italian, having been stripped of his senses. Antonio freed his cock and pushed inside her. She moaned his name. "Say it," he growled as he drew her hips forward again and again. He had her cradled, one arm on her hip, one across her shoulders. Then his words softened. "My darling, Sophie, please. Say it."

Sophie smoothed a hand over his face and whispered it softly, a hitch in her throat. "I love you." She swallowed. "I'm sorry. I didn't mean to. I know this isn't permanent but—"

"The hell it isn't permanent. You're mine, mi amore. I love you, Sophie," he said in English. His accent was thick and rich. "I love you. You are mine, my love. And I'm yours."

Antonio started to come because this felt way too good. Sophie was hot and slick and so tight. She hooked her ankles behind his back, one heel pressed into his ass as she yanked his hips forward, taking him deeper. She reclined on her arms, her breasts arching upward as she started to climax. He cut loose, going hard and deep, and she gasped for air as her body contracted around him, her legs pulling him in deep. "Come, Antonio. Please."

That did it. He popped her off the counter and held her up, pulling her small body up and down as she rode his cock. Then he fractured, his soul exposed as he let go inside her. Antonio cradled her to him, whispering to her as she nestled her face in his neck, "Mine, my love. You're mine."

THEY LAY ON HIS BED, SPENT FROM LOVING EACH OTHER. "I LOVE you, Sophie. I love you so much, it consumes my very soul every time we make love. You are mine to protect. Can't you see that?"

He held her close, kissing her hair and stroking her. They fell asleep for a time, then began to stir in each other's arms. It was then that they both realized they hadn't used a condom.

Antonio looked between them. "I didn't think, Sophie. Jesus, I'm so sorry." But part of him wasn't. It was the closest he'd ever felt to someone. She was pale, shaken by the possible consequences. He suddenly felt awful. Like he'd betrayed her trust.

Sophie wasn't sure why she hadn't run out of the room screaming and into the shower. She looked at Antonio's beautiful face and somehow found the calm to say, "We both forgot. And it's okay. I mean, it's not exactly okay, but it's not a tragedy, either. At least not for me. I know I should be panicking right now, but I'm okay. It will be okay," she repeated, trying to convince them both. She smiled so sweetly that it tore something deep inside him.

Antonio felt himself stirring, needing her again. And after all, the damage was already done. At least for the next couple weeks. A wave of longing rolled through him. Visions of Sophie swollen with his child. Of Sophie wearing his wedding ring. Of her at St. Clare's. He brushed her mouth with his, and she felt his arousal against her belly. Her eyes glazed over, her mouth and cheeks blushing with desire. She rolled on her back, opening herself. Letting him in.

"Come to me, Antonio." Sophie whispered the words, and it made his entire body tremble. He never broke eye contact. He wouldn't have looked away for anything. This time, his orgasm rolled through him like a soft tide. Urging her to join him. Her eyes grew frantic with need. His breath stuttered, and she felt his erection kick inside her, his warm seed releasing. Antonio took her chin in his palm as he watched her come. Watched her take from him. It was the most beautiful moment of his life. More beautiful because this time, it had been chosen.

❧ 18 ❧

Antonio didn't give a fig who knew about him and Sophie. At least now that his grandmothers weren't here to take turns boxing his ears and calling the local priest. The first time he wrapped his arms around her and kissed her between the eyes, she'd been surprised. But he needed her close to him. To rub his lips along her hairline, absorbing her scent. Feeling the solid warmth of her.

Giuseppe threw his arms up. "Finalmente!" he shouted. Antonio wouldn't let her go as she hid her face. Marcello and his siblings all came around the corner to see what was happening. Giuseppe repeated, "Finalmente!" and gestured to them.

Catarina said in English, "Finally, indeed."

While Marco said, "I was afraid you'd lost your touch, Antonio."

Marcello just smiled warmly, and it was tinged with sadness. Maybe for his lost love. But when the men left the kitchen to the women, Marcello pulled him aside.

"Antonio, do you love this girl?" Antonio tensed. He didn't like that chiding tone.

"Why are you asking me this?" he said defensively.

"Because she's a beautiful soul. And if you are just going to leave and go back to Brazil, I wish you wouldn't ..." He wanted to be mad at him, but he couldn't muster it. His father was protecting Sophie. Even if it meant offending Antonio. He thought about that bastard who had taken advantage of his mother.

"I do love her, Papa. With all my heart. I know it's only been a few weeks, but sometimes that's all it takes. I felt it as soon as I met her. And it's only grown stronger as I've gotten close to her. I love her, Papa. If she'd have me, I would be with her always."

He was shocked to see his father's eyes mist with tears. "It was like that with Margarite."

Giuseppe said, "And your grandmother. She was always meant to be mine."

It was strange, this unchartered territory. They spoke not as a child and a father or grandfather. They talked as men. And this alone had been worth traveling an ocean to discover— knowing them as men—his youthful pride and anger set aside for something much more precious.

SOPHIE SAT AT THE SOIL-DUSTED TABLE OUTSIDE THE POTTING shed, carefully working on the rootstock she'd harvested. She was trying to graft the new Sangiovese stock that she was going to plant with some dormant rootstock from the oldest vines on the grounds. Much easier than doing it in the field to already-planted vines, but she wasn't sure it would take. Later, she'd been getting on the ground and grafting scions to existing rootstock.

Catarina watched her closely. "When your hand gets tired, you must ice it. If you show me, I can do some and give you a break."

The corner of Sophie's mouth turned up slightly, but she suppressed the smile. Catarina was dying to try her hand at this. Normally, Marcello handled the grafting. So, she broke it down into slow steps. It was tedious work, but she could get them done faster with help. "I'll have to come back and visit in a few years. To see the fruits of our labor and my Frankenstein vines."

Marcello had done as he promised, giving her a small parcel of land that was, as of yet, unplanted. It was on a part of the slope that couldn't be cultivated with a tractor. She'd spent the better part of yesterday working the soil with two men from the batch of seasonal workers. She noticed, too, that Marcello had come along. And his hunting gun was never out of reach. *You never come up here alone. It's too isolated.* And she'd listened. She wasn't careless with her own life. Carelessness put everyone in danger, not just her. Her parents were on holiday, having decided to take a short cruise through the Greek Islands. She'd have liked to meet them at one of the ports, but there was too much work to do. And this family had closed ranks around her. Protected her. She would stay put. Let law enforcement handle Richard.

She hadn't noticed Catarina's stillness until now. "What's wrong?"

"You said you'd come back and visit in a few years. Does this mean ..." She clamped her lips shut tight. "Are you using my brother? I know he's very handsome. I'm sure you wouldn't be the first, but he is my brother."

Sophie was sitting there like an idiot, not sure how to respond. So, she opted for the naked truth. "Catarina, I love Antonio. I've never been in love before, but I know what I'm feeling. I would never use him like that."

She seemed to settle. "So, what is the plan?"

Sophie sighed. That was the million-dollar question. How in the hell were they going to make this work?

They heard someone approaching. Catarina asked, "Antonio, how is Nonno?"

He kissed his sister's head as she stood up to greet him. "He's better. I gave him some of the ginger rice and he's keeping it down."

Catarina said, "I'll go help Papa with lunch."

Antonio took her place on the bench as she worked, and Sophie finally looked up to see that he was following her motions, grafting the two vines together as his sister had done. She put her work down. "Nothing like making it look easy. It took me two semesters to get this right." It was very meticulous work.

He gave her a sexy, sideways grin. "It took me four years of surgical residency to get this right."

"Touché, Medíco." And she continued to work. She would watch him now and again. Antonio had long, smooth fingers. Strong, steady hands. The hands of a healer.

"I saw you tending Nonna's flowers and kitchen garden. That was nice of you," he said. Sophie was so at ease with him here, like nothing in the world could touch them. She glanced up.

"It's the least I could do, I would think, given I've chased the poor woman off her estate." As she said it, the oak tree above their heads sprayed them with leaves. A bird landed near her feet and she froze. It was beautiful.

Antonio watched the bird and said, "Upupa or a Hoopoe in English. It's likely going to fly toward Africa soon. They have to migrate for winter."

She said, "He is a pretty boy, isn't he?"

"How do you know it's not a girl?" he asked. "It's not like some birds where the male looks more vibrant. Watch now."

The bird's top feathers fanned out as its mate showed up. Sophie said, "Well now, he's showing off for her. Perhaps he'll get lucky."

Antonio smiled over his work, saying, "Maybe I should try teasing my hair up like that."

She gave him a dry look. "As if you'd need it. I'm sure you've had no problem attracting the ladies."

"It's not all I am, you know." She looked up at his words, stunned to see a bit of vulnerability with that statement.

"I know that, Antonio. I won't apologize for liking how you look, but you are so much more than that to me. You are a wonderful man. Smart, kind, and loyal. And if no one has ever told you that, then I will."

"It's been said by a few women." Antonio watched her tense and narrow her eyes. He smoothly added, "All sisters at the abbey, of course. And girls at the orphanage. Little girls love me. They like to brush my hair and put ribbons in it."

"I was getting ready to throttle you, but then you say things like that and it makes me rather mushy inside," she said.

"Say things like what?" He shrugged, as if every man on the earth would let little girls brush their hair and put ribbons in it.

Sophie pulled him by his ears and kissed him. When she released him, he saw tears misting her eyes. She looked down, not wanting to make a display of it. "Your sister was afraid I was using you for your body. She got very protective of you." She said the words without thinking because he'd want to know how that conversation came about.

"Why on earth would she think that? That doesn't sound like her. She loves you, Sophie." She tried changing the subject, standing to collect the grafted specimens into a gardening bin. "Sophie, you didn't answer me."

"It was nothing. I said something about coming back to visit in a few years, to see how my vines were producing. It doesn't matter. I shouldn't have said anything."

He thought about what she'd said. "So, she took that to mean you were just in this for a fling. That you'd leave after the internship was over." She just nodded. "I'm sorry she put you on the spot like that, Sophie. I mean, I'd thought about it myself. Not the using me for my body thing, but about where you'll go."

"I don't know. I'm afraid my plans have gotten out of my control. I don't know what I'm going to do because I don't think I can go home."

Out of nowhere, he asked, "Have you menstruated?" She jolted at his words because she'd also been thinking about their last week together.

"Jesus wept, Antonio. Could you sound more like a doctor?" Sophie was blushing like mad. "It's not due for a few more days. And I've never been regular." She looked at him, her jaw tight. She was almost thirty. She'd never met anyone she'd thought about having kids with until Antonio. "Don't worry, Antonio. I'm sure it's okay. But we should be using something."

He knew she was right. "I have them. I just ..." He shook his head and smiled sadly. "It was wonderful having nothing between us." It was nice to pretend they both wanted a baby. He was thirty-six years old. He wanted kids. And to his surprise, he realized he wanted them with her.

"Just so you know, mia cara. My father gave me the same lecture that Catarina likely just gave you. He adores you. Everyone does. You could stay here, Sophie. They'd let you stay."

"I couldn't do that to them. Look what's happened. Nonna is away while Giuseppe needs her." She closed her eyes, and the tears finally did come. "I'm the one who should have left."

He pulled her to him and kissed her then. Soft and sweet. "Never, Sophie. I told you, mi amore. You are mine to protect. And when the harvest is done, we will not just turn you out." He had plans for this woman.

❄ 19 ❄

"A person with increasing knowledge and sensory education may derive infinite enjoyment from wine." — *Ernest Hemingway*

S ophie was in the blending room now, and the very special selection of Sangiovese needed to be blended and bottled. She asked, "Why three sips?" She'd watched Antonio working with his sister, and instead of one drink, where he let the wine wash over his palate, he took three smaller sips.

He swirled the new mixture, looking at the color through the light. "When you begin with a new wine, and have cleansed the palate, it can be a shock ... that first sip. A burst of flavor, at least for me, which can overwhelm the senses. It's like kissing."

Sophie narrowed her eyes. She leaned in and said quietly, "Must you make everything about snogging or shagging?" He gave her a rakish grin, his eyebrows twitching up just once.

"Get your mind out of the gutter, *mia cara*. This is serious. You are supposed to be learning."

Her mouth tilted up on one side. She said, "Yes, please. Do go on."

"The first kiss is a surprise. The first meeting of two mouths. You are on unsure footing. But it's during the second kiss that the tasting begins." He took a second sip, rolling the liquid in his mouth. "But the last kiss. That's where you explore the depths of your lover's mouth. The hidden hints of pleasure. The subtle tastes. It lingers, even after it's over."

She'd never seen this technique, but it was the best lesson she'd ever had. She'd taken the sips along with him. Two small, informative sips. Sophie was ready to climb over the table and taste his wine-soaked lips.

Antonio took the final sip, closing his eyes. He made an appreciative noise. "The last sip of wine lets you know if you really love it. This wine is magnifico. The addition of the vines from the northern slope ... it has added something. The old vines are exquisite, and the new ones are really fine from a few years past. But that third section, yes. I think this is it. I think we should try less from the new vines, add a bit more from each of the other two. What do you taste, Sophie?"

She said, "Dark, ripe fruit. Plum, cherry, and berries. Soil and a hint of spice. The tannins are there, but not overdone." She felt the telltale signs on her tongue. The sharpness and slightly astringent feel. It was a flavorful explosion, with some minerality. "There's a strong acidity, but it's not off-putting. It's almost perfect. Almost."

Catarina was standing in the doorway, having run to the processing shed to help with a jammed destemming machine. "Molto buona, Sophie. Let me taste this one, so I can compare with the adjustments you both are proposing."

Catarina didn't need three sips. "This is possibly the best wine we've ever made." Her eyes were so intense. "This will put us back on top. And just think ... this year's harvest is magnifico. It's going to be even better, I think. The old vines produced such beautiful fruit this year. We had just enough rain and sun. It's all coming together." Then something occurred to her. "The barrel you took the old vines from was in a newer barrel, yes? The interior had a medium toast. What if we take the other wine from a high-toast barrel? Let me show you."

They went into the room of the cave that held the two-year barrels. She put her hand on one. "This barrel is a high-toast barrel. We only have one. But I think we could bottle a very limited amount of this *Riserva* with the wine from this barrel if it has the effect I think it will. Just enough to get that higher vanilla note. It'll smooth it out a bit. Maybe soften up the tannins a smidge."

Sophie gave a single, hard clap. "You are a genius. You know that, right? Let's give it a go!"

❦

ANTONIO REACHED ACROSS THE OLD, WORN TABLE. A TABLE THAT had been in the cave for five generations. "You made something very special, Catarina. Let us finish it."

He carefully siphoned from the three barrels, all marked and sorted based on the age of the vine and where they were grown on the estate. The 225L barrels were French Oak but made by a local cooper so that Catarina and Giuseppe could oversee the making of them. They were a diminutive vineyard when compared to the major growers, but every bit of the process was carefully thought out and overseen.

Larger growers who had multiple vineyards had an endless variety of samples to blend. Multiple estates gave a broader spectrum of vines to choose from in the pursuit of perfection. The terroir varied in minute ways throughout Chianti Classico, offering a broader variance of the one type of grape. Subtle differences in the minerals in the soil, sun exposure, and the sloping of the land.

Viti del Fiume was smaller. A single estate with modest production. But his father and grandfather were as good as any grower in the country. His sister's palate was unmatched as far as he was concerned. Antonio brought the three carafes. Catarina altered the blend, peeling back the amount of wine from the newer grapevines. *She is like a chemist*, Antonio thought. He looked at Sophie, who was smiling. She said, "Your sister is either a genius or a mad scientist ... maybe just enough of both." Catarina's mouth twitched.

She swirled the wines together, making it one. Uniting the best of Viti del Fiume in one bottle. They all looked at each other, nervous and exhilarated. Sophie held it up to the light, her glass tilted to see the spectrum of ruby. "Look at that color." She was in awe.

They all sipped. Sophie knew it as soon as it hit her tongue, rolling to all parts of her mouth. She looked at Catarina. In her best Italian accent, she said simply, "Bravo."

IT TOOK APPROXIMATELY EIGHT DAYS IN ALL FOR MAGDALENA Rinalto to put her foot down. She showed up, her son-in-law giving them all a look of apology as both grandmothers came into the house with their bags. Apparently, she'd threatened to take the bus. "This is my home!" She yelled the words in Italian, but Sophie understood every syllable.

What would it be like to have a home for so many years? The same home, with family all around. Sophie knew what a happy home felt like. But her parents had moved on after their retirement, and that beloved family homestead was gone. One generation of Bellamys had bought and sold it. But Viti del Fiume was a legacy. Generations of love, fertility, death, and all of the other things that happened in between those things. She was rather proud of Nonna. After all, you couldn't build such an empire without strong women. They'd convene for dinner, letting Nonna feed them. It was her joy in life to fill a large table with love and her home-cooked meals. But first ... there was the wine.

They were all gathered around the dining table. The rest of the family, and the foreman for the seasonal workers, all had a glass in front of them. Sophie held Catarina's hand. "This is perfection, my friend. Don't go doubting yourself now."

Antonio watched as they all sipped, and even Marco's brows shot up. He didn't have the refined palate needed for Catarina's job, but he knew good wine when he tasted it. His father smiled so broadly that Antonio was startled to realize he hadn't seen that smile in ten years. Since his mother was alive. "This is the one, Catarina," Antonio said. He looked at his own father.

Giuseppe said, "This! This is the one that will go before the judging board. This deserves the Gran Selezione label."

Catarina blushed. "Please, Nonno. No small vineyards ever seem to compete well. I don't think we should."

"If we all thought that, then no one would try. No one would show those big growers what is possible at a quality, family estate. What the Rinalto family is creating is brilliant. Yes, my dear. This *will* go before the judges. Because he who does not try, does not gain. And we fear no man's judgement."

SOPHIE FELL ASLEEP BEFORE ANTONIO EVEN CAME INTO THE house. He didn't want to disturb her. He'd been bottling until late in the night for the last few days. He had dark circles under his eyes from the work ... and the stress. The officer who had been following up on the assault had come to the house today. He'd spoken with the liaison at the London branch of Scotland Yard. Richard Devereaux was missing. He'd missed his check-in date with his parole officer.

Nonna had followed him in, demanding that he let her change his sheets. If she noticed that the bed hadn't been slept in since the last time he'd handed the sheets over, she tactfully kept her own counsel. Antonio helped her put the new sheets on the bed, watching her fluff his pillows. The tenderness he felt nearly buckled his knees. He'd missed her. "I love you, Nonna."

She turned to him, her dark eyes and soft, lined face so precious to him. She took his face in her hands. He had to bend low because he towered over her. She kissed his cheek. "My baby, Antonio," she said. "You look so much like your mother. So beautiful. But your heart is strong. So much stronger than hers. Strong enough to live and love. You will grow old and have many children and grandchildren." He started to speak and she shushed him. "But you aren't getting any younger. If you know what is good for you, you will keep these sheets clean and curl up next to that Englishwoman."

"Nonna!" Antonio was shocked. She was a staunch Catholic.

"I'm not so unaware of things as you all might think. It puts the cart before the horse, so you get working or I will call the priest myself." She smiled. "I like Sophie. She makes you glow with love." And that was that. She walked away, her arms full of clean bed linens.

SOPHIE FELT THE WARMTH OF HIM BEHIND HER. ANTONIO SLEPT, his breath warm and steady on her hair. She also sensed the evidence of his desire, even as he slept. She arched back, and he came awake in slow degrees. He ran his hand along her hip, urgency building. Then he slid his palm down the plane of her belly, slipping softly between her thighs. He moaned, and then she felt him rip her cotton knickers sideways with one jerk. Antonio pressed her on her belly, keeping his palm against her slick heat. He pushed one leg upward with his knee and slid inside her just as she tilted her ass up, seeking. She cursed and he laughed a husky growl against her ear as he came to her in long, deep thrusts. "I'm going to come inside you. Fill you up." She arched her hips up, over and over, taking him deep as he pumped his hips. "Fuck, Sophie. I'm so far in and you're so tight." He propped up on his fists and took her so hard and so deep, she gripped the edge of the mattress and bit down on the pillow. She had to stifle the scream.

Antonio gazed down at Sophie, half animal as she clawed and bit and growled into the pillow. This small, spritely Englishwoman took all of him. Raised that pretty, little ass in the air like a cat. Creamy, white hips meeting him, round and pale against his skin. Seeking what only he could give her. She came so hard, she clamped down on his cock to the point of pain. Exquisite pain that caused the tension in his balls to coil and his orgasm to come without warning. He didn't afford her the courtesy of stifling his own screams. He cried out, deep and throaty, as he released himself to her completely.

❧ 20 ❧

The next night, Antonio stood watch in the rain, letting Sophie rest from the marathon sex they'd had in the early morning. He was taking a big risk. She'd end up pregnant if they kept this up. He wanted her pregnant. Wanted to bind her to him. Flesh and blood and the sort of love that came with making a family. He'd heard about this sort of thing happening to other people. Struck dumb on sight. A connection of the souls that couldn't be measured in time. He felt like he'd known Sophie forever. That she'd always belonged to him.

But Antonio had a life. He was needed, but he thought that maybe Sophie needed him, too. He knew he needed her. But there was a genuine threat to her. He could help her disappear. It wasn't ideal because she was, in fact, a viticulturist. But she had experience in fermentation and horticulture. There could be a place for her in Brazil. And he could hide her there. He stood there, peering out into the wet night, vowing that he'd find a way to keep his Sophie. Keep her for good.

Sophie heard Antonio stirring in the room. She was exhausted. More tired than she'd ever been in her life. She didn't think it was five o'clock yet, so he must have come in for a snack or to get out of the dampness for a time. She felt guilty about them all working so hard, then standing guard duty. Especially tonight. The huge estate was difficult to guard. They had four-man shifts, Marcello paying overtime to some of their work crew. Tonight, it was just the family, though—Antonio and his father and grandfather. The crew needed to sleep. They'd worked hard this week in order to beat the rain, and the men needed to go home to their families. She thought about getting up, but her limbs were like lead.

Sophie knew why, of course. How could she not. She'd lied to Antonio. A white lie to avoid undue worry. They'd played fast and loose with their coupling. They hadn't used birth control since the first time they'd forgotten. The lie was a source of guilt. She wasn't irregular, ever. You could set your watch by her cycles. And she was six days late. Her breasts were heavy. And she was just so tired. Even as she thought it, she started to drift off again.

The body pressed on top of her was wrong. All wrong. Another nightmare? She moved her head, but she tasted the raw smell of tobacco smoke and rough skin in the space between them. Panic hit her full force as she came awake, knowing she wasn't dreaming. His breath was hot on her face, and the acid boiled in her stomach. "You thought you could hide from me, Sophie love. But I get what I want." She felt the tip of something sharp against her jaw. Felt her skin give way just a prick. He wrenched her head to the side and licked. Tears were pouring out of her eyes as she fought and tried to scream.

"Keep your mouth shut, or I will gut that pretty boyfriend of yours." His Manchester accent was thick and low and all too familiar. She'd heard it in her nightmares for ten years. "I've been watching you whore yourself out for this nice cottage. Letting that bastard put his cock in you. But that all ends tonight. After tonight, this will be all you need." He ground his erection into her hip and she nearly vomited. She thrashed, but the knife pressed in again. She froze, rage and panic warring inside her.

He shifted his hand, and now her nose was covered, too. That's when she went completely apeshit. She worked one arm loose from over her head and clawed his face. She didn't care if he cut her throat. He growled with anger and punched her so hard, she almost lost consciousness. Her cheekbone felt like it split into a hundred pieces. She had to get away, but she was fighting the urge to pass out. Threats or not, Antonio was armed. He could take this piece of shit out for good if she could just stay conscious and reach him. He had his hand over her mouth and nose again, and things started to get fuzzy.

❦

ANTONIO HEARD A SNAPPING TWIG BEHIND HIM RIGHT BEFORE someone pounced. The man grabbed him in a bear hug from behind, but his arms weren't strong enough to hold him. Antonio dropped low, coming out of the grasp just in time to hit the asshole in the gut with the stock of his shotgun. Then he turned and butted the motherfucker in the face for good measure. *First, do no harm* rang through his head as he considered putting a bullet through the man's intestines. They'd obviously released him from jail. Instead of shooting the man, he kicked him. "That's for Sophie." Antonio stepped on his wrist as he tried to get up and pressed down with all of his weight until the man was howling. "And that is for the three stitches you gave me."

Antonio did a signal shot in the air, ejecting the round and letting the next slide into place. Marco and Catarina had their orders. Even if they heard the warning shot over the storm, their job was to protect their grandmothers. But Nonno and Papa would come.

He pointed the rifle at the man. "How many are there besides you?"

The man was dazed, but he'd heard him well enough. He wasn't talking. Antonio raised the butt again. "I will enjoy cracking your skull, you piece of shit. I asked how many!"

He threw up his arms. "Basta!" he begged, then dropped his hands, letting the rain pelt his face. "It is just me and the Englishman. The others wouldn't come. Too many police." He groaned, touching his busted nose. "You are too late. He's already got her." Antonio used the flex cuffs the local police had given them, then froze when he heard a scream cut through the sheets of rain.

No, no, no! He'd cable-tied her wrists. "I will cut your throat rather than let you stay here one more day, so keep your hole shut. If you don't want my men to dice up that old woman and that pretty granddaughter, you better start walking." He had her by the hair, leading her out the back door and into the depths of the vines. She'd only caught a glimpse of him in the dark. Richard looked like he'd aged twenty years, not ten. His hair was thinning and he had a scruffy beard. The knife made another small cut. He hadn't meant to do this one, and he shifted the blade. "Sorry, love. I'd rather have you alive. I have plans for you. Somewhere out of this hot hellhole. Then you and I will go about plowing a new furrow through you. I'll wipe any trace of him away. You've made me wait so long, after all."

"You are insane. We barely even knew each other. This is all in your head, you twisted asshole! I will never be with you, so you may as well end this now." Brave words, but then a stab of panic. What if ...

They were headed toward another part of the vineyard, where it bordered the riverbed. The overhead light poles made just enough illumination to maneuver the ground and vines. They came to the river and she was shocked. It had been a dry trickle for the entire season, until now. The rain had finally come, pouring onto the land in sheets like she'd never seen before. The water slushed between the rows of vines like small creeks. The smell of mud and overripe fruit had her stomach roiling. The sky had been grey all day, the rain coming harder as every hour passed, but it was okay because they'd finished the harvesting just yesterday. There were no stars or moon to see by, and Richard stumbled and slipped in the dark behind her. She heard gunfire in the distance. On the other side by the saffron field. That was where Antonio was standing guard. It was not far from the road, and they'd tried to take her that way before.

"Please, Richard. Let me go. You are free. You got released early. You don't need to do this." She hated begging, but maybe he didn't know they could tie him to a murder in England. She certainly wasn't going to tell him.

"I do need to do this!" he shouted. "You betrayed me, you stupid cow! You snubbed me like some rich little college bitch and then you had me arrested. You stole my life from me!"

She struggled then, turning her face to scream at him. "You broke into my flat and attacked me, you fucking pervert. And you are going to decay in prison when they catch you. You killed a woman. You almost killed another. I hate you to the depths of my soul, and I hope you rot in that prison!"

So much for not tipping her hand. She was so angry that she could barely catch her breath between the words. He punched her, closed fist, in the face again. Then to her horror, he slammed his fist into her gut. She doubled over, her knees sinking into the mud. "Oh, God. No!"

What had she done? Oh, please God. What if she was pregnant? She gasped for breath. Just as he bent to pick her up off the ground, she rolled and screamed at the top of her lungs. He dove at her, but she was on her back and she landed a kick of both feet squarely in his chest. He flew back. She barely got to her feet when Antonio burst onto the path, shotgun pointed in front of him. Richard pulled her by the hair, putting the knife snugly under her jaw. Antonio saw a small line of blood trickle from the floodlights above.

"I will gut her right now before I let you have her. She owes me!" He moved the knife and put it facing in toward her belly. "So, if you don't want to see what her intestines look like, you better turn around and walk toward the house, and you can leave that shotgun at your feet." Antonio was frozen, looking at where he had the knife. The moon had come out, and his face was pale as the pieces started coming together.

"Don't hurt her. Please, let's just talk about this. My family has money. We can get you out of Italy. Somewhere they can't extradite." No way. This bastard was dead. Antonio might be a doctor, but he'd learned a thing or two about men like this in South America. He lowered the muzzle, but he was not giving up his gun. Sophie was shaking, wearing a tank top and pajama pants. She was soaked to the bone and her face was tight with fear.

"You think I want money?" The man spit on the ground as the rain started to come down harder. "I make more than enough money. She is mine." Sophie trembled, feeling that knife at her belly. Feeling the cold mud engulf her feet.

Antonio's gaze was fixed on Sophie's abdomen, and it wasn't until then that Richard Devereaux fully understood. "Interesting," he said so calmly it made Antonio's nape tingle with danger. Then he saw them. His father one way and Nonno coming about ten yards the other way. Both behind Richard.

He had to get Sophie away. Get them both out of the line of fire. Antonio slung the gun on his back, putting his hands up. "The gun is away. Just let me take her and you can go." The man had been inching sideways, but he had to stop. The river was fierce and high. Where there had once been a brook, as Sophie had called it, the water rolled and bubbled with life. It was fast, and there was a lot of debris. Logs and other things. It was dangerous to get this much rain all at once, especially after a dry spell.

The man continued. "Tell me, Dr. Rinalto, you rutting whoreson. How will it feel knowing that somewhere far from here, your child will die with a rush of blood on the floor? I will not raise another man's bastard. I'll beat it out of her if I have to. She and I have plans. She owes me." He took her neck in the crook of his arm, licking her mouth.

Antonio said his next words in a voice Sophie didn't recognize. "You will not live out the day, *cazzo di merda*." Sophie struggled to get away, even with her hands bound tightly behind her. Antonio wondered if she'd sensed his father and Nonno behind her. This was it. Marcello moved first, and Richard saw him raise his gun just as Sophie bit him to the bone on his forearm, then she head-butted the piece of shit, the back of her head crunching bone. A nose or maybe teeth. He screamed in rage as he let go out of pure self-preservation. Sophie's adrenalin was keeping her upright as she got clear of him. He brought the knife down in an arc. She turned away, shoving him with her shoulder, causing him to lose his balance. Antonio ran toward her, snatching Sophie off the ground and clearing the way for Giuseppe. He and Sophie were in the line of fire for his father, however. Marcello couldn't shoot.

Richard turned toward the closest threat, and Antonio watched in horror as the man ran toward his father. That's when Nonno fired his Benelli. Richard jerked at the impact, but Nonno kept coming. His words were like nothing Antonio had ever heard come out of his grandfather's mouth. Gutteral, like an avenging angel. "You stay away from *mio famiglia*." Antonio heard the sound, like a train coming from up river. *No!* His father heard it, too, but Nonno was single-minded. He shot the man again, watching him fall.

Antonio screamed, "Papa! Flash flood!" He picked Sophie up because she wasn't wearing shoes and her hands were still bound. He ran like hell toward the house. Away from the downward-sloping trenches of rainwater that emptied into the river. And away from the swollen river, where a wall of debris and water was tearing up the part of Viti del Fiume that bordered the bank.

Antonio slipped, falling to his knees. He slung the shotgun more securely over his back, picked Sophie up again, and turned just in time to see the river take Richard's body up and away. But not before it swept his grandfather's feet out from under him. The water snatched him before Marcello could grab him. He heard his father's screams, and then he heard his own. "Nonno!" The river was so fast and swollen that within seconds, his grandfather was out of sight.

Sophie hadn't seen it happen, but the anguish in Antonio's voice, and Marcello ... Oh God, not Giuseppe.

IT WAS JUST AT THE START OF DAWN WHEN THEY FOUND THEM. They'd called their closest neighbors and the police, and the search had begun as soon as the grounds were passable on foot. Marco had dragged his father into the house, sobbing and yelling. Once they'd checked everyone for injuries, and the ambulance had been called for Sophie, they headed out on foot. The police collected the man who had attacked Antonio, still tied up where he'd left him. The rest of them took the path downriver. Some carried medical supplies and lanterns, some were still armed.

The sun was starting to come up just as the body of Richard Devereaux was found hanging in the thick branches of a riverside tree. His eyes were vacant, having traveled on to the hell he so richly deserved. He had a fondness for dumping women in the river, and it was a just end.

Antonio had screamed himself hoarse, hoping to hear his nonno's voice answering back. He also silently wept until the well was dry. For his family and for Sophie. She'd blame herself. She'd been inconsolable and badly beaten. He was trying not to think about her right now. Or what Richard may have done to her. He failed to keep her from his thoughts, but he had to give everything he had to Nonno right now.

They traveled through the thick mud, downriver to a neighboring vineyard. Giuseppe was there. He was limp, having exhausted the last bit of energy to climb into an old olive tree. Possibly older than the one on their own property. Antonio waded through the thick mud. "Over here!" he screamed hoarsely. His grandfather was covered in mud, his eyes crusted shut. The men took as much care as they could, bringing him onto high ground into an olive grove. Antonio took water out of his pack, wetting a cloth. "Wipe his mouth and nostrils," he ordered his brother.

Catarina came next to them. "Nonno! Wake up!" She sounded like a girl, and it gutted Antonio. He cut his grandfather's favorite shirt open, taking the cloth and wiping his chest. "Get the thermal blanket out. He's hypothermic."

"Why is he so cold! Is he gone?" Catarina was creeping up on a full panic.

"Shush, little duck," he said in Italian. He checked his grandfather's pulse and said, "He's alive. His pulse is not where it should be. It's sluggish. I need that blanket."

Within a minute under the thermal blanket, Giuseppe started to shake. "His body is fighting to keep him warm. It hasn't given up and neither will we." Antonio tended to a cut on his head, cleaning it and securing a rolled bit of bandage from his bag. "Catarina, do the same with the one on his leg. First, cut his pants and clean the mud out of the wound. I think his leg is broken. Don't move anything. If you see bone, tell me and then stop what you are doing."

It helped, giving her a purpose. She wept silently. That's when his papa caught up to them. They'd used the mobile radios that were normally for the workers and their boar-hunting parties. His father was so winded he couldn't speak, and Antonio finally saw him for what he was—a man who would turn sixty this year. "He's alive, Papa. The ambulance is coming. We shouldn't move him. I think he has at least one broken bone and his lungs are compromised." An ambulance had already come for Sophie. This was really starting to become a habit with this family.

His father took his coat off, putting another layer on Giuseppe. Marcello wept openly, "Papa, no. Please, don't leave me. Don't leave me." Antonio looked at Marco, who was stricken with grief. Catarina wept over the wound, unable to look up. To see her father's agony. That's when Giuseppe stirred. His hand came up to thread in his son's black-and-silver hair as Marcello sobbed with their foreheads together.

"I will not leave you, my son. I'm not going anywhere." His words were hoarse.

Antonio glanced at Marco, smiling through tears. "Take Nonna and Martha and meet us at the hospital in Florence. We need a trauma team, and it's where they took Sophie. And tell the police where to find the body. Get that piece of shit off Nonno's land."

ANTONIO WAS ALLOWED TO OBSERVE, BUT LIKE ANY GOOD hospital, he couldn't directly treat a family member. His grandfather had internal bleeding. His spleen was saved, but much worse for the wear. They'd inserted coils to cut off the bleeding. He had two broken ribs as well, one having punctured a lung. His oncologist assisted, and the lung tumor they'd been attempting to shrink was removed. Surgery on a man in his eighties was risky, and they weren't going to do open surgery twice if they could avoid it.

It was a strange experience, seeing his vibrant grandfather so still. So broken. An orthopedic surgeon had set and pinned the leg, remarking how he seemed to have strong bones for a man his age. They'd also bound his wrist, which had been twisted in the debris. No break there, small favors. Now they waited. He told this all to his family. Infection was the big risk, second only to pneumonia. It had been dangerous taking the lung tumor, given his injuries, but this recovery would be long. He was old. And they wouldn't likely risk surgery again for another six months. All of this had been explained to Giuseppe. He was, after all, extremely lucid. His only other questions. *How is our Sophie?* And, *Is he dead?*

Giuseppe seemed relieved at both answers. Now Antonio walked down to the wing of the hospital where Sophie was occupying a bed. She was asleep, her brow furrowed. There was an angry bruise on her cheek. The son of a bitch had punched her in the face more than once. He'd checked her over before the ambulance had taken her. What he hadn't seen was another angry bruise forming on her belly as the nurse adjusted her gown. He remembered Richard's words. *How will it feel knowing that somewhere far from here, your child will die with a rush of blood on the floor?* Sorrow washed through him.

The doctor came in, taking in Antonio's scrubs. "Dr. Rinalto, how is your grandfather?"

"Rather beat up, but he is strong. He will live." Antonio's voice was sure because they just couldn't lose Giuseppe.

"Dr. Rinalto, I know you were concerned about the attack. Her face isn't fractured, and she doesn't seem to have any internal injuries other than some horrific bruising. Any other blood you see is from her monthly courses."

Antonio shut his eyes. "Maybe not," he said, swallowing. "She may"—his voice hitched and he took a deep breath—"she may have been pregnant."

"Dr. Rinalto, I know that was a possibility. She was out of her mind with grief. She kept screaming that he'd hit her in the belly. She didn't want X-rays or medications. I tested her before we did anything, and she had never been pregnant. If she was pregnant and miscarrying, it would have still shown in the bloodwork. I don't know how you feel about it, but I think we should all be glad. That blow to the abdomen could very well have caused a miscarriage if she had been pregnant. So, you see, she will be fine. And you can try again when she is feeling better."

"She's not my wife," he said stupidly, "but I did hope. It's crazy, I know. But I had hoped. Now I'll thank God that my hopes were ignored. You are sure she's okay? That the bleeding is —"

"I'm positive. I had an obstetrician come in while you were in surgery with your grandfather. I also swabbed her mouth and will tell the coroner to check him for any sort of communicable diseases. It's a precaution, since she broke the skin when she bit him."

Antonio shook his head. He should have been here with her, but he couldn't be in two places at once. She'd been adamant that he go look for Giuseppe, even as battered as she'd been, because he'd be able to treat his injuries immediately. And how could he do less? He had to find his nonno. They'd given Sophie something for the pain and something to calm her. She'd had a blow to the head. *The second one in as many months*, he thought, remembering that she'd headbutted him. "Any concussion?"

The doctor shook his head. "Very mild. She is hardheaded, I think."

Antonio let out a sound that was both a laugh and a sob. He said, "She is extremely hardheaded."

The doctor smiled and remarked, "I've found those are the best kind. They keep you humble." He looked at her, lying so still. "She should be coming around any minute. We pulled back on the meds. She'll be confused."

Antonio cleared his throat. "Who was the OB who examined her?"

Behind him came a woman's voice. "An old student of mine, as a matter of fact."

Antonio turned as his grandmother, Martha, was coming into the room. He took her gently in his arms. "Thank you for being here with her. They wouldn't let anyone else in with her. We aren't her family."

Martha leaned in closer, her words serious but soft. "She wasn't raped. She made it very clear and the exam showed nothing. I wanted you to know that, Antonio. And she's going to recover from everything else."

A second wave of relief washed through Antonio. It was something he'd feared. That while he'd been standing guard in the rain like a useless dolt, the man had raped her in their bed. He exhaled a shaking breath. "Even if she had been, she'd have survived that, too. But good God, Grandmother, I'm so glad. I couldn't think about it at the time, but I'm so relieved."

She continued. "The police have come and gone. She gave an account, but it was hard on her, and she'll likely be fuzzy about everything. They plan to do a press conference. They want the word to reach the drug tradesman, I suppose. The tales of stolen treasure being false and all that. What a rotting bastard."

The young doctor choked down a laugh as he was checking Sophie's IV. Apparently, his English was proficient. That was good. Sophie was too traumatized to interpret for herself. He hugged his grandmother again, feeling like an utter fool. He'd stayed away for so long. They were a wonderful family, and he'd never abandon them again. He was lucky to have them.

Antonio heard Sophie stirring. She opened her eyes, looking around. When she saw the morphine pump, her eyes bugged out. "I shouldn't have this!"

He took her hand. "You have some injuries, mi amore. Remember? And you can have the medication. You're not pregnant." Her eyes were wild, and he said quickly, "And no, you didn't lose the baby. You were never pregnant. So, all of our careless abandon was not rewarded. Not yet," he said with a secret smile that was just for her. She put her head back on the pillow, not wanting to blink. Not wanting to take her eyes off him.

Sophie smiled, her eyes welling up. "I remember now. Thank God. When he hit me in the stomach ..." She shuddered, collecting herself. "I suppose it's a good thing. I don't know where I'll be. Where is Richard? Did they get him? Is anyone alone at the house?" She didn't remember. It had all happened so fast and she'd had a blow to the head.

"He's dead. Giuseppe shot him twice when he went after Papa. I found him washed up not far from where we found Nonno. He's dead, Sophie. It's over."

"Oh, God." She put her hand to her head. "Now I remember. The river jumped the bank. Giuseppe was caught in the current. Is he okay?" she croaked, the tears starting again. "This is my fault! He was after me! Oh, God. Giuseppe!"

Antonio rubbed her hair back with one hand, taking her hand in his with the other. "No, Sophie. This was Richard Devereaux's fault, and he died for his crimes. Giuseppe protected you because you are family. Don't take that from him, my love."

With a calming stroke to her forearm, Martha said, "Giuseppe is a tough, old goat. No worries on that account." She winked and squeezed Sophie's shoulder. "Everything is better from this moment forward, my dear. This is where the good stuff starts."

❧ 21 ❧

The seasonal workers were able to extend their employment by another two weeks. The rain had stopped, but the mess it left in its wake was significant. It hadn't damaged any buildings, as they were well away from the river. Just a section of their blending grapes would have to be replanted when the earth wasn't a thick pile of muck. For now, they cleared debris and fortified the riverbank with sandbags. The entire region had felt the effects of the flash flooding, and Viti del Fiume had sustained little damage in comparison.

Sophie walked a little farther every day, making it down to the bottling. The concussion was mild, and she wasn't the sort to stay down for long. She'd been luckier than her friend Morgan. The good news was that Morgan had regained consciousness and had been released a few days ago. Sophie's academic advisor hadn't been as lucky. The thought of Sophie washing up on the riverbank, lifeless and still, continued to wake Antonio at night.

Giuseppe was another matter. Antonio said, "Nonna, speak some sense into your husband!"

Marcello tried to intervene. "Papa, you can't go hopping

through the vines on one leg. Let's get in the truck, and I can drive you to the cave. They are blending the *Riserva* and could use another taster. You can do your exercises on the flat part of the estate, in the orchard. Later."

Giuseppe scowled at his son. "I will not be treated like an invalid."

"You are the textbook example of an invalid! You are broken from head to toe, old man! Give yourself some time to heal!" Marcello was standing with his hands on his hips, doing a standoff with his father.

Antonio just shook his head. Tough old goat, indeed. "How about we walk down and then ride up? Then you can work your lungs a bit." It was a compromise, and he could see his grandfather considering it. Crutches on these slopes were not easy, and he might just ask for the truck halfway down.

Giuseppe said, "Okay, but I want some *sfuso*." Marcello's lips twitched, and he was trying not to laugh.

Magdalena intervened, patting her husband indulgently. "One glass. You are still on medication. In case you forgot, you almost died and left me!" she said with feeling. Giuseppe leaned down and kissed her like she was a girl, not a woman in her eighties.

A pang hit Antonio deep in his chest. He looked at his father and was suddenly sad for him. "It's not too late, you know. You could find that again."

His father shrugged. "I'm too old."

"You aren't too old. You aren't even sixty, Papa. Not yet. There's no age limit on such things. It is too precious."

Marcello said, "And what about my pigheaded children? Will I ever see any grandchildren out of you?"

Antonio's face fell. Then he said it out loud for the first time. The thought that weighed heavily on his mind. "They don't make wine on the Amazon River, Papa."

His father leaned in, suddenly serious. "She's worth it, Antonio. Find a way to make some sacrifices—both of you—and make this work. Good God, boy. You almost lost her!" And his father knew what that was like. Antonio saw the truth of that loss flicker across his father's face.

༄

ANTONIO FOUND HER ON A LADDER, ELBOW DEEP IN A fermenting tank. He laughed. "Did you lose something?"

Sophie smiled at that and said, "As a matter of fact, I did. I was trying to scoop a sample for a photo and lost the blasted ladle. Ha, I've got it! Thank God it floats!"

"Are you testing a sample?" he asked.

"No, I'm taking a picture of the *must* for my intern documentation. I've been keeping a sort of photo journal. Photos and video clips to accompany my written work. I called the university. I had to. With my advisor ..." Sophie closed her eyes, putting a tight rein on her emotions. "With her gone, I needed to tell the university what was going on. Apparently, the head of the department knew about our arrangement. She was keeping a hard copy of my student file in the boss's office. He has a secured file cabinet." She shook her head. "Anyway, it isn't a secret anymore. Not after what happened."

She was scrubbing her hands when her mobile rang. "Could you get that, love?"

Antonio answered the international call. "Yes, she's right here." And he put it on speaker. "It is an officer from Scotland Yard."

The Englishman got right to the point. "Yes, Ms. Bellamy. We've been in contact with the local *polizia*. Top notch. Very professional chaps. I just thought we owed you a call. It's an ongoing investigation, but I thought you had a right to know."

Sophie's stomach dropped. "What's happened?"

"Nothing to anyone you know, miss. No one else, that is. I just ... I've just been exploring the database. We've been trying to piece together other potential victims. Unsolved assaults or murders. You see, we searched his current residence and made a rather disturbing discovery. He had locks of hair. Different samples from different sources. He kept them in envelopes and tied off like little pigtails. He labeled them with just first names. Yours was found ten years ago, but there were others. That is, besides your friend and your"— he cleared his throat—"your advisor. So far, we've used the names and hair color to identify two other women who were sexually assaulted. They remembered him cutting their hair."

Sophie was shaking so hard that her teeth were chattering. She felt Antonio's arms come around her, and she just let him hold her tight. The officer continued. "And at least one Jane Doe who washed up on the coast. I think we've found out who the girl was. It's been a while, but I believe we've identified her. She was a nine-teen-year-old woman who'd run away from home at sixteen. Serial rapists and killers often escalate as time goes on. Get more brazen. This woman disappeared just before he met you, if our timeline is correct. She may have been his first murder. You are very lucky, miss. You helped us lock him up. God knows what he would have done in those ten years."

"And why the bloody hell did they let him out!" she screamed, then stifled a sob. "I'm sorry. I know it wasn't your doing."

"I don't know why, miss. Nor do I know why they didn't give you your day in court. They should have pursued those assault charges. I think his parole case fell under some effort to decriminalize marijuana. And because they didn't pursue the assault charges, they were free to release him early. But make no mistake, he was deep in the drug trade. He'd become a much more prevalent dealer inside the prison than he had been out of it. I got this information from an informant in the same cell block. Anyway, I just wanted you to know. Don't lose one moment of sleep on that bastard. Not anymore. You've got some good people watching out for you, it seems."

"You're very right about that. Thank you, Officer. I appreciate you taking the time to call me about this. I hope you identify all of them. They deserve the same closure." Her voice was quavering by the end. Then she rang off and cried. She cried for all the women he'd hurt. For Morgan and for the cheeky, vibrant academic advisor whose life was cut short because of her. "It was all so senseless. And it could have been me. It was by sheer luck that first time. Maybe that's why he became obsessed. He didn't feel like things were finished between us."

Antonio said, "Whatever he intended for you, it didn't happen. We stopped him. And your friend Morgan is going to be okay. Maybe you can call and check on her now? That might make you feel better."

"Would she even want to hear from me? And this may not be over, Antonio. That son of a bitch put the word out that I'd stolen and hidden a bunch of money and drugs. What if more men, like that one bloke, come after me again? Or show up here, threatening your family?"

"The media coverage should put that rumor to rest. But ..." He caught himself. She was upset. He was not going to bring this up now. Or maybe that was his cowardice talking.

"But what?" she asked.

"Nothing. It's nothing, mi amore. But I think it's time for a riposa. You are still healing." But his eyes held different plans when he got her back to the cottage.

THEY HADN'T BEEN TOGETHER SINCE THE ATTACK. TENSION prickled between them in their little, temporary home. Sophie broke the silence. "He didn't rape me."

Antonio just nodded, his eyes bright. "My grandmother told me." He paused. "But there are other ways to violate someone. He bound you. He hit you. Just because he didn't ..."

She bit the words out. "He made me feel helpless! It was London all over again. And he touched me. I woke up with him on top of me." Her words were guttural. "Grinding himself on me." Antonio wanted to raise him from the dead just so he could murder the son of a bitch. But he kept silent. She was entitled to her anger. Hers and hers alone.

Sophie started pacing. She said, "When I fought him, the threats started. That he'd go in and do horrible things to Catarina and Nonna." She wiped angry tears away. "That he'd gut you because I'd been whoring myself out to you for this house." She screamed again, "He made me feel helpless! He paralyzed me with those threats. I'd take just about anything—any beating, any torture —and I would keep fighting. But I wasn't going to let him hurt this family. Then I thought he'd ... ended the pregnancy. God, I hate him! I'm glad he's dead. I'd kill him again if I could. A thousand horrible deaths! He took something from me! When he pinned me down and bound my wrists. When he touched me, he stole some-thing from me! And most of all, I hate that I let him take some-thing. That just because he could overpower me physically, that he somehow had power over me. The power to take everything."

Antonio was angry and hated the feeling of impotence. He'd failed to protect her. If he felt this way, how much harder is this for Sophie? She was small. She was a woman. No matter how tough she was, Richard Devereaux had taken her control over her own body and her own choices.

He said calmly, "Then take it back, Sophie. Feel your power. Feel the innate dominance that is in your personality. The domi-nance that made you headbutt me that first night we met. Take it back."

"I don't know how!"

"Yes, you do," he said softly.

She narrowed her eyes at him. "I won't use you to work out my anger, Antonio."

He got up close. Too close. In her space. Provoking her. "Take it back. Take what you need!"

Sophie launched herself at him and they went to the floor. She slammed her mouth down on his. "Take what you want from me, Sophie. You're in control," he said against her mouth.

She took his cock in her hand and he hissed. Then she shocked him by climbing down his body and yanking down his shorts. She didn't even tease. She sank his cock deep in her mouth, and with a few good strokes of her mouth, he went off like a cannon. "Fuck!" He bucked off the floor, his whole world shorting out in an electric light show behind his eyelids. When he looked up, she was rubbing her hand over her chin. He almost came again. "Let's go to the bed, Sophie. This was about me, not you."

"I wanted that. I wanted you under me, helpless and out of control. So, I took it." Her eyes were sharp. Her words clipped and so fucking hot coming out of that little, pink mouth.

Antonio said, "I'm going to go get on that bed, and you are going to take everything. Everything your proper, little English mind is too afraid to voice. You are going to take it."

He was digging in his bureau drawer when she came into the room behind him. When he turned around, she was shocked by his arousal, already at full salute again. And by the silk ties in his hands. "I can't do that, Antonio. I can't be tied down. Not now. Maybe not ever."

Antonio tilted his head. "They aren't for you." He purred the words, stabbing her deep in her belly. Her eyes bugged out, and he gave her a wolfish grin. "Don't worry, my Sophie. This isn't some kink I've been keeping a secret. It'll be a first for me, too. As you've probably noticed, I'm a dominant lover."

She swallowed. "I noticed." She loved every minute of it.

He wasn't Richard. She knew that. He didn't have to do this. "I'm okay, Antonio. We don't need to ..."

He ignored her, walking to the bed. Then, like a lazy cat, he stretched out, completely comfortable with how very fucking naked he was. He extended an arm, daring her. Offering the binds that would, if only in a symbolic way, have him at her mercy.

Lust pooled in her belly and she felt the desire sweep like warm honey between her thighs. Sophie tied the first one, leaving enough looseness not to hurt him. He watched her, almost predatory. Like he'd change his mind and throw her down on the bed and cover her. Not a bad idea, but she was wrapping her head around this one right now. When she pulled the second tie to bind his other wrist, spreading his arms out like a sacrifice, he hissed. "Did I hurt you?" she asked.

"No," he bit out, his hips rolling. "I just didn't know how fucking hot this was going to be. Get up here, Sophie."

She looked down his body, a bead of wetness at the tip of him. And he rolled his hips, turned on that she was staring at his hard length. Sophie knew he wanted her to sink onto him. "Not so fast, Medico." She ran a finger up his shaft, and he pulled against his bindings.

She slid her pants down, then off with her top. She could see the tension in his jaw. "Whatever you want, Sophie. Don't be shy. You're hot and wet between your thighs. I know it."

Antonio knew what she liked. Nothing more than to have him spread her thighs and have her with his mouth. But he was tied down and on his back. She'd have to take this for herself. The thought of it had his erection kicking. "Take it, Sophie. Ride your slick sex against my mouth. Climb up here where we both want you." She actually blushed that he'd read her so easily.

Sophie was throbbing between her legs. The smug bastard inched down and laid his head flat against his pillow. Making room. Waiting for her to take him like this. She could see it all. Coming hard against his tongue. Slipping down his body and riding him again. Her chest was pumping. She didn't feel a bit guilty because he was so turned on, he was raw with it. "Get over here, or I'll break these binds and pull you over my face." He was grinding his teeth, aroused to the point of madness.

Sophie started at the foot of the bed, climbing. When she got to the place where her core met his sex, she brushed herself fleetingly against him. He hissed and bucked. She leaned down and kissed him deeply, just letting the heat and slickness of her make the slightest contact with his tip. His breath hitched in his throat as he tried to curb his natural dominance. Let her take what she needed at her own pace. He was ready to explode.

She continued up, hesitating every few inches. Shy, but wanting this rather badly. It was when she was finally in place, knees on either side of him, hands dug into the wooden headboard, that he raised his mouth and brushed a soft kiss over her heated flesh. She shook with desire. Then Antonio used the tip of his tongue to lick up to the top of her sex, rubbing his mouth on her. Moaning and rolling his hips, he was gentle and coaxing, until she couldn't take it anymore.

Sophie sank down into the contact, arching as she sighed with pleasure. He stayed with her, finding a rhythm. She held on to the headboard with one hand splayed on the wall. She started climbing, rolling her hips and making little gasping noises. She heard the sound of tearing fabric as he reared his upper body off the pillow and his hands pulled her hips tight against his face. Sophie was suddenly so glad she hadn't tied those binds tight as she felt him take deep draws on her. She put one hand against the wall and one in his hair, pulling his thick mane and keeping him hard against her. She screamed as she came, her hips jerking against him. Antonio moaned and kept taking the last shuddering bit of her climax into himself. Feasting like a starving man.

She didn't even give herself time to recover. Sophie moved down his body, and he took her nipple in his mouth just as she slammed herself down, seating his thick length to the hilt. She fucked him like an animal. Digging her fingers in his chest even as the marks on her wrists still showed. Antonio met her thrusts with his hips, going so deep it almost hurt. Until he hit a spot that made her bow her back. He caught her, leaning her back as she rode him in short, thrusting jerks. Thumbing the slick, swollen pearl of her sex until she was liquid heat, climaxing over and over. Then he joined her, spilling himself deep in her womb. Giving her everything.

Lazy and satisfied, Antonio said, "You cheated. You didn't tie them very tight. You knew I'd want my hands on you."

"You don't use your hands to hurt or control me, Antonio. You use them to comfort and to keep me close. I did it for me. I knew, at some point, I'd need to feel your hands on me." And although she understood why he'd done it, she didn't ever want to suppress his dominance. Although ... it had been rather exciting seeing Antonio at her mercy. Body tight with lust and unable to just grab her and take what he wanted. It was the teasing that had heightened the lovemaking, and she felt more at ease. They'd both been through a lot, and she'd been healing. But she'd missed him. His physical passion was like a drug, and she'd happily succumb to addiction.

He stroked her all over. Kissing her wounds, and letting her feel the love he had for her. He could be rough and he could be gentle. He'd be whatever she needed him to be. The next time she took him, it was warm and sweet. Her wavy hair shrouded them both as she breathed against his mouth, whispering words of love to him and letting him touch her gorgeous, Boticelli curves. He said her name like a prayer. Like an achingly quiet plea as they slipped back into oblivion together.

22

That evening, Catarina retrieved Sophie from the cave, wanting her to come up to the house with her.

"What sort of surprise?" Sophie asked Catarina. "Is it food? Because I am starved, and I wouldn't mind a huge table of Nonna's food."

"You'll get that regardless. This is so much better." Catarina was excited, and it made Sophie very curious about what was waiting for her.

Sophie turned to Antonio, who shrugged. "Don't look at me, mia cara. She hasn't told me, either."

They heard voices shush just as they came into the kitchen, and whatever Sophie had been expecting, it hadn't been this. She cried out and ran across the room, into the waiting arms of her parents.

"Everyone is okay? You're okay?" Sophie sounded like a hysterical idiot, but she wasn't in control of her emotions just now.

"Yes, we are both fine, ma cherie. We had a burglary, but it was some children in the village." Her father's lovely French accent washed over her. He was warm and smelled like home. Like soap and fresh air. She squeezed him tighter, and he held on to her for dear life.

Her mother smoothed her hair back, kissing her head. "They were looking for some sort of gaming computer. I think they did it on a dare, to be honest. We noticed some wine missing after the fact. The little shits."

Sophie laughed, and if it sounded a little hysterical, no one said a word. Laughter rumbled through the group, and relief swept over Sophie like a cool breeze.

❦

MARTHA AND SOPHIE'S MOTHER HIT IT OFF IMMEDIATELY. THEY had a lot in common, despite their age difference. Sophie was so happy, she felt like her face would burst. "Catarina, I think we should give Kate and Sophie a chance to catch up. Let's go see what your grandmother is up to in the kitchen."

They left the women in the garden, a pitcher of fresh-squeezed lemonade between them. Her parents had taken the red-eye, and it was just after breakfast when Marco had picked them up at the airport. "I'm surprised Papa didn't rent a car," Sophie said, watching her mother savor the freshly picked lemons.

"He was going to, but your host family wouldn't hear of it. And honestly, I can't imagine wanting to leave this place." She eyed her daughter speculatively. She reached over, tracing the faded marks where Richard had cut her neck and chin. "Someday, you'll have your own children. I hope you never have to see them hurt the way you've been hurt. If Giuseppe hadn't killed the rotting bastard, I'd have done it myself. Your father would have, come to that."

Sophie just took her hand, pressing her mother's palm to her face. She smiled, comforted by her mother's touch and by the mere fact that she was here. Sophie hadn't really let herself dwell on what might have happened if Richard came looking for her in France.

Her mother tilted her head, meeting her gaze as she continued.

"You can take a breath now, Sophie. A full, easy breath. It really is over." Sophie was afraid to speak, lest she weep like a child. She nodded. It was over.

Her mother said, "You've fallen in love, haven't you?"

Sophie smiled, clearing her throat. "I have. Viti del Fiume is a beautiful place."

Her mother's mouth turned up at its corners. "You have the worst poker face, Sophie darling. It's why you could never get away with anything as a teenager."

"And you've become a nosey pensioner," she said, eyes narrowed.

Her mother laughed. "Cheeky," she said, and took another sip. "You've fallen in love," she repeated when she'd set her glass on the table.

"You can't possibly know that in this small amount of time," Sophie said.

"I can. You are my only child. I've made it my business to study you most intensely. And I must say, Sophie, full marks. A doctor and absolutely gorgeous. I swear, he's the tallest Italian I've ever met."

"That apparently comes from Martha's side," Sophie said with a grin.

"And that's another point in your favor. This family is wonderful. I think I'd like to see my grandchildren running through those grapevines."

"Mum, stop," she said, her cheeks getting hot.

"Don't Mum me, Sophie. It's long past time you were happy. This life you've been living, it's taken a toll. It's made you wary of people. There's no trace of that girl here. You seem so happy and content with this family, even after everything that has happened."

"He doesn't live in Italy, Mum." She said the words out loud, which made her want to cry. She'd known this day would come.

"I see. Where does he live?" All teasing was gone from her mother's voice.

"He lives on the Amazon River." She barked out a sorry laugh.

"He went there as a missionary and never left. His life is in Brazil, and mine is nowhere."

"Then you make it work, Sophie. Jesus wept. Look at your father and I. He was French, for God's sake. My parents nearly had a stroke. And look at Martha. She left England to be with Antonio's grandfather. Do you know the kind of struggles a female doctor likely had back then? You make it work because you love each other. Go with him! They may not grow grapes in that part of Brazil, but they don't grow Antonio Rinaltos in England!"

"He never asked me to go with him," Sophie said. And the words were like a weight on her chest.

"And would you go? I mean, God knows England isn't much better than Brazil for wine. If you really don't want this, then come to France. But somehow, I don't think that would make either of you very happy."

"I suppose I would go, but I'm not going to press him for such a thing. I mean, I'm a modern woman and all that, but I couldn't, Mum. I just couldn't."

The voice came from behind them, and Sophie wanted to crawl under the table and die. His voice was soft and thick with emotion. "I was afraid to ask." She turned to look at Antonio and his eyes were full of longing. "You'd given up so much because of that horrible bastard. I just wanted you to have ... everything, I guess. I wanted you to finally have everything on your terms. It seemed selfish to ask."

"I'm going to go find your father. I think you two need to talk," her mother said.

Antonio said, "Thank you, signora. Your husband is in the cave, doing a wine tasting."

She walked away, down toward the place where the barrels of their best wine were kept under lock and key. Antonio turned to Sophie. "Will you walk with me, amore?"

"Antonio, I don't know how much you heard, but—"

He cut her off. "Please, my love. Come with me. I need you just now. And I want to talk, before I lose my nerve." Antonio gave her a self-deprecating smile. They started down the path toward the oldest part of the vineyard. He held her hand, pulling her along until they were away from prying ears. Then he began to talk.

"When I moved to Brazil, I was young. I'd just turned twenty-six. It was new and exciting. Manaus isn't like some of the more affluent, touristy parts of Brazil, but it was edgy compared to this place. Not so refined as Firenze or Milano. I got a lot of attention from women, and that was okay for a while, but I'd never been what you'd call a promiscuous sort of man. It was a balm, at first. I was in pain with all that had happened here. But I wasn't a youth. I eventually wanted something else.

"That's when the class system started to become more prevalent. There are ridiculously wealthy men in Brazil. Money buys women as easily as it buys jewels. But there's also the other end of that spectrum. Such poverty as you and I will never know. Poverty that I couldn't even wrap my mind around at first. Doctors make a good living there, but I am not rich. I'm not sophisticated. I grew up in a small village. A farm boy at heart, really. My family does well, but we are upper middle class at best.

"I found myself between the wealthy and the desperately poor. Women who wanted the former, well ... they'd be happy to take me to their bed, but nothing more. I work constantly. I have a pool I don't swim in and a kitchen I barely use. My villa is beautiful, and I'm proud of it, but it's empty of everything that matters." He swallowed hard. "Then there are the other women. So poor that they have to turn to prostitution or the drug trade if they want any real money. The young girls at the orfanato are sheltered. We prepare them for college or to be a bride of Christ or teach them office skills. Anything to keep them off the street when they age out of the orphanage. Their mothers weren't so lucky. They died of disease because that is always a danger. Malaria, Zika, Yellow Fever. All of it. Or they die in some derelict hut with a needle in their arm. Or they just leave."

Sophie was stroking his arm, letting him talk. Her heart was breaking for him, but this was going somewhere and she had to let him lead her there at his own pace. Antonio said, "So, you see, it's not that I never wanted to marry. To have a family. I just was stuck in the middle of these two worlds. Not rich enough for some. An uneven power dynamic between myself and the other. And I worked a lot. One job out of necessity, one job out of duty. I love my work. I just never found a way to balance my life with ... love." He turned to her. "But it doesn't mean I don't want it. After I lost my mother, I was skeptical it actually existed, but I hoped it did."

"There was never anyone?" Sophie asked, sadly. "No one you ever wanted?" She couldn't

believe it, although she'd never been in love, either.

"There was one woman. She was an American. Prior military and a brilliant surgeon. But she wasn't meant for me. I know that now. I watched her fall in love with my friend, and I'm happy for them. I thought I loved her. I mean, I do love her. But it wasn't the sort of love on which you build a life. I was infatuated." His voice grew hoarse. "I realize that now because I never felt for her what I feel for you."

Sophie's throat ached, and she heard a small sound come out of her. Antonio said, "I know you have a whole life to plan. You've worked so hard, Sophie. And you are good at this." He motioned along the sweeping land of Viti del Fiume. "So, I find myself in that same awkward space—wanting something that isn't going to work. I can't give up the missionary work. I would die a little every day if I turned my back on the Sisters of Saint Clare and the children. But I'm not sure I can live without you either, my sweet Sophie." She could tell he was fighting his emotions. "When I thought I might lose you ... or that you were pregnant and he'd harmed you" —he ground his jaw—"my life would have ended right alongside you. I know we haven't had long together, but sometimes you just know. And the thought of separating from you is like being torn in two." She took him in her arms and he melted into her.

Sophie said against his chest, "My mother is right. I have lived a half-life during the last ten years. Looking over my shoulder. I was actually relieved when my parents moved to France. I missed them every single day, but they just seemed safer there. I don't want to be afraid anymore. I don't want to be alone anymore, either. I've lived without a lot of things in my life, Antonio, but I don't think I could part with you."

Antonio shuddered in her arms, his face in her neck. Then he rose above her. "Your mouth, Sophie. I need your mouth," he begged. She went up on her toes to meet him, slow and lazy, giving him her mouth. He kissed her until they both could barely breathe. "I want you with me, Sophie. We could work something out so you didn't have to give up your career. You could come here during the summers and during the harvest. As long as you needed. I could come with you for part of it. But I want to show you my life, mi amore. My home and the mission where I've dedicated my best life's work. You've got a background in horticulture, right? Maybe you could do something there. Help the sisters earn some money with the local plant life. Or not. It's your choice. But I think we could make this work. You'd be giving up more than I would, though. I don't want you to think I don't realize this."

Sophie put a hand over his mouth and said, "Whatever we do from this moment on, we will do together. Whatever I give up, it will not compare to all that I will gain."

Then he pulled her to him. "I love you, Sophie. I love you and I want to marry you. Please, mia cara. Please say you'll be by my side. I want to be yours. Marry me here at Viti del Fiume, where my parents took their vows. I promise you that you will never regret this." They sat under a tree that skirted the rows of vines. Antonio took a piece of the grapevine in his fingers.

"What are you doing?"

His concentration was fierce, then he looked up with a smile. "Making you a ring. I'm making this official before you come to your senses."

IT WAS NONNA WHO SAW IT FIRST. THE BOND AND THE RADIANCE shining between them. Then her eyes fell on Sophie's hand, her homemade ring curling around her finger. She cried out with the joyful vigor of a young girl. She raised her hands in the air and walked to greet them both. "Promesso sposa!" She knew, and she burst into happy tears.

Marco came to his brother's side. "She's a good woman, Antonio. You chose well." Antonio met his eyes, understanding that Marco had secrets to share with him. Sometime when they were alone. But not now. Not today.

Catarina hugged Sophie so hard, it made Sophie squeak. "I finally have a sister. Oh, Sophie. You were always meant to be in this family."

Marcello watched from the doorway and thought, *I wish you were here, Margarite. They are just as wonderful as you said they'd be.* Sophie walked to him, tilting her head. He felt the tears in his eyes. "She would have loved this. She was a hopeless romantic."

Sophie hugged him, whispering in his ear, "I think she wasn't the only one. Thank you, Marcello. Thank you for giving me the safety and shelter of your home."

"This is your home now, bellisima." He kissed her on both cheeks. "And thank you for making my son so happy."

They had a wonderful dinner, everyone squeezing in to make room for her parents. Not just at the dining room table, but in the house. Antonio moved into his brother's room very discreetly. Then the second bedroom in the pool house was conveniently vacant. Over a bottle of their best wine and a spectacular bit of veal, the family got to know each other. Later, Sophie would wonder how the thought popped into her head. But the question was out of her mouth before she thought better of it.

"Antonio, you called him something." Her face was serious, so they all knew who *he* was. "What does *cazzo di merda* mean?" Marco was walking from the kitchen and spit a mouthful of wine out before he could control it. Nonna crossed herself. Catarina capped a hand over her mouth, and Giuseppe's belly rumbled with laughter. Marcello gave his son a chiding look.

Antonio said, "Sophie, darling. It's not for polite company, as you say. I'll tell you later."

Sophie's father said, "Oh no, Antonio. This I have to hear. Out with it."

Sophie actually felt a little guilty. *Sorry*, she mouthed.

Antonio's face was redder than she'd ever seen it. He cleared his throat and said, "Now, take into account the circumstances. Sophie was in danger, and I was violent with anger." He had been trying to impress her parents. *Damn it.*

Marco had no such scruples. "You can wash your mouth out with soap later, Antonio." Then he said with a grin, "Losely translated, it means a dick-faced piece of shit."

Talk about dancing on the bastard's grave. The giggles started with Sophie. Laughter rolled through the entire group, all but for Nonna, who gave Antonio a swat on the back of the head on the way to get dessert. Then another for Marco.

THEY MARRIED IN THE LEMON ORCHARD, AS IT WAS HARVESTING time for the olives. Sophie looked so beautiful, there was a collective gasp as her father walked her down the aisle to where Antonio waited for her. Marco stood next to Antonio, the happiest he'd ever seen him. In his suit coat, he had his mother's wedding ring, a simple gold band that his father had taken from his bureau on the night Antonio had proposed. Martha had taken off her sapphire engagement ring the night of the engagement and told Antonio that his grandfather would have wanted her to have it. "Your grandfather had a weakness for Englishwomen. He would have loved your Sophie."

Her dress was plain linen, coming to just above her ankles. She had a lovely ring of flowers in her hair, and the sight of her nearly undid him. She looked like a woodland fairy. Her hair was long and wavy down her back. It had been three weeks since he'd proposed. Time enough to cut through the government red tape, secure a priest, and get Sophie a Brazilian visa that they'd pick up in England.

Sophie watched this beautiful man speak his vows to her, and she could hardly believe it was happening. He was dressed in a summer suit. The only dressy item he'd brought in his luggage. He looked rather dashing in a suit. Among the buzzing insects and vibrant fruit trees, they bound themselves to each other before God and family. This was the beginning of something so unexpected and exciting, sometimes Sophie wondered if she was dreaming.

They wanted to get to Brazil before Christmas so he could be there to lavish the children and staff with gifts from his homeland. Sophie's internship ended in a week, and then they would leave to start their life together.

He said his vows in Latin, and she said hers in English. No one minded, of course. Not the priest or the family. When he slid the ring on her finger, he kissed her hand right over the ring. Connecting, in a small way, with his mother. This was the band his father had slid on Margarite's finger. His mother had loved his father. Deep down, Antonio knew this. And for Marcello, the love had traveled beyond death, into forever. He understood now. He said, "Forever, my sweet Sophie."

ANTONIO TOOK HER HAND, LEADING HER AWAY FROM THE GROUP to the old olive tree. The one that's trunk bowed and slanted to form a seat of sorts. He just wanted a moment alone with her, away from the crowd. But when they came to the special spot, they both slowed and just stared in awe. Seated within the embrace of the tree was Giuseppe. His eyes were closed, and he was humming softly to Magdalena. She was curled in his lap, and he held her so sweetly that they could have been teenage lovers. "Oh, Antonio. Look at them," Sophie said.

Sophie teared up, and he understood it. His grandparents had been together their entire adult lives. How many times had they sat like this over the many decades of their marriage? Magdalena spoke, "You were hurt. You are sick. I shouldn't be sitting on you." The laughter rolled, soft and deep, from Giuseppe's chest.

He said, "I will never be too old or too weak to hold you, my darling." Then he kissed the top of her head. Sophie caught the gist of it, and she couldn't take much more. They were so beautiful. She wanted to grow old like this with Antonio. Antonio seemed to agree because his eyes shone with tears of love as he looked at her.

He and Sophie slipped away, not wanting to intrude on their time together. Magdalena tried to be strong, but Giuseppe's illness scared her. She'd be lost without her beloved Giuseppe.

So, Sophie and Antonio strolled among the vines, content to walk as he told her more about Brazil. "I'm going to make you very happy, mia cara. I promise you. And you will love the children. They just added a new baby to the family, and two of the older boys are leaving to go into the military. It's a good job for them, and it will keep them out of the mines."

"Is working in the mines so bad?" she asked.

"It is. They aren't like your English mines or in America. They'd practically be slaves. It's dangerous, too. Our boys are too good for such a life. I'm going to miss them. But there are new children. There are always new children." His voice sounded sad.

"I can't wait to meet them." Sophie stopped, wrapping her arms around his waist. "I always thought I was a decent person. Maybe even better than most. But I feel like you are going to teach me what it really means to be a good person. You are going to make me better, Antonio. And I love you so much for that."

ANTONIO STOOD BETWEEN HIS SIBLINGS, LOOKING AT THE SMALL grave just outside the village. She'd been buried in the Rinalto plot, and it occurred to Antonio that his grandparents would be here someday. And his father would someday take his place next to his wife. He didn't like thinking about it.

He went to her stone, *Margarite Maria Rinalto, Loving wife and mother*, and put the sweet-smelling mixture of lilies at the head of the grave. The sun was setting, and he remembered all the Tuscan sunsets he watched with his mother. Antonio said, "I was married today, Mama. I think you would have liked her. She's smart and funny. She's brave, too. Very brave and loyal. I'm a lucky man. You always told me I'd fall in love one day, and you were right." He wiped his nose, just letting his tears fall. "I love you, Mama. And I think I understand you better now. You always felt things more intensely. You shined brighter than most. And I know you'll be waiting for us all someday, lighting our way with your vibrant spirit." His voice broke and his father's arms came around him. "I miss her, Papa. Oh, God. I miss her."

Marcello's voice was rough and low as he said, "I know, my little rabbit. I miss her, too." He scooped his other two children into his arms, all of them with their heads together. Marco and Catarina wept silently. Marcello said, "It is time for you all to start your own families. Your own lives. And whether that happens here or somewhere else, I will love you enough for both your parents. And I'll keep *Viti del Fiume* safe for your return."

❦ 23 ❦
MANAUS, AMAZONAS, BRAZIL

Antonio parked his Land Rover in the garage of his villa. He paused, the key in his hand. He looked at Sophie, giving her a quiet smile. "This moment is when it happens. Two lives merge. Thank you for this, Sophie. Having you here feels like a dream."

Sophie leaned over, taking his face in her hands. She kissed him, slow and sweet. "I love you, Antonio. Wherever you go, I go."

He said, "I'm going to remind you of this conversation the first time you see a Goliath spider." She laughed against his mouth.

"Or a bullet ant? Or a lancehead viper?" she said, smiling.

His face grew serious. "Jesus, you must love me to put up with all of this."

She said, "Head over heels, my love. Now, are you going to let me out of the car park? Because I could use a shower."

❦

ANTONIO PAID THE GROCERY DELIVERY BOY AND CARRIED THE bags into the kitchen. He'd missed all of this fresh fruit. Mangos, passion fruit, and guava. Fresh herbs, potatoes, nuts, and some very good beef. He was going to cook for his wife, then they'd christen their bedroom properly. He washed some of the fruit, then started chopping it all for a light snack. It was perfectly ripe, and he took a slice of passion fruit in his fingers, ready to sample.

Then all thoughts left his head when he looked up to see Sophie standing in the doorway to the kitchen. She was pink and scrubbed clean from the shower. Her hair was wet and wavy over her shoulders, and she was wearing one of his scrub shirts. The sight of her in his kitchen, wearing his shirt, hit him hard in the gut. She belonged here. She was his, and he was absolutely hers. He reached out an offering. A ripe slice of passion fruit. When she let him feed her, her eyes registered shock. "That's the most gorgeous piece of fruit I've ever tasted."

Antonio pulled her to him, and she tilted her head. She didn't quite understand the pain she saw in his eyes. "What is wrong, love?"

His voice was hoarse. "Nothing, Sophie. Everything is finally just right. Having you here with me makes this a home." He kissed her, slow and deep. She tasted like passion fruit and something uniquely Sophie, and it fueled his need. He lifted her onto the counter, deepening their kiss. "I need you."

"You have me." She ran her hands up the back of his shirt, and he swayed as he felt her palms roaming his body. Sophie whispered, "And you're mine, Antonio. All mine."

They hastily peeled each other's clothes off, and she arched as he kissed her neck and collarbone. She ran her hands over his beautiful, smooth skin and then slid one hand into his thick, dark hair. She smoothed the other over his tightly muscled ass.

He ran a hand up her thigh until he could rub a thumb over the sensitive top of her sex. She gasped and closed her eyes. Antonio balled a fist in her hair. "Open your eyes," he pleaded. She did, and they were damp with tears. It was his words. She was safe and she was home.

Antonio sheathed himself into her and felt himself quake with desire. And so much love that he thought he'd unman himself by weeping. He pulled her to him, over and over again. Sophie made little mewling noises, just as overcome as he. He saw how much pleasure she took in his body. Her eyes were hazy with it, her body liquid in his arms as he took her, hot and demanding. "Look at me while you come. I'd see it in your eyes, mi amore. I want to see into your soul." She let go in his arms, and he knew it was his words, not his thrusts, that drove her over the edge. Words of love and desire were their own sort of magic. "I love you," he croaked, his voice tight with lust and love combined. Antonio looked into her eyes, searching. Blue green and frantic with cresting pleasure. And he dove deep into her body, spilling himself. He pressed her forehead to his, his orgasm going on and on as he gasped like a dying man.

⊛

Antonio was cooking some potatoes and grilling steaks. He was wearing a pair of low-slung shorts and a T-shirt. He was beautiful in this casual, domestic setting.

He said, "We should sleep after dinner. It will help us get on a different schedule. It will take a while, though. It's a big time change for you. Tomorrow, we'll go to the mission. I'm still techni-cally on emergency family leave, so a couple more days won't hurt."

Sophie loved the villa. It had three bedrooms, three bathrooms, and a big swimming pool. It was very beautiful, but he wasn't one of those well-to-do types whose home had ten bedrooms and a jacuzzi in every bathroom just to prove he could afford it. He had enough for guests ... or perhaps a couple children. She felt the evidence of their countertop session, slick against her flesh. She cleared her throat. "Antonio, do you want me to go on the pill?"

He stilled, then he turned the burner off. He swung around to her and asked, "Do you want to go on the pill?"

She squirmed. "I asked you first."

"Truthfully, Sophie, I don't know how to answer that question. I'm turning thirty-six years old next month. I want children, yes. I've always wanted them. But I want you to be ready. This isn't just about me. I have excellent doctors I can recommend."

"I don't want to go on the pill." There. She'd said it. "I'm pushing thirty. I want children, and I think we should just let nature take its course. I love you, Antonio." She paused. "I don't want to go on the pill."

He took her again, right there on the floor.

THE FOOD REHEATED, THEY ATE THEIR FIRST MEAL TOGETHER IN their villa. Antonio told her about his work at the private hospital. She said, "It sounds like they were lucky to get you right out of medical school. I think what you do is absolutely amazing, Antonio. You save lives. You go into their bodies and ... repair. Heal on a very physical level. I can't imagine it."

He was embarrassed by her praise, she knew. He shrugged as he played with his food. "Yes, well, my work at St. Clare's is a little broader on the spectrum."

She asked, "What is the most outlandish case you've ever handled?"

So, he told her. The day was branded in his memory. "There was a fire in one of the indigenous villages, far from any sort of fire-fighting services. The logging company had been doing a controlled burn, and it got away from them. The thieving bastards just take without thought to what it means for this place. For the earth itself. And they ignore safety regulations." Antonio shook himself.

"Anyway, one of the injured people was a pregnant woman who was burned horribly. The trauma of it put her into labor. We were cut off from the boat, and the fire was gaining momentum. We took her and the other villagers over the rope bridge that crossed a branch of the river. There's a sacred spring there. It's a fertility spring, or so they say. And I believe it. A waterfall is fed from an underground river. The tribal mothers thought if they could get her to the spring, the mother of all things would spare the woman and child. We held her up, her feet planted in the water. She was near death from the burns, but she seemed to draw strength from the holy place. She wanted to save her baby."

Antonio stopped, his throat working. Sophie should stop him because he was getting emotional. But she couldn't. She had to hear this story. She felt that it was important. That it would explain why he did this work and why he couldn't walk away from it. He said, "She gave birth, despite catastrophic injuries. The fire raged near us, and the river was so high, they almost couldn't rescue us. But she saved her child. She drew strength from someplace inside herself that was beyond the physical shell that had been so horribly injured. She drew strength from the waters of that spring. I felt it. We all did. A sort of warm hum that filled the water and the air between us. It was a miracle, Sophie. They both lived. The baby was healthy, and the mother recovered. She is scarred, but she lives to care for her child."

Sophie watched him relive the experience with tears misting his eyes. "That's the most incredible thing I've ever heard. Oh, God." She grabbed him, hugging him tightly. "I thought you were going to tell me about pulling some big bug out of someone's nose or reattaching a limb. My God, Antonio. You and the other doctors are risking your lives to serve these people."

"That is why they call it missionary work. If it was easy, everyone would do it. But we were all called from God, I believe. From the nuns who inhabit the abbey to the gardener. From the doctors to the teachers. God brought us all there to do His work— work that others wouldn't do." Antonio smiled, trying to lighten the mood. "The baby was a beautiful little girl." He met her eyes.

"I'd like a daughter. And sons, of course. I'll need three of each, at least."

She raised a brow. "Oh, really? Only six?"

"Well, we are getting old," he said with a shrug, then he dodged a blow from her. He caught her wrist, kissing her soundly on the mouth. "I wouldn't want to grow old with anyone else."

✿ 24 ✿

ST. CLARE'S CHARITY MISSION, AMAZON
RIVER, BRAZIL

S ophie knew she was gawking, open-mouthed and ridiculous to anyone who cared to watch her. The city was old and exotic looking, a little rough around the edges in some parts. But as they reached the outskirts, she was taken aback by the poverty. Houses literally stacked on top of each other. Waste going directly into the river. But the people recognized Antonio's car. He stopped on occasion to introduce her.

When he started toward the mission, he explained, "I have taken care of many of these people, both at the mission's hospital, if they can make it there, or at the mobile clinic for routine care. Vaccinations, wound care, well-child exams. They are poor, but they have their pride. They give the mission what they can, even if it's in goods instead of currency. One man helps maintain the vehicles. Another gives them eggs. The woman I introduced to you in the green dress, she mends clothing for the children. The *orfanato* relies heavily on used clothing. And they are children, so accidents occur. Ripped knees and missing buttons. She fixes these things." He shrugged. "It works. Normally, one of the sisters does the work, but

294

she's diabetic. She wants to pay but she can't. So, this gives her a sense of dignity."

Sophie said, "That's kind of you all. Dignity is important. If they didn't barter like this, maybe she'd stop coming for care."

"Exactly," Antonio said. He turned off the main road, and suddenly the vehicle was enclosed in green.

"Oh, my! This is unbelievable. It's so thick. I mean, you hear things about the density of the canopy. I studied it in school. But it's different when you see it." The air was suddenly balmier, but fresher. Like grass and decaying leaves and rain-soaked bark. "This is ... indescribable."

"Wait until you hear it at night. When the hum of the engine isn't masking the sounds. This forest is a living thing, more so than the forests in Italy or in England. This system is perfect. From predator to the smallest flower. It is ruthless and dangerous. It is beautiful and bountiful. They've discovered important medicines. Something nature provided, but that we had to hunt to find. And it's all disappearing."

"The loggers and developers," Sophie said bitterly. "I know it's not the same, but if you went to Ireland, England, and Scotland hundreds of years ago, there were trees from shore to shore. But then the British Navy came into power, and they needed to build more ships. They stripped it bare. We are fortunate, I suppose, that ships are made of metal now, and not lumber. Maybe we'll get some of it back."

"Maybe," Antonio said. "But humans always find a way to take more from nature than they give."

THEY FOLLOWED A ROUGH ROAD FOR SEVERAL MINUTES. THEN IT opened up suddenly, and there it was. Antonio stopped the car for a moment, just taking in the sight of their little, self-sustaining compound.

Sophie felt like she'd been hit in the chest. Here it was. This place that had healed her husband. The place and people that captured his heart forever. Her eyes filled with tears as she looked at him. The relief and the joy she saw in his face. Home. This was home. He'd said that she finally made his villa a home, and now she understood. This place was his safe haven. These people were his family.

There was a screech from a child, and Sophie saw the children start to point, recognizing the Land Rover. The teachers held them back so that Antonio could safely drive to the parking area of the hospital. There was a school to the left, and what looked like a dormitory. With small windows spaced evenly. The children's rooms, most likely. Between that and the hospital was the abbey and the chapel. Finally, there was a small hospital. Two stories and made of stuccoed stone and wood. There were nuns in full habit, tending to the children. To the far right of the property, she noticed new, wooden cottages, raised off the ground about five feet. *The married housing.* Antonio had told her about this. There was a walled garden with an old doorway and a kitchen garden that was well tended.

No sooner had they opened the door than a long-haired, drop-dead-gorgeous man came running out of the hospital. He launched himself at Antonio and hugged him. *Liam. This is his friend Liam. And Izzy, whom he loved.* She amended, *But not the way he loves me.* She was lovely, though. On the tall side of average and athletically built. Golden skin and cropped hair that was thick and full of soft, loose curls. It looked like spun caramel. Sophie didn't have time to be jealous. After a second tackle by this woman, both doctors turned to her. Liam raised a brow. "And who is this lovely lass?"

Antonio thought about how to answer. This was Liam O'Brien. The Irishman who'd been rescued out of an unending tragedy, into the arms of his mate. Because the lore of the O'Brien clan was clear. They had only one true mate. Til death and beyond. He wanted to make Liam understand. She was more than his lover or his wife. He said simply, "She's my mate."

Liam reared back in surprise, as did Izzy. Then Liam noticed the rings. His dazzling smile was mirrored by Izzy's. Liam grabbed him for another hug and a whoop. Izzy snatched Sophie close for a hug, holding nothing back. She whispered in Sophie's ear, "Oh, God. We prayed for you to come." She had tears in her eyes as they separated, taking Sophie's hands. "And now you're here."

Liam approached her. "I'm sorry, lass. We are huggers. I'm Liam O'Brien."

She smiled. "Sophie Bellamy," she said. Then she corrected, "I mean Sophie Rinalto. Still getting used to that, actually."

Liam's eyes widened. "And an Englishwoman to boot. Antonio, I can't wait to hear this story. But for a start ..." He grabbed her up and swung her around. "Welcome to St. Clare's, Sophie." He kissed her on the cheek, just to get under Antonio's skin. Then he grinned at him. "He's the jealous sort, don't you know. I can't resist." He narrowed his eyes, giving her a more serious appraisal. "Men like Antonio mate for life. You must be quite a woman to have earned such a love."

"I don't know about that, but I do know that I mate for life as well. And I am extremely lucky to have earned his love." That seemed to please the man. She jumped as she heard someone approaching from behind with booming footsteps. She was still easily startled. Something that would heal with time. The man who approached looked like a Viking raider.

Antonio yelled, "Hans!" Cue another big-man hug.

Three more people neared. All, as it turned out, were Irish citizens. Two O'Briens and one woman whom they called Doc Mary. She was married to Hans, a retired US Marine. It was quite an eclectic collection of humans who made up St. Clare's. It was all so overwhelming, and Sophie hadn't even met the children or any of the sisters. This was going to be difficult without name tags.

Antonio felt her a moment before she appeared. Like sensing

the presence of an angel who came to watch over you during times of trouble. They all parted like the Red Sea, and she came to him.

Sophie watched as the lovely, commanding woman approached. Well into her advanced years, Sophie was surprised to see no hint of frail bones and diminishing muscle. She was tall for a woman and straight-backed. She had intelligent, sharp-blue eyes. She enfolded Antonio in her arms. "Welcome home, my boy. We've felt the absence of you most keenly." Antonio melted into her, and Sophie felt the tears prick her eyes. This motherless boy had come to her. Not really a boy, but when we were injured in our hearts, the child shone through. The abbess had taken him into her loving shelter and given him a purpose. Maybe this place did this for everyone. Maybe it could do it for her. The abbess turned to Sophie. "I am Reverend Mother Faith. And who might you be?" Her words were kind and curious.

Sophie smiled. "It's a pleasure, Reverend Mother. I've heard so much about you and your mission. I'd be the new wife." She felt her cheeks flush pink.

The woman's eyes widened and her mouth turned up on one side. "Are ye now?" She had the loveliest Irish lilt to her voice. She turned to Antonio. "I always wondered what kind of woman would see your worth. Ye went all the way to Italy to find yourself an English lass?" She smiled, rubbing his cheek. "Well done, lad." She turned to another woman, petite with red hair. Liam's mother, Sorcha. "It appears I owe you that five euro. As it turns out, we won't have to import a nice girl from the old country."

Liam laughed. "Mam, ye didn't wager with the abbess?" He shook his head, looking at Sophie now. "Irish women are nothing but trouble, lass. Mind your wits around these two."

The Reverend Mother gave him a sideways glance, but Izzy gave him a swat. Then his mother, Sorcha, just winked at Sophie. "My well-behaved son is getting married in two weeks, so we don't have too much time to corrupt you. In case you're wondering, Liam is not the well-behaved son." Liam smiled and gave his mother a kiss on the cheek.

The abbess said, "And we are sorry to see you go, Sorcha. I hope we can persuade you to come back to us." The abbess then turned her attention to Sophie, her gaze warm but direct. "I hope you're hungry, my dear. Gabriela has made a fine feast for Antonio's home-coming. We weren't expecting a wedding celebration, but we will celebrate double the blessings. The children are beside themselves, wanting to see him. I'm rather afraid you're going to be overrun with hoards of them."

Sophie smiled. "I can't wait. I've heard about them. About you. All of you. We've just spent several months with his family, but I think St. Clare's is his home."

The abbess's eyes misted. "He is a permanent part of this family. We would be lost without him. And now we have you, and which-ever of your gifts the Lord sees fit to bless us with, my dear. Welcome to our home."

❧❦❧

In between obscenely stuffing herself, Sophie watched with unhindered wonder and joy as the adults of St. Clare's inter-acted with the children from the orfanato and neighboring villages. There were two young girls attached to Antonio and Liam, braiding their hair in a sort of hairstyle contest. Liam poked the one child in the ribs. "Why can't ye choose one of the women for this? The indignity of it all." The one child obviously spoke little English, and Sophie warmed to her toes as Antonio interpreted the dialogue in Portuguese. The girls giggled.

There was a small boy with glasses. Cristiano was his name, she thought. And he was nestled between Doc Mary and Hans like he belonged there.

Izzy pointed and told her, "Normally, the children eat over there at their own tables, and the adults eat together. But since the children all missed Antonio so much, and they are so curious about you, the sisters have bent the rules for lunch."

There was a small girl next to her, touching her long ponytail. An older girl came with a baby, and Sophie's eyes lit up. The girl said in broken English, "I am Rosalis. This is my new sister, Hortência. I won the honor to name her. I could say the Hail Mary in English and Latin without mistakes," she said proudly. "Her name means the gardener. She was left in our walled garden by God." Sophie's eyes darted to Izzy's.

Izzy cleared her throat. "Yes, she was ... found in Reverend Mother Faith's personal garden. She is indeed a gift, Rosalis. You are very right." Her eyes pleaded with Sophie not to break the girl's illusion. Someone had left the child in the walled garden, hoping the orfanato would take her. Save her. What would it be like to be so desperate?

Rosalis asked, "Would you like to hold her?"

"I'd love to hold her. But she seems very attached to you, so maybe you could sit here right next to me and make sure she's happy."

The girl handed the baby to Sophie, and she nestled the child in the crook of her arm. Hortência's wide, dark eyes just stared at her, as if trying to decide whether she would settle for this stranger's attentions. Sophie rubbed her lips on the baby's soft head, then she put an arm around Rosalis. Sophie said, "I think you are a gift from God as well, Rosalis. You are a very good girl. She's lucky to have such a loving big sister."

Then she kissed the girl's head softly. The child beamed with pride. She was about fifteen. Small, but maturing. She was such a pretty child. Sophie glanced at Antonio, and the look on his face caused her breath to seize up in her chest. He just mouthed, *I love you.*

AFTER A THOROUGH TOUR AND AN INTRODUCTION TO EVERY MAN, woman, and child on the property, Antonio was called in for a surgical consult. Sophie was fascinated by the flora of this part of the world, and she asked Paolo, the groundskeeper, if he would take her on a tour of the gardens and the surrounding property and explain the different plants and edible wild things.

Her first attempt at university, when she'd been eighteen, was coming back to her. She'd begun studies in horticulture and floriculture. It wasn't until later that she'd decided to become a viticulturist.

The diversity of plant life was overwhelming. Nuts, tropical fruit and berries, cacao, medicinal plants, and an endless collection of gorgeous flowers. In the gardens, he grew cassava, yucca, beans, eggplant, onions, corn, and the property had acai berries, passion fruit, and plantains.

He foraged for wild ingredients on the uncultivated portion of their land. It was all interesting, but it wasn't until he explained everything that he knew about the Aguaje, or moriche palm fruit, that Sophie's wheels began to turn. It grew wild on the unruly palm trees that lined the river and dotted the wetlands. The super fruit was harvested during the rainy season and had to be picked from a canoe, according to Paolo. It had many uses, not the least of which was an indigenous wine.

❦

ANTONIO HAD BEEN PETTING SOPHIE FOR HOURS. BETWEEN THE jet lag and their rigorous bed play, she'd fallen asleep—hard. He loved the feel of her skin, smooth and warm under his fingers. Under his lips as he rubbed them along the cap of her shoulder. He couldn't get enough contact. As if sensing his need, she rolled over and into him, where she fell asleep nestled against him like a kitten. "I love you," he whispered.

Sophie stirred, tipping her face to him. "I love you, too. Thank you for this."

"For what?" he asked, lifting up her chin to look into her eyes.

"For trusting me and loving me enough to bring me here. Giving me them. The sisters and the children and everything that comes with them. For giving me all of you."

❧ 25 ❧

THREE MONTHS LATER

Sophie wiped the rain out of her eyes. Antonio had been adamant that she wear raingear, which was stiff and uncomfortable. She looked at Paolo, who found her outfit amusing. "Don't say a word. He's insufferable."

Paolo said, "I don't know this word."

"Hard to tolerate, a pain in the butt," she said.

He gave her a chiding look. "*Senhora*, you don't need to be out here. The boys and I can handle the picking. If you are buying the fruit from the abbey, you shouldn't have to pick the fruit, too." He said this half in English, half in Portuguese, but she followed it.

"But I like the picking. It's part of the process. Granted, it is usually grapes, but ..." She shrugged. *One works with what one has.* She raised her arms up with the long pole to cut the heavy clusters of fruit that hung off the palms. Sophie asked, "Why don't we get the fruit off the really high ones I saw? There's more to take there."

"Too high to pick safely, Ms. Sophie. The trees are over a hundred feet. I suppose we can leave those for the animals, no?"

Sophie smiled and said, "I suppose. For now." She was a woman on a mission. And she was looking at the possibility of a jaboticaba orchard as well. A tree that normally grew in the hilly region closer to Rio de Janeiro but was nicknamed the grape tree. The fruit grew right out of the bark and made even better wine. Paolo had created a monster. If she couldn't grow them here, then maybe she could travel down to the orchards to buy the fruit in bulk. She'd continue experimenting. Keep buying as much as she could off the abbey, selling it in order to keep the revenue coming into the mission. She smiled as she worked, loving how this new work pushed her to learn more. Showed her how to work with the indigenous plants.

Her smile waned as a flush of heat went through her. Then her stomach jerked. The canoe was rocking a bit, but surely she wasn't getting seasick? She never got seasick. She loved the water. But it seemed she was, and with only a second to spare, she turned to the other side of the canoe and lost her lunch. All that gorgeous cheese bread was now fish food. She heaved twice more, then sat up. She opened her mouth, catching the pouring rain to rinse the sour taste from her mouth.

She turned to find three sets of eyes looking at her. Cristiano, Hans, and Paolo. "What? I'm just a bit seasick. It's nothing."

It was Doc Mary's husband, Hans, who smirked openly. She scowled at him. He put his hands up in surrender. "If you say so, Momma."

She just sat there in the rain, momentarily speechless.

❦

ANTONIO RAN DOWN THE HALL WHEN THE CALL CAME IN. JESUS, it never seemed to calm down nowadays. Izzy was on her day off, but being Izzy, she ended up running alongside him, tying the cord to her scrubs. "No workout for you, it appears."

"Multiple casualties, all hands on deck. This is its own sort of workout, I suppose. Give me the details."

"A crane collapsed on the edge of the city. They took some of the wounded to the public hospital, but they sent three here.

Impact injuries, mostly, but they kept the head traumas where they had the better radiology department." St. Clare's radiology department consisted of one good X-ray machine and one archaic one they kept maintained for situations just like this.

"Ages?"

"No idea. They just told us we were getting three trauma patients. Adults, I'm assuming, as it was a worksite."

They came into the triage area and stopped dead in their tracks. Not three. Six. And two of them were children. Antonio yelled, "I need Quinn!" Quinn was the pediatrician, but he had trauma experience from doing several missions in South America and Africa.

Quinn yelled behind him, "Already on it, brother. Jaysus, I thought this was a construction zone?"

The EMT from the city said, "It was a school bus. There were two children and the woman was the driver. They were passing under the crane when it collapsed. There are more men trapped under rubble. I must go. The girl child is the most critical." Then he was gone.

Izzy said, "You have more pediatric experience. I'll take the three adults. Mary can assist."

Mary came in next. "I'm ready, love. Tell me where you need me." Mary was a family practice doctor, but her time at St. Clare's had taught her more than she'd ever learned in her small county in Ireland.

Quinn's voice was grim. "The boy needs X-rays on his clavicle and his humorous. Right side. He's alert, abdomen soft, legs are okay. Laceration to the right scapula. He'll need stitches." A nurse came in and took him right to X-ray.

Meanwhile, Antonio was assessing the small child. Quinn came next to him. "What is this?"

Quinn jerked. "It looks like some sort of bolt. Christ, that's really close to her liver."

Antonio started moving. "We need to open her up. She won't

make it to the city hospital. They should have taken her there first thing."

Quinn was next to him. He yelled back to Pietro, the lab tech, "Tell the sisters to call the school and find her parents!"

The total was seven hours in surgery and every bit of their stored plasma. At some point, Izzy had come in. Two surgeries already, yet she insisted on helping. "You've done everything you can, Antonio. It's time to close. It's in God's hands now."

Antonio had run out of the energy to be angry. They'd had no choice, but the girl should have never been brought there. They'd just piled six of them in one ambulance when they couldn't take any more to the city hospital. Despite what they'd said, they hadn't triaged beforehand. If he'd been at his private hospital, they would've had more equipment at their disposal. Still, he was a good surgeon. So was Izzy. He wasn't sure about a lot, but he knew that much. He just wasn't sure it would be enough.

"We are out of plasma, so I'll need the O-Neg on standby in case this doesn't hold." Whole blood transfusion was their only option. They didn't have enough plasma for something like this, and the platelet supplies had passed their expiration. The city hospital was supposed to keep them stocked, but they didn't always prioritize their little hospital. They'd typed the girl, but O-Neg was the universal blood donor and carried the least risk. "How are we doing on that supply?" Antonio asked.

"Good enough," Izzy said as she counted sponges. Antonio was sewing the girl's incision closed. "The abbess sent your bride to bed. She was feeling poorly. She wouldn't leave, so she's in my cottage, curled up next to Liam." Antonio froze. "Just kidding. Liam's doing rounds with Doc Mary."

"Smart ass," Antonio said with a grin. The nurse started stirring behind him. "What is it?"

"Blood pressure is dropping fast, Doctor."

The alarms started going off and Antonio yelled, "Get that blood!" He said to Izzy, "I'm opening her back up. Stand by with a fresh clamp!" That's when her heart stopped. "No! No, bambina. Don't leave us." He started compressions while Izzy got the paddles ready.

"Clear." Izzy zapped the child, her chest jerking. "Come on, baby girl. Don't do this. Your parents are waiting for you."

"Again, Izzy."

SOPHIE CAME INTO THE SMALL WAITING AREA JUST AS A WAIL SO sorrowful rang through the building, sending chills through her whole body. *Oh, God. No.* Antonio was kneeling at the feet of a small woman, seated in one of the worn chairs. His head was down, and he rubbed the woman's back as she wailed inconsolably.

Her husband was one of the men they'd brought in. He'd live. The little girl was being dropped off at his construction site because her mother worked as well. He'd escaped with several broken bones and lacerations. But his daughter was gone. An unsafe work environment was a reality in Manaus. It was senseless and tragic. Another heart-wrenching wail came from one of the rooms down the hall, no doubt where Izzy was telling the father. One of the sisters took the mother in hand, leading her to her husband. She watched Antonio rise to his feet, slower than she'd ever seen him move. His shoulders were set in a slumping position of defeat and despair, then she went to him. There were others waiting for better news of their loved ones. They'd all heard, of course. The women knew each other. Right now, their eyes were fixed on the still, devastated figure standing in surgical scrubs. They were pristinely clean, which means that he'd had some reason to change clothes before he saw the parents.

Jesus, this was unlike anything her small, safe life in England had prepared her for. A child gone. A community of women who were used to the dangers their husbands faced, but likely hadn't prepared for those unsafe work places to reach a tentacle out to snag a small child. Snuff out a life that had scarcely begun.

Sophie approached him, smoothing a hand down his arm as she felt a shudder go through him. "I'm so sorry, love."

Antonio pulled her slowly to him, snaking an arm around her waist and putting his forehead to hers. So gentle compared to his normal treatment, when his hands were on her body. She thought about the scorpion he'd carefully retrieved from her bedroom in Italy. *The world is full of parents who don't care for their children. And I see enough death. This was an easy one to prevent.* She'd wondered, at the time, just what Dr. Antonio Rinalto had seen to make him say such a thing. Now she knew. In this instance, the parents had loved and cared for their child. But in the end, it hadn't been enough.

❦

ANTONIO HAD FALLEN ASLEEP IN HER ARMS. SHE'D DRIVEN HIM to their home, knowing he'd want to be in his own bed. He didn't cry, but he was quiet. Now he was stirring, nuzzling her and pulling her tight to him. Not in lust. He just needed contact. She smoothed his hair back, not sure what to say. He smiled. "Thank you. I needed you and you seemed to know."

"I did. You were in surgery so long, I just thought you'd want to go home to your own bed. I'm sorry. I wish I could help." Then she thought about the thing she'd asked Doc Mary for earlier that day. "I want to ask you something. I don't want to make you feel worse, but it might make you feel ten times better."

"Tell me," he said, curious now.

Antonio watched his wife get off the bed and start digging in her daypack. When she took out the item she was searching for, he popped off the bed. She put her hands up. "I don't know for sure. I just wanted us to do this together. I lost my lunch on the canoe today. And ... I'm late."

He jumped out of her embrace and began dragging her into the loo. She said, "Oh, no. Get out. I'm not ready for urinating to be a spectator sport. Out with you."

Antonio knew he was grinning like an idiot. He let himself be banished from their bathroom reluctantly, but she was entitled to privacy for this part. He heard the toilet flush and was in the room before she had her hands washed. Seated on the tub, he looked at his watch. One minute.

At thirty seconds, both blue lines were there. They both stared stupidly. Then he met her eyes. She was radiant. How had he not noticed that she was glowing? "When you set out to cheer some-one's mood, you don't use half measures, mi amore." He laughed. "I'm going to be a papa. A papa!" He let out a whoop. "Come here, Mama. Come let me hold you."

EPILOGUE
GREVE IN CHIANTI—AUTUMN

Antonio was ready to gag and bind his wife, scoop her up, and tie her to a chair. Indoors. In that order because she had a mouth on her when she was feeling feisty. She waddled down the aisle of grapes, tasting and assessing the berries for harvest. She said, "These aren't ready. Let's try the vines farther up the slope."

Antonio said, "Get in the truck, Sophie. You aren't walking. You shouldn't even be out here on your feet. It's too warm."

Sophie gave him an indulgent look. She was so adorable, it actually pained him to look at her. In bibbed overalls and a baggy T-shirt from his old alma mater, she was radiant. She was also very, very due. The child's due date was tomorrow, for God's sake.

"I feel fine, Antonio. Relax. You said it yourself. First babies usually go over the due date. Go check on Nonno. He's looking pale," she said, not meaning a word of it.

"He is not looking pale. He's as strong as ever." He wasn't, actually. He became out of breath much easier after the lung surgery. But he was cancer-free, at least for now. "Don't try to distract me."

"I would never," Sophie said innocently. She was far from it.

She'd woken up this morning like a she-cat. Pregnancy hormones had put her libido into overdrive. Her belly was so big, they had to get creative, but her every demand was his wish. His groin stirred just thinking about it. She was no wilting flower. After her initial morning sickness had ebbed, she'd been a force of nature.

Brazil held endless fascination for her. She'd begun fermenting her first experimental batch of Aguaje wine a few months ago. But Autumn was for Italy. She'd flown to Italy ahead of him, escorted by Catarina, three months ago. Catarina had finally visited when she'd heard about Sophie's pregnancy. His sister loved Brazil, as he knew she would. And she loved the entire motley crew of St. Clare's Charity Mission.

Sophie wouldn't have missed the harvest at *Viti del Fiume* for anything, and so they'd decided to have the child here. Antonio put his hand on her belly. "Please, my darling. Humor me." He kissed her thoroughly.

When he let her come up for air, she narrowed her eyes at him. "Just because you are servicing my every whim with your body doesn't mean you can boss me around."

He moved his hand up, running a thumb along the underside of her ever-growing breast. "Of course not," he said with a rakish grin. She sucked in a breath, and he swelled with pride that after a year, he could still arouse his wife to the point of breathlessness. Or so he thought.

He felt her abdomen draw up tight like a drum. She bent forward, groaning. So, the old wives' tale was true about sexual release inducing labor. Because she'd released, all right—twice last night and once this morning.

Antonio said calmly, "Okay, mia cara. It looks like our morning session has started things along."

She grunted. "Don't look so proud of yourself."

He laughed, but his heart was racing. This was it. She was going to have their baby. "Nonno! Pull the truck around. I need to take Sophie up to the house. Now!"

Catarina skidded to a halt, her father close behind her. They took one look at Sophie and their faces blanched. Sophie said, "I'm not dying, for God's sake, I'm in labor. Someone, get the truck." She was feisty. A good sign. No fear in sight ... until her water broke all over her overalls.

❧

SOPHIE GOT OUT OF THE CAR TWO DAYS LATER, ANTONIO LIFTING her gently by one arm. She said, "I'm okay. Just get Maggie." Magdalena Martha Rinalto was caterwauling like the world was ending. "I can carry her if you get her out of the car seat."

Antonio said, "I will carry her. My girls need a big, strong man to help them. I'm not totally useless." Antonio smiled at her smirk. Maggie recognized two types of people in the world— Momma and the rest who were delegated to the lesser group known as Not the Momma. The benefit of having the milk she wanted and the body that had created her from a few small cells. She was absolutely a mommy's girl. At least for now. He carefully freed her from the child restraints. Tawny hair and a red face, flushed with righteous indignation. She was a masterpiece.

"Oh, there, there, my angel. You are too pretty to cry so loudly. What will the neighbors think of us?" He crooned to her in Italian, making it a mission that she learn it before English. Sophie, having a naturally competitive nature, would take that challenge, gladly. She thought this, smiling to herself as she watched them.

Antonio held Maggie snuggly with one arm and prepared to hold Sophie with the other. But his father beat him to it. Marcello ran out of the house as soon as they pulled into the drive, and he treated Sophie like a queen. It was rather heart-warming, Antonio had to admit to himself. And if he thought about it, he remembered the doting, pampering husband he'd been when Antonio's mother had been pregnant with Catarina. He was a good man, and Antonio was so grateful that he'd finally come home to reconcile. Marcello said with wonder, "My first grandchild. Bellisima!"

Catarina came outside, shaking her head. "This child will be spoiled. Marco is no better. The size of that rocking horse is ridiculous. She's too small to even play with it."

Marco came out next. "But she will see it and know that she has the best uncle in Italy. And someday, she will be big enough to ride it. Then I will buy her a real pony. We can keep it next to Fabio."

Catarina rolled her eyes, but she smiled at Marco. He really was a good brother, despite their bickering. And he'd be a very good uncle. He came next to Antonio like a spotter, obviously worried Antonio would drop his precious, little parcel and Marco would have to dive and catch her. The intensity on his face was comical.

As they settled in the kitchen, Antonio knelt down and placed the baby in his grandmother's arms. "This is your *bisnonna*, sweet girl. Your great-grandmother who is your namesake."

Nonna wept joyfully, muttering a prayer to the Blessed Mother. She looked up, smiling through her tears. "She is so tiny. It is easy to forget how small they are." She looked at Marcello, as if remembering a time when she was a new, young mother and holding her first baby. Then her eyes went back to little Maggie. "I will teach you to cook, sweet Magdalena," she said in Italian. Sophie might lose that bet just yet. Nonna adjusted the little bundle in the crook of her arm like a pro, crooning to her the way only a woman could do.

They would all teach her something. She'd be multi-lingual and loved so much that she'd never want for anything. They'd return to Brazil after Christmas. Maggie was too small to travel now, and Sophie's parents would visit from France. Her mother had been beside herself on the phone. Down with the flu, they hadn't wanted to travel or to expose anyone. So, they'd had to postpone their trip. Yes, little Maggie Rinalto was going to be as loved as any child had ever been. Especially when the nuns and children of St. Clare's got to meet her.

Martha had come into town for the birth and been allowed in the delivery room with the happy parents. She leaned down, rubbing the soft hair of her great-granddaughter. "Margarite would have loved you, sweet darling." Martha wasn't prone to sentiment, but her voice was hoarse. "And I know they say you can't tell this early, but I think she's going to have our eyes, Antonio. Just past the dark blue, do you see it? Waiting?"

"Yes, I did notice. She'll have my eyes and charm and her mother's hard head." Sophie elbowed him, and they all rumbled with laughter.

❦

"ANTONIO," MARCELLO SAID WHEN THEY STOOD ON THE BACK patio alone. "Your most important job from now on is to make sure that your family is okay. Happy, safe, and healthy. It must come above all things."

"It will. Just as you did. You couldn't fix everything, Papa. No one can do that. But you loved us well, and you loved her well. You and Nonno have cared for this family. I will do the same for mine, and we will not stay away. I promise you." His father's eyes welled with tears. And for the first time in over a decade, there was nothing but love between the father and son.

AUTHOR NOTES

Thank you to my readers, whom I also consider my friends. You offered so much support during arguably the roughest year of my life. This book is a long time coming.

I went to Greve in Chianti in the summer of 2000 with my soon-to-be husband. A honeymoon of sorts, two months before our wedding. Cart before the horse, but I never said I played by the rules all the time. We did a day trip into Tuscany during our time in Florence. We stopped at vineyards, drank wine, had lunch, and visited the little towns that speckled the map of the Chianti Classico region. I love Italy, and just like the West Coast of Ireland, the rolling slopes of Tuscany captured my heart and my imagination.

Given the twenty-one-year gap, it took some research to recapture the magic that Italy wove into my mind. I couldn't visit due to the COVID-19 pandemic, so I had to depend on books and the Internet. I read a wonderful article by Lauren Mowery in *Wine Enthusiast. A Beginner's Guide to Chianti and Chianti Classico*. It refreshed my memory and taught me more about the subzones of Chianti wine. Jump ahead several months, and my husband buys the Great Courses course on Italian wine. Specifically, *The Everyday*

Guide to Wines of Italy instructed by Jennifer Simonetti-Bryan, Master of Wine and Certified Specialist of Spirits. It helped me to renew my love for Italian wine and taught me a little more about the tasting process.

I'd like to thank my beta readers, as always. Ya'll are amazing. I also wish to thank my dear friend and designer, Christine Stevens. You turn vision into reality, and I've loved every single one of my book covers.

Also a long time coming, I have forged a relationship with an excellent copy editor and proofreader. Joyce Mochrie helped me get this book out just in time for the harvest. Thank you, Joyce. I think this will be the beginning of great things.

Finally, I'd like to thank my mother. She was such a supportive influence in my life. She loved my books. This is the first one she won't read. She won't giggle on the phone about the sexy parts.

I'm a little lost without you, Momma. I'll miss you every day. Tell Daddy and Randy that I love them.

IN MEMORY OF
MENERVA JOYCE CLAYTON

June 6, 1945–January 9, 2021

Made in United States
North Haven, CT
12 July 2024

54680269R00183